PESTILENCE
RANDALL WOOD

PESTILENCE

For information contact:
Tension Bookworks
PO Box 93
Nokomis Fl, 34274
www.tensionbookworks.com

⫯ensionBookworks
and the portrayal of the screw are registered trademarks of TensionBookworks.

Book and Cover design by Derek Murphy
Formatting by Jayne E Smith

Cataloging-in-Publication Data is on file at the Library of Congress

Wood, Randall, 1968-
Pestilence / Randall Wood—1st ed.
ISBN-13: 978-1-938825-13-2
First Edition: August 2012

10 9 8 7 6 5 4 3 2 1

For all the D-boys, past and present

pes·ti·lence |ˈpes tə lən(t)s|
noun: a destructive infectious
swiftly spreading disease.

I looked, and beheld, an ashen horse; and he who sat on it had the name of Death; and Hades followed with him. Authority was given to him over a fourth of the earth, to kill with sword and with famine and with pestilence and by the wild beasts of the earth.

– *REVELATION 6:4*

Disease is the retribution of outraged nature.

– *HOSEA BALLOU*

WORLD POPULATION PROJECTED
TO REACH 7 BILLION IN 2011.
October 20, 2009—CNN

–ONE–

MUZZAMMIL HASSAN WAS ONE week past his sixteenth birthday. If the day went as planned he would not see his seventeenth. As he watched the men work he thought of the small party his parents had thrown for him. Like most families in his country, his was large and poor. His mother and father had worked hard for the extra food to serve that day. His father had spoken proudly of his son to all that were present, but Muzzammil knew he would never rise to the successes his father had predicted. It was enough to simply stay alive in his country. Muzzammil knew suffering. He had lost a sister and uncle to AIDS, and two brothers to the tribal warfare that often plagued his country. His hope was that his decision would not only bring pride to his father, but provide for his family. He had been promised repeatedly that they would be well cared for and would never again suffer from hunger or lack of medical care. That his family name would be spoken with honor and reverence and he himself would be elevated to a place of distinction few of his people could hope for.

But the price was great. He thought of the words he had spoken into the camera a short time ago. He had delivered them with force and volume as instructed and could only hope that his fear had not shown through. It was a speech he had heard growing up from others before him. He had learned the slogans before he was ten and delivered them with a fury he had not felt before today. The men he now watched working had observed silently until he was through, and then applauded his performance before returning to their shovels and buckets.

The men worked tirelessly as they had throughout the night. The bags were pulled from the pallet left by the forklift. There had been over two hundred total, but they were now down to the last ten. The bags were emptied into bathtubs that had been pulled from the rubble of the city. The mixing was performed by men wearing masks and supervised by the Arab. Muzzammil did not know his name, and neither did any of the others. While the man spoke his language, it was obviously not his native tongue. He barked at a man holding a jerry can of diesel and the man quickly poured some more into the tub until barked at a second time. The mixing resumed until it was to the Arab's approval and he signaled to other men waiting nearby. They reached into the tub wearing leather gloves over the plastic ones they had donned first. This protected their hands from the nails and other small pieces of metal that had been added to the mix. The fumes were strong, and the Arab positioned himself in front of one of the multiple fans they had set up to circulate the air. The men packed the thick slurry into five-gallon buckets that were carried to the truck. Here the buckets were handed up and then down into the large tank where Muzzammil briefly saw the hands of his friend, Hanni, accept them. This was followed by the muffled noise of him packing the mixture inside the tank. Muzzammil smiled at his friend's discomfort. Being young and skinny as he was, he was chosen for the job of packing the truck, as he was the only one who could fit through the opening. At least he had a gas mask that kept the fumes at bay. The heat could not be escaped. The empty buckets soon emerged and were passed back for another load.

Muzzammil's thoughts were interrupted by a hand on his shoulder and he turned to see the robed man they all looked to for guidance standing over him. His one good eye sparkled with pride at Muzzammil, and he smiled at the boy before watching the last of the bags of ammonia nitrate being mixed in the tub. As the mixing process was finished and the last bucket loaded, the men slowly approached and offered their prayers and admiration to Muzzammil. All under the careful eye of the robed figure standing behind him. Hanni, his skinny friend, was the last to leave. Muzzammil looked from his friend's sweaty face to the red irritated skin of his arms and legs. The mark of the gas mask ringed his face and gave a comical frame to the lopsided smile he offered. What little he had to say would not come, he simply smiled, clasped his friend's hands in his own, and with a nod departed the garage.

The robed man took a seat next to Muzzammil and they both watched silently as the Arab moved around and under the fuel truck. Although less than half the size of a semi-truck, it still carried a 5000 gallon capacity. More importantly, it was indistinguishable from the other government owned gas trucks in his country. The steel reinforcements added to the front end and heavy bumper were hidden to all but the most careful observer. An effort had been made to preserve the well-used appearance of the truck, as anything out of the ordinary would compromise their mission. The Arab had been insistent on every aspect of the operation, and all of his wishes were followed. The fertilizer had been purchased in various quantities from several places and stockpiled until it was needed. The diesel fuel had been slowly siphoned from several trucks and saved as well. While the fuel was not necessary for the reaction the Arab desired, he had explained that its addition would increase the chemical energy of the mixture, hastening the violence of the detonation, and providing more of a shock wave. Now the man was busy completing the wiring he had started a day ago. After a few minutes in the cab of the truck, he walked to the two men and took a seat facing Muzzammil.

"You remember the instructions?" he politely asked.

"Yes."

"Good, please tell them to me one more time?"

Muzzammil recited the instructions he had memorized the night before. "I drive the truck on its normal route at its normal time. I obey all traffic laws and do not speed any more than the other traffic. At the last intersection, I attach the cord on the wheel to my wrist and grip the wheel. I then wait for traffic to open up in front of me before using the space to speed up as much as possible. Others will help by shooting at the guards. I drive through the barrier and get as close to the building as possible."

"Good, and then?" the Arab pressed.

"I simply pull my hand away from the wheel," he replied.

"…and grasp the hand of Allah as he welcomes you to paradise," the robed man finished.

"Yes, Teacher."

The Arab looked at the boy for some time. Muzzammil met his gaze without faltering.

"They will speak your name around the world, my young friend. You are already known to Usama, he speaks of you with pride," the Arab lied.

Muzzammil's back straightened with the statement. He stood as the other men did.

The Arab adjusted the boy's clothes before stepping back to look him over.

"The clothes fit you well." He checked his watch before looking at the robed man.

"A prayer, before you depart," the man announced.

Mats were pulled from nearby chairs and the three men knelt together on the floor. When finished, the boy was escorted to the truck and the two men watched as he climbed into the driver's seat. They looked for any hesitation or muscle quiver. Any sign of the boy changing his mind. The Arab pointed out the cord on the steering wheel and the boy nodded. A squeeze of the shoulder before the man left to open the garage door.

"I am very proud," the robed man stated.

"Thank you, Teacher. I am proud to serve our cause."

"The world will know your name tomorrow. All of your brothers and sisters await you. Allah be praised, go now, my son."

Muzzammil started the truck and with only a slight jerk eased it out the door and into the rising African sun. The door was quickly pulled shut behind him.

The Arab searched his pockets for a cigarette as he walked back to the robed man.

"He will do it?"

"I have no doubts," the robed man replied.

"If he develops any, we will help him." The Arab pulled the remote detonator from his pocket.

"I do not think that will be necessary, but we cannot have him captured. It is becoming more difficult to find men willing to do these things. You will take care of the family as promised?"

"Funding is becoming more difficult, but improving the lives of his family will cost little. The boy is a fool, but it will be done. After all, we may need more 'volunteers' in the future. Come, my friend. This building will burn in less than thirty minutes. We must depart. And I wish to be well on my way out of this country. By the end of the day it will not be safe for either of us."

"Yes, the Americans," the robed man replied. "Let them come."

"Oh, they will my friend. You angered them once before, and they robbed you of an eye. I imagine they will want more this time. I would not underestimate them."

"Yes, I will be leaving as well, but not for long. I will see you again?"

"Perhaps, Allah willing, but most likely not." The Arab offered no explanation.

"I understand."

*   *   *

Djimon increased the speed of the forklift after rounding the corner. After driving daily for three months now, he considered himself an expert. He had not spilled anything since his first day. He had feared that day was his last, but the Americans were forgiving, and he had been given a second chance. He had been offered the job after befriending one of the many officials who worked there. His sister was employed by the woman and watched over her child while she and her husband worked. While Djimon's job did not allow him access to the embassy itself, he worked right next door in the warehouse, moving supplies all day and loading and unloading trucks.

Djimon was very proud of his job and worked hard for the Americans he had come to respect. The constant flow of humanitarian items he moved every day had removed any doubts he'd had before. Other boys his age would curse the Americans, saying they were taking over their country and treading on their beliefs. Djimon knew better. The job he did every day had proven it. How could he deny the generosity of his employer when he himself moved every pallet of food, medicine and clothing that came through the building? He saw the destinations on the crates. All for his countrymen and all for free. They paid him well, treated him with respect, and fed him twice a day, also for free. He had discovered chocolate from the Americans, and they would often dip into certain crates before they left the docks so he could take it home to his younger brothers and sisters. Not once had they questioned him on his religion or interfered with his prayers. No one had tried to convert him, or offered him anything that went against his beliefs. While his employers drank alcohol and ate things he found foul, he had soon realized that his people also did some things that the Americans found unpleasant. But he had come to accept them as he had been accepted by them.

Today his supervisor was a man named Ken. A simple name he had easily remembered. Ken, he had learned, did not work for the American government, but for one of the drug companies that were supplying the medications that fought AIDS. Medications his country needed desperately. Ken was a stern man, not as friendly as his other bosses. When the medications arrived they were always brought by the same three men: a driver, a passenger, and a man who rode in the back with the pallets. All of them were heavily muscled and heavily armed. They were polite but serious men, and Djimon feared them greatly. Violence in his country was a fact of life, and Djimon knew the look of men who were no strangers to the deliverance of death. He always worked quickly to unload the crates when they arrived, the sooner to get the men on their way. Today was no different, and Djimon was now placing the crates in their proper locations according to the numbers stamped on each.

But he had a problem. He had been treated to a good breakfast by the Americans. Complete with orange juice, which he loved. He had drunk his fill to the amusement of the bosses and was now going on several hours of driving back and forth with a full bladder. There were three crates left, but he had to pee. Now.

The current pallet on his lift contained shrink-wrapped boxes of medicine vials. Today they were yellow tops, as opposed to the red tops that had arrived last week. It had confused him at first. The vials were the same in every other way. Same size, same shape, same number on the side. Yet he was told he could never mix the boxes. The yellows went in their designated area, the reds in theirs, and were stored in separate ends of the warehouse.

Surely he could park the lift in the red zone for a moment? Just long enough to pee. He looked around for Ken, who usually watched his every move when moving the drugs. He saw him at the other end of the warehouse. He was talking on his cell phone and not looking his way. Djimon quickly parked the forklift in the red zone, leaped off and ran toward the bathroom on the other side of the office. He only needed a minute.

*   *   *

Muzzammil stared at the street light. Normally he was impatient and often would run the lights, but today they seemed to be blinking green just for him. He dared not run it. His truck was heavy and slow, and the cargo too precious.

He squeezed his eyes shut in a silent prayer and mopped the sweat from his face. He had always been comfortable in the African heat. It was all he had ever known. But today he was sweating. Despite the sweat in his eyes, his vision was unusually sharp today. He found himself noticing every little detail of life swarming around him. He was also keenly aware of his heart beating in his chest. Something also unusual, but it had been with him since he had departed the garage. The act he was about to perform was keeping the adrenalin flowing through his system.

A blaring horn forced his eyes open. The light was showing green.

"Allah Akbar," he mumbled as he slipped the truck into gear.

He could see his target over the cars in front of him from his elevated position in the truck. Keeping his acceleration slow, he opened a gap in the traffic in front of him. He looked for the promised snipers on the buildings around his target, but saw nothing. Soon the gap was large enough and he floored the gas pedal, working the clutch and gears, coaxing as much speed as he could from the heavy vehicle. The weak point in the concrete barrier was marked with graffiti and he kept his eyes focused on his target. He was within one hundred meters when he heard the first shots. Two of the guards at the gate fell to the pavement, and the third took cover behind the kiosk. As he shifted gears, Muzzammil ducked down as low as possible as bullets from the embassy rooftop shattered the windshield into a spider web of cracks. The truck had reached its top speed and he angled not toward the gate and its snake-like concrete entrance, but to the outside barrier ringing the building. The embassy had not upgraded the perimeter with concrete and steel posts as other embassies had, and was instead utilizing pre-formed concrete fencing of the type seen on highway projects. They were not anchored down and the graffiti directed him to the joint where two barriers met. Muzzammil sat up and braced himself before impact, gripping the wheel tightly. He must not let go too soon. Shots continued to ping the truck around him, but the shooters had the wrong angle to reach him in the driver's seat.

The impact threw him forward and his nose crunched as his face impacted the wheel sharply, almost causing him to lose his grip on the wheel. His view was a kaleidoscope of sun, glass, and the interior of the truck as he was thrown violently around the cab. His face struck the wheel a second time as the truck suddenly stopped and listed to the right.

Muzzammil pulled himself up and assessed his position. It was strangely quiet. As he gazed through the shattered windshield he discovered he had penetrated the barrier and come to rest against the wall of the embassy itself. He looked down to see his hand still gripping the wheel in a white-knuckled grasp. The wire was still attached to his wrist. His hearing suddenly returned as a bullet impacted his chest. He saw his blood pour down the front of his shirt to join that streaming from his nose. He breathed deep and coughed, adding more blood to the mixture. His gaze once again fell on his left hand.

*　　　　*　　　　*

Ken Gates was not pleased. He had just received a verbal lashing from his boss half a world away and was now looking at an empty forklift. Worse yet, it was parked in the red zone with a load of yellow tops still on the skids. He'd told the boy very plainly how important it was to not mix the two. Something he kept an eye on at all times. The goal of this drug treatment was too important, and while Ken was sure he wasn't privy to the whole plan, he had received the lecture and taken the shot. He was committed. He really had no choice. Everyone was committed, one way or the other, everyone.

He was about to hop on the forklift and move the pallet himself when he heard the sounds of gunfire. He stopped and listened closely, but sound was dampened in the large warehouse. As he listened he heard the sound of the toilet flushing. He turned to see Djimon hurrying around the corner from the bathroom. He opened his mouth to admonish the boy for his violation, but before he could do so, the wall in front of them disintegrated in a ball of fire, throwing debris across the room, crushing them both.

*　　　　*　　　　*

The Arab smiled as the sound of the explosion echoed across the city. His view of the building was now one of a giant dust cloud that moved toward him, assisted by the dry wind. He had given the boy as much time as he could, and while he would get the credit for his sacrifice, the Arab had been forced to use the remote device. He now carefully disassembled the device and added it to a small metal waste can he had previously filled with paper and bits of wood. Only when every surface was exposed, both internal and external, did he set the paper aflame and place it out on the balcony. He did not worry about being seen as the sky was now blacked out by the dust cloud rising from the embassy and traveling on the wind. He left the room and, wrapping his head in cloth, exited the building into the chaos of the street. Joining a group of fleeing people, he moved swiftly down the street away from the embassy. The wind moved the small sandstorm he had created along with him.

His day would now consist of a long walk out of the city, followed by a day and night in the African bush. He would then be given new papers and smuggled on a truck across two borders before arriving in Sudan, where he would be welcomed as a brother. A hard journey, but a small price to pay.

90% OF THE OCEAN'S EDIBLE SPECIES
MAY BE GONE BY 2048.
November 13, 2006—USA Today

-TWO-

JACK CUPPED BOTH HANDS around his coffee mug as he leaned on the railing and gazed out over the deserted beach at the Atlantic. The only movement he saw this morning was the wind blowing snow across the dunes and the slow progress of a container ship on the horizon. It was the same view he'd had for the last month of his mandatory vacation.

He sipped the coffee and tried to think of what was on his list for the day. Not much. After his last investigation had come to its climactic end on live television, he had been in the press for some time, again. Not something his wife had approved of. The FBI had been forced to initiate an internal investigation into him and his team under the pressure of a few politicians, all hoping to score some political capital against their rivals in the current administration. The hearings and depositions had become regular additions to the news cycle for several weeks. They had picked through every aspect of his past, from his days in collage through his time in the military, his inherited business, and finally his days with the FBI. Thankfully, a member of the Senate had become exposed in a nasty sex scandal, and the press had turned their attention to a juicier subject.

The fact that Jack had been under the bare light bulb of the investigation that produced no wrongdoing by him did not sit well with the oversight committee. Despite the Director of the FBI backing him, the Attorney General had suggested some time off. It was delivered with a medal no one would ever see, and a personal letter from the President himself, but it still did not ease the pain of being sidelined. He had tried to look on the bright side. It did give him the time off he had promised Debra. She had been forced to leave her teaching job due to the press following her every move. The charity work she did had at first suffered also, but had enjoyed a surge in donations once the story got out that the FBI's hero favored their cause. Their time together had been strained, but they had gotten through the tough part, and were now finding new routines to replace the old. Well, at least she had. While their relationship had improved greatly since his last case, there were still some things to work out. They were both trying.

While his wife spent her full time at her charities now, he had surrendered the house in Kenwood to escape the press and placed himself in exile at the beach house he had inherited from his father. The drive was too far for the Washington press, and the winter cold meant his seasonal neighbors were not due for a month yet. Jack had the entire dead end street to himself.

He'd avoided the TV for the first couple of weeks, but soon his thirst for news overwhelmed his dread of seeing his own face on the screen. He had found time to read the directions for the remote and had discovered his father had programmed the same "favorite" channels in as he would have selected. Something he hadn't come to a complete opinion on yet.

The problem was Jack had nothing to do. He was no longer a corporate business man. Although he kept tabs on his father's company, (his now, but he would never see it that way) he found little pleasure in reading quarterly reports and expansion summaries. The people he had left in charge when he left to join the FBI were doing fine work, and would most likely be better off without him jumping back in for what he hoped would be a short leave of absence.

He had already skimmed through the library his father had gathered and gone through four novels. He had made $17.00 in the process as his father had a habit of using whatever bill he had in his wallet at the time as a bookmark, only to be left behind for the next reader. Jack had actually counted the books, and using an average based on his earnings so far, estimated a profit of a couple grand if he read them all.

The wind had a bite and was picking up, so Jack retreated into the beach house to refill his cup. He was searching for the remote when the phone rang. He eyed the caller ID suspiciously, but it showed his wife's cell number. He thumbed the button for the speaker phone.

"Hi, honey."

"Are you out of bed yet?" she asked.

Jack smiled. "Aren't you funny today?"

"Well, you were up late last night, thought you may have slept in a little." He could hear her smile as she poked at him.

"You know there's no coffee maker in the bedroom," he shot back.

"Sorry, I forgot. Should I pick one up for you?"

"No, I'll manage somehow."

"I plan on leaving early today so I should be out there by four or so. How about dinner?" she asked.

"Out or in?"

"You feel like cooking?"

"Out it is. How about The Half King? I feel like a steak."

"Okay. Any word from the office?"

Jack could hear her tone. She asked the question because she knew it mattered to him, but her tone said she hoped the answer was no.

"Not yet," was all he replied.

"It's not fair, Jack. They can't just leave you hanging like this forever. I don't like you being there and me being in town. If they won't call you back in then I think we should talk about some options."

"Not yet, Deb, let's give it some time."

"Then when, Jack? You can't keep putting it off forever. Sooner or later you may have to accept that your time with those people is over."

Jack didn't like the "those people" comment, but he didn't feel like fighting about it now, especially on the phone.

"Let's talk about it tonight."

"Don't brush me off, Jack. I have to call you just to get you to talk about it. It's the only way I have your attention. It's not right and it's not good for you or us. Promise me we'll talk tonight," she pushed.

"Okay, I promise."

"Good, I'll see you about four then. I love you."

"Love you, too."

Jack frowned at the phone as it emitted a dial tone over the speaker. He was forced to admit that she was right as he pushed the button ending the call. He knew what her options would be. Return to the board of directors, make more money, come home every night, play golf, schmooze with her rich friends, and repeat. Everything he had worked hard to avoid. The children conversation hadn't come up in awhile, but he was sure that as soon as one of her socialite friends got pregnant it would be on her tongue the next day. Jack didn't hate the idea of kids, he just wanted to do some other things first. Dinner was not going to be fun.

Jack refilled his mug and wandered into the living room. He found the remote under the book he had left on the end table next to his favorite chair. A "man-chair" his wife called it. Large, leather, and very comfortable, Jack had spent several hours a day in it over the last month. He thumbed on the big screen and hit the favorite button. Robin Meade of CNN appeared.

"…possible new evidence in the Leslie Evans case. The five-year-old went missing from her Virginia home three months ago and investigators are no closer to naming a suspect…"

Click.

"…the Dow is expected to open lower today as the housing market continues to struggle. New home sales are at an all time low, a full 58%

down from this month last year..."

Click.

"...local city Councilman Warren Dickerson has been charged by a grand jury today with five counts of embezzling city funds and three counts of falsifying records. Two other councilmen are also expected to face similar charges involving the use of city funds for personal reasons..."

Click.

"...Hello America! Billy Mays here..."

Click.

"...just in from our state department desk. The United States Embassy in Tanzania, Africa was bombed by terrorists early this morning. It is reported that a fuel truck carrying explosives broke through the perimeter barrier and exploded against the south wall of the building. As you can see from the footage on your screen, at least half the building is in ruins. I'm told that the sections destroyed housed the main offices and work areas of the embassy. The staff quarters and housing are located in the back and appear to be still intact. The warehouse structure adjacent to the building was also partially destroyed. The warehouse held mostly relief supplies for a country plagued by food shortages and disease. There are twenty-two confirmed dead and as many wounded at this time. That number is expected to rise. An hour after the bombing, a group calling itself Al Qaeda in Africa has claimed responsibility. A video, showing a young man believed to be the driver of the truck, delivering a speech denouncing the presence of American influence in the small country, aired on the *Al Jazeerah* network and was picked up by the wire services. No other information is available at this time. Stay tuned to the BBC for further updates as this story develops."

Jack thumbed the mute button as he scrambled out of his chair and raced down the hall to the bedroom. He fumbled through his clothes on the floor, searching the pockets. Where the hell had he left it? Was it even on? Did the battery die? He fell to the floor and searched under the bed. There, that pair of jeans. He dragged them out and riffled the pockets.

There it is. He looked at the screen and saw nothing.

"Damn it!" He palmed the dead device and raced back down the hall to the kitchen junk drawer so full he could barely open it. He rummaged through the mess, but didn't see what he needed. Now what?

The remote?

He returned to the man-chair and pulled the back panel off the remote. He stole an AA battery, swapped it for the dead one in his department pager, and turned it on.

"Come on, baby, work for me," Jack pep talked the device and the tiny screen lit up, and after blinking for a few seconds, delivered a message.

"888"

"Yes!" Jack pumped a fist in the air.

Now where the hell was his cell phone?

*   *   *

John Kimball ignored the looks he got from the passing platoon of paratroopers as he ran down the packed orange clay of the firebreak. The North Carolina winters were mild, and while the temperature was good for a run, the damp clay stuck to his running shoes and made for a slippery surface. He noted a couple of paratroopers sporting orange coatings on their otherwise gray PT uniforms, the victims of their own carelessness. He caught up to another platoon running in his direction and matched speeds to the cadence of the sergeant leading them. He enjoyed the off-color song, knowing it would have to change to something more traditional as they neared the post again. He turned north after a mile and headed back to his own duties.

While he wore military clothing similar to theirs for his morning run, his longer hair and non-regulation mustache marked him as one of "Them." The fact that they were in area J of the Fort Bragg training zones, just south of the Delta Force compound, gave credit to their assumptions. While the compound appeared on the maps as an impact area—clearly marked off-limits due to live gunfire and possible unexploded munitions—everyone knew what it was and who it supported. The triple-fence perimeter and snake-like concrete entrance just added to the mystery. Rumor had it that the majority of the space was underground, and they were right, especially all the latest editions. One of which John Kimball was in charge of. .

As he neared the gate, the guard waved him down from a distance. He complied by slowing to a jog, placing his hands on his head, and jogging backward for a few yards. Picking up a walk for the last thirty meters, he pulled his ID out from inside his shirt and held it up.

The guard held out a laptop-size item similar to a computer. John swiped his card before wiping his hand on his shorts and placing it on the screen. The computer announced with a beep and a green light that he was allowed and the guard let him pass. Passing through the airlock-like double gate, he then stretched out his stride till he was past the Delta buildings and into his own. Like theirs, his had no label of any kind, not even a number to distinguish it from the others. All the buildings were simple red brick with windowless metal doors. Some of his people used the last two numbers of its grid location to identify it, but that was as far as it went toward getting a name. His building only differed in the amount of climate control equipment on the roof. Obviously much more than was needed for a building of its size, it was not unusual in this neighborhood. But only the people working there knew the real reasons for the equipment.

The sound of the door chime was drowned out by the C-5 Galaxy aircraft passing overhead as it took off from Pope Air Force base, probably carrying a load of gear, or troops, or both, heading over to Afghanistan. The flights were regular now, or so he was told. He couldn't hear the planes from his office.

Proceeding through another set of doors that automatically locked behind him, he didn't bother glancing at the cameras that followed his progress to the elevator. Once on board, he slid his card again through a slot on the wall before punching his floor. The doors shut and then sealed with a hiss before descending. What the neighbors did not know was that while the building had four stories above ground, they were all utilized for air handling purposes. A variety of pumps, filtering units, electrostatic dust collectors and climate control equipment crowded the space. All functions were backed up and then backed up again. There were technicians stationed in the spaces twenty-four hours a day, and the facility had the ability of being sealed off entirely from the outside world for up to six months.

It was staffed much like a nuclear reactor, as it was even more dangerous. Thus it had been placed where everyone accepted secrecy, and no one dared to question.

The elevator arrived at S-12, or sub-floor twelve, and the doors broke their seal before opening. Kimball stepped out a few feet and turned to enter the men's locker room. Here he disrobed completely and after a quick shower, moved to the large locker at the end of the room. Removing a jumpsuit in his size he peeled the sealed plastic from around it. The plastic went into a specially marked bin and he quickly donned the garment. Once dressed, he passed through another door into a glass airlock. Holding his arms up, he was blasted repeatedly by jets of air, similar to what one would be subject to passing through a security checkpoint at a major airport. He waited while the air was sucked up through the floor and the computer processed the sample. It took a few seconds for the advanced biosensors to do their job, but eventually the glass door opened with a buzz, allowing him to proceed.

"Good morning, Mr. Kimball," a guard greeted him.

"Yes," he simply replied. He had long since ceased caring what others thought of him. The man was just a guard, not worthy of his time.

He proceeded down a sealed concrete hallway devoid of any decorative additions other than the ominous biosensor every ten meters until he reached his office. Here he was greeted by the usual pile of paperwork stacked neatly in his IN basket. Everything else in the office was neat and orderly. John Kimball was a detail man in a detail business, one where the smallest mistake could mean death. It showed in every aspect of his life.

He had not even sat down when he heard a knock on the door behind him. He turned to see one of his operations people. Although he was dressed the same as John, the similarity ended there. The baggy jumpsuit did little to hide the man's physique or body language. If that didn't say "field operative," the haircut certainly did.

"What is it?" John asked.

"We have a problem, sir. Terrorists have bombed P-13. Our storage there has been compromised. We are unable to locate the caretaker. He may be dead."

Kimball absorbed this without emotion. They had little threat of exposure at this point. With the caretaker gone they would have to move fast to clean up the agents before they were mishandled, or worse, compromised and sold on the black market.

"You have people in the area?"

"No, sir. The team is currently at P-18 setting up a secure storage facility. If we pull them out it will raise some questions, and possibly leave the agents without a caretaker," he replied. "We have a transport crew of three within twenty hours distance, but that's all."

Kimball thought this through. One of the big disadvantages of the project was the lack of personnel. While need-to-know was applied, some always *did* need-to-know, and one cover story did not work for all contingencies.

"Safeguard the agent in place at P-18 and move the crew to P-13. Assign a new caretaker and get those three men there as soon as possible. I want updates every half hour."

"Yes, sir."

Kimball rounded his desk and sat down. Picking up the remote, he thumbed on the TV and surfed till he found CNN. A helicopter view of the embassy rubble slowly moved across the screen. He waited patiently till he saw a view of the warehouse next door. One end was in rubble while the other was intact. He knew exactly where every vial ever made was and the picture gave him reason to suspect that the vials were not mixed. He debated taking more measures to secure the agents, but chose not to. Secrecy was still their best option. The program was almost at the point it could be deployed if the time came. He could not afford to attract attention at this time.

He considered calling some old contacts he maintained from his days with the CIA. But then he would owe favors, and they would be curious as to what he'd been doing since he had left. Hard to collect a favor if you didn't know what someone was capable of. One of their best biological warfare hunters just disappearing in the middle of an armed conflict was not unusual, but for him to stay gone was. There were still plenty of people that needed watching. North Korea, Iran, China, Pakistan, our new/old friends the Russians, the new government of Iraq, and, of course, every terrorist group out there. He decided he would just stay quiet and off the radar. He would most likely get what he needed from the press anyway. It would just take a little longer.

He turned the TV off and picked up a report on Arctic Tern migration. They had been tracking them very closely this year.

—THREE—

"IT'S ABOUT TIME, JACK, I've been stalling for a couple of hours now. Where the hell have you been?"

"Sorry, sir, I was at the beach house to get away from the press, and I kind of let my pager die," Jack confessed as they turned to walk down the seventh floor hallway of the Hoover building. Jack had broken a few speed limits on his trip in from Delaware.

"Let your pager die?"

"Well, you're the one who put me on vacation, sir."

"Touché, thanks for pointing that out. You can consider that vacation over as of now. You saw the news this morning, I take it? The AG wants a team sent to figure out if Osama's boys are behind this as they claimed, or if it's somebody else using their name. You can pick your people, but you'll have some additions from State and the CIA. No arguments right now, Jack, just hear me out. This is big and we need to move quickly. There was some protest when your name came up. You're lucky to get this assignment at all. This is your chance to get back in the game."

"Why me, sir? I really don't have that much experience in Africa."

"I know. And I mentioned that, but they didn't debate it very long and you got the green light. You care?"

"Not yet. Something tells me I might later," Jack replied.

The Deputy Director stopped walking and looked around. Jack straightened his tie while he waited. His boss lowered his voice.

"Look, Jack, it's like this. You pissed off a lot of people when they found out the shooter we were chasing was your personal friend." He held up a hand before Jack could interrupt. "I know it wasn't your fault, but the way things ended on live TV didn't make you or the Bureau look good. That senator had a lot of friends. I'm not sure why your name came up for this, but Africa is a long way from DC and maybe that's why, they could just want you farther away. If you find something and do well, they can say they always had faith in you, and they look good for backing you and the FBI. If you screw up, they can use it against you and the Bureau and give the investigation to another agency. Some of these guys are hoping you drop the ball. I know you hate the politics, but that's the way it is. So, when we go through those doors, just be a good little soldier, toe the line, and we'll get you back on the front line, okay?"

Jack nodded. "Okay."

"That's my boy."

They turned and entered the large double doors. All conversation stopped as Jack found himself in the Bureau's largest conference room. It was used for meetings involving the upper echelon or the elected committee members. The walls were richly paneled in dark wood, and oil paintings adorned them, depicting highlights in the FBI's history. A large portrait of Hoover himself looked down from one end of the room. The windows were floor to ceiling, and the faint buzz of elevator music vibrating the glass to foil eavesdropping devices could be heard if one listened closely. The table was larger than any Jack had seen in his corporate days and it was ringed by high-backed leather chairs. Two empty ones sat waiting for him and his boss, and they took them facing several men and women. Jack couldn't help but note that there were no aides standing on the sidelines taking notes. Some of the people he recognized, but most he didn't.

"I apologize for the delay everyone," his boss addressed them. "We can proceed whenever you wish."

The room shifted its collective gaze to the man seated on the opposite end of the table. Jack recognized the man as Senator Kenneth Teague of Texas, the longtime chairman of the Senate Arms Services Committee. He was infamous for being a hard-ass, both for and against, when it came to the military. The senator had very clear ideas on what he thought the military needed and didn't need, and billions of dollars rested on his yea or nay votes. Now that the Department of Homeland Security had been added to the country's defensive arm, he had gained influence into the intelligence and anti-terrorism world. There were many who felt he wielded too much power, but few that had the cover to oppose him. No president had won Texas without his support, and the current president was a personal friend of the senator.

"Mr. Randall, I have no doubt you know why you were summoned here today. This embassy bombing is another setback in our war on these terrorists. I have your file here—" he placed his hand on a thick manila folder on the table in front of him, "—and I can see you've had a short, but impressive career here at the FBI. Normally I would expect the CIA to rectify their mistake of not averting this type of attack by bringing in those responsible for it. But I'm afraid they are focused elsewhere at this time. An investigation into this bombing is just that, an investigation. We have determined that the FBI has the best resources to execute and complete this task. I'm also told you are the man we need to conduct it."

Jack forced himself to not look to his boss for support. The questions in his mind were popping up faster than he could process them. How did he get my file? Was it my FBI file? My military file? Who cares, he has it. He can have it anytime he wants. Why are they so eager to send me? He recalled something an old teacher had told him. When it all goes to hell, just fix one thing at a time.

"Thank you, sir," Jack offered.

"You have some special operations experience?" the senator probed.

He already knows what I have, Jack thought, this was for the others present. Or it was a test. Don't be a pushover.

"Sir, I apologize, but I don't know every party present here. I feel it would be inappropriate to discuss that here today."

"Fair enough. Ever been to Africa?"

Jack hesitated again, but the senator let him off the hook.

"Simple yes or no will work, Agent Randall. I've been six times myself."

"Yes, sir, just not to Tanzania."

"Know a lot about bombs, do you?" The senator smiled as he asked.

"I know the fundamentals pretty well, sir."

"Very well. You know what to look for. I think we can get you some help from some of our people in the area?" He directed the question to a man seated across from Jack.

"Whatever he needs," was the man's reply.

It suddenly dawned on Jack who the man was. Anthony Beason, the newly appointed Deputy Director of Operations for the Central Intelligence Agency. The man responsible for every field spook the agency had deployed. He saw every piece of intelligence that came in from every asset they had. A powerful man in his own right, yet he seemed to defer to the senator.

"Good. Mr. Randall, you will assemble your team and depart as soon as possible. The Bureau will be the lead agency on this investigation and I expect all others represented here today to back him up. Are there any questions?" The senator didn't look around the room when he asked it, and a tap of Deacon's foot against Jack's ankle erased any from his mind. After a pause, everyone rose with the senator and filed out of the room. Soon Jack was left with just himself and his boss.

"That was quite a show," Jack ventured.

"Yes, it was. Look, Jack, the senator is a hard man, but he gets the job done. He's managed to cut a lot of pork from the defense budget while still giving up a lot of money for what he thinks they all need, and if the bastard wasn't right every time he wouldn't be where he is today. Hell, he hasn't had a real challenge to his seat since he got elected. Today he sees a mission that needs to be done, and he's stepping on some heads to see that it doesn't get used as a stepping stone by some bureaucrat, or bungled due to interservice rivalry. He pressured the others to get you the job."

Jack thought about it and the full definition of his new position came into stark clarity. His name had no doubt been discussed at length before it was mentioned to the suits that had just left the room. With his current public-hero status combined with his internal problems, he was good for all contingencies. They could point out that their hero had done it again if he succeeded, or they could ease him right out of the Bureau if he failed. He was disposable, if necessary. The right man for the job, huh? From their point of view, he was perfect.

"I get to assemble my own team?" he asked.

"I have a letter from the Director and the Attorney General to that effect. Your budget is out of Homeland Security and is basically a blank check. You have temporary rank as an O-7 with access to whatever military support you need. You have some mandatory attached personnel, but you can assemble your own team."

"Mandatory attached personnel?" Jack frowned at that. "You mean babysitters?"

"The CIA has people who are familiar with the area. They'll assign someone to be on the team. It's not negotiable," his boss replied.

Jack sank back in the leather chair and flipped a pen through his fingers. It was either accept the mission or return to the beach house—possibly forever.

"All right, here's who I want."

*   *   *

Crack!

Sydney Lewis rode the recoil into her shoulder and brought the sights back in line with her target, her finger already taking up the slack in the trigger. She steadied her sight picture and did her best to not jerk the trigger.

Crack!

"Good," she heard the instructor say behind her. "Improve your memory."

She knew he was referring to her muscle memory and not her brain. Although those memories were the reason she had devoted so much of her free time to the range over the past month. She had almost shot her boss in the middle of an important investigation! The fact that they had been a couple once didn't help things either.

She had never been a good shot, favoring the science aspect of her job more than the law enforcement portion. Jack had taught her himself in the beginning, and thanks to him she had somehow made it through her qualifying shoot to make it into the FBI. The brief romance that followed was passionate, but had ended with their graduation. They both just had different paths before them at the time. Being teamed up with him years later had been both pleasant and stressful, but so far their past had not interfered with their ability to work together. At least not too much. Since then she had picked up her weapon only when she'd been required to do so.

Her near-miss had changed her mind on shooting. The instructors here at Quantico were the best, and she had improved quite a bit in the last month.

Crack-Crack! She finished off the clip with a double-tap and automatically ejected the spent magazine and reloaded with another she pulled from her belt. It was empty and the reload was just practice, but it was something the instructors insisted upon. Only then did she relax, and still keeping the barrel pointed downrange, pulled the clip from her new automatic. She laid both down on the pad in front of her with the slide locked back. The safety was built into the grip and already engaged.

When she had first approached the instructors about becoming a better shot, they had all listened politely and then watched her shoot a few times. It was quickly determined that her current Glock was just a little too big for her small hands. They had tried her out on a few different models before she found her fit.

The Heckler & Koch P7 was small, chambered for a 9mm round, and featured a built-in safety mechanism that was disengaged just by her gripping it. She could cock it manually or with the grip mechanism, and this worked perfectly for her as it took a lot of doubt out of her mind and let her concentrate on improving her marksmanship. It had been further modified for her by the instructors to fit her specific trigger strength and outfitted with tritium sights for low-light conditions. She had purchased two and was practicing with the backup today. Behind her was Dave, her favorite instructor. She pulled her ear muffs down around her neck and shook her long black hair back behind her shoulders so she could hear his critique.

"Much, much better today, Sydney. I saw a few go a little right, so we need to get that trigger pull of yours a little smoothr, but other than that I think you should be happy with your progress. I may even take you out on the combat range and start working with you there. Let's see how you did."

Sydney pushed the button on the side of the lane divider and watched as her target came rushing at her. Sometimes Dave worked the button while she shot, simulating a rushing attacker. It was a little unnerving at first, but she got over it. The targets today were standard silhouettes. Dave had eagle eyes that missed little, and she wondered how far to the right she really was.

The target stopped in front of her and was backlit by the range lights. Most of her shots were center-mass—right in the chest, with a couple in the head when she had double-tapped.

"See here?" Dave pointed to two holes that were on the outside line of the innermost circle. "There, a little right. We need to work on your trigger pull, you're still jerking it after the first five shots." The shots were still in the center and would have been lethal if real, but Dave was a perfectionist in a serious business, and if he said she was off, then she was off.

"Okay. Any changes?" she asked.

"No, I think more practice will take care of it. Your reload speed is better. This is your backup, right? Do we need to get the well beveled?" They'd had the magazine well of her primary machined to accept the clips easier. It helped when loading a new clip in a hurry or in the dark. Her backup had yet to visit the machinist for that alteration.

"No. I think we'll just practice that more, too," she replied. Dave smiled, obviously pleased with her answer.

His smile was replaced with a frown and she followed his gaze to the rest behind her. Her pager was vibrating toward the edge and threatening to fall on the floor. She intercepted it before it could. Thumbing the button, the screen lit up and revealed three numbers.

"888"

Her expression changed from one of curiosity to a smile. 888 was code for "Report for a mission." She could finally get back to work.

"Raincheck, Dave?"

"Anytime," was his reply. "I'll clean your backup. You can pick it up later. Go see what they got for you."

"Thank you!" she called as she left the range, trying not to run.

*   *   *

Eric scrolled the code across the monitor screen, looking for what he was sure was a typo in the latest upgrade to his crime scene software. His schedule at the FBI was more hectic than most and he hoped to finish the software upgrade today so he could concentrate on other things.

His arrival at the Bureau had been rather untraditional and he was working hard to change everyone's perspective. Less than a year ago he had been a promising student at MIT, but a conflict with a professor over a prank had resulted in his being asked to leave for a short while. He'd been spending the time helping his father at the Las Vegas police department when he was discovered by Jack Randall. It had led to a job offer and now he found himself taking an accelerated course at Quantico on top of his other assignments. It was a heavy schedule, but he knew he would never find anything more interesting than what he had been exposed to in the last few months. The training and influence of his instructors showed as he had done away with the spiked hair and earring and replaced them with a more conservative cut and better wardrobe. He had also packed on a few pounds of muscle, most of which was sore and causing him to squirm in his seat.

He looked up from his computer screen as the buzzing broke through his concentration. He checked his pager, but the screen was blank. Puzzled, he looked around his cubicle for the noise. No lights on the phone. His cell was not ringing. He waited for it again.

Bzzzzzzzzz.

Some quiet cursing was heard from the cubicle next door. He pushed his chair out into the aisle and leaned it back in order to see around the corner.

Larry was holding a file in one hand and a cup of coffee in the other. A man with decades of experience, he was the detail man that Jack needed to back up his up-front style of leadership. The years had not been especially kind to him and duty at headquarters had added pounds around his midsection. He accepted the fact that he would never make it to the top of the ladder years ago and that was fine with him. Larry preferred good solid investigative work and would have been surprised to know that Jack had fought hard with several people to get him on his team. Some found Larry's unkempt appearance, peculiar wit, and lack of protocol a negative, but Jack knew better. Larry got results, and to Jack that was all he needed to know. Larry had taken a shine to Eric and they now had side-by-side cubicles.

He was currently making a concentrated effort to ignore the pager on his belt as it continued to vibrate.

"Larry?"

"Yeah, kid?"

"Your pager's going off."

"You sure?" Larry continued to pretend to read the file.

"Uh …yeah. You don't want to answer it? Could be important."

"No."

Eric smiled and pushed his chair farther into the cube. "Why not?"

"Ever been to Africa, kid?"

"No?"

"Well I have. It sucks. Hot as hell. Steam room humidity. Everything's dirty. Food gives you the shits. Bugs big as your head. Every disease known to man, and let's not forget, people who don't like us."

"And?" Eric was puzzled.

"Somebody thinks I should go and they're paging me. I hate Africa."

"They're just gonna keep paging," Eric pointed out.

"You don't think they'll get tired and call somebody else?" Larry pulled the pager from his belt, but refused to look at it. "You're good with this kinda stuff, can't you disable it for me or something?"

"No, not without somebody asking me why."

"Please?"

"Could be an adventure," Eric coaxed. "Who is it?"

Larry frowned at Eric. "You're a big help." He looked down at the offending device and reluctantly pushed the button. Eric watched his face and unexpectedly saw a smile.

"Not Africa?" he asked.

"No, it's Africa all right."

"So why the smile?"

Larry held up the pager for Eric to see. "It's Jack's number."

"He's back?"

"Evidently. You have a passport?"

Eric frowned. "Yeah, but no page for me."

Larry's reply was interrupted by the pager buzzing again. He snatched it off his belt and read the screen again. He handed it to Eric with a smile before turning to lock all his cabinets.

Eric looked down at the little screen: "Bring Eric with you. Jack"

"Hurry up, kid. Jack's back. Let's not keep him waiting."

Eric scrambled to lock his cube and follow.

*   *   *

"All right, let's quiet down people!"

Deputy Director Deacon's voice carried to the rear of the briefing room and silenced the multiple conversations. He scanned the room as everyone found a seat, ticking off names against the list in his head. Satisfied that everyone was present, he moved to the front of the room and waited till all eyes were on him.

"Okay, as you all know, the US Embassy in Tanzania was bombed today. The current numbers we have are 24 dead, 102 wounded, mostly Tanzanians working in and around the building. I'm told that the ambassador was among the dead, as well as FBI agents Bill Goecker and Steve Park. Both were working in the embassy at the time. Some of you knew these men. My hope is that we can bring some justice to the people who did this. That said, I give you your team leader." Deacon stepped aside and Jack took his place.

"For those of you that may not know me, my name is Jack Randall and I've been assigned to lead the team that'll be investigating the attack. The goal of the investigation is to find evidence leading to the identity of the attackers and the people who supported them. Following this briefing you'll be excused until nineteen-hundred to pack. You will then report here and we'll all depart for Andrews where we'll board planes to Africa. I don't know how long we'll be gone, so pack accordingly. Security is very tight, people, refrain from telling anyone where you are going. The press will be on us soon. Anyone found commenting to the press, on or off the record, will earn a ticket home and you can explain your comment to the Director."

Jack paused to let his comment sink in.

"You've all been chosen for your expertise in your field, your experience, and your ability to operate on no sleep." Jack got a courtesy laugh, even though they all knew he wasn't kidding. "You'll need all of it in the coming days. I've asked a few of you to intro yourselves and cover some key points, so let's get started. Syd?"

Sydney rose from her seat against the wall where she had been scanning some documents. She walked to the front as Jack retreated to a corner where he could watch her speak and observe those listening.

"Hello, my name is Agent Sydney Lewis and I head the forensics team. I'm here to give you an idea of what type of environment we'll be going into medically. A brief is being prepared covering all the other basics and will be available for the plane ride. I'm giving you this in person because it's important. East Africa is one of the most dangerous places on earth for disease. This doesn't mean you *may* be exposed, it guarantees it. Typhoid, leprosy, yellow fever, blackwater fever, cholera, tuberculosis, amoebic dysentery, tick borne fever, malaria, bilharzia, elephantitis, ancylostomiasis, Marburg, Ebola, and AIDS just scratch the surface of what can be acquired in Tanzania."

A hand shot up and Sydney waved it down.

"Yes, you will all be inoculated, several times." She paused to break open a medical kit in front of her on the table. She noted that she had everyone's undivided attention. She held items up as she lectured.

"Halazone tablets. They counteract all the bugs in the water, most of them anyway. Mefloquine. Anti-malarial tablets. You'll start them tonight and continue them for two weeks after we return. Don't forget them. It's the first thing you'll get. The rest of these items are antibiotics. We can't trust the local stuff. Tetanus toxoid injections. You'll get a booster before we leave also. Snakebite kit. I'll have anti-venom with me. Remember, of the thirty-three types of snake in East Africa, thirty of them are poisonous."

"How do we tell them apart?" someone asked.

"With a ratio like that, I suggest you avoid them all," she answered. "The hospitals over there have limited resources, and we'll be working in a hostile environment. Be careful when you're climbing around the embassy. Cuts and broken bones can turn to gangrene or sepsis quickly in that climate. If you end up bleeding and need a transfusion, well, you figure it out. I'm told an air ambulance will be on call, but that takes time. My point is, be careful. You don't want to get sick or injured over there." She reached inside her shirt and pulled out a chain with two tags hanging from it. "Dog tags. Everyone will be issued two pair. Wear them at all times. No exceptions. Something happens, they may just save you. Any questions?" She scanned the room. No hands. She turned to see Jack stepping forward.

"Take it to heart, people. The hospital is overwhelmed. If you get sick or injured that's one less of you on the team, and we need everybody for this one. Our security on this investigation will be run by Agent Greg Whitcomb. Greg comes to us from the Hostage Rescue Team and he will be second in command. What he says goes." He nodded to Greg who took Sydney's place in front of the room and proceeded to outline the threats they faced and the procedures they would all follow.

Jack looked from face to face as Greg gave them the bad news. A few frowns, but no one looked like they were having second thoughts.

"A lot of strange faces, Jack," Sydney whispered from her place next to him.

"Yeah, but we need them."

"You pick them?" she asked.

"Most. Some were added by the Director."

"On whose order?"

"Exactly. I didn't really have a choice. But most of them make sense."

"And those who don't?"

"I'll keep an eye on them," Jack replied.

They watched Greg give his talk for a few minutes and Jack scanned the new faces in the group. The strangers among them were sitting quietly and taking in the lecture. He reviewed the files he had briefly read on each as he thought about Sydney's question.

An attractive young woman sat in the front row, actually taking notes. She wore short dark hair that was simply brushed. No highlights or stylish cut. Subtle makeup. She possessed the healthy figure of one who was no stranger to hard physical labor. Intelligent eyes sat behind wire-rimmed glasses. Her name was Heather Sachs, and she was from the Center for Disease Control in Atlanta. Although only twenty-eight, she held dual degrees in Microbiology and Genetics from Duke University. Her attachment to the group was due to her being one of the United States government liaisons to the disease fighting groups in Tanzania. She coordinated with the CDC, WHO, Red Cross, Doctors without Borders, and all the other groups attempting to fight the diseases plaguing the area. Although a civilian, she had numerous contacts, and some pull with the military, and seemed to be respected by her peers. Several glowing letters were included in the file, and she had spent considerable time in the field, mostly East Africa. The embassy had been one of the hubs of the disease fighting effort, and she was hitching along to salvage what supplies could be saved from the building and adjacent warehouse. Jack was not quite sure as to why she had been included in his group as she offered no real skills pertaining to the investigation. Other than taking the place of someone else, he hadn't seen any harm in her going either. Attempting to cut her was not worth the fight, so he had simply kept her without question. Jack had watched her during Sydney's lecture and waited for her to interrupt. But she had simply listened politely and not offered her expert opinion. Jack took her in now as she listened. She caught his gaze and returned it with a nod before returning her eyes and attention back to Greg.

Jack moved his gaze to the back row and found the figure of Dennis Murphy of the Central Intelligence Agency. Tall, mid 40s, red hair, and Irish through and through. He also had an impressive file and Jack had tried to absorb more than the highlights, but had been pressed for time. His job description was that of an analyst. One who took the raw data gathered in the field and figured out what it all meant. He had been at the Africa desk for several years, and although the file claimed he'd had no military experience, Jack didn't believe it. He had watched the man enter the room and climb the stairs to the top row before selecting his seat. Something an operative did out of habit—his back to the wall and everyone in view. He also had the build of someone who had carried heavy loads at one time. Military people ran a lot. They also had strong backs from long marches with heavy rucksacks. Mr. Murphy had the telltale signs of well developed calves and lower back muscles. Either he had an out-of-proportion workout regimen, or he had spent some time in the trenches. Jack suspected that the file was a phony, or at least a half-truth.

Murphy was along to coordinate between the CIA and the investigation team, following up on anything they found and getting it to people who could do something about it. Jack wasn't wild about his presence, but he understood the need. Nevertheless, he would keep a careful eye on Mr. Murphy.

Jack moved his gaze to a man in the second row, an FBI man by the name of Bradford Williams. An explosives expert, complete with a missing finger. A former US Navy Seal, he had transferred to the FBI after ten years with the teams. Jack was impressed with his record. Combat tours on three continents, some nice letters from the admirals that steered the navy, and one from the King of Saudi Arabia that was heavily blacked out. Somehow he had found time to complete a Masters degree in electrical engineering, and so far had worked with HRT and other departments of the FBI on other bombings ranging from abortion clinics to the Murrah Federal Building in Oklahoma City. His purpose on the team was self explanatory and Jack was happy to have him.

The others were familiar faces, some of them picked by Sydney from her team, three of Greg's shooters, a documents analyst, and some communications people. All in all, a good team. Jack would see what they were made of quickly. They were all about to be thrown into the deep end.

WORLD CAN 'SAFELY' BURN ONLY
25% OF REMAINING OIL, COAL.
April 29, 2009—Reuters

–FOUR–

"MAY I JOIN YOU?"

Heather looked up to see Sydney standing over her. They had boarded the G5 at Andrews and everyone was finding their place for the long flight. She had secured herself a window seat, and was buckled in and reading when Sydney approached.

"Sure, be my guest."

"Thanks. Nice to sit with one of the girls for a change. We haven't had a chance to meet yet. I'm Sydney Lewis." She offered a hand for a quick shake.

"Heather Sachs, nice to meet you too."

"Sachs as in Saks? If that's true, you're my new best friend," Sydney inquired.

"No such luck I'm afraid. My parents are hippies from the Midwest," Heather replied. "You're the forensics team leader, the one who likes shooting dead people?"

"Yes, you heard the rumors already I see. That's good." Sydney grinned. "I understand you like bugs?"

"Also true, the microscopic sized ones anyway." Heather laughed. "I got interested from a friend of my father's. Mom was an oceanographer. I grew up in a science community. I started hunting diseases with Dr. Peters of the CDC when I was still in school. Been in it ever since."

"How'd you get attached to us?"

"Well, after I finished a hunting trip for Marburg I had a few months off. A forced vacation actually. But I'm not one who sits still so I stayed in-country with a doctor I met and helped out with the AIDS/TB program, vaccinating people and setting up clinics. Then, somehow my name got to someone at Homeland Security, the bombing happened and they called. So here I am."

"What do you think so far?" Sydney asked.

"I'll give you this. You guys really know how to travel. The CDC flies commercial, or we hitch rides on military transports. This is a nice change."

"Yeah well, the Bureau doesn't really own this plane. At least I don't think it does. It was seized by the DEA from one of the cartels. So if you find a bag of cocaine under your seat, don't be surprised. We've used this one before and it's pretty plush. The best thing is it already had the best communications gear possible. They added the scramblers so we can talk in the clear, but other than that, it's just like we got it. I have no complaints."

"I wouldn't either. Flying commercial takes forever. Last time it took me something like thirty-six hours or so. That's with a connection in Sao Palo, Brazil. Not a pleasant trip."

"Coach?"

"Of course. Our budget is always tight. We're lucky to have travel money. The Homeland Security budget helps offset our cost and The World Health Organization helps a little, but money is always a big factor."

Sydney took this in as she looked at the woman next to her in a new light. She wore no expensive jewelry, no flashy clothing. A Timex watch adorned one wrist, the kind a jogger would wear. Her clothing had the durable look of something you would find in a sporting goods store rather than a department store. Well-worn canvas shoes covered her feet, and there was no hint of perfume. Her face had minimal makeup, but then not a lot was really needed. A floppy hat and a pair of sunglasses protruded from her handbag, also made of canvas and showing years of use. She looked just like the person she claimed to be, Sydney decided. She also noticed Heather wore no wedding ring.

"So this doctor you stayed with, he wasn't the young and cute type by chance was he?" she asked.

"Maybe," she admitted. "But he was married to his work. You know the type?"

"Oh yeah." She sighed, glancing behind her.

They both settled into their seats as the engines screamed louder and the plane accelerated down the runway, ending the conversation.

*   *   *

"Spook huh?"

Larry found himself sitting next to Dennis Murphy in the middle of the plane. Eric was on the opposite side, but he was already settled in with his earphones on and laptop open. Larry knew he'd be in his own little world for the majority of the flight.

"Yup, over fourteen years now," Murphy replied. "You?"

"I stole Hoover's stapler on my first day," Larry dodged. "How'd you get attached to us?"

"I'm the guy who gets all the East Africa stuff, everything from tribal war scoreboards to who's overthrowing what government to new pirate safe havens. Believe it or not, it's a busy place for a guy like me. Nothing ever makes the news in the States coming out of East Africa, but when it does. Well, you know, the occasional Hollywood movie about genocide at a hotel or diamond smuggling gets some attention. But mostly it's a forgotten area of the world."

"Not anymore."

"True, but for how long? They'll be back to their lattes and celebrity gossip by the weekend. Anyway, somebody higher up than me got a call and here I am. Gets me out of the office."

"That happen a lot?" Larry probed.

"On occasion," Murphy replied, revealing nothing. "You been to Africa before?" he asked, changing the subject.

"Yup, during my early days. Can't say I'm a big fan."

"Ever come outside of duty?"

Larry snorted. "No, can't say that's ever crossed my mind."

"You should. The Serengeti and the highlands are beautiful. And they're disappearing. You should see them while you still have time."

"Maybe. So what do you think we're gonna find?"

"Depends on your people, really. We have reports of Al Qaeda operatives in the area, but nothing concrete. If you can get me some leads I can follow them up with agency contacts in the area, and maybe track it up the chain. The African cells are not as tight as the Asian cells, and the communications there are easier to compromise. That could help us. The hard part is the languages. While English and Swahili are the national languages, the people speak hundreds of local dialects, and that makes translation take much longer than normal. We only have so many people on the East Africa desk. I'm told we have numerous intercepts, but it may take days or even weeks to translate and analyze all of them."

"What about the government?" Larry asked.

"The Tanzanians? They actually have one of the more stable governments in the area. They're fortunate to have less of the tribal warfare that plagues the other African nations. Leftovers from the stupidity of the European colonial rule. When they divided up the continent they paid no attention to tribal boundaries and there's been constant war among them ever since. They're also lucky to have Kenya for a neighbor, one of the few nations to get past the tribal disputes and secure their country's future. No, I believe the Tanzanians are truthful in their desire to help us. They ultimately know that the future of their country, as well as all of East

Africa, rests in the hands of America."

"How's that? They really have no strategic or political strength. They can get guns, or oil, or whatever from somebody else. Why do they need us so bad?" Larry was confused.

"Drugs. Disease is slowly killing Africa. AIDS and other diseases are rampant. The average woman produces four children, and the population is still declining. American pharmaceutical companies have the drugs and the manufacturing capabilities to produce them on the scale that's needed."

"Okay, so ship the drugs."

"Not that easy. These drugs require a strict regimen of three different drugs being taken at precise intervals in a twenty-four hour period. They also cost about sixty bucks a day."

"Bullshit. That's just what they charge."

"Not necessarily, the pills cost about four dollars a dose to produce today. That's the pills made now. The *first* pill cost over 400 million in research and development costs. The companies can't afford to just give them away. Shipping them to the capital is a negligible cost, but after that they are subject to corruption and theft for resale on the black market. On top of that, our biggest effort to combat AIDS has backfired on us."

"What was that?"

"The highway. The Kinshasa highway runs across central Africa. Most aid doesn't make it to the people it's intended for because there aren't sufficient roads in Africa to deliver it to them. So we built the highway."

"I don't get it. How did that backfire?"

"While the road helped speed the delivery of supplies, it also spread the disease faster. Sick villagers would no longer stay in place. People trading goods traveled the highway and spread the disease quicker. Truck drivers and prostitutes are the main culprit these days."

"Wow," was all Larry could offer. He sat back in his seat to think about it for a few minutes. "You said that the drugs could be delivered now, right? So why are the people still dying?"

"The drug companies have shown a reluctance to send them. They feel that even if they were to send all that were needed, it would make little difference."

"Why? Because there's more money in Viagra?"

"The people have no education, and no watches. They can't read the labels or tell time."

"That's it, lack of a watch and some simple education?"

"That's it, simple as that. That young lady who's sitting up there with your friend? I've heard of her. While I applaud her efforts, I sometimes feel like she's fighting a lost cause."

"Sounds like you've dealt with this a lot. You sure you're a spook?"

Murphy smiled. "You can't avoid it in Africa. It's both a scourge and a business there. But on this trip we're hunting terrorists, and I hope we find the bastards."

"Me, too. This thing has a full bar, how about a drink?" Larry offered.

"My new boss won't mind?"

"Not on a flight this long. Just be ready when we hit the ground. Jack's a results kind of guy. You get the job done and he'll overlook a lot. Whiskey, I'm guessing?"

"My names Murphy, isn't it?" he shot back.

"Two to go." Larry heaved his considerable frame out of the seat and went forward to the galley. He noticed Eric was already asleep with his headphones still blaring loud enough for Larry to hear. Jack had asked Larry to get friendly with their CIA attachment. So far he hadn't found anything unusual about the guy. If anything, he seemed very knowledgeable and forthcoming. Well, he had a few minis of Bushmills and several hours to work on him some more. He'd see what he could do. On the way back to his seat he noticed Sydney talking and laughing with her new friend. He hoped she was having better luck with her assignment.

*   *   *

Jack sat in the back row of the plane with Greg and Bradford Williams. Every hour they had received multiple faxes as the home office updated them with new information. The latest included a series of pictures that Brad scrutinized with a magnifying glass for several minutes.

"Well, Brad, what do you think?" Greg asked.

"The damage is consistent with what the eyewitnesses say. Most likely the truck was packed with ammonia nitrate and diesel fuel. It's cheap and you can probably get it easier than ammunition over there. One dedicated driver to deliver it and that's all you really need. That embassy was built in the days before we had to worry about such things. The perimeter wasn't upgraded, I see, possibly why they chose it. Timing was a factor too. The government is in the process of moving their capital from Dar to Dodoma. Most of the embassies were choosing to follow. Good excuse to upgrade the building and get better security at the same time. In about six months this building would have been vacant."

"Was that common knowledge?" Jack asked.

"I doubt they did a State Department release, but there really isn't a way to hide it. New construction is guarded from day one by United States Marines, otherwise you get a building full of bugs like we got in Moscow."

Jack remembered reading about that. The contract for the new Moscow embassy had been handled by a company that used a private security firm. As a result, the United States was the proud owner of a building so infested with electronic listening devices the phones couldn't function. It sat empty for years before being sold for pennies on the dollar.

"So what should we look for?" Greg asked.

"I'll determine the epicenter of the explosion, which won't be hard. Get some measurements and estimate yield and what not. Then I'll send it all to your man Eric. He can combine what I find with the building's blueprint and run it through his computer to come up with a map of where the items we want most likely are. Nothing else to add to this list?"

"No, not so far. They didn't have a remote view camera there either."

"Damn, that really would have helped."

Jack referred to a camera that had become standard at most embassies that was set up about a block away and recorded a constant view of the embassy. Some had multiple cameras. Most likely, the cameras hadn't been set up due to the impending move.

"So we want the two cameras that viewed the front, the east wall camera, the lobby camera, the stills from the ATM across the street, and all the news footage from the local station. Are we going to have a problem getting that?"

"I understand we have it already. The station gave it up on order from their president. He seems to be backing us very strongly. We'll have to dig for the rest," Jack answered.

"CNN cameras tend to bring that out of a person," Greg commented.

"I'm told it's more than that, but we'll see when we get there if it's just lip service or not. What's your security plan?"

"Well, we have some pissed-off Marines for perimeter control. The locals have given us control out to a block away. Any extra Marines will be sifting through the rubble. We have an earthquake recovery team flying in with their dogs. Heavy equipment is on the way from local mining operations, but we can't use it till we determine if there are any survivors left. The airport donated klieg lights so we can work non-stop. The Navy is moving the Mercy offshore in about a day. It was on its way back from India after that small tsunami they just had, so that solves the medical problems. We get a bunch of rooms at the Kilimanjaro Hotel, built by the Israelis about a hundred years ago. Touristy, but nice. Security will be okay. Tanzanian military, but we'll have Marines at the ends of the halls and in the lobby 24/7. I'll set us up a comm center on the best balcony. No uniforms for us, we'll try to look like tourists. The Marines will take us in groups to and from the site. I want one of my people with any group that travels. Same if somebody needs to go somewhere alone."

"You brought all your toys, right?" Jack asked.

He got an evil smile in return. "And then some. First thing I plan on doing is taking a little toy of Brad's on a drive around the city. It's a little box that sends out signals on all frequencies. It tends to set things off prematurely. If there're any more remote detonators in the city, it'll find them."

"Sounds like a plan," Jack agreed. "Let me know if something changes, I'm going to try and absorb this before we get there." He held up a two-inch stack of paper. He adjusted the overhead light and settled back in his chair. Outside the sun was going down over the ocean, but he had no time to enjoy it.

*　　　　*　　　　*

The plane circled slowly over Dar es Salaam and Jack looked down on the port city, attempting to find the embassy. The downtown area was quickly passed and Jack was given a view of the city extending to the west. The homes were all the same size and shape, sporting blue or red tile roofs and whitewashed exteriors. All the buildings looked the same from a thousand feet up, and the billowing dust carried by the offshore breeze obscured details. It was a month before the wet season, and Jack was thankful for that. The plane straightened and leveled off, flying directly over the city on its approach to Julius Nyerere International Airport. Jack pulled his attention back into the plane and observed his team.

Despite the luxury of the Gulfstream 5 aircraft, they all looked haggard and worn out by the journey. Flying east was always harder then flying west. The jet lag was worse. It was easier to go to sleep later than usual rather than try to force the body to sleep earlier. Dar was a full eight hours ahead of Washington, DC. They would be out of their circadian rhythms for a few days.

Jack tucked the file he had been reading into his overstuffed briefcase. He had saved it for last and was glad he had finally found time to read it. It was a six page summary on Tanzania, a cut-and-paste document thrown together by a junior staffer somewhere in the bowels of the Hoover Building. Jack had absorbed it in the last hour and had been appalled by the numbers. For a country roughly the size of California, it held a population of forty-one million people, 470,000 of which were refugees from the neighboring countries. The life expectancy was only forty-nine years for the average male, this due primarily to the diseases that ravaged the country. An estimated 32% of the people were infected with AIDS. Despite an aggressive effort by the government and several aid groups, the number was still climbing. He returned his gaze out the window in time to see them touch down on the main runway. The plane taxied off the runway and soon followed a pickup truck flying the green and blue national flag on the rear tailgate. It proceeded down the taxiway to a large hangar. The plane stopped just outside the hangar doors, and the co-pilot emerged from the cockpit to open the door.

Jack watched Larry out of the corner of his eye. Larry didn't respond well to heat, and Jack knew he was in for a spectacle when the door opened. With a hydraulic hiss it broke its seal and the stairs were lowered slowly to the ground. The heat flooded the interior, removing any remnants of air conditioning that remained. Larry's face scowled, his eyes rolled, but he said nothing. The thick humid air contained the smell of the tropics and emphasized the fact that they were no longer in DC.

"It's not bad," Jack offered. "At least it's not raining all day."

"Hate Africa," was all Larry had for a reply. His face was already starting to sweat. He put on his sunglasses before grabbing his bag and moving toward the door. He unconsciously rubbed the knot in his ass as he moved forward. They all had one from the shot of gamma globulin Sydney had administered the day before. Larry thought it was cement, or maybe peanut butter she had injected instead. Between the knot in his butt and the upset stomach due to all the pills, he had not had a pleasant flight.

Eric however, was the first one off the plane. He had taken Jack's advice and was sporting a pair of rip-stop pants similar to military fatigues and a new khaki Columbia brand fishing shirt. He had stopped at the Century City Mall before they departed and picked up several pair, mostly the same color since they were out of season. So he would dress like Einstein for a few days, big deal. Jack had also mentioned he would probably not wish to return with some of them. He swung his bag over his shoulder and did a quick one-eighty, taking in the view. There seemed to be two terminals, one, a modern structure with a vaulted concrete and steel roof several hundred yards to the west, and another, older, red brick building with neat white trim. It featured a short control tower just off to their left.

"No welcoming party?" he asked Sydney.

"I guess not. We're supposed to be low profile, remember?" she replied. She removed a tie from her wrist and gathered up her hair for a more comfortable ponytail.

"Can you *be* low profile in a G-5?" Eric asked.

She looked around the tarmac and the only plane she saw bigger then theirs was a commercial DC-9 with the Air Kenya logo on the side. Everything else was propeller driven and very old.

"Maybe not," she conceded.

Larry joined them and dropped his bag on the hot asphalt. "What is it you think, about a hundred?" His shirt was already stuck to his back and sweat stains adorned his armpits.

"Maybe, may cool off into the ninety's tonight. Good sleeping weather," Sydney offered.

"Very funny. Who's this guy?"

"That would be our embassy contact," Jack answered. "Follow me."

Two men approached from the hangar door, a white man of about forty and a black man of the same age. The black man wore the uniform of the Tanzanian military and stood at least 6'5" with a heavily muscled frame. He was not sweating at all.

"Mr. Randall? Peter Brooks from the embassy. This is Major Arusha from the Tanzanian Security forces. He'll help us through customs and get us into the city."

Jack shook both the offered hands. "You're from the embassy staff?"

"Yes, aide to Ambassador Green. I was fortunate enough to be out of the building the day of the bombing. I was meeting with the Major here to discuss medication delivery. I'm afraid it requires security as a vicious black market has developed."

The major spoke with a deep voice that carried over the sound of the jet engines in the distance. "I wish to express our sympathies on behalf of my country. My president asked that I extend you any courtesy you may need to help bring these criminals to justice."

"Thank you, Major. I hope our people can work together to make that happen," Jack replied.

"Like an English Darth Vader," Eric whispered.

"Shut up," Sydney hissed back.

"If you will just follow me, please?" the major bellowed at them. He turned and led them through the hangar and into the red brick building. The customs facilities were bypassed and airport security scrambled to get out of the major's way as he led them with long strides out to the street. Two buses waited, accompanied by two Jeeps sporting mounted machine guns and three-man crews. A police car led the motorcade with lights flashing.

"A precaution. We don't expect further trouble," Brooks quietly offered Jack. "They feel embarrassed by what happened. We can't really say no without offending them." Jack just nodded in reply. He'd been briefed. The Tanzanian government saw the terrorist as a threat to their nation as well. While the island of Zanzibar had a high Muslim population, the mainland people were mostly Gratian or Tribal in their religious beliefs. The current government was like all governments—they wished to remain in control.

"Why the wire?" Eric asked Larry. The buses came with thick wire over the open glass windows.

"To keep the grenades out," Larry answered.

"Oh."

"Did I mention that I hate Africa?"

DROUGHT AND FAMINE
IN NORTHWEST AFRICA.
August 9, 2009—USA Today

—FIVE—

SYDNEY STOOD UP FROM her seat in the front of the bus and turned to face the group. She consulted a list she had put together while on the plane and addressed them in her loudest voice, to be heard over the open windows and street noise.

"Everybody listen up! We're making a stop at the hospital on our way in. We have some supplies for them, and those of you who can will be asked to donate blood. Supplies are critical and the local donors can't be screened thoroughly. I have all your types here, and these people need every drop." She paused, expecting some resistance. There was none. She got an encouraging smile from Heather. Sydney realized she was the wrong person for the rest of the speech. "Heather will fill you in on what you'll be seeing and what we'll need of you." She let go of the overhead rail and dropped into her seat with the help of the potholed road. Heather struggled to take her place and quickly grabbed the vacated rail.

"I don't know all of your backgrounds or what you may have been exposed to, so forgive me if I'm talking down to any of you," she began. "The hospital here has been overwhelmed for some time, mostly due to AIDS. When the beds are all full people end up on the floor or in the hallways. Now with all the victims of the bombing, they are barely hanging on. Supplies are being flown in from outside the country, but they take time to load and ship. So we beat them here, is what I'm trying to say. People are being treated in a tent city that was set up for the overflow, but until the Mercy docks in the harbor, the situation won't improve. Those of you that did not require new vaccinations will be asked to donate blood. The local population is full of HIV and other diseases, so any outside donations will be priceless. I'm told that the Americans that are stable enough to be flown out are being moved in the next twelve hours or so. Those that can't are being treated as best we can here. They need blood and platelets mostly, so please donate."

"The hospitals range from a modern facility here in Dar, to tents in the bush country. Medications are very limited. You're going to see some people suffering. That doesn't really cover it, but just know what's coming. Try not to touch anything you don't have to, keep your gloves on, and just be careful. I don't know what else I can tell you." Heather shrugged and looked to Sydney for help.

Sydney stood and took her place. "Any questions?" She got nothing but head shakes from the team. It was hard to know what to ask when everything was an unknown. Those who knew just watched out the windows as the bus made its way through the busy streets.

The hospital came into view as they rounded a corner. A building of modest size with little thought given to aesthetics, it sat in the city surrounded by a large group of people. Most sitting quietly in whatever shade they could produce while others crowded around the entrance, pleading their case to the military guards controlling access to the door. Children and adults, some covered in blood, milled about aimlessly, unsure as to what they should do as they waited to see if they would be allowed into the hospital. The bus closed on the bumper of the Jeep in front of them and they slowly forced a path to the front door. The crowd of refugees, disease victims, and the recently wounded parted slowly. From their elevated position, the passengers of the bus could see over the square and down the side streets in every direction. The sea of humanity stretched out as far as they could see. The mass of bodies moved like a single living organism. Most of them dressed in rags, some carrying children, or what few possessions they still had. Some lay still in the dirt under the open sky and merciless sun. The smell and sounds of the living and dead filled the bus, and they all heard the fragile, erratic coughing of sick adults and children coupled with the moaning of the wounded and the wailing of the mourners as relatives died. It was as if they were crossing a battleground just after its horrible conclusion. The fine cloud of dust stirred up by the mob did little to hide the scene from the team.

"My God," Eric whispered. He looked down on a young boy of no more than four years as he clung to his mother's leg. The boy gazed up at Eric with one eye, the other glued shut by dried blood and filth. The sun's warmth and the size of the crowd had attracted a great swarm of flies. As the boy watched Eric pass, flies landed in his mouth, his nose, his eyes. Anywhere there was moisture. He brushed them away but they immediately returned. Too many to deal with, the boy couldn't afford to waste his strength and the flies were ignored. Eric watched him until he disappeared into the dust.

Their attention all turned to the front of the bus as it stopped in front of the hospital. Eric stood and then bent to retrieve two boxes of supplies that had been assigned to him to carry. He shuffled forward until he was at the front.

"Can you handle one more?" Heather asked.

"Sure."

Heather added a small box to the top of the two in his stack. Her height did not let her carry too much without blocking her view. Eric did not have the same problem.

"Where do we go?" he asked her.

"Just follow the major until we're through the gate. Don't let anybody grab you or the boxes. They're like gold, and these people are desperate," she warned.

"Okay." He got an encouraging look from Sydney as he passed her and followed Heather out of the bus.

The smell was overpowering and the flies were on him instantly. He squinted and shook his head to keep his eyes clear long enough to follow her through the corridor of armed men and past the gated wall into the hospital compound itself. Here the walls of the building offered some shade from the sun, and he found himself walking past a long line of people waiting to see two men under a tarp stretched out in the corner closest to the door.

"What's the line for?" he asked Heather.

"Food and medicine are limited. Some of these people have walked for days to get here. Most have a disease of some kind, or are too mal-nourished to be treated. The doctors give them a quick physical assessment to determine if they are healthy enough to be saved. If they are, they get a paper chit that means food and medicine. If they aren't...." She let her thoughts fade, unwilling to voice the alternative.

Eric stood and watched as a young woman handed a baby wrapped in rags to the doctor under the tarp. The doctor pinched the skin on the baby's back, then on her thighs. The child did not stir or even blink the flies away from its clouded eyes. A stethoscope was placed on its chest and the expression on the doctor's face clouded. The baby was too far gone. The doctor turned his attention to the mother. She was very emaci-ated, beyond what little help the food bank could provide. The doctor handed the baby to a large black man assisting him before facing the woman. The woman held out her hand for the paper chit, but the doctor just shook his head. The woman trembled and again stretched out her open hand. But the doctor again shook his head. The assistant grasped the woman by her shoulders and spoke to her in her native tongue. Small tears appeared as she listened to his deep voice, and she allowed herself to be slowly led away.

"What will happen to her?" Eric asked.

"Sometimes the babies die and the mothers carry them for days. They can't bring themselves to put them down. He'll find her a place out of the sun to rest. Provide some water. She'll most likely be gone by morning. Every day at sunrise the dead are loaded into a truck and taken to a mass grave somewhere outside the city."

"I never imagined." Eric shook his head.

"There are too many people," was all Heather replied.

Eric watched the doctor as he steeled himself before seeing the next person in line. Eric met the man's gaze briefly and was shocked by how young he really was—barely older than himself. The man nodded in return before wiping the sweat from his eyes and facing the next refugee in line.

Eric turned and followed Heather and Sydney into the building. The crowded lobby gave way to corridors filled with stretchers lining the walls. Most held people who quietly suffered while others wailed or moaned to whoever would listen. Native nurses pushed through the masses to attend them as best they could. Mosquito nets hung at intervals in the hallways and eventually the flies dissipated. The hallways revealed rooms with people occupying every available space. Eventually they arrived at an intersection that was divided by a half wall that kept the traffic from the three desks on the other side. A tall, thin white woman dressed in worn scrubs and the expression of one who was overwhelmed, stood on the other side and she watched as the parade of white faces approached. When she saw Heather's face among them her expression changed to one of recognition and delight.

"Heather, I thought I would not see you for some time!" She rounded the desk and came through the gate to embrace her friend.

"Sister Mary!" Heather replied. "I come bearing gifts." She barely managed to set the boxes down before the woman wrapped her in a hug.

Sister Mary released her friend and eyed the rest of the group. "All Americans? Can they donate?" she asked.

"Some," Heather replied.

"I have their types with me," Sydney added, holding up a notebook.

Sister Mary turned and spewed a torrent of Swahili at two nurses standing at the desk behind her. One immediately picked up the phone, while the other sprinted down the hallway. A third unlocked a room behind the desk, revealing shelves for supplies, many of them empty.

"Please leave the boxes here and then follow me. The Americans are in surgery and the blood supply has run out." She turned and walked away at a pace that was surprising for her age. She did it without looking back.

The group looked to Jack for guidance and he simply replied, "Get moving."

They all dropped their boxes on the wall by the desk and sprinted to catch up. After two hallways and three flights of stairs they found themselves outside a surgical ward. Sister Mary spoke briefly with the nurse before turning to address them.

"We only have three surgeons right now. One of the hospital's surgeons was attending his father's funeral in England. I'm told he is returning as we speak. The others were in country as part of the humanitarian efforts. They have been in the OR since the attack. We've exhausted our blood supplies and tapping the local population has proved to be too dangerous."

"How bad is it Mary?" Heather asked.

"The last few patients have required auto-transfusion. They're in recovery but …we need blood." The nurse returned to Mary's side and handed her some papers. She scanned them quickly and looked up, searching for Sydney.

"I need two, maybe three, type A positive?"

Sydney consulted her notes and barked out the names. "Murphy and Randall, Eric, you're last. Everybody else just stand by. You need help in there?"

Jack and Dennis moved to the front of the group just as a doctor pushed through the doors behind them. His face was masked and his bloody gloves were clasped together against his equally bloody surgical scrubs. He had tired eyes behind wire-rimmed glasses that perched on a sweaty nose. His feet were wrapped in booties and left a trail of bloody footprints. He corrected his posture and worked his neck from side to side before addressing them in American English.

"I'm Doctor Dahli. Sorry to be brief, but I have an embassy Marine on the table who's bleeding out and I don't have anything to replace it. Who can donate?"

Jack stepped forward with Murphy. "Right here, doc."

He nodded and turned to Sister Mary. "Get 'em prepped and in here now."

"Take off your shirt and shoes and put these on," Sister Mary ordered as she flung two scrub tops in their direction. They scrambled to comply. Sydney began stripping down as well, oblivious to the men surrounding her.

"Sydney?" Jack asked.

She looked up to see Jack giving her a curious expression. She met it and turned to Sister Mary. "I'll need one, too. I can help."

Her tone left no room for argument and the scrubs were provided.

The three of them pushed through the doors and followed the footprints to the second OR. Here Sydney pulled a box of latex gloves off the wall and handed them out. Once they were all gloved, gowned, and masked, she put her back to the door and pushed it open, holding it for her boss and their spook.

"Don't touch anything. Just find a spot in the corner till I need you," she told them. Once they had complied, she looked the room over. The surgical team was busy working on the Marine. Her paramedic eyes took in the injuries and the vital signs on the monitor. The Marine was a large man and muscular in the way most Marines are, but his color was poor, and the amount of blood on the floor combined with the blood pressure reading on the monitor told her he was close to bleeding out. She noticed a stretcher pushed against the wall that was adjusted to its highest setting.

"Jack, get up on that stretcher," she ordered. She walked to the supply cabinet against the opposite wall and began going through the drawers. It was actually a tool box, just like they used in the States. In the third drawer she saw what she needed. She removed alcohol preps, iodine, IV tubing, saline, and two 16 gauge catheters. She couldn't find a tourniquet, so she grabbed another glove from a box on top of the cabinet.

She paused long enough to look over the doctor's shoulder and see where the patient's IV was before approaching Jack.

"Show me your antecubital fossa," she told him.

"Do I have one?" Jack answered.

"I mean make a fist so I can see the veins in your arm."

She wrapped the glove around his biceps for a makeshift tourniquet. While he pumped his fist she hung the bag of saline and flushed the tubing, clamping the end when it flowed freely. She scrubbed his arm clean and then eyeballed the catheter by habit before unwrapping it. It was three months past its expiration date, but that couldn't be helped.

Fortunately, Jack had always stayed in shape and possessed prominent veins. She held the needle up to the light to determine the bevel angle—it also allowed Jack a preview of what was to come. Before he could say anything, she grabbed his wrist to steady his arm and plunged the needle into the vein. Getting a flash of blood, she advanced the catheter with her forefinger, clamping the vein above it with her thumb. She removed the needle and attached the IV tubing. Taping the tubing in place, she retrieved the other end.

"We're ready," she announced to the surgical team. Doctor Dahli looked up as if he had just noticed her. He quickly took in the scene and her preparation.

"Excellent, use the femoral line," he ordered.

The team parted long enough for her to attach the tubing to the central line in the patient's left femoral vein. She pulled back and opened the roller clamp. Immediately the saline from the bag mixed with the blood from Jacks arm and began flowing to the patient. She watched the monitor for signs of improvement and was soon rewarded with a climb in the systolic pressure. She turned to Jack and saw him steadily pumping his fist. The smile on his face was evident, even from behind the mask.

"Nice job, Syd," he offered.

She attempted a shrug. "Riding a bike."

"Very good," Murphy added.

"Thanks, let's get you ready. He's going to need more than Jack can give. Eric is smaller than both of you so I'm saving him till last." She watched the drip chamber and attempted to get a flow rate, but soon got lost in the math and pulled out her pen to scribble it out on the sheet. Jack would give a pint, maybe a little more, Murphy the same. Then Eric, if they still needed more. She began laying out the equipment for her next IV attempt. She paused long enough to check her watch and observe the surgeons.

*   *   *

Larry sat on a bench next to a nurse working on a clipboard in the hallway and watched as the boy wandered toward him. He was barefoot, and wearing a tattered pair of shorts with a T-shirt that was too large by two sizes. He seemed to take the chaos and the suffering people in stride. He paused at each bed, saying something to the person occupying it that Larry couldn't understand. The boy stopped when he saw Larry and they observed each other for a few minutes. Larry finally couldn't help but smile and he got one in return.

"*Mzungu!*" the boy declared as he pointed at Larry.

"What did he say?" Larry asked.

The nurse looked up and smiled when she saw the boy. "He said *mzungu*, it means novelty, or something new or unusual. It's a Swahili word for white people. You may be the first he's ever seen."

Larry nodded and returned his gaze to the boy who had now ventured a little closer, obviously both cautious and curious. Larry didn't move, just offered a smile. With a nod from the nurse providing reassurance, the boy closed the gap and slowly reached out a finger to touch Larry's bare arm. He quickly withdrew and a stream of Swahili came forth. The nurse chuckled as she translated.

"He wants to know how your white skin keeps the rain out."

"Tell him I don't know. It does it just like his."

The nurse translated for the boy before shooing him away. The boy retreated, but not before giving Larry a grin as he disappeared around the corner.

Larry's grin was replaced by a look of determination when he saw Jack approaching. He noted the bandage on Jack's arm as well as on a few others. Larry hadn't been allowed to donate due to all his new vaccines.

"We're done here, time to get to the site before we lose what's left of the daylight," Jack declared. "Back on the buses. We're meeting Greg and Bradford at the embassy."

"Okay," was all Larry could say. He rose and followed. He spotted his new friend and offered a wave of good-bye. He got one in return.

"Making new friends, Larry?" Sydney asked.

"Yeah, I can always use some more," he replied.

*　　　　　　*　　　　　　*

The pictures they had seen on the plane did little to prepare them for the real thing.

The six-story structure still stood, but any resemblance to its former self was gone. The entire front of the building lay open and naked to all viewers like the bare thigh of a murder victim lying in the street. The blast of the truck bomb had exposed every facet of the structure. Wires dangled from ceilings and walls, pipes that once brought water and took away waste stuck out at odd angles from every floor. Papers still fluttered in the breeze and people were attempting to gather them. Tar paper that once coated the roof now hung down like a torn sheet as if the building were attempting to hide its shame from those below. Everywhere they looked the living crawled over and around the building's remains, looking for the dead. Three people were unaccounted for, and the search would go on until they were. The city's fire trucks used their ladders, not to go up into the building, but to provide a safe passage across the rubble into the first and second floors. Everyone wore a mask over their mouths, all streaked with dirt and sweat. Ambulance crews stood by waiting, but the look on their faces was one of dejection as the chances of finding anyone alive at this point were nil. The crater left by the truck was surrounded by paths on both sides, cleared first by dogs, and then bulldozers, to provide access to the building.

Eric watched as one tired dog sat panting in the sun while his handler changed the leather booties the dog wore. The dog lifted his paws obediently to help and when all four were changed the handler removed the dog's mask, allowing him to drink from a collapsible bowl of water before they returned to the pile.

He detached himself from Larry and Sydney to join Jack, Greg and Bradford at the side of the crater. He was surprised to see that it was half full of water.

"I'm estimating that truck was maybe three-quarters full, maybe more. Definitely had some diesel included. Crude, but it gets the desired effect. We'll have to pump out that water soon as we can," Bradford commented.

"Okay, I'll get someone on that. What are you looking for?" Jack asked.

"Anything. Trucks are full of parts with serial numbers. We just need one and we can track it. Probably stolen, but we have to start somewhere," he answered. "Best thing would be part of the detonator. Most bombers don't realize that their fingerprints will survive the explosion. We'll get a few, try to track 'em down."

"That's Sydney's department. Just give her what you find and she'll do the rest," Jack stated. He looked up from the crater and noticed Eric had joined them. "Eric, I need you to do a repeat of what you did in Vegas. I know it's a bigger scale so keep it simple this time. Can you do it quickly?"

"Actually, I already finished the software over the last few weeks. I just need a zero point and a grid. The rest is just cataloging the pieces and the location they were found. It should be close to what you got in Vegas, sir."

"You finished the software already?" Jack asked.

Eric shrugged. "Thought we might need it."

"Good thinking." Jack caught Greg's eye and they left Eric and Bradford to meet with Sydney to get organized.

"Any luck with your toy?" Jack asked when they were alone.

"Not on the first pass," Greg answered. "But we plan on a sweep twice a day in the area with random trips around town in between." Greg and Bradford had broken away from the group at the hospital and driven around the city in a borrowed van, using the device they had brought along that triggered remote devices. Other than setting off a lot of car alarms and opening a few garage doors, they had not managed to trigger any explosions.

"Okay, keep your ninjas ready. I'll feel better when we have more security here," Jack commented as he looked out over the city facing them.

"You thinking they might try again?" Greg asked.

"Wouldn't you?"

"…Yeah."

*   *   *

The three delivery men that Djimon had feared were observing Jack from a building several blocks away.

"You sure it's him?"

"Yes, I'm sure. The guy's famous. Pick up a newspaper sometime," the man retorted.

The driver frowned, but held his tongue. The three of them had driven all night from Nairobi and were tired. Getting back into the city had been difficult due to the bombing. Luckily, they had become familiar with the border guards and had talked their way through. The guards assumed they were on official business, despite the fact that their truck was empty. The detour they had taken to rearm themselves had made the trip even longer. They had arrived in the city and located a place to observe from a safe distance, and were now taking notes on what they saw through the binoculars.

"So we have Jack Randall from the FBI. Who's the other guy?"

"He moves like a shooter, too. I'm guessing Hostage Rescue, or maybe a SEAL. The perimeter includes the warehouse. We need to find a way in there, and soon."

"They may want us to destroy it in place," the third man spoke.

The first two men pulled their attention from the scene below and faced the third man.

"What? Kill more Marines?"

"You know what they'll say to that. We need to be ready for either contingency. The agent can't be compromised."

-SIX-

PEOPLE STOOD IN LINE with objects in their hands waiting to get them checked in at the van. The canopy that had been set up wasn't large enough to accommodate them all, and they subconsciously bunched up in an effort to reach the shade quicker. They stood with floppy hats and sunglasses shading their eyes and faces from the merciless sun. The dust caked their skin and found every sweaty patch, creating a sandpaper effect. Race had ceased to exist as they were all now a shade of gray that blended into their current surroundings.

When one finally reached the van, the object they held was examined by both Bradford and Eric. If determined to be a piece of the truck or the device that triggered the explosion it was then digitally photographed, its location was cataloged and entered into the computer, and it was assigned a number and barcode tag. All pieces were then transported to the airport where a hangar had been donated by the government. There, laid out on the floor, they slowly began to resemble a truck.

Eric looked out the door of the van as the pump started up again. He could see Sydney standing on the rim of the crater, supervising the crew pumping the water out. She was wet from the waist down and shielding her eyes from the sun with her hand. He felt a moment of guilt as he had the relative comfort of the air-conditioned van to work in, even though the van was more to protect the computers from the dusty environment than it was to provide them comfort. Working at night under the glare of the lights was far better than under the hot sun, and Sydney was going on her eleventh hour.

"Come on, kid, she's got her job and we got ours," Bradford prompted him. He nudged Eric back to work with his elbow.

Eric turned his attention to the piece in Bradford's hand. It looked like some kind of valve.

"What you got?"

"I think we have a valve from the bottom of the truck, the one that's used for filling the underground tanks." He carefully wiped the mud off the twisted metal object until he had a better view of it. Leaning close to several pictures of an intact truck on the wall of the van, he compared the object in his hand to what he saw.

"Yup, right there on the back end near the bumper. Looks like a match. Location?" he asked the person who brought it.

"In the crater on the south side, maybe about a foot from the bottom," the tired Marine replied.

"Okay, thanks," Eric acknowledged, his fingers flying across the keyboard. Bradford took photos of the object against a white backdrop, one of each side, top and bottom. The pictures were automatically fed into the computer where the software slowly rebuilt the truck piece by piece.

"Only about 60% of it left," Eric informed Bradford.

"Don't tell me that, kid, it's depressing. Let's just keep at it. A lot of people want to know who did this, me included."

"Yeah, me, too. What's next?"

"Looks like a speedometer, maybe?"

*   *   *

Jack climbed through the debris of the warehouse with Larry behind him doing his best to keep up. From the looks of it, the wall facing the explosion had been blown into the building, crushing most of the supplies stored there. They had found two bodies, one a young native boy, and the other a civilian drug representative handling the vaccines and other treatments coming through the embassy. He noticed Heather crawling through some boxes next to an overturned forklift. As Jack got closer, he noticed a large pool of dried blood on the floor. Evidently one of the victims had died here.

As he picked his way closer, he noticed that Heather seemed upset about something and was pointing around at several vials on the floor as she addressed the cleanup workers. She did not notice Jack's approach, and he strained to hear what she was saying over the sounds of the equipment running all over the site. The workers turned to leave or do whatever she had asked, and Jack was puzzled as he watched her scoop up a few vials of medications and slip them in her pocket.

Larry finally caught up to him. "What a mess. Can we salvage any of this stuff?"

Heather turned to the sound of Larry's voice and saw them. "Hello. I didn't see you there."

Jack decided not to mention the medications in her pocket. He asked Larry's question again. "Can we save anything?"

"It looks like we can get some of these supplies out of here and over to the hangar or the Canadian Embassy. Some are damaged or just compromised, others are date sensitive. Some will require repackaging, but I'm actually encouraged. I thought it would be much worse," she answered.

Jack carefully looked over what was left of the warehouse before speaking to Larry. "Larry, I'm gonna have you handle this. It looks to me like the wall gave way due to the blast wave, so I doubt we'll find too many truck parts here. Once Sydney and Bradford have gone through here and we're sure there are no bomb fragments, let's get these supplies out of here and on their way to wherever they were going. Heather, you help him, but he's the man in charge, okay?"

"No problem," she replied.

"I'd start by seeing if we have enough hangar space and what the Canadians can do to assist," he added.

"I'll stop there on my way to the hangar." She turned and picked her way out of the building.

"Take one of Greg's guys with you!" Jack called after her.

"Okay."

Jack watched her go and when he was sure she was out of view, stooped down to see what it was she put in her pocket. He picked up two vials of medication from the mess on the ground. The labels didn't give a name, just a number. The fluid was clear and one was topped with a red cap, the other a yellow cap. He shook them. The contents had the consistently of water. Why was she so worried about it, and why had she pocketed some? He decided to do the same. He would ask Sydney about it later.

"What ya got there, Jack?" Larry asked.

"I'm not sure. But do me a favor and keep an eye on Heather while she's in here. I want to know what she's doing."

Larry opened his mouth to ask more, but then thought better of it. Sometimes Jack had reasons that couldn't be explained.

"You got it."

"Quite a mess we have here!"

Jack and Larry turned to see Dennis Murphy picking his way carefully though the rubble toward them. They watched as he stumbled and almost fell into a crate of mosquito nets. He saved himself from falling and scrambled the last few yards to join them.

"So, what's the plan for all of this?" he asked.

"We'll try to determine where it was headed and get it shipped out of here. Is there anything the CIA can do to assist in that?" Jack asked.

"We sometimes used the charities to move our people around, without their knowledge, of course. We may have someone who can help. I'll make some calls," he replied. "Is there anything else I can do?"

Jack traded a look with Larry. "I don't know. What can you do?"

Murphy smiled at that. "Fair enough question, I guess. Well, I can help trace any numbers your technicians may find. If the truck came from out of the country I can help get around the red tape. If it proves to be local, I have some contacts that we can question."

"If it's something that's say ...out of our jurisdiction?" Jack probed.

"I don't think that will be a problem, unless you need it all neat and admissible in court?"

"Just as long as the information is good," Jack answered.

"Ahh, a results man. Or so I've been told. I like that. Then you know how it works. Quality information requires time and patience. Information obtained in a hurry tends to be acquired under ...stress, shall we say? Its accuracy is always questionable. All I can say is tell me what you need, and I'll do the best I can to get it."

"Fair enough. I'll let you know about the other thing."

"Right. So who inherits all this?" He spread his arms to indicate the entire building. Jack just pointed to Larry.

"My job now," Larry answered. "Soon as Syd and Brad clear the place, we'll get an inventory and then try to get it all shipped out. We have some hangar space at the airport to store some of it, and the Canadians have offered to help, too. We have security at the airport, Marines and locals, plus the usual airport security. Stuff should be safe there till we can get it out of here."

"So you need trucks," Murphy stated.

"Yeah, I guess I do," Larry answered.

"Trucks I can do."

*   *   *

"They seem to be getting ready to move the warehouse items somewhere." The driver spoke on the satellite phone while the others listened.

John Kimball was sitting alone in a small restaurant just off of Yadkin road and was listening to his subordinate from half a world away. He appeared to be just another military bachelor that didn't feel like cooking

for himself that night. Not an uncommon sight in Fayetteville. The waitress would have been shocked to know the topic of the conversation.

"Yes, my source called and says they're moving the agent to the airport tonight. It's damaged, but still intact. The Reds were mixed with the
Yellows. Can the agent be recovered?"

The driver shared a look with his partners before answering.

"Maybe."

"If you have the means to do so, recover the agent. If not, it must be
destroyed at all cost."

The driver frowned at his boss's choice of words. But he knew there
was no arguing the point.

"Yes, sir."

"Inform me when it's done," he answered. He closed his phone, ending the call just as the waitress approached.

"More iced tea, sir?"

"Yes, thank you."

*   *   *

"It'll have to be done on the way to the airport," the Deliveryman said
to himself.

He watched them load the truck through the binoculars. One of
them had kept a constant watch on the structure and the progress of the
crew as they worked throughout the night and into the next morning.
The search for survivors had been called off at dusk last night, and the
bulldozers and cranes were now digging into the pile with more urgency.
The forensics team headed by the woman could be seen stepping into
every newly cleared opening, their flashlights probing for pieces of the
truck. They had finally pulled a bulldozer from the main embassy building long enough to clear a path to the warehouse for a newly arrived
pair of Bobcats, both fitted with scoop shovels. They soon had enough
room cleared for the forklift to be uprighted and put back into service.
Crates and pallets of supplies had been seen being loaded into the trucks.
The trucks had then been followed to the airport three times. The driver

estimated they had until later tonight before the forklift got to the agent. They had to have a plan ready by then. He put down the binoculars and picked up his cell phone.

*   *   *

The next truck should be back in about twenty minutes, Larry thought to himself. He consulted his clipboard and tried to determine what he could fit on the next one. Over the last twelve hours he had been slowly clearing the warehouse of material and moving it to the secure hangar. Larry had almost pointed out to Jack that his assignment had nothing to do with the investigation, but then had thought better of it. He was not a forensics expert, a bomb expert, or a computer expert. His skills would come into play once the evidence started being gathered. Until then he could contribute little, and it was hard to not consider the loss of all these supplies after the few hours they had spent in the hospital. So Larry would change hats and become a logistics expert for a day or two.

Trying to organize the pile of crates and pallets had been his first job. Some of the crates still had the packing slips attached; some had been damaged in the collapse of the wall. Many had to be pried open to determine their contents. Larry had found everything, from boxes of shoes from some guy named Tom, to crates of mosquito nets from Bill and Melinda Gates. Four crates containing manual water pumps had baffled him until Heather had explained that there were people who came to the country just to drill wells for drinking water. She said these pumps were from a guy named Doc Hendley.

"The guy from the Eagles?" he asked.

"No, Hendley, not Henley, and he's a bartender, not a musician," she had answered.

"A bartender?" he muttered to himself. He just shook his head and made another notation on the clipboard as the pumps were loaded onto the truck.

One of the Marines approached him with a large box in his arms. It was full of the vials of medication that had been strewn across the floor.

They had picked up every one they could and saved them. He looked into the box and estimated at least a few hundred of both red and yellow capped vials.

"They both have the same number on 'em, sir. Should we separate them?" the soldier asked.

Larry looked the vials over. They looked identical in every way except for the colored caps. No name for the medication. If the numbers matched they must be the same, he decided.

"No, just ship 'em together with the rest of the red ones. We saved the yellow ones from the other end of the building so they can all go together. Let's try to keep all the meds in one area and under a tight watch. I'm told the black market is pretty bad here for this kinda stuff," Larry answered.

"Yes, sir," the kid replied before hoisting the box to his shoulder and walking away toward the stack of meds awaiting the forklift.

Larry's attention was pulled away from the clipboard again as he was addressed from behind.

"Any problems, Larry?"

Larry turned to see Dennis Murphy mopping sweat from his face with a T-shirt he had sacrificed and turned into rags. He had been helping in the warehouse all day.

"No, we seem to be making progress. Nice job with the trucks by the way. Do I want to know what it's cost Uncle Sam to have 'em?"

Larry and Jack had listened in while Dennis had made several phone calls, speaking to many people before finally reaching the person he wanted. The conversation had taken place in many languages, but when finished, the spook had simply smiled and asked to talk to Jack for a few minutes. Jack had nodded after the brief whispered conversation and soon provided Murphy with several envelopes that he immediately tucked into his pants under his shirt. Murphy had then disappeared into the crowd of people surrounding the embassy, only to return two hours later with three US Army surplus 2-1/2 ton trucks, complete with drivers. A heated discussion had then occurred between the lead driver and Murphy. More envelopes had been offered, and now the three men sat in the passenger seats while Marines drove the trucks. Their smiles gave away their opinions on the arrangement.

"The *baksheesh* you mean? It's the way things get done here in Africa. Goes with the territory," he replied.

"*Baksheesh?*" Larry questioned.

"It's an Arab word, actually. It means bribe or payoff."

"Spoken the world over," was Larry's only comment.

"True. So what's next for us here?"

"Well, I figure we can get this last load off before Jack sends us to the hotel. It'll be dark by then, but we want the valuable stuff at the hangar as soon as possible. The rest of this stuff was for the embassy. Toilet paper, Post-its, and what have you. It can wait. I'm told we should have enough pieces of the truck by tomorrow that we can start doing some real investigating."

"Not liking your present job?" Heather asked as she joined them.

"Not my reason for being here, but I see why it needed to be done," Larry neutrally replied.

"I've been making some calls. A lot of the medications were bound for Nairobi, and from there on to Darfur. They're looking at alternate ways of shipping them out," Heather informed them.

"Good. Let's just get them to the hangar, then it's somebody else's gig from there," Larry replied.

"Trucks are here," Murphy pointed.

"Good." Larry waved and got the attention of the closest Marine. The forklift was manned and the three of them watched as the medications were loaded onto the last truck of the day.

*   *   *

Jack was once again standing next to the crater. He had been dividing his time between ground zero, the evidence van, the warehouse and the hangar. So far he was happy with the progress they were showing. The truck was over sixty percent recovered, and he was told the rest would be small parts with little forensic value. The truck had carried the charge on its back, and that had resulted in the majority of the debris being driven into the ground by the explosion. They were at the sifting stage now, and the backhoes were working hard under Sydney's watchful eye. He had made rest a mandatory item and the HRT shooters had been escorting the Marines and crew back and forth to the hotel for sleep, food and clean clothes. He had even taken Eric's laptop away from him at one point. He knew the kid wouldn't sleep unless he did.

On his last visit to the hangar he had been joined by Major Arusha, who immediately decided the security at the hangar was not enough and had strengthened it without asking. He now stood next to Jack and watched the crew at work.

"Your man Bradford, he understands explosives. Where can I get my people trained in such matters?" he asked Jack.

"I wouldn't know. I have just my military experience to draw on. That mostly involved how to blow stuff up, not figure out how someone did it."

"Are they not the same thing?"

"Not really. But feel free to ask him."

"Thank you, I will," the major replied.

"Your accent, Major, it's not South African. You've spent time in England?"

"Yes, during my school years, then again with the British Army. I attended many of their excellent training facilities before returning to serve my country. I return on occasion to learn new things," he explained.

Jack knew all of this already, but it never hurt to hear it from the source himself. Corruption was rampant across the entire continent, and Tanzania was no different. The British had spoken highly of the man, and so far the major had been as advertised. Still, Jack would be careful what he said around him.

"You speak very well. I'd like to thank you for the help you have provided. It's proven invaluable."

"These terrorist are the scourge of the world. While it was your embassy that was bombed, it was in my country, and that angers me. Men like you and I will be the ones who defeat them, Mr. Randall. I fought hard to keep my country intact when threatened by tribal war. I will not see it torn apart by terrorists. Tanzania will not become Somalia. If your president asks for my help, then he shall have it."

Jack absorbed the statement while he watched the crew under the fading daylight. He wanted to believe the man. He just didn't know him well enough yet.

"I can't speak for my president, Major, but I for one will thank you for the assistance, and maybe I can get some help from the Bureau on the explosives thing," Jack replied. "I'm going to the hangar with the last truck. Care to join me?

"Very good," the major replied. He shifted his sidearm around his belt and followed Jack into the warehouse. The truck was almost ready. The major pointed at the native passenger and gestured that he leave. The man saw the uniform, and taking it into account along with the size of the man wearing it, beat a hasty exit.

"Okay." Jack shot a look at Larry as the major climbed into the cab next to a bewildered Marine. "Let's go."

–SEVEN–

THE THREE TRUCKS LEFT the warehouse with one Jeep escort. The setting sun was in Larry's eyes as they pulled away. His truck sat in the second position behind Jack's with the major's bringing up the rear. The trip had become routine for the men in the Jeep and the gunner no longer stood behind the mounted machine gun but instead sat in the seat, smoking a cigarette. Traffic still parted for the convoy and they moved with considerable speed over the potholed road. They came to the decision point of which route to take and the Jeep turned to the right to lead them down a street lined by warehouses. Traffic was much lighter here and the speed on the convoy increased.

Jack found himself getting edgy. The lack of streetlights and the thick cloud cover helped the darkness descend quickly. It was over ten miles to the hangar, and that meant plenty of opportunities for trouble.

"What's your name?" he asked the driver.

"Sullivan, sir."

"Jack. You've gone this way before, Sullivan?" he asked the Marine.

"Yes, sir, three or four times now. No problems so far."

Jack eyeballed the M-4 rifle lying on the seat between them. He picked it up and slid back the bolt far enough to see gleaming brass in the chamber. The rifle, the Marine's sidearm, and Jack's own 9mm pistol were all they had inside the truck.

"Grenades?" he inquired.

"In my gear." Sullivan pointed to the floor between the seats.

Jack picked up the LBE and found two fragmentation grenades and an HC-White smoke grenade attached to the webbing. He straightened out the spoons so they could be separated from the gear quicker.

"Didn't want to lose one," the Marine explained.

"I understand. But if you need it in a hurry, you're screwed. Better to be ready," Jack lectured.

"Yes, sir."

Sullivan double-clutched and downshifted, holding the deuce-and-a-half tight into a left hand curve that led to a slight incline. The road then turned to dirt and flattened out. He double-clutched again and slipped into a higher gear in an effort to stay tight on the Jeep.

*   *   *

Five blocks up the road, the Driver was counting down the distance from a second story window. One of his fellow deliverymen sat with three local hired guns waiting to participate in what they thought was an ambush of U.N. supplies. Something they had done many times. The third sat at the wheel of a truck very similar to the ones being driven toward him by the unsuspecting Marines.

"The prize is in the third truck," he spoke into the radio. He received clicks of the mics keying in reply.

The driver of the waiting truck tightened the straps holding him into the seat one more time. He didn't like the plan, but they were short of manpower, and had no choice but to keep it that way. He wiped the sweat from his hands before gripping the wheel tightly, and watched for the signal from the building across the street. The idling truck hid the shaking of his hands.

"Get ready," the radio squawked.

*   *   *

Jack saw the truck in the alley as they passed and he immediately grabbed for the radio.

"Ambush! Floor it!" He then punched Sullivan in the arm and yelled, "Get off this road!"

The Marine complied immediately, standing on the brakes and spinning the wheel into a right hand turn. Jack grabbed the overhead handle with one hand while he pawed for the M-4 with the other. The deuce tipped up on one set of wheels as it rounded the corner only to slam down hard after impacting a parked car. The car did little to slow the truck down and it bounced back into the road as Sullivan fought to regain control. He worked the clutch and the gears to regain acceleration. Jack grabbed the rifle and the LBE.

"Keep moving and try to circle around!" he ordered.

"Got it!" the Marine replied. He pulled his gaze from the road long enough to see Jack bail out of the passenger side and roll in the dirt. He was lost from sight in the rearview mirror immediately as the dust and darkness swallowed him up. Sullivan gritted his teeth and hunkered down behind the wheel as he heard a crash followed by shooting behind him. Working his way through the gears, he made another right hand turn onto a street with a few lights. He shook his head at his luck. He'd thought he was all done with this ambush crap when he got out of Iraq.

*   *   *

Larry's eyes widened as he heard Jack's warning on the radio. His driver hesitated as he saw the nose of the truck emerge from the alley and quickly narrow the opening.

"Go—go—go!" he yelled to the driver. It seemed to happen in slow motion. First his brain said they wouldn't make it, but then the ambushing truck seemed to slow. The Marine angled for the gap and gunned the engine. Larry planted a foot against the dash as his eyes judged the narrowing gap. Maybe.

Maybe not. The ambushing truck surged and caught the right rear wheel of the deuce and the impact flipped it onto its left side. Larry tumbled into the windshield, spider-webbing its surface and cutting his forehead before falling toward the driver and pinning him to the driver's side door. The truck continued on its side for a few meters, throwing up a cloud of dust and gravel from the secondary road, before impacting a building.

Larry struggled to untangle himself from the driver, but they appeared to be stuck. Larry managed to turn his head far enough to see his face. It was covered in blood and his nose had an awful twist to it.

"Corporal, can you hear me?" Larry got a moan and some movement for a response, but the soldier was not fully awake. Larry was contemplating his options when the decision was made for him by automatic weapons fire from a few meters behind them. The corporal groaned loudly as Larry twisted his body around and planted both his feet against the shattered windshield. He started kicking.

*   *   *

The driver of the ambush truck had revved the engine and released the hand brake before popping the clutch and holding on. The truck jumped from the alley and out toward the middle of the road just as the first truck passed. He caught sight of the white man in the front seat looking at him with wide eyes before he flashed by and the street was empty. It distracted him for a split second, but that was all it took.

The truck hesitated and took one hop before stalling. He realized he had slammed it into the wrong gear.

"Idiot!" he screamed at himself. He cranked the starter and the engine caught as it continued to coast forward. He chose the lower gear and turned to check on the target. He was horrified to see it coming even faster and angling for the gap he had left in front of him. He mashed the accelerator and the truck lunged forward, clipping the passing deuce in the ass and flipping it over. His own truck continued on before he could stop it, jumping the curb and impacting the building across the street. Again it stalled, coasting backward over the debris left by the impact. He let it go until he had the road sufficiently blocked. Yanking the hand brake, he wiped the sweat and blood from his face before grabbing an AK-47 off the floor and bailing out the driver's side. The third truck was fast approaching.

*   *   *

The major reacted instantly to the radio call. Scanning ahead, he saw the ambush site and quickly deduced they were committed to entering it. Muzzle flashes winked at them as they approached and the windshield shattered as bullets entered the cab, seeking the driver. The major shifted his considerable bulk down below the dash, but was unable to avoid all the incoming rounds. A bullet creased his forehead, opening a gash that bled freely while another found his shoulder just below his neck. He turned his head in time to see the young Marine at the wheel take several rounds in the chest and face, showering the cab in more blood. He slumped over the wheel and his lifeless foot depressed the accelerator. The truck sped up even more and the major chanced a look through the cracked glass. Seeing the muzzle flashes concentrated on the right side of the road, he reached out and grabbed the steering wheel. With a bloody grin, he drove the truck right at his attackers.

*   *   *

Jack's lungs were straining as he sprinted down the street. He had twisted an ankle when he dropped out of the cab and automatically performed a PLF, or Parachute Landing/Fall, and had luckily scrambled to his feet without a head injury. The ankle was complaining, but he couldn't listen to it now. He slowed as he reached the corner and stopped to put on the LBE. As he scanned around the corner, his hands took inventory of what the Marine had included. He felt five full magazines for the M-4.

A Ka-bar knife mounted cross draw on the left shoulder. Two combat bandages and the three grenades he had seen earlier. He thumbed off the safety on the M-4 and proceeded around the corner into the dark. He had heard the crash as he was running and now the sound of his approach was covered by the automatic weapon fire from down the street. He looked for the escort Jeep, but it was nowhere to be found.

"Up to you, Jack, don't get dead," he whispered to himself.

The roar of a truck engine at full throttle helped cover his boot falls on the packed dirt. The second truck came into view and he slowed to a walk. He could make out movement in the cab and as he got closer he saw Larry smashing both feet against the shattered glass of the windshield. He was about to sprint across the opening when he saw movement at the front of the truck. A man approached, ducking around the still spinning front wheel. The approaching lights silhouetted him for a moment and Jack saw the outline of a large man. Not skinny like the locals. An American? The man raised his weapon and Jack saw the familiar outline of an AK-47. Larry didn't see him through the cracked glass. The man stepped forward and took aim at Larry.

*   *   *

The Deliveryman with the hired guns was at first pleased with the accuracy of the gunman. He watched as the bullets shattered the glass in front of the driver, thereby improving their chances greatly. This changed to a look of horror as the truck sped up and swerved right at them. He saw no one in the passenger side and the driver was obviously dead at the wheel. But wait, the top of the passenger's head could be seen in the faint light provided by the muzzle flashes.

"Shoot him, you idiots!" he screamed at them. But like most bandits, they lacked the discipline of trained soldiers and had expelled their first magazines and were now reloading. The truck gained on them quickly and he realized they had nowhere to run. He grabbed the device at his feet by its handle and retreated to the doorway of the building.

"Keep shooting!" he screamed at them before firing a burst from his own weapon. He left them pinned in place, all of them thinking they could stop the big truck if they just pumped enough bullets into it. The Deliveryman knew better and retreated into the concrete structure to escape the coming impact. He took shelter behind a large pillar. He heard the scream of the passenger just before the truck impacted the building, crushing two of the ambushers against it and pinning a third to the wall. As the sound of the impact subsided, it was replaced by the pinned man's screams. He used the noise to cover his escape out the back and began circling around the building, looking for a way back to the truck that would provide him concealment. The mission had just changed.

*   *   *

Larry felt the frame of the windshield finally give way and he turned his head away from the flying glass as it fell into the street. He was reaching for the frame to pull himself through when he saw movement over him. Looking up, he saw a large man with an equally large rifle pointed at him. Larry opened his mouth to say something, but before he could get the word out the man's face exploded into a mist and his body fell forward to land in Larry's lap. He quickly pushed the bloody mess away and scrambled out of the cab, dragging his too large frame to his knees. He saw a large man moving toward him in the dark and automatically reached for where his sidearm usually was.

It was gone.

Larry dropped to his knees and felt blindly in the shattered glass for the Marine's rifle, cutting his hands repeatedly. He was about to change his decision to retreat when a voice stopped him.

"Larry, it's Jack. You okay?" the voice hissed.

Larry realized he had been holding his breath, waiting for the bullets. He now let it out and sucked in another. He pulled himself out of the cab and examined the glass stuck in his palms. If it wasn't for that he'd of put them together and prayed.

"Yeah, I'm okay now," he answered.

Jack was now standing over him. "Pull that glass out of your hands.

This isn't over yet. Your driver dead?"

Larry looked the man over. "No, breathing okay. I don't see any holes in him. He's unconscious, though."

"Grab his rifle and gear and follow me. Be quiet," he added. Jack was already moving toward the sound of the screaming man.

Larry found the rifle and combat vest. He put it on, but it was like he was wearing a kid's lifejacket. He didn't have time to adjust it so he took one arm out and slung it over his shoulder. The rifle was in the glass, too, and he shook it off as best he could before checking to see if it was loaded. His sidearm was MIA. He quit looking for it and followed Jack, this was his kind of game, and Larry didn't want to be left behind by himself.

*   *   *

The major woke up on the floor of the truck. The taste of blood in his mouth combined with the acrid smell of smoke pushed the darkness away. While his injured body said rest, his combat trained brain screamed wake up. He forced himself to do a quick self inventory and deduced he had been shot at least twice and there was pain in his head and back also. But everything seemed to work. Pain was better than numbness. He reached for the dash and pulled himself upright in the seat. Wiping the blood from his eyes and face, he also succeeded in pulling several glass fragments from his forehead. The blood now flowed freely down his face. He found his beret laying on the dash and used it to stop the flow long enough for him to clear his eyes and look around.

He was seated in the passenger seat as before, but the view was now one of the destroyed facade of the building seen over the crushed hood of the truck. The engine was on fire and thick smoke churned out from under the buckled hood. The loud noise was coming from the man pinned to the building by the truck's heavy bumper. He saw an arm and the lifeless torso of two other men sticking out from under the rubble. He couldn't help but grin and in the process discovered some missing teeth. That was okay, he decided, he had still won. He placed a foot against the crumpled door and pushed twice to get it to open. The screech of bend-ing metal carried across the street and the screaming man paused long enough to see the bloody apparition of a man emerge from the truck. His eyes widened as he recognized him, and he briefly forgot the pain of his crushed legs.

The major stood on wobbly legs, but was soon circling the truck and approaching the trapped man. He drew a knife from his belt as he got closer.

The pinned man resumed screaming.

*   *   *

Jack scanned the street and made a hand gesture to Larry that he didn't understand. The shooting had stopped at the sound of the second truck crashing, and Jack was moving *toward* it with Larry reluctantly following. Larry thought they should be leaving, but there was the matter of the Marine and the third truck. Where was Jack's truck? What about the Jeep with the three government bodyguards? Larry had all these questions and more, but he also knew there was a time and a place for them and this wasn't it. Jack was in his element and Larry knew both his and the wounded Marine's best chance lay with him. So he followed without question and ignored his aching body. Jack had them down behind an abandoned car while he was in a pushup position looking under it at the burning truck. Larry watched back the way they had come because he figured that was what he should be doing. He pulled out his shirt and wiped the blood off the pistol grip of the M-4 before repeating the process on his hands. He didn't want to lose his grip on it when the time came, and he had a feeling the time was coming soon.

He glanced at Jack and saw him still in the pushup position—one hand on his rifle and the other a fist in the dirt. Jack angled his body down and to the right to get a better look at whatever it was he was looking for. Larry shook his head. He could not even remember the last time he had done a pushup. He thought hard, but it wouldn't come. He made a mental note to do some soon.

Jack pushed himself up and rolled to a squat next to Larry.

"The third truck is into the wall and has one of our attackers pinned. He's screaming his head off, but I think it's more fear now than pain," he whispered.

"How's that?" Larry whispered back.

"Come on, I'll show you. Just keep looking out behind us, okay?"

"Yeah," Larry replied. He hadn't been sure if Jack had noticed.

"Let's go."

*   *   *

The Deliveryman paused in the darkness of a doorway and surveyed the scene before him. The flames from the truck lit up the street, and the screams of the pinned man kept the locals from coming out. He had not encountered anyone as he circled the building. Somewhere in the scramble to get out of the way of the truck he had lost the radio. He looked now over the truck and to the window where his fellow Deliveryman sat. He saw no movement, but had no doubt the man was there. He would not give away his position unless he absolutely had to.

But the mission was up to him now. The truck with the agent was totaled and they had neither the time, nor the means, to transfer the agent to another truck. He had to get closer if he was to finish the mission. He was about to make a dash to the next doorway when some movement caught his eye. A large black man in an army uniform emerged from the burning truck. He looked like a man brought straight from hell. The blood from his head and shoulder stained his torn uniform, and the grin on his face made him look evil in the flickering light of the burning engine. The Deliveryman watched as the man willed his heavily muscled frame erect and slowly circled the truck, approaching the once screaming man. The light from the fire reflected off the blade of the knife as he slowly drew it from his belt and held it up for the man to see.

The screaming began again.

*   *   *

The Major smiled at the man's fear. He had some idea of what he must look like in his current condition. He also knew the deep rooted fears of the tribesmen in his country. He let the blood from his wounds flow over his skin and pushed the blood in his mouth out through his white teeth to better scare the man. He also took in the man's injuries, and it was apparent that he would soon be unconscious. He would have to start the questions now.

"Who are you?" he roared.

"M-M-Mashiq."

"Who sent you?"

"The man …from, from the embassy."

The major turned the knife in his hand. There was now blood dripping down the blade. The man's eyes caught every drop.

"What man?"

"The men from the truck …the …the ones who bring the cure," he cried.

"Major?"

Major Arusha spun and brandished the knife, only to see Jack and Larry staring at him.

"You live, Mr. Randall. As do I. This man was just telling me who I will be visiting soon." He returned his gaze to the pinned man as he continued in Swahili. "So that I might kill him quickly." He spit blood on the ground before grinning at the man and thumbing the blade of the knife.

The man's eyes widened even more as he stared at the devil before him. He opened his mouth to beg for his life, but it was taken as a three round burst of rifle fire tore into his chest.

Larry spun and returned fire at the windows of the building across the street as Jack tackled the major and pulled him under the burning truck. The muzzle flash and distinctive sound marked the rifle as an AK. Jack and Larry returned fire until all the windows were shot out. They both stopped and waited for more, but none came.

Something landed in the back of the truck over their heads with a loud thump, making them all flinch. They spun around in the dust as they heard the sound of running footsteps retreating into the darkness. Jack scrambled out from under the truck on the side away from the buildings and peered into the interior. He saw and heard the active fuse connected to the satchel charge lying next to the crate of medications.

"Run!" he yelled. He grabbed the major's bloody hand, dragging him to his feet and propelling him toward the cover of the abandoned cars. They had just made it when the charge blew, destroying the truck and everything in it.

They traded looks with each other as the debris rained down around them. What the hell was going on?

The sound of gunfire down the street and well off into the darkness did little to answer their question.

*   *   *

The Marine driver of the second truck was still unconscious. This was a good thing as the pain of his wounds would have been augmented greatly by the potholed road he was currently being dragged down. Jack and Larry had retrieved him from the cab of the truck and were pulling him down the street on a large piece of canvas torn from the rear of the deuce. The major had stopped his own bleeding with the help of the battle dressings and was now walking point with an M-4 gift from Larry. They had gone only two blocks when they saw the figure of a man, dimly lit by the partial moon, lying in the street. They approached cautiously to find a large black man with three bullets in the center of his chest. Jack looked at the wounds closely and smiled.

"What are you grinning about now?" Larry asked.

Before Jack could answer, a voice addressed them from the darkness.

"You guys want a ride?"

Jack pushed the barrel of the major's M-4 down as a figure approached from the dark.

"About time you showed up," Jack said.

Corporal Sullivan stepped out into the light with a grin on his face. "Yeah well, I couldn't find a place to park."

—EIGHT—

"YOU GUYS ARE FOOLS!" Sydney announced her opinion to all in the room. "What made you run off without some of Greg's ninjas with you? I mean really, what the hell did we bring them for anyway?"

"I'm afraid I gotta side with her on this one, Jack. You should have let me know," Greg added. He was not shy about voicing his opinion.

Jack sat in a chair with his twisted ankle propped up on another. Ice packs were both over and under it, and he could no longer feel anything. He had been thankful for this a few minutes ago, but now was starting to regret the fact that he couldn't get up and walk away from the double scolding he was getting.

"And what happened to your escort? They find them yet?" she continued to rant as she plucked more glass from Larry's backside. Larry grimaced, but said nothing. He knew it would only make things worse. He had first been scrubbed with a stiff brush by a nun, before being stitched by a doctor who could barely stay awake. Sydney had finally stepped in and sent the man to bed. He didn't argue. She had finished the sutures and was now plucking shards of glass out of his sizable butt. Larry had lost count at nineteen.

The major had been first and his wounds were not as bad as they first appeared. The forehead was bloody and would leave a nasty scar. The neck wound was more severe and had been cleaned and bandaged. The hole in his trapezoid muscle was through and through. They packed it off and probed for bone splinters. Finding none, they had stitched him up and, after a shot of antibiotics, had sent him on his way. He would visit the dentist later.

"They will be found," he spoke from a bed across the room, "but most likely they are dead, also." His tone left little doubt to either point.

Jack stayed silent as he thought about that. He had ordered the recovery of all the bodies from the ambush site. The Marine driver had been sent to the Mercy docked in the harbor. Word of the ambush and abandonment by the escort Jeep had reached the Marines working at the embassy and they were in a foul mood. Jack asked Sullivan to leak the story of the major's actions. Once the word got around, any talk of retaliation ceased. The Tanzanian Army's presence had doubled around the embassy site, and the hotel was now sporting a tank in the parking lot. Greg made a few suggestions to the new commander which were all executed without question. One of his heavily armed HRT shooters stood in the hallway outside the room. Passing hospital workers gave him a wide berth.

Jack started thinking out loud, as he was prone to do. "I can understand the ambush if they were just after the supplies for black market resale, but these guys went beyond that. Why?"

"Deny the competition?" Larry ventured.

"Maybe, but why waste the ammo? I know it's plentiful in this part of the world, but a satchel charge rigged like that shows some sophistication. That wasn't some Molotov cocktail he threw in the back. They wanted to make sure it was totally destroyed."

"What was in the truck?" Sydney asked as she dug deeply for another piece of glass.

"Larry?" Jack passed the question.

Larry was busy biting his lip while Sydney probed and didn't answer right away. Sydney shot an evil grin at Jack as she tossed another chunk of glass in the metal pan. Larry took a couple of breaths before he finally answered.

"The medications. We grouped them all together before we sent them out. You about done yet, Syd? You're killing me."

"Couple more," she replied as she swabbed the area with alcohol. Larry clenched his teeth as well as his cheeks against the burn.

"Relax," Sydney told him. "I can't get these last two if you fight me."

"Fight you? I'm fighting you? My ass was already sore from that damn shot of cement you stuck in there before we left! Now you're sticking a pair of salad spoons in there and I'm the one who's being difficult?"

"Just hold still, ya big baby," she teased as she pulled another piece free. "There, all done." The glass pinged in the metal tray.

"About time," Larry groused as he started to push himself up.

Sydney got him with another swab of alcohol. "Stay put till I get you bandaged up!"

"Damn it!"

Jack watched with a smile he couldn't avoid as Sydney prepped another syringe of antibiotics, keeping it out of Larry's view. Larry caught the look on his face.

"What?" he asked suspiciously.

Jack just shook his head and tried to appear innocent.

Sydney plunged the syringe into Larry's left cheek and quickly shot the plunger before retreating even quicker as Larry leaped off the stretcher.

"Jesus Christ, woman! I swear you enjoy that!"

The rest of the room laughed at Larry's discomfort, including a roar from the major. It was the tension relief they all needed.

*   *   *

"You're not going to like this."

Jack looked up from the papers he was reading. Sydney and Bradford were standing in the makeshift office they had made in one of the larger hotel rooms. He had his ankle propped up per Sydney's instructions and was told he couldn't come out till the next day. Almost through all the paperwork, he had watched the latest update of Eric's electronic reenactment of the attack twice. Two of the cameras had been found, and the data was being reviewed. He was told they would have more tomorrow. The truck was slowly being rebuilt in the hangar on a large wood and steel frame. Progress was slow, but at least there was some.

"What am I not going to like?"

"I did a quick exam of all the attackers' bodies. Took some pictures and gave them to the major. He says one is a well-known thief and smuggler. Two others they are trying to track down, but the other two…"

"Yeah?"

"I think they're Americans, Jack."

Jack looked to Bradford who nodded his agreement. He didn't look pleased.

"What makes you say that?"

"Look at these." She handed him several black and white photos. "This guy has a mess of dental work. All professionally done, and the bridge and fillings appear to match an American manufacturer. Look at these tattoos. They also look professionally done and American made. This guy has some scarring that looks to be from laser tattoo removal surgery. I put it under my magic light and this is what I got. It's just a faint outline. I faxed it to the home office and this is what they sent back." She laid a paper over the photo. "Says it's an old US Army tattoo. Special Forces. You recognize it?"

Jack stared at the blob-like shape until it became clear. He could just make out the crossed arrows. "Yeah, I see it now. Is that all you got? Kinda thin."

"The other guy had a plate in his leg from a previous fracture. I pulled it and I *know* it's American made. There's just one thing. The serial number's been removed. Nobody does that unless they need to remain invisible. That bridgework on the first guy? No number on it either."

"Okay, so run their prints and faces through the database," Jack said.

"We did. Nothing."

"Nothing? Not even a codeword clearance?"

"Absolutely nothing, Jack. We've all heard of Black Operations, but even those guys exist. You just never find out the truth about them, it's always some cover story file full of whatever it needs to say that week," Bradford added. "I know. I used to be one of those guys. These guys just plain don't exist."

Jack nodded in agreement. He used to be one of them, too. "You think they had something to do with the bombing?"

Sydney and Bradford exchanged a look before she answered. "We don't know, but we think it's something worth looking into."

Jack tapped the photos with his pen while he thought it through. Could be some ex-CIA or Special Ops guys who were now freelancing for themselves, or just hiring out their skills to whoever could pay for them. But who could pay for guys like that in this country? And why did they go after the medications? He slipped a hand in his pocket to make sure the vials were still there. Something wasn't adding up, and Jack's instincts were telling him to track it down.

He looked up at the two faces waiting for his answer. Sydney had a look that he knew well. She smelled a rat, too.

"Okay, let's do this. I'll make a call to Deacon and we'll set up some secure commo to talk about it. Who else knows about this?"

"Just us three right now. The major knows a little."

"Murphy or Heather?"

"No."

"Let's keep it that way for now. I'll bring Greg into the loop and tell you when it's safe to talk to him. No more communication with the home office until we get secure comms. We'll dig into it, but the primary mission is the identification of the bombers. We can't stray from that. Clear?"

"What about Eric?"

Jack shook his head. "Not yet."

"Okay, Jack." Sydney gathered up her pile of photos. "What about the bodies?"

"Bag 'em up and seal them as evidence. Find a cold locker on the Mercy and put a guard on it."

"Won't that raise some questions?" Bradford asked.

Jack smiled. "Let's hope so."

*   *   *

"The agent is safe?" Kimball asked.

"I think so," the Deliveryman replied.

"You *think* so? What happened? You told me you had sufficient funds and personnel."

"We used most of the funds for the deserters and the equipment. The personnel we brought in for a share of the take. They weren't very well trained, but we didn't have a lot of time to shop around. The truck ran them down. One of my guys managed to place a charge in the truck. It blew the cargo to hell and back and the truck burned for over an hour. I feel confident the agent is destroyed. The man was shot trying to flee the scene. There's only myself left."

"No one who can be traced back to you?"

"I finished off the one survivor myself. He didn't have time to say anything."

Kimball pondered this for a moment while the Deliveryman waited. He didn't ask about the other men. He knew they were untraceable, but the locals were no doubt in a computer somewhere or just known by sight to the local police. It was something to be concerned about. Unfortunately, there was little he could do. Stealth and secrecy were still their best options. There was always his hole card if things went really wrong. The Deliveryman was not aware of that asset.

"Get out of there. Head for Nairobi and stay at the safe house there until I contact you."

"Yes, sir."

Kimball pushed a button, breaking the satellite link before cradling the receiver. Drumming his fingers on his desk he thought of his options. The two dead operatives didn't cross his mind other than a brief thought of how fast they could be replaced. Two dead men were nothing in this operation. He had to focus on the main objective. It was the big picture to beat all big pictures.

He glanced at the clock on the wall. He was inspecting the Level-4 bio lab in thirty minutes. That gave him just enough time to make the needed calls he needed and still stay on schedule. He couldn't afford to interrupt production any longer than was planned.

*   *   *

Eric rubbed his eyes for the fourth time in the last few minutes. He considered reaching for the aspirin bottle that beckoned him from the shelf next to his computer, but thought better of it when he remembered how his gut had ached the night before. He was still compiling information at the embassy, but the parts where coming in slower now. At least it kept the air conditioning inside longer. He was surprised the van kept running. It had sat in place since they had gotten here, much like Eric.

At least he had the internet. A high speed satellite connection, installed in the van, allowed him to run serial numbers through various databases in an effort to track down the van. The answers came slowly and Eric resisted the temptation to snoop around in places he didn't really belong. Playing video games would just be insulting to the people out digging in the hot sun. So, he checked and double checked his work, sent a few emails to motivate the people on the other end, and basically forced himself to be patient.

But it wasn't easy. Sydney and Bradford had given him the full story on the ambush, and as much as he was relieved everyone was all right, he craved being out there with them—not staring at a computer screen all day. The program could be run by almost anybody at this point as he had refined it to be very user-friendly. Although the Bureau was using it for free at the moment, Jack had advised him to approach the subject with the bean counters when they got back. He had even given him a phone number of a business lawyer in DC to call. Eric had already called him from the van, and after dropping Jack's name, an appointment was set up for whenever he got back to DC. Eric smiled when he thought about it. Evidently Jack was still a businessman, too.

A prompt on his screen started flashing and interrupted his thoughts. He pulled himself up and clicked on the email icon. It was from Freightliner, the maker of the gas truck. He scrolled the document as he read it before finally getting to the part he needed. Eric scribbled the numbers on a scrap pad he had and then stuck the pencil in his mouth as his fingers flew across the keyboard. He soon had a list of names on the screen. He compared the names to the list he had been given yesterday.

The seventh name was a match.

Eric stabbed the button on the printer to fire it up and tapped his leg in irritation as he waited. The printer announced it was ready with a beep and Eric soon had it spitting out the information. Soon as he was done he gathered it up, put a file folder around it to protect it from sweaty hands, retrieved his sunglasses from the shelf next to the aspirin, and bolted out of the van. He stumbled as he was blinded by the noon sun.

A five minute search finally located Sydney and Bradford watching two Marines pulling something out of a pile of rubble. They both looked happy. Before he could say anything they pulled the object onto a nearby table and began prying it apart.

Eric couldn't help but ask, "What is it?"

"The last camera," Sydney replied. "The one with the best view of the bombing. If the data card isn't destroyed, we may just get a few clues out of it."

Bradford smiled also as he forced the housing open with a crowbar. "Looks like it's okay. It was only a few feet from where your software said it would be. Nice job."

Eric shrugged. "Thanks."

Sydney stopped looking at the camera as if finally noticing Eric. "What brings you out here in the dirt?"

Eric held up the papers he had. "Take a look at this." Eric laid the file down on the cleanest corner of the table. They looked over his shoulder as he pointed out various things. He turned pages for them to keep them clean.

"We need to find Jack," Sydney said.

"Now?"

"Right now."

*   *   *

Jack was currently pacing in his hotel suite, trying to see how hard he could push his ankle. Larry also had taken up the practice of working while standing, just for different reasons. He stood in the small kitchen area with papers and photos covering every surface. Jack preferred to read while he walked.

A knock on the door pulled their attention away long enough to see it open and the team walk in. They were led by Eric and the rear was brought up by Major Arusha. They were smiling.

"Tell me you found something," Jack asked.

"We found the truck, sort of," Eric replied.

Jack laid down his file and sank into a chair. Larry joined the group from the kitchen but remained standing. The others gathered around the coffee table where Eric laid out the file.

"We were able to find two serial numbers on the truck. Both of them were partials, but after we determined the make and model we were able to track it down to a specific production period. Then we used process of elimination to determine which trucks are someplace else. Twelve trucks from that group were shipped to Africa. I managed to account for eleven of them. This is our truck." Eric pointed to a highlighted item.

"Okay, who owned it?" Jack asked.

Eric pulled another file from his pile and laid it out. "The truck was originally purchased by an oil company here in Tanzania. I accessed their records and found it was sold to a subsidiary and used for cross border transport. So I accessed the Tanzanian government's vehicle registration records." Eric paused as he glanced at the major. The man sat in his chair and made no comment. "It's owned by Kamill Oil. A Yemeni distributor based out of Nairobi."

"So what do we know about Kamill Oil?" Larry asked.

"They have some loose ties to extremist groups. Their owners are actually Saudi. Nothing concrete, but Homeland Security has them on their watch list. Kamill also has operations in Sudan. Curiously, their building here in Dar burned to the ground the day of the bombing."

"You mentioned some prints?"

"The partials were merged and a possible hit came up. It's not enough to stand up in court, but they came back to Mohammed Ahmed Al-Nasser," Sydney said.

Sydney watched Jack closely as he took in the information. She had known him longer than the others, and as they had been a couple at one time she could read him better than anyone else. She could see the wheels turning. They were leaving.

Jack looked up and caught Sydney looking. He smiled back before addressing them.

"Very good, Eric, you get an extra dessert. Okay, people, we're leaving. Greg, tell our pilots to warm up the jet. Bradford and Syd, I'll need your report on the bomb and what we know up till now and we'll have to leave a skeleton crew here to finish the recovery, so pick out your people. Eric, I need all this packaged nice and neat and ready to send to the Deputy Director in about one hour. I'll inform the new ambassador that we're leaving and have somebody from the State Department call Nairobi. They're about to get visitors. Let's go."

Everyone rose to leave, creating a brief bottleneck at the doorway. Jack watched them for a moment before a thought occurred to him.

"Major, would you mind staying for a moment?" Jack asked.

Larry turned and gave Jack his patented one-eyebrow-raised look. Jack just waved him away so Larry left the room, shutting the door behind him.

The major walked back to his original chair and filled it. The chair groaned under the weight of the man.

"How are your injuries?" Jack asked.

"I will live. Your ankle is recovering well?"

"Yes, thank you. Major, this conversation won't leave this room and I have no right to ask this, but I'm going to ask it anyway. Have you had any dealings with any American CIA or Special Operations people in your country?"

"I knew your CIA man at the embassy. He was an agricultural attaché, I believe is what his card read. We were not friendly, but we knew one another."

"Anyone outside of an official capacity?"

The major paused for a moment before addressing Jack. "Mr. Randall, you are asking for a great deal of trust. We have known each other for only a short time." He raised a hand to stop Jack before he could reply. "I, however, feel you are an honorable man. Your people obviously respect you, and your skills, shall we say, are proven. I would hope you are not using the leverage of your government's aid to influence me."

"I have no such power or intention, Major. I simply ask for an answer. It is your choice whether to provide it or not. We'll just have to trust one another."

"You ask for trust, yet your man breaks into my government's computers?" the Major replied.

"I apologize for that. Eric is, well ...impatient, and he was somewhat of an expert at doing that before I found him. I will have a word with him."

They sat in silence for a moment before the major spoke. "I understand that you and your man, Larry, could have easily left me behind at the ambush site, and I may not have escaped the sniper or the explosion if you had. So I will say this first. I give you this information myself, not in my position as a government official. Do you understand what this means for me if others would know I told you this and not them?"

"Yes, sir, I do."

"Then please listen closely."

SEA LEVEL RISE COULD COST
PORT CITIES $28 TRILLION.
November 23, 2009—CNN

—NINE—

SYDNEY STRETCHED HER LEGS and stuck her feet under the chair in front of her. As a result, her laptop almost slid off and onto the floor. Eric snatched it before it could complete its fall.

"Thanks," she said.

"No problem. You want to share the pullout?" Eric referred to the table that folded out of the wall of the plane.

"No, I think I'll try to get a nap in. It's only a short flight, and it feels so good just to be clean and in the air conditioning for a change."

"Yeah, I felt kinda guilty sitting in that van all day while you were out in the heat."

"Good." She smiled. "You should."

"Not sitting with your new friend?" Eric asked with a nod toward Heather.

"No," she whispered. "She seemed a little preoccupied for some reason. I thought I would just leave her alone."

"Sure loves her cell phone," Eric commented.

"What makes you say that?"

"Seems like every time I see her, she's on it."

"Well, she was coordinating the movement of all that stuff out of the warehouse. That would be hard in the States, probably a nightmare to get it done here in Africa. Why, is something bothering you?"

"No, I don't know, maybe. It's just that she seemed a little distant. I walked up to her once or twice and the phone conversation always got cut off quick. It was like she didn't want me to overhear anything," Eric explained.

"Were you maybe *trying* to overhear something?" Sydney teased.

"No," Eric deadpanned.

"Well, if I were you, I'd be more suspicious of our spook. He kept disappearing for a couple of hours here and there. I don't know if Jack knew what he was doing or not. I haven't had time to mention it yet. I'm not sure about that guy. Maybe it's just his CIA odor or something."

"CIA odor?"

"Normally I'd say aura, but since he's CIA…"

"Right."

"I think you're wrong about Heather, she seems too sweet. Let's just you and I keep a watch on both of them. At least until I can talk to Jack."

"Deal."

With that said, Sydney reclined her chair back as far as it allowed and, twisting her gun out of her ribcage, closed her eyes, leaving Eric to watch the CDC and the CIA.

*   *   *

Sitting in the back of the plane with his own laptop in front of him, Jack was watching footage recovered from the security cameras. He had retained all that they had recovered, and so far it supported the identity of the bomber as the one in the video on *Al Jazeerah*. The video wizards back at headquarters would enhance the picture, clean it up, and provide a positive identification, but Jack was sure it was the same kid. They were still looking for his friends and his mullah, but the major said it was most likely they were in hiding whether they were innocent or not. They all feared reprisal. It would be some time before they returned.

Jack glanced around the cabin and assured himself that everyone was either busy with their own assignments or sleeping before he reached in his pocket and pulled another disk out. He slid the disk in the drive and adjusted his screen so no one could see it if they walked by to the lavatory. While it was booting up, he pulled the visor down over the oval window to eliminate any reflection.

He was soon looking at a number of video files labeled by number and corresponding to the embassy cameras they had searched for the last few days. These files were from a few days prior to the attack. Jack had come up with the lame excuse of needing them for comparison purposes, and had been given them without question by an embassy staffer. He reviewed the footage from the warehouse, fast forwarding through periods of non-activity. He noticed the young native boy on the forklift and the drug company representative. He located the meds and watched them come and go. The angle of the camera did not cover the loading dock and Jack could not see the identity of every truck driver that brought supplies. He froze the image of the ones he could see and saved them to another file. As he became better at scanning the video he sped it up, hitting the pause key every once in awhile to catch something. He once slowed it long enough to watch a conversation between the drug representative and a deliveryman. The deliveryman stayed just off camera, as if he knew it was there. Jack was beginning to think he wouldn't see any of their faces when he was suddenly treated to a close-up of the forklift driver's face. His nose filled the camera's view before he leaned back and rubbed the lens clean. With each circular motion the camera edged a hair to the right. The boy checked his work when finished and Jack could see right up his nose for a brief second. He then disappeared down the ladder and Jack was treated to a different view than he'd had previously. He had gained about five feet of view to the right into the loading dock. Curiously, there was a painted line on the floor where his view had ended before. Jack fast forwarded ahead until another truck arrived. The boy was quickly on the forklift, unloading more medications and stacking them at the far end of the warehouse. After a few trips, the pharmaceutical rep walked to the far end, leaving the boy alone. The boy suddenly stopped his trip and appeared to be listening to someone. He parked the forklift and ran into the office, returning with three bottles of water from the refrigerator inside. Jack watched him walk toward the line on the floor where he was met by the deliveryman stepping forward.

Jack quickly paused the film. Tinkering with the video options he found the zoom feature and focused it on the man's face. He lost some picture quality as he blew it up, but it retained enough for him to get a good look at the man.

Jack reached for the file Sydney had given him and shook out a few photos. He paged through them until he found the one he wanted. He compared it to the face on his screen.

The man in the photo was the man Corporal Sullivan had shot in the street, the same one who blew up the truck with a satchel charge. The same one who'd had laser surgery on his Special Forces tattoo. The one Sydney claimed didn't exist.

*   *   *

"This isn't so bad, feels more like ninety-eight or so, beats a hundred any day." Larry commented as they left the plane in Nairobi. He painfully hoisted a bag over his shoulder and stalked off toward the waiting embassy vans. Eric and Sydney shared a smile before they followed, Heather close behind, all of them just taking the heat in stride. An embassy staffer approached them.

"Mr. Randall?" he asked.

"Over there," Sydney pointed. "The tall guy with the fishing shirt and the limp."

"Thank you."

Sydney paused and watched the man run on until he met Jack and handed him a large envelope. Jack scanned the first few pages before waving Greg over. They had a brief conversation before they quickly gathered their bags and followed the rest of them. Sydney watched his face and was surprised to see a grin. Must be good news, she thought.

She fell in behind Jack and Greg as they passed and found a seat behind them on the van. She leaned over their seatbacks so they would know she was eavesdropping.

"They're sending the team over now?" Greg asked.

"That's what it says. Should be in place within twelve hours," Jack answered.

"Are you guys gonna share, or are you just holding out on me?" Sydney asked.

Jack craned his neck to give her a look. She shot it right back with a smile. Greg held up a picture for her to see. It was a grainy satellite shot of a man standing next to a Jeep in the desert. Without saying anything he flipped to the next shot, a full frontal. Then the next, a head shot. The last thing he showed her was a wanted page from the FBI.

"Mohammed Ahmed Al-Nasser again? Is this our bomber?" she asked.

"We think so. NSA got some intercepts and some of them foolishly dropped his name. We also know he was in Somalia a few weeks ago, with a possible sighting here in Nairobi a few days before the bombing," Jack explained. "He's Al Qaeda's resident explosives expert, son of a rich Saudi family, educated in Europe with a degree in engineering. He ditched the family business in favor of terrorism about six years ago. Since then he's been spotted in their propaganda tapes, and he's believed to have helped with the Cole bombing. The Bureau's been after him for years."

"So where's he now?"

"These photos show him getting out of this Jeep near the Sudan-Kenyan border. The Jeep was followed since it crossed the Tanzanian border a day after the bombing," Greg answered.

"Followed? By what?"

"A Predator drone and some satellites." Jack smiled. "We think he's headed for a safe-house in Sudan."

"More like a safe-tent, but it won't matter either way," Greg added.

Sydney nodded as she took it all in, then it dawned on her.

"You guys are going after him," she declared. "I don't mean some team of super-troopers. You two are going after him."

"Well, we hope to, and we'll be sure to take some ninjas with us," Greg answered.

Jack didn't say anything. The look he was getting from her was bad enough. They hadn't been an item in many years, but that didn't stop her from becoming the concerned girlfriend. There was nothing he could say, at least not here. There would be a talk sometime in the future. They both knew it.

"I'll brief everyone when we get to the embassy. We should know a lot more in a few hours." *We can talk then,* his look said.

Sydney dropped back in her seat and looked out the window. The African dust obscured her view of the passing city. The window reflected the concern on her face.

*   *   *

"NSA confirms it. It's him!" Greg stated as he hung up the phone.

Jack nodded, but did not take his eyes off the three flat screen monitors hanging on the wall in the basement of the embassy. With the permission of the ambassador, they had commandeered a large conference room, and it was now being used to help coordinate the attack on the small camp in the Sudanese bush country. Jack had a Navy Seal team commander on one screen and a Joint Operations Air Force general out of Fort McDill, Florida on the other. The general's aide was listing the assets they had for the operation.

"Twelve Navy SEALs and two Air Force Close Combat Control people will HALO into the target off the carrier *Reagan* , currently in the Gulf of Aden deterring pirate activity. They'll do the initial assault on the camp and be supported by two Cobra gunships from the same carrier battle group. The security and extraction team will then come in from the Kenyan border using two Pave-hawks. We are allowing for five minutes maximum on the ground before all units leave. For support we'll have medical standing by using the embassy Blackhawk at the border. A Hawkeye and a squadron of Hornets off the *Reagan* will provide air superiority. If we should have any prisoners, they'll be extracted to the *Reagan*. Alternate airfields have been sent. All assets will be in place in three hours. Once everything is in position, the chairman will notify the President. We go on his word, any questions?"

Jack had a few, but he kept them to himself and let the SEAL commander speak. They discussed frequencies, approach contingencies, alternate extrications, door thickness at the target, and a few other items before he paused. Here it comes, Jack thought.

"Mr. Randall, I mean no disrespect, but are you sure you wish to join us on this?" the commander asked.

Before he could answer, Greg spoke up. "He's been doing this longer than you, Charlie. You just try to keep up."

Jack had to smile. "Back in my day we only had to send four guys in to take one out. You guys are taking forty? That's just sad."

The SEAL team commander took the jab with a knowing smile and read between the lines. "Okay, we'll see you when you come get us."

"We'll try to be on time."

"Everybody happy?" the general asked. He got yes sirs all around. "I want final operation plans in one hour." He signed off.

*   *   *

Jack rubbed his hand through his hair as he strode down the basement hallway, looking for a bathroom. He had been in the conference room for the last two hours ironing out details and drinking coffee. He left Greg with Murphy and his Kenyan embassy counterpart behind and managed to find a bathroom at the end of the stairs.

Looking at himself in the mirror, he noted the red and tired eyes. A new shirt would be a good idea, also. He made an effort to put his hair back in order but soon gave up. He looked himself over again.

"You still got it?" he asked his reflection. He got no answer.

Pushing the door open to return to the conference room, he found himself ambushed by Sydney. She calmly waited, leaning against the wall with her arms crossed, a look of concern on her face. He let the door fall shut and it revealed Heather standing behind it. This was not going to be a pleasant conversation, Jack determined.

"Yes?"

Sydney pulled her eyes from Jack and nodded toward Heather.

"Sir, if you don't need me any further, I was wondering if I could possibly return to the States? I've rerouted all of the supplies from Dar and well ...there just doesn't seem to be anything here for me to do."

Jack nodded as he thought about it. "Okay, I see no problem releasing you at this point. The director will need a full report once you get back, and of course I'd like to see it first. I know this wasn't what you signed up for, but I think you handled it real well. I'll be sure to say something to your boss."

"That's very kind of you. Is there anything I can do before I leave?"

"No, I don't think what's happening will call for your skills."

Heather nodded. "Yes, I would have to agree with you there." She stuck out a hand which Jack shook. "Thank you and good luck with ... well, you know." She turned and proceeded up the steps. Jack shared a look with Sydney for a moment before turning and calling out.

"Heather?"

Heather turned at the top of the steps. "Yes?"

"Just curious, is there anything missing from the warehouse here in Nairobi?"

Heather scrunched her face at the question. "No, sir, it appears to be fully stocked as normal."

"Okay, thank you."

"No problem." She turned and proceeded up the steps and out the door to the embassy.

Once the door shut behind her, Sydney asked, "What was that all about?"

"I'm not sure yet, but follow me." He led her up the stairs, but turned the opposite way and entered the embassy warehouse door. After finding the lights and turning them all on, he strolled down the aisles slowly, hands in his pockets.

"You have something you wanted to say?" he asked Sydney who was trailing behind.

"Jack, why are you going on this raid?"

"I'll be with the extraction team, Syd, gathering intelligence. I'm not kicking in doors or anything. I don't do that anymore."

"You don't?"

"Okay, yes, I did kick in a door in DC, but that wasn't the same thing and you know it."

"Jack, you left with a group only to ditch them and take off on your own. You almost got shot by your own guys. Why can't you just let the SEALs do this?"

Jack spun to face her, startling her to the point she stepped back.

"Because we're at war, Syd, that's why. You need to understand that. Just because Congress hasn't declared it, doesn't make it less so. How do you declare war on a group of people? They aren't a country or some rogue nation-state. They're the same thing that all men who cause wars are—greedy, fearful men. They want to ruin us because they covet our power. This isn't about Islam or a fanatical way of thinking. It's about greed and power. They want something and we are in the way. They want to rule over the Middle East, plain and simple. They want the money and the power that comes with that and to do it they're willing to exploit the ignorance and religion of their own people! Why do you think the bombers are all kids and religious students? The leaders never sacrifice themselves, do they? Well, today I found an enemy that I can kill, and I'm going to do everything I can to end him."

Sydney stayed silent until Jack calmed down. "Okay …okay, I understand. I'm sorry, I just …I just still worry. I thought I'd lost you that night in DC, and I don't want to go through that again."

Jack took a deep breath. "No, I'm sorry. You didn't deserve that. I've just had too much coffee and not enough sleep. Let's just drop it for now.

Come on, take a walk with me." He turned and led her down the aisle between the stacked crates and pallets. He once again put his hands back in his pockets. She followed in silence for a minute before speaking.

"It was nice of you to let Heather go home."

"I'm having her followed."

"What? Why?"

"You notice the drugs at the last warehouse?" Jack asked, looking around the warehouse for unseen company as he spoke.

"Yeah. Pallets of them. Why?"

"I noticed one pallet at one end of the room had yellow caps, and another pallet that was partially destroyed at the other end had primarily red caps with a few yellows mixed in."

"Okay?"

"Well, they both had the same number. No name on the vial, just the number. Heather seemed quite upset that the reds were damaged. I saw her slip some in her pocket before they got cleaned up and boxed."

"Why?"

"I don't know. But I can tell you this, the pallets that were destroyed in the ambush were the red top vials. But what bothers me the most is what the major told me before we left."

"What?"

"The guy who was shot by his own men at the scene? Before he died he told the major who hired them to do the ambush."

"So, who?"

"The same guys who delivered the medications in the first place. I reviewed the warehouse surveillance tapes. Your dead invisible American was one of the delivery guys."

Sydney absorbed all this as they walked. Jack kept pace silently, giving her time to think it though.

"What was so special about the red top vials?" she asked.

Jack smiled. "I don't know, but I aim to find out."

"How? They were all destroyed."

"Simple. By giving them to you." He pulled his hands from his pockets and handed her the vials he had carried for the past few days. "I'm going to be very busy tonight. When we get back to the States, I need you to come up with a way to analyze just what's in these. Somewhere outside normal channels. I don't want to use any FBI labs or the CDC. Find somewhere independent. I'll pay for it out of my pocket. Nobody knows except you, me, and Deacon. Understand?"

"Yes."

"Notice anything on our little walk here?"

"Like what?"

"There's a stack of yellow tops over in that corner." He spun and faced the other end of the room. "And a fresh empty space over in that one."

Sydney's mind was racing, but she pulled herself together and just nodded. Jack was passing the ball to her. She wouldn't drop it.

"Okay, let's get back before the rumors start flying," he joked.

She smiled and slipped the vials into her pocket before following him out of the warehouse.

GLACIERS A CANARY IN THE COAL
MINE OF GLOBAL WARMING.
August 8, 2009—CNN

—TEN—

LARRY WATCHED THE SCREENS in front of him while chewing on a toothpick. He had skipped his pain meds so he could concentrate better and his sore ass was keeping him awake and on his feet. Not that the current situation wasn't stimulating enough.

"Any second now," Eric said from his position at the conference table.

Larry turned and Eric indicated the third monitor that was showing nothing but static at the moment. It was the satellite feed that would offer them a bird's-eye view of the action. Eric had been brought in at Jack's insistence. He had wisely listened to his briefing without a question before immediately working to improve the link and signal of their communications.

Sydney pulled her eyes from the floor long enough to see the screen come to life. It showed a group of three large tents in the middle of the Sudanese bush country. The view went to infrared and several prone figures could be seen inside the tents of the camp while two others seemed to be moving around outside the largest tent. One of them flared briefly in the infrared as he dragged on a cigarette.

"Count hasn't changed," Larry observed.

Sydney checked her watch and compared it to the mission clock on the screen. Mission was two minutes ahead. The plan was to hit the camp at 3 a.m. local time, when the body's circadian rhythm was at its lowest functions. The terrorist would be asleep.

But Jack was awake, as he'd been for over twenty-four hours. What about *his* circadian rhythm? She had watched silently as he and Greg had suited up. The black fatigues, the armor, the boots, knives, guns, and radios. She hated watching it. But she said not a word as she taped up his ankle before it all. His face was a mask and she didn't want to distract him from what he needed to think about. Now she sat silently in the room, trying not to picture him flying through the dark in that damn helicopter. She had held it together as long as she could as they all watched them load up and leave. He had offered a big reassuring smile as the Blackhawk lifted off the roof of the embassy and she had done her best to return it. Yet the tears had welled up as soon as it disappeared into the night sky. She had turned away, but not before Larry caught a look.

"Just don't say anything okay? Just don't…" She had walked away and Larry had kept silent.

Now she sat on the floor with her legs drawn to her chin, trying to tell herself Jack would be fine. He has Greg and Murphy with him. The SEALs will have the place safe before they arrive. They have planes and gunships over their heads. He'll be back in a couple of hours.

Her thoughts were pulled away as she heard radio chatter coming from the screens. She pulled herself up and joined Larry and Eric as they watched.

"There!" Eric pointed.

They looked closely and saw shapes moving through the bush from two different directions. It looked like a choreographed dance as some stopped, only to have others move. Eric pushed a button and the view widened. They could now see two men lying on a rise overlooking the camp.

"Sniper and an observer," Larry spoke. "Their count is good, too, everyone made the jump okay."

The groups had slowed and were now approaching the camp in two lines at a snail's pace. First one stopped and then the other.

"The gunships are orbiting a few miles out. No reports of activity in the area," Eric voiced.

"Any second now," Larry whispered.

"The first guard's cigarette glowed brightly in the screen before a flash from the sniper's position sent it flying to the right. Another flash from the man closest to the other guard resulted in both of them lying prone in the dirt. The teams immediately moved forward and took up positions surrounding the tents.

"Two, three…" Larry spoke.

The tents with the prone figures disappeared as the camera was overloaded by the flash-bang grenades the SEALs used. The picture returned seconds later as the cameras readjusted and they were now looking at a confused picture of shapes moving inside the tents. Muzzle flashes added to the confusion and it was just as quickly over. Figures were seen moving over and around others lying still on the ground and the flashes repeated. Sydney was shocked until Larry explained.

"Cameras."

Most of the SEALs immediately left the tents and formed a loose circle around the camp as two infrared strobes began blinking just to the south. The sniper and his observer were now aiming themselves out in the opposite direction. Before they could make sense of it, the whole scene was blotted out by a large heat signature. Eric once again adjusted the view and it showed three helicopters flying over and landing just outside the camp. The SEAL perimeter expanded like an amoeba and surrounded them as well.

"There's Jack," Sydney croaked.

She followed three figures as they emerged from the smallest helicopter and ran toward the largest tent. They moved about for a full minute before leaving, pausing only for a few seconds at the Jeep parked outside.

They then ran for the waiting Blackhawk as the SEAL team collapsed their perimeter into the larger birds. They rose from the ground as one and quickly disappeared from the picture. The satellite picture slowly changed angle as it kept its gaze over the now still camp. The bodies of the first two men already cooling in the camera's view.

"Less than five minutes," Larry noted.

"Amazing."

"It's not over yet. Watch."

Their eyes returned to the screen for another minute only to see the view disappear in a large flash. The cameras again swiftly compensated and the view now was one of destruction. The tents were gone, and in their place was a large crater surrounded by burning brush. The telltale shapes of bodies could no longer be discerned.

"Parting gift from the *Reagan*, those Hornet drivers don't miss."

"Why?" Eric asked.

"Deniability. All they will know is that a bomb hit them. Now they won't know if we got their guy alive, or if he's part of that smoking hole in the ground. Hopefully they chalk it up to a Predator and never clue in on the fact that we got him."

"Did we?" Sydney asked.

"We'll know when Jack gets back. You can breathe now, Syd." Larry offered a grin. She couldn't help returning it. But she knew she wouldn't be happy till she saw him get out of that damn helicopter.

*   *   *

Her first sight of him actually made her feel worse. The sun was up by the time they landed on the roof again. As Jack stepped off, Sydney saw that he was covered in blood from chest to waist. He quickly waved her off with a smile, letting her now it wasn't his.

"Jack, what the hell?" she shouted as the engines shut down, she couldn't help staring.

"Not mine, Syd, belongs to our friend Ahmed. He made the mistake of reaching for a gun so the shooters had to pop him. He was still alive when I got there, so we pulled him out with us. Other than cursing us all to hell, we didn't get much out of him before he opted for paradise. We got a lot of intel though. Some good stuff."

"Good, can we go home now?" she asked.

"Lemme get this bloody gear off and then we can talk."

"I'm fine, too, by the way!" Greg added.

"Sorry, you guys are all okay?"

"One of the SEALs broke his wrist on the drop, didn't tell anyone until we were out. Typical. Another one got some flash burns from a grenade he was too eager to follow, but he'll be fine. Normal cuts and scrapes, but they expect that too," he answered. "Actually, out of all of us, Jack *looks* the worst."

She just sighed and shook her head as she followed them down the stairs. They encountered the ambassador in the hallway, but after one look at Jack he turned and retreated into his office.

"I know noth-ing!" Greg did his best Sergeant Shultz impersonation.

"Leave him alone." Jack smiled.

Sydney waited outside the men's locker room until Jack emerged. She caught sight of Greg scrubbing blood off his weapon while blood and camouflage paint still streaked his face. Priorities she didn't understand.

She followed Jack down the hall to the room he had been assigned. She took in his toweled body, still looking for injuries and almost got caught as Jack spun around.

"Can I get dressed?"

"Go ahead, not like I haven't seen it all before," she replied with a grin. Jack gave her a look till she turned her back with a smile.

"So now what?" she asked the wall.

"Now, I get dressed. Some coffee, and then Murphy and I go over what we found. Then I plan on some food and a long nap."

"No coffee."

"All right, no coffee. But if that's your plan you better get all that stuff bagged and filed as soon as possible. The sooner we get it to the labs, the sooner we have more answers. If you can make it all portable, we can evaluate it on the plane."

"Deal. Why don't you take a quick nap while I process all that stuff. You shouldn't handle it until I do anyway?" She chanced a look over her shoulder. Jack sat on the bed in a pair of BDU pants. Clearly tired, he seemed to be thinking it over.

"Okay. Twenty minutes, no more. Then we go over everything." He lay back and put his bare feet up on his duffle bag.

"Okay, I'll wake you."

"I'm serious, Syd, twenty minutes."

"Okay! I promise."

He had closed his eyes and slowed his breathing so she moved to leave the room. Before she made it to the hallway he stopped her with a question.

"What happened to Heather?"

"She caught a flight out last night to Madrid."

"All right …and send Eric to wake me up. I have something I need him to do for me."

"Okay." She waited for a follow-up but got a snore instead. She indulged herself with another look before she retreated down the hall.

*   *   *

"You're sure?" Kimball asked.

"Yes, they cleared the warehouse out and sent everything to the safe house. We'll have to distribute it though other channels. Only the yellows remain."

"Good, did they question you?"

"No, I thought he was going to, but he just moved on. They had other things on their minds. I think we're safe. As far as I know they never even went into the warehouse."

Kimball thought this over. Could they afford to assume this much? The program had been in operation for many years and this was the closest they had come to being discovered. They had to be careful.

"You'll be coming back soon?"

"Yes."

"Come see me when it's safe to do so. We need to evaluate this threat."

*   *   *

Jack let himself sink into the soft leather seat of the Gulfstream as they passed over the Mediterranean. Larry summarized what they had found.

"Well, it's safe to say that he did the bombing. I mean look at what we got here? A map of Dar with the embassy highlighted. This building he has circled has a direct line-of-sight to the impact point. A hand-drawn circuit that matches the wiring we found in the trigger mechanism. We also have the name and address of the driver and all his family members. Something tells me we'll see some economic improvement in their lives real soon! There's even some paper here tying him to Kamill Oil. He entered the country on one of their ships. This is the jackpot!"

Smiles were evident on the faces of his team as Jack looked around the cabin. Murphy and Greg were obviously tired from the long and nerve-racking night. Eric flexed his fingers as he had spent the last few hours they were on the ground feeding copies of the documents into the secure fax machine at the embassy. Sydney reviewed the catalog of evidence and double checked that they had not left anything behind. Bradford fingered his copy of the trigger mechanism (he had asked for a personal one) and compared it to the one he had drawn. His face held a look of personal pride as the drawings were virtually identical.

Jack was happy his team had accomplished their goal. He was also personally content as this would help ease the pressure off him due to the outcome of his last assignment. Although it would have been better to capture the target alive, killing a terrorist would not affect his sleep.

He tuned Larry out for a moment and watched Sydney as she read a bloody handwritten message wrapped in plastic. He waited till she looked up and caught her eye. He gave her his questioning look.

She shook her head and Jack read her face. She had no new information on the vials. Of course she hadn't had much time, so what did he expect? He'd have to wait until they got home.

He listened to Larry as his tone became more joyous with each new finding. He couldn't tell if he was happy with their success, or just glad to be going home in an air conditioned plane. Maybe it was both. Jack wadded up his fleece jacket and stuck it behind his head. He was soon asleep.

CAN OIL PRODUCTION
SATISFY RISING DEMAND?
November 24, 2005—USA Today

—ELEVEN—

THE SENATOR LOOKED UP from the file in front of him and saw the room all waiting for him, just as he expected. He leaned back in his chair and removed the reading glasses before carefully folding them and placing them in their case.

"Looks like you had a rather interesting time in Africa, Mr. Randall. I am, however, pleased with the results, as is the President. The intelligence you gathered is being put to good use. I'm afraid I can't elaborate on that, but let's just say we'll be reducing our Tomahawk missile inventory in the near future. I'll need you to keep that to yourself, of course. The President will announce this from the Oval, I'm sure, as soon as the BDA is available. I understand all the players involved will be getting a nice letter of commendation or something to that effect from their superiors, as well. A job well planned and well executed. Everyone comes home and no banner headlines. Very good."

"Thank you, sir," Jack answered.

They all waited again as the senator consulted some notes. He addressed the room without looking up this time.

"Could Mr. Randall and I have the room please? Please stay also, Mr. Deacon."

Jack shared a look with his boss as the others gathered their papers from the table and filed out past them. The senator watched them go and when the door closed he waved them closer to his end of the table.

"Use your young legs and come down here so this old man doesn't have to shout." They moved to oblige him.

"I'm too old to candy coat things, so I'll just say it. You really pulled yourself back from the edge on this one, Jack. The committee was ready to hang you if you hadn't. But you probably knew that already."

"Yes, sir."

"Smart, smart I like. You may have noticed that we didn't talk about the drug thing? I'd like you to tell me your version."

Jack couldn't help but look at his boss. It was supposed to be between the two of them.

"Don't blame him. He answers to his boss who answers to me. It's still a tight circle and I know everyone in it. I think you were right to keep it to yourselves."

"Sorry, Jack, the director thought it was important enough to brief the senator."

Jack just nodded a hasty agreement before telling the story of the ambush. He spoke slowly and provided detail when needed. He was careful to separate fact from his own opinions. He also cataloged what evidence they had up to that point.

The senator took it all in with only two interruptions to clarify a point. He now sat back in the chair and crossed his hands over his growing spare tire.

"This Tanzanian major, he's the only one who heard the man speak before he was killed?"

"Yes, sir, and I believe him. I'd like to point out that he was shot twice in the attack, and performed bravely on our behalf. If you could possibly get someone from State to send a letter to his boss, my team and I would appreciate it."

"The President is in a letter writing mood. I'm sure it can be arranged. What about these drugs? Were all of them lost?"

"Yes, sir. The charge they used was a big one. What the blast didn't destroy, the fire did. We really weren't in a position to try a put it out. There was still some gunfire happening. Luckily it turned out to be one of our guys."

"Yes, I think my thoughts would have centered on leaving also. Still, good work all around. I'll have some people look into this drug business and see just what's going on there."

"You don't think the Bureau should investigate it, sir?" Deacon asked.

"I think you have enough on your plate and there are other assets that have more contacts in the area that we can use." The senator rose to leave and Jack and his boss joined him. "I'll shoot a memo your way if we find something. I have another meeting, gentlemen, so if you'll excuse me?"

The senator left the room and was immediately accosted by one of his aides brandishing a cell phone, leaving Jack and Deacon alone in the conference room.

"What do you suppose that was all about?" Jack asked.

"I'm not sure. He sure steered us away quick."

"A little too quick if you ask me."

"You *really* don't have any of the drugs in question?"

Jack caught the tone of the question. He collected his briefing material and moved toward the exit.

"*I* don't, sir."

Deacon smiled as he watched the door swing shut behind Jack.

*   *   *

Heather shivered against the air conditioning as she stepped out of the jet way and into the terminal. As tired as she was from her layover in Madrid and the long flight to Atlanta, she still chose to avoid the moving sidewalks crowded with travelers, and instead opted for a leisurely walk through the terminal. She knew her way by heart from her numerous trips and let the passing throngs of travelers flow around her as she made her way through Customs to the baggage check. Her fellow travelers were there waiting and she gave herself a pat on the back for not rushing as they had. She visited the bathroom as she knew they had even longer to wait and was appalled by her appearance in the mirror. The last few days in the African sun and dirt had been hard on her pale skin, as usual, and she now sported a face with a sunburned nose, tan lower half, and a pale forehead from wearing her hat all day. She made an effort to comb her hair into place with her hands but soon gave up. It was glued to her head on one side from sleeping in her airline seat for most of the flight. She wore no makeup as a personal principle, but admitted that she could use some right now.

She dug in her canvas purse for a hairbrush but soon remembered she had lost it. Stolen most likely by a hotel maid, but that was okay. It was not like it was going to help much anyway. She spotted her cell phone in the bag also, still off from the flight, and decided not to turn it on just yet. No doubt her boss was wondering where she was. There would be a long bath and a cold drink before the phone came on, she decided. A couple more hours wouldn't kill him. She left the bathroom and walked to the baggage claim to see people snatching bags off the rotating belt. She watched hers go by once from the rear of the crowd and waited until an opening presented itself before approaching. She noticed a young man in a suit coat and jeans waiting as she was and they shared a look recognized by veteran travelers. Some people had patience and some didn't. She watched her bag make its way around toward her and stole another look at the man. He was kinda cute. And of course she looked her worse. She forced herself to look away and grabbed her bag before it passed her again. She shouldered it and spun on her heel, heading for the tram that would take her to the exit where she would catch a bus to the long term parking lot. She hoped her trusty Nissan was still waiting for her. After stepping out of the terminal she stopped on the curb to wait.

Glancing up and down the busy terminal, she caught sight of the cute guy, now wearing sunglasses and looking in her direction. He carried a small carry-on and still wore his coat. Kind of odd, she thought, spring in Atlanta was no time to wear a coat if one could help it. Maybe he was an Air Marshall? She shrugged off the thought as her bus arrived. She waved the driver off as he offered to help her with her bags and recited her parking spot zone from memory.

Fifteen minutes later she was in her Nissan Exterra, which still needed a bath from her latest wilderness excursion. After thumbing on her iPod and pulling up her favorite list, she put the SUV in motion and was soon headed home, relaxing for the first time since she'd left Africa. Traffic was light as it was after rush hour and she made good time, arriving home as the sun began to set. She was lucky enough to find a spot right in front of her building and pulled in quickly to claim it. After unloading her bags, she struggled to pull them up the stairs, the treads of her canvas shoes slipping on the tile floor. Once the door was defeated and she had gained entrance she flopped on the couch and savored the feeling of home. The cold drink came to mind so she forced herself up and to the fridge. Its bare interior greeted her with a minimum of options, but at least there was Coke and ice. A bottle of rum was in the cabinet and she soon had item one on her coming home checklist done. She was about to flop on the couch again when she remembered the car. Had she locked it after she unloaded her bag? She walked to the window as she sipped her drink and parted the curtains in order to see it parked on the curb. She thumbed the remote and was rewarded by the lights flashing back at her.

She was about to turn back away from the window when she saw a dark sedan moving down the street. She watched its approach as the driver leaned out the open window, looking up at the apartments on her side.

It was the cute guy from the airport.

*   *   *

John Kimball compared the reading on the gauge to the paperwork in his gloved hand. The production numbers were only slightly below the predicted output of the bioreactor, and although he was pleased by the accuracy of their prediction, he would still push his people to meet the expected number. He bent over to see the output liquid as it flowed into the collection vessel. The liquid settled in the bottom and had the look and consistency of corn syrup.

"Incredible," he said to himself inside his space suit. In this one small glass jar was enough highly concentrated agent to change the world. For good or for bad was defined by one's own personal opinion. That decision was for someone else.

He listened closely to the bioreactor. It seemed to be functioning fine, the quietly running pump gave off a gentle hum. Although no larger than a standard-sized refrigerator, it produced enough agent to meet the ordered production without strain. There were two others exactly like it in the room. Only one ran at any given time due to safety and staffing issues. The bioreactors were the best that man had invented so far. No cost had been spared in their acquisition. Theoretically they could be sterilized and used for beer production if and when that time ever came. John shuddered at the thought. He hoped to see the bioreactors shut down permanently one day, but to get to that point would require that the agent be used. The world was not to that point yet.

John made a few notes before showing the production foreman what he had written. It was easier than shouting though the space suit. The man quickly read the instructions and nodded in agreement.

"How long?" John mouthed silently through his face shield.

"Two days," the man mouthed back, holding up two triple-gloved fingers to be clear.

John gave him a thumb's up before moving carefully past and walking to the door of the production facility. He then found the stairs and holding the railing carefully ascended one flight to enter an animal testing lab. He was late for a demonstration, but they really weren't going to start without him.

After passing through the door and connecting to one of the overhead air hoses he was noticed by one of the lab techs who patted the arm of the department head. John recognized him from his body language. With everyone dressed in blue space suits, body language became the chief way of identifying coworkers in a hot zone. The department head waited until he approached and leaned his head forward. John did the same while crimping the air hose to his suit to stop the roar in his ears. The men touched helmets to better conduct the sound of their voices. They still had to speak up as the plastic was thick.

"The test is all ready. We have four different subjects this time and we'll be testing the newest delivery system."

"The canvasbacks?"

"We added them, plus the terns, gulls, and Canadian geese."

"Okay. Lead on."

John unplugged his suit from the overhead hose and followed the man into the next room where they were joined by the man's team plus a couple of engineers. Everyone plugged back in before lining up outside a large window that looked into an enclosed area.

John saw eight sets of wire cages resting on stainless steel topped lab benches spaced evenly around a central bench holding what looked to be three large rocks, each about the size of a football. The cages held a total of eight birds, two of each breed, one male and one female of the types he'd been told. The birds were restless. There was no way they could know what their purpose was in the room, yet somehow they knew it was not good. All were making a variety of noise, although it was the equivalent of having the TV on mute as none of them could be heard by the spectators.

John felt a tap on his shoulder and turned to see one of the engineers beside him. The man carried a remote control device and a small dry-erase board. He quickly scribbled out a message.

"Range improved to two miles." The man smiled when he held it up.

John offered a nod to indicate he understood but no more. You could send the signal all day from two miles away, but if the device didn't respond it was worthless. Actually worse than worthless as it could not be left in place if it failed to function. Someone would have to recover it, and it sure as hell wasn't going to be John Kimball.

The engineer looked right and left and received a thumb's up from the people manning the video cameras. Once he was satisfied they were on, he pointed to the man at the control board. The man threw some switches and they all felt rather than heard the air control units shut down over their heads. The room they were looking at, while sealed tightly, had just lost its negative pressure. There was no movement of the birds' feathers as they grew quiet in their cages.

After one more look around, the engineer pushed the first button on the remote device. John watched the rocks on the table and was pleased to see a steady cloud of vapor emanate quietly from the closest one. The stream shot visibly from the surface of the rock to a height of about three feet before it dissipated and was no longer seen. After half a minute the first rock stopped and the second began, followed by the third. John checked the reading on the decibel meter hanging over the cages. The needle had barely moved. The noise and vapor stream had hardly startled the birds who now sat quietly in their cages, oblivious to what had just happened. The birds showed no signs of change for the next five minutes until the air units came back to life and the room again was under negative air pressure.

John was offered the dry-erase board again.

"Have #'s in 1 day" it read.

John took the offered board and erased the statement with his gloved hand before taking the offered pen.

"Good job, everyone." He held it up for the room to see. He received smiles from their glass-encased faces in return.

John carefully danced his way though them and made his way to the stairs. He was two flights away from the airlock and had been in his space suit for several hours. More than he was accustomed to. In a day he would have data on the delivery device. If it worked, the vapor would have delivered the right size droplets without destroying the agent. Then it was just a matter of waiting to see if the birds became hosts. That should only take a few hours more.

As he entered the decontamination shower and pulled the handle to start the seven-minute ordeal, he reviewed the migratory data he had committed to memory. With the addition of the canvasback ducks he felt they should now have the entire world covered. He raised his arms and rotated under the shower while the numbers raced through his mind. He looked for any holes in their coverage as he did the dance of death in the chemical deluge.

✻   ✻   ✻

Dennis Murphy sat back in his chair with a sigh and watched the computer power down. He shook his head at the time it took. Security. He knew it was necessary, but sometimes it was just a pain in the ass. He never understood the logic behind the commands either. What was the first step to turning a computer off? Click on START. He was sure it made perfect sense to somebody. His mind was too tired to dwell on it any more.

After returning from Africa he had spent an hour on the seventh floor in the office of the Deputy Director of Operations recounting everything that had happened over the last few days. The Deputy Director of Intelligence had joined them and he had been grilled with questions for another hour after that. Finally they had ended it with instructions to write a report on everything they had just covered for the director's desk tomorrow. It had turned into a long night.

Now that the computer was off, he became aware of the silence in the room. The other department analyst had gone home hours ago and his desk was now the only one lit.

"Good idea," he voiced aloud to the empty room.

He gathered the report off the printer and slipped it into a file of the proper color and border tape before depositing it in his secure cabinet. Giving the lock a spin as he stood, he fetched his coat from the back of the chair and headed toward the exit. Making sure his badge was visible for the night security, he started the long walk to his car.

The corridors of the CIA would never be described as having any semblance of décor. The floor was tile and echoed the footsteps of the third shift workers and security personnel as they strode their lengths. Everyone was strangely quiet as conversation was not encouraged in the common areas. The walls bore no decorative artwork and no sculptures filled the open areas. The only thing present being the large mirrors mounted high in every corner, used both to prevent a collision with a fellow spook as well as assure that no one was listening from around a corner.

Murphy listened to the echo of his feet as he rounded a corner and passed a small kiosk manned by a blind attendant. The man sat quietly and offered a nod to Murphy as he approached.

"Goodnight, Bobby."

"Good night, Mr. Murphy," was the immediate reply.

Murphy smiled. Bobby never got a name wrong. He'd learn a new one in a matter of days and it would be stored in his vault-like memory forever. Something that had not gone unnoticed by a few people and a paper explaining how he did it had been authored and distributed to a few people at the Farm, as the CIA's training center was known. A thank you letter from the director himself hung on the wall in Bobby's kiosk and he made sure it was free of dust every morning.

After sliding his pass through three turnstiles, Murphy finally arrived at the gate to the parking garage. Here his seniority and rank bought him a spot on the second level and he was spared the rain as he unlocked the driver's side door.

He was soon on his way down the Dolly Madison in the light drizzle, heading for his home in Sterling. Since it was late, he chose to use the Hirst Brault Expressway as traffic would be light.

He first noticed the car as he entered 267 and headed west. It had been behind him since he had gotten on the Dolly Madison and training had him in a habit of checking behind him.

"Probably a fellow spook," he told himself. He thumbed on the radio and was assaulted by Green Day at high volume. Evidently his daughter had used the car while he was gone. He turned it off as the rain increased along with the traffic. He was sure the presets had been changed as well and didn't want to deal with it right now.

Checking the mirror again, he noted that the car was closer now. The rain had dropped visibility and the other cars around him had opened up some space. Yet this one was closer?

Murphy changed lanes and the car soon matched his move. But the move had also placed the car behind him and in silhouette from the headlights of the car behind it. He could make out two men in the front seat. The car was just a car, it didn't look government bland, but it wasn't flashy either. The plates were civilian tags, but the car was too far away to make out the number.

He drummed his fingers on the wheel as he neared Reston. "Watch out for monkeys!" he could hear his daughter say in his head. Something she always reminded him to do when he left for work. She was referring to the Reston Monkey House where, in 1989, the entire population of primates had died from Ebola, a deadly hemorrhagic viral disease. Rumors of escaped monkeys running through the suburbs had become folklore in the area. Right now he had other things to worry about than stray monkeys.

Who was it? The FBI? Why would they be following him? He had just completed a job with them. He even had a nice letter of commendation to go with it. Maybe even an intelligence star from his own agency. Maybe it was his people checking up on him. Could be that he was just the subject of a training exercise by some new recruits who picked out the wrong car to follow? The NSA maybe? He hadn't made any phone calls that would trigger a tail. DIA? The alphabet soup of possibilities was endless.

He finally chose to put aside the identity and reason for the tail and find out how dedicated they were. He made another quick lane change and exited the expressway. The car did not follow. He pulled into the first gas station he came to and found a space at the pump farthest from the road. Exiting the car, he proceeded to casually top off his already three-quarter-full tank. He used the reflection in the glass of the rear window to watch for the tailing car, but it failed to show before the pump shut off. Despite the fact that he had paid with his credit card already, he capped the tank and strolled to the convenience store. Here he found a place in an aisle where he could shop for junk food while watching the road outside. After a few minutes he decided he was being paranoid and grabbed a bag of chips for appearance's sake before approaching the counter.

Back in his car he made it as far as the entrance ramp before he saw them. This time they had no choice but to pass him and he quickly made a mental note of the tag number before catching a glimpse of the occupants. Both of them were young men in their twenties with close-cropped hair, clean shaven, wearing suits. They both avoided looking at him as he passed. Might be students from the Farm, but could be anybody, he decided.

He kept an eye on the mirror the rest of the way home, but the car never reappeared. Was he wrong? He didn't think so, but to be sure he would run the plate number in the morning and file a contact report per policy. He had been out of the field for some time, but his instincts said he had been followed tonight and he usually trusted them. The real question was who was doing the following and why? Should he just flat out ask Jack Randall? Or maybe call some of his recent teammates and see if they had some tails, too? Maybe just keep it to himself and see if it happened again?

He failed to spot any monkeys, also, something he reported to his daughter when he got home.

NATURE CAN'T TAKE UNRESTRAINED
ECONOMIC GROWTH.
July 8, 2009——Reuters

—TWELVE—

JIM MILES HAD SOLD out, but few could blame him. He had lived
a life of great success as well as great disappointment. Once one of the
army's leading researchers into biological warfare, he had been on the
cutting edge of research and development during the late sixties and early
seventies. Serving his country for over thirty years, he now had little to
show for it. Once a leader in his field, he was quickly shunned and quietly
retired when he started speaking out against the use of the very thing
he was helping to make. Two failed marriages and some bad financial
planning had found him on the street with nothing but a modest pension. Blacklisted by the military, and unwanted by the CDC, he turned to
the only place he could and began teaching microbiology at Vanderbilt
University. After three years he had lost his taste for the classroom and
accepted an offered position with a large pharmaceutical company. The
head of research and development had a wife who was a psychologist
and after meeting with Jim a few times, made the tentative diagnosis of

Asperger's syndrome. His boss, soon realizing the kind of man he had, provided Jim with his own small lab where he was left alone to pursue the virus research that had dominated his life. He proved to be proficient at the development of vaccines, and in just two years time had provided the company with the means to make millions. For this he was given all the equipment and funding he requested, and left alone with his Petri dishes and microscopes, his boss confident that another multi-million dollar breakthrough was soon to arrive.

Sydney parked outside his modest house in the pine barrens of New Jersey. It was an old farmhouse with a wide porch and peeling white paint. An equally ancient barn sat in the backyard, leaning precariously to one side. The fields around it were bare, but showed signs of being tended. The house did not, surrounded by trees that needed trimming and grass that was far too high. Weeds grew up through the gravel driveway and brushed against the underside of the car as she pulled up to the front porch. She took in the grime coated windows and closed curtains. A light shone behind one so she got out and walked up the creaking steps. She knocked on the door as hard as she dared—it looked ready to fall off by itself.

"Who the hell is it?" a man's voice called out from inside.

"Dr. Miles? It's Sydney Lewis, from Vanderbilt."

She heard some muttered cursing as he made his way to the door. It seemed to take him awhile. The curtain pulled back from the glass and she was treated to her former professor's face glaring at her over his glasses.

"Who?" he asked. "What the hell do you want?"

"It's Sydney Lewis, sir. You taught me advanced micro in school?" she prompted.

His glare remained before his memory kicked in. He withdrew his head and she heard several locks turning. The door was swept open and she was treated to the smiling face of her former professor.

"Sydney Lewis! Why it's been…"

"Eight years, sir, how are you?"

"Oh, I'm doing just fine. Come in, come in."

Sydney carefully stepped through the door and took in the room. The locks were all reengaged behind her and he joined her, following her gaze.

"I'm not much for housekeeping. Just ignore all this stuff and come to the kitchen. I just made a batch of sweet tea. Gotta make it myself. Damn Yankees drink it plain, but we know better don't we?"

"Yes we do."

Sydney understood why it took so long for him to get to the door as she followed him through a path of stacked books, journal articles, and old furniture. A cat watched her every move from a hiding place between the stacks. A fireplace went unused against one wall and served as a depository for more clutter. It was a relief to finally enter the kitchen. The professor moved to the refrigerator and removed a large glass pitcher. Setting it on the spotless table, he fetched two glasses from a nearby cupboard, inspecting them carefully before adding ice and setting them down.

Sydney watched him work, for that is what he was doing. The kitchen was the exact opposite of the room she had walked through and it didn't surprise her as she already knew the man. A kitchen was just another laboratory to the professor, and this one was as clean and in order as any she had ever worked in. She watched him move about in his usual uncoordinated way, but there was never a wasted moment. He knew where everything was and everything was in its place until needed. The man had worked out his priorities several years ago.

Sydney sampled the tea and it was exactly as she remembered it.

"So what brings you to New Jersey? Are you with the New York office now?"

"You know where I work?"

"Well of course I do. I get television, even way out here, in color and everything."

"I'm sorry. I just figured you lost track. I know how busy you keep yourself."

"That doesn't stop Stacie from calling. Nothing really stops Stacie from calling. Called me one night about a couple of months ago and told me all about how you were working for the FBI and flying around in a big jet. I was happy to hear you'd finally found your niche."

"It is rewarding. I like my job. How are you doing?"

He paused for a large sip of tea before jumping to his feet. "I'm doing okay now. Found a job where they just leave me alone and let me tinker." He pulled out a box of cookies from a shelf organized by size, shook some out onto a spotless glass plate and set it on the table. "Pays well, too. Finally realized money wasn't my thing and hired a guy to take care of mine for me. Not like I need a lot, but he tells me I'm getting rich. He gives me an allowance, believe it or not, like I'm some kinda kid."

"Are you bored?" she asked.

Professor Miles munched a cookie as he thought about her question. "Am I bored? Yes and no. I basically have my own lab, Bio level 4 even. I can do whatever I want. They give me stuff they want me to work on, but it only eats up maybe half my time. I do some experimenting and I publish a little. A lot of it gets classified and that still pisses me off, but I don't tilt at windmills anymore. If I do bitch they pay me off with a raise or a vacation. I'm content, I guess you could say."

"What if I said I had something mysterious for you?"

He let his chair fall forward as he reached for another cookie. Sydney recognized the pattern. He was using the cookie to buy him some time to think. She waited patiently.

"Is this secret FBI stuff?"

"Maybe. We're not really sure yet."

"We?"

"My boss and myself," she answered.

"Who's your boss?"

"Jack Randall."

"Tall dark-headed fellow, I saw him on the TV with you. Stacie said he was a straight shooter. Just what is it you need?"

Sydney pulled the vials from her pocket and set them on the table.

He looked at them and then at her before he brushed the crumbs off his hands and picked one up. He looked it over carefully and held it up to the light.

"I don't recognize the numbers. No name on the label. What is it?"

"We don't know. Some type of vaccine, we believe. We found it in an East African warehouse. We were attempting to transport it when somebody ambushed the trucks. They were fought off, but the ambushers destroyed the remaining supply rather than let us keep it."

"It's not any vaccine I know of, and I know them all. Somebody killed for this?"

"Yes, and we don't know why. Black market drugs are big in Africa, but they really took a big chance destroying the truck."

The professor rolled the vial around in his hand for a moment while he thought some more.

"You say they were inoculating people with this?"

"The yellow top vials seemed to move in and out, but the red tops just seem to sit once they arrive."

"Like it's waiting for something," he stated.

"Maybe, but what?"

"Good question. They both have the same number on them, just different lids." He was just speaking out loud as teachers were prone to do when they're thinking.

"They were always stored far apart, never in the same area."

"Strange. I could run it through the lab and see what it is for you. That what you need?"

"If it's no trouble. We're willing to pay you."

He took his eyes off the vials long enough to frown at her. "Who, you or the FBI?"

"Jack has money. He said he'd pay whatever you need. We'd like to just keep this quiet for now, just the three of us."

"Tell your friend he can keep his money. I've got the time and it'll be nice to have something different to play with. I can run it through a little gizmo I helped invent not too long ago. It's a new biosensor. You just

park a little drop in and it breaks it down to the DNA and compares it to
a database, takes just a few minutes. Somebody took my idea and they're
working on a handheld model for the military and TSA and whoever
else they think needs it. I'm told I'll be rich for that, too, but I'll believe it
when I see it. You got a phone number where I can reach you?"

Sydney reached in her purse and pulled out a card. She wrote her
private number on the back. "Use this one, not the one on the front."

"Okay, you hungry?"

She smiled at his rapid change in thought. "Sure."

"Good, let's go down to the Hide-a-Way and eat. They got a cheese-
burger big as your head." He jumped up and grabbed his coat, placing the
vials in the pocket.

They took the shorter route out the back door, bypassing the obstacle
course of the front room.

$$* \qquad * \qquad *$$

Professor Miles was up early the next morning after a sleepless night.
He'd lain in bed listening to the cats chase one another around the house,
the loose boards of the barn banging in the wind, and the sound of the air
conditioning turning on and off. His thoughts kept returning to the vials
his former pupil had dropped off.

What a life she must have, he thought. She had been one of his best
pupils, but what he had liked best about her was that she had no sense
of entitlement. She was the exact opposite of the rich kids who were the
sons and daughters of legacy graduates. A former paramedic, no less,
maybe it was her age and street experience that gave her the attitude they
had all noticed. While the other medical students had aimed at plastic
surgery or lucrative careers as specialists, Sydney had wanted nothing
more than to return to public service with the FBI. Stacie, her friend
and mentor, had been cut from the same cloth and he had followed the
careers of both of them over the years. He had been overjoyed to see her
on his front porch and he'd had to bite his tongue to not bring up the
subject of the vials over their cheeseburgers. The mystery of the vials was

just what he needed right now.

The drumming of a woodpecker on his aluminum downspouts told him the sun was creeping up, and he pulled himself out of bed and turned off the alarm well before it was set to ring. The cats stood quickly to avoid the flying blanket then just as quickly settled back down on the bed to sleep the morning away. They knew that food would await them in their bowls when they chose to awake, and it was best to stay out from underfoot during their owner's high speed morning ritual.

Jim quickly showered and shaved before walking around the bedroom with an electric toothbrush running in one hand as he pulled whatever was on top from a multitude of drawers with the other. Whether the items matched or even went together never crossed his mind. His trademark Detroit Red Wings baseball cap went on over his unruly hair and he made it back to the sink in time to spit. He had mastered the art of brushing his teeth and getting dressed at the same time years ago.

A quick stop in the kitchen for an energy bar and a bottle of Gatorade and he was out the door, only to immediately return and fill the cats' bowls to overflowing. He looked at the mess on his clean floor, but quickly decided he could clean it up later if the cats didn't finish it all. He had a new puzzle to work on, and he loved puzzles.

The twenty-minute drive to his office and lab took him only fifteen minutes today in the light early morning traffic. The average driver would have taken thirty, but Jim always sped wherever he went as he considered time spent traveling to and from as time wasted. He looked forward to the invention of the molecular transporter so he could just beam himself wherever he wanted to go, but he doubted it would exist in his lifetime. His eight-year-old Mercedes held up just fine to the brutal treatment he dished out daily.

Arriving at his lab he stormed through the office area, snapping on the lights. His assistant, lab techs, and secretary weren't due for another hour yet. He paused at her desk to leave a short message before advancing to his own office. First he took off his coat and hung it on the hook next to his framed "The Terminator" marquee poster before he retrieved the vials from its pocket. He set them down on the blotter and forced a deep breath. He moved his nose down until it was an inch from the vials.

"Who's first?" he asked them.

Recalling what Sydney had said about the yellows being the ones that were moved in and out of the warehouse, he chose it first. Picking up the red top vial he placed it in his personal safe. One he'd had reprogrammed by a "visiting consultant" some time ago. He just didn't trust his employers to keep their noses out of it. Palming the yellow vial, he proceeded out the door and into the lab. He had made the decision to work on the vial in his Level 4 lab last night. He had two reasons. One, he had an unknown substance and he felt safer playing with it under those conditions, and two, he would have total privacy.

The lab here was only a few years old and modeled after the Russian biological warfare labs discovered after the Cold War ended. The labs had the same levels of containment, 1 through 4, but whereas the CDC had different labs for different levels, this design was proven more efficient and safe and had been adopted by the rest of the world. It was basically a series of rings, the outermost being Level 1 and progressing to the core which was Level 4. Any virus being worked on in the core would have to get past three levels of containment in the event of an accident.

Jim paused at the first gate to slide his ID card through the reader. The door opened with a hiss and he felt the slight tug of air pulling him into the lab. All of the lab areas were under negative pressure, the air being constantly sucked toward the core to prevent the escape of airborne viruses. The air from the core was processed through sealed ductwork lit by powerful ultraviolet lights that served to destroy the genetic material of most viruses. It was then pulled through a chemical shower and an electrostatic dust collector before being processed by a series of High Efficiency Particle Arrestor—HEPA—filters. The entire system had multiple fail-safe measures and backup power sources that were maintained and guarded twenty-four hours a day.

He waved to the surprised guard reading a paperback in front of a group of video monitors.

"Good morning, Charlie."

"Morning, sir, you're starting early today?"

"Yeah, got an idea. Don't worry, I'll try not to moon ya."

Charlie grinned, it was their standard joke. Security cameras were everywhere, even in the locker room. Charlie had a view of the doctor's bare ass every day.

Jim didn't pause or break stride as he moved on through the Level 1 lab and entered the locker room. It was a small room with a few lockers, a bench, and a large sink. A full-length mirror hung on the wall. Jim opened his locker and removed all of his clothing, including his underwear, his watch and his Red Wings hat, which he carefully placed on the top shelf facing out. Standing completely naked, he walked to the last locker and removed a sterile set of surgical scrubs and a surgical cap. He first donned the cap and, using the mirror, made sure every strand was tucked underneath. He then put on the pants and shirt before tying the drawstring to just the right tightness, which he tested with a deep knee bend to ensure it wouldn't ride up his ass when he sat down. Once he had donned the space suit there was no way to fix such a problem, and he didn't wish to be stuck with a distracting wedgie all day.

Now, standing in his bare feet on the cold epoxy-painted floor, he pushed the button for the Level 2 door. As it opened, he again felt the small breeze that preceded him into the next room. He moved through the staging area that was lit with blue ultraviolet light, passing a decontamination shower with its hotel bars of soap and sample-sized bottles of shampoo. He paused long enough to force a last pee and grab a pair of socks. He then walked across the room to the bio Level 3 staging room door. Once through, he pulled a pair of rubber surgical gloves from a box and slipped them on without powder (he hated powder) before pulling a roll of tape off the wall and carefully taping the sleeves of his scrub shirt to the gloves. With practiced hands he diligently repeated the process on his socks and pants. Finished, he inspected his work in another mirror before deciding it was satisfactory. At this point he had only one layer of protection.

He then proceeded through another swing door with large windows into another locker room. Here he reached for his space suit hanging on a rack, marked with a piece of tape and a black marker. He placed the vial in a special carrier with a large handle before spreading the suit out on the floor. He then stepped into it and sat down, placing his feet into the legs and carefully pulling them up, inspecting the suit as he did. Holding the suit with both hands, he then stood and pulled it up to his armpits, sliding his arms into each sleeve until his fingers passed the connecting gaskets and entered the brown rubber gloves. Once both of his hands were in and snug, he spent a full minute inspecting both. This was his most vulnerable point. With these gloves he would be handling sharp objects, glassware, and syringes with needles attached. He had never taken it lightly, and as a result had experienced only one minor exposure in his entire career. If he had even the slightest doubt about the integrity of his space suit, he would destroy it and get another. He slipped his feet into a pair of thick yellow boots and taped them as he had his socks and scrubs earlier. He added three six-inch long strips to his right forearm to serve as emergency seals if he should somehow rip a hole in his space suit. Once done with the tape, he added another set of surgical gloves over the suit gloves. This put three layers of protection over his hands.

He performed a quick mental checklist before pulling on the soft plastic helmet. Once in place, he pulled the lubricated zipper closed across his chest with a series of popping sounds. He quickly snagged a coiled yellow air hose hanging from the ceiling and plugged it into the suit. He immediately heard the roaring air and his suit blew up till he resembled the Michelin Man. The condensation on his faceplate disappeared as he pirouetted in front of the three-way mirror looking for leaks. Finding none, he picked up the tray and stepped to the airlock. Pushing the button for the door, he unhooked the air line as it opened and walked through the small stainless steel corridor. It was lined by stainless steel plumbing leading to stainless steel nozzles over a stainless steel floor. Several large red buttons were spaced down both walls and it was lit by the same eerie blue ultraviolet light. This was the decontamination chamber. If he hit one of the buttons he would be locked in for a full seven minutes and deluged with water and chemicals. Something he would do on the way out. For now he walked its length quickly and opened the far door of the airlock. He stepped through, and was in the hot zone.

*   *   *

As Doctor Miles entered the hot zone, Sydney was speeding down a New Jersey back road in her new Mustang convertible, a treat to herself after their last case. She couldn't understand why anybody would buy a sports car without getting a convertible top. It just added to the thrill. She loved her little car and gave it a little extra as she came out of a sweeping curve.

The illegal speed resulted in a breeze that almost drowned out the ring of her cell phone. She slowed down to a safer speed and pulled out her Bluetooth headset before she thumbed the button.

"Hello?"

"Syd? It's Jack. Where in the hell are you?"

"New Jersey."

"Are you standing on the beach or something? Sounds like you're in a wind tunnel."

"I've got the top down!"

"Okay," he bellowed back. "What do we know?"

"Nothing yet, I just gave it to him yesterday, give him some time."

"I figured you two would run straight to the lab with that stuff. I know it's been burning a hole in your pocket."

"Yeah, but you can't just barge in and order an old friend down to *his* lab. We had some dinner and caught up. I'm sure I piqued his interest, he's probably in the lab already."

"Okay, you're sure we can trust him?" Jack had to ask.

"Yes, he's a good friend." She let her exasperation come through a little.

"How much is he nailing me for?"

"Nothing, said he'd do it for free. He makes plenty himself."

"Well okay then, how long till you get back?"

"I was gonna just take the back roads and enjoy the ride. Why?"

"Both of our friends disappeared. The tails lost them."

Sydney thought about this as she slowed even more. Something was going on with their newest team members. Jack's instincts weren't often wrong.

"I'll be back as soon as possible."

"Good."

ACTION NEEDED TO AVOID
WORLD WATER CRISIS.
March 12, 2009—Reuters

–THIRTEEN–

DOCTOR MILES CONSIDERED HIS options. Based on Sydney's theory that the sample was a vaccine of some sort, that meant it was most likely made up of a weakened version of a live virus. He decided to run it through his new bio analyzer to identify it by its DNA.

After laying out a variety of equipment on the bench in front of him and pouring a large bowl of EnviroChem and placing it on the table, he was ready. He first held the vial up to the light one more time, sometimes the DNA would clump up and one could actually see it with the human eye. As he had tried several times already he was not surprised to see nothing again, just a clear fluid with the consistency of water. He gripped the vial in one hand and pried off the yellow top. It broke its seal under the pressure and he was treated to a view of the gray membrane material that was common for this type of vial. It would allow a needle to pass through to draw out the fluid, yet would seal again on its withdrawal. Using a syringe, he withdrew half the fluid and placed equal portions into five small test tubes, each about the size of his little toe.

Once that was accomplished, he disposed of the needle in a red plastic box full of EnviroChem and switched to a micropipette. He had turned the machine on when he had entered the lab and selected a disk of the most common vaccines to try first. It loaded quickly and the machine now announced its readiness with a green light. He drew a small drop of the fluid from the first test tube and placed it on a sample card which he then fed into the machine. The solid green light began blinking as the machine worked on it, and Jim watched the screen as the dry air roared in his ears.

Soon he was treated to letters scrolling across the screen—only four letters, in seemingly random order—T, C, A and G representing the nucleotide bases thymine, cytosine, adenine, and guanine, the building blocks of DNA. The letters scrolled faster as the machine worked and were soon going too fast to read. This could take some time. A small virus can have over 7,000 bases, a more complicated one over 200,000.

After a five-minute wait he felt he had enough to try for identification. He pressed a few keys on the machine and a larger computer monitor to the left came to life. The machine would automatically link via the internet with an organization know as GenBank, located not too far away in Maryland. Its purpose was to maintain a large database of genetic sequences. If you were looking to identify an unknown strand of DNA, this was like asking the Library of Congress of genetic codes for help. With a few more clicks on his part, the GenBank computers accepted the data and began matching it to its database. He soon had answers popping up on the screen.

Knowing he would have to run several samples he forced himself not to look and began prepping another sample on a slide to look at through his microscope. Again using the micropipette, he placed a small drop onto a slide and utilizing tweezers secured a cover slide over that. This he placed under his microscope and reached for the fine adjustment. He saw various shapes, but nothing he could readily identify. He had not really hoped to get too much as this microscope was not powerful enough to see something as small as a virus. For that you needed an electron microscope, something they had in his lab, yet he was not an expert at running it. For that he had a talented lab technician who should be along in a couple of hours. He would do what he could to prepare for him what he needed.

He separated the last two test tubes from the other three and placed them into a separate holder. Uncapping the lids, he added a quick-drying plastic resin. The resin would freeze any virus particles in place. The tech would then take these small tubes of plastic and slice them utilizing a diamond bladed microtome. Much like a machine one would see in a deli, it would produce incredibly thin samples no bigger than the head of a pin.

Once the resin chore had been handled, he rose and walked the length of the room to a large door next to the airlock. He stopped to gather several biscuits and other food from a small closet before opening the heavy door and entering the room. He was greeted by the hoots and hollers of several monkeys. There were two banks of cages facing each other across a narrow walkway. The monkeys always went crazy at the sight of him early in the morning. They performed as they always did, rattling their cages and leaping back and forth. Their high pitched screams penetrated the thick plastic of his space suit and overpowered the roar of air in his ears. He checked the cleverly engineered door mechanisms to ensure they were all still locked as they should be. The mechanism had to be easily manipulated by a human with a triple layer of gloves, yet unable to be released by curious primate fingers. He moved down the walkway, shuffling his feet on the concrete floor with its multiple layers of thick epoxy paint.

"Hello ladies," he greeted his two control monkeys as he carefully dropped monkey biscuits into the feeding chutes. He watched as they scrambled to pick them up and immediately start eating. They still never took their eyes off him, watching every move he made. Unknown to them they were the only two in the group that were safe from him as they were always isolated and never experimented on. They served to inform him of unexpected airborne pathogens, much like the canary in the coal mine. Their names were Thelma and Louise.

He continued down the row feeding the monkeys and the noise level dropped somewhat as they now divided their time between screaming and eating. He carefully observed all of them for any signs of disease, but they all appeared normal and healthy. He finished providing water for them also and quickly left them to their breakfast.

He exited the monkey room and entered a smaller, much quieter room housing a variety of animals. Here he performed the same feeding chores for a multitude of mice, rats and guinea pigs. He stopped to observe a cage of six white mice he had injected last week with a new vaccine. In three more days they would be exposed to a form of cervical cancer to test its effectiveness. Someone had beaten him to the discovery already, so this was more of a personal mission, and who knew, perhaps his version would be better? The mice looked no different then they had yesterday.

He selected six mice from a small cage next to the original six and separated them into a portable cage. He wasn't ready for them yet, but he wanted to separate them now just to save the time later. He observed them as they climbed around and over each other as they explored their new home. They all looked healthy. Soon they would get an injection of Sydney's mystery vaccine. He truly hoped they stayed healthy.

A virus to Jim Miles was both a beautiful and a deadly thing. He'd been fascinated with both aspects of their existence his whole life, and to this day the appeal kept him researching them for their secrets.

He called them Terminators, after his favorite movie character. Like many scientists, he was a science fiction fan. When the movie had come out he had been captivated by the writers' invention of the man-machine with its single goal, and the cold, efficient, and deadly means to carry it out. To him, the Terminator was the ultimate virus. It existed for one purpose: to kill the main character and therefore ensure its own survival. A virus was much the same. With eternal patience it would lie in wait, much like a machine, only to spring to life and begin the process of taking over a host for the purpose of self-replication, ensuring its survival.

He often recalled the soldier's description of the Terminator as he described it to the woman it was pursuing. "It's out there. It can't be reasoned with. It can't be bargained with. It doesn't feel pity, or remorse, or fear, and it absolutely will not stop, ever, until you are dead!" It helped him to remember the words when he worked in the hot zone. They kept him safe.

While they may have been similar in their mission, on a structural level the fictional Terminator and the real virus were very different. While the Terminator was the product of the computer age, a virus was made up of a single strand of DNA or RNA, encased in a membrane of protein. The genetic strand was simply a long molecule containing the instructions for making more viruses. There was much debate over whether viruses were actually alive or not as they existed somewhere in between life and nonlife. They switched from one aspect to the other as their environment changed.

A virus that was outside a living host might form a crystal or protective barrier and have no metabolic activity. Essentially they were dead. If this virus should come in contact with a living cell and managed to attach to its surface, the cell will feel the virus's presence and engulf it, drawing it inside its own membrane.

This was to the cell's own demise as the virus was a parasite which cannot survive without the aid of another living cell. Once inside the new host, the virus comes to life and quickly takes over the cell's processes, reprogramming them to do nothing but manufacture copies of the virus. This goes on until the cell can no longer contain the population of virus within its membrane and it simply explodes, destroying itself, and releasing millions of viruses to repeat the process on other cells. If enough cells are destroyed, the host dies. Any virus particles that are unable to find a new host will either die, or adopt the dormant stage, awaiting the opportunity of a new host.

This made it easy for Dr. Miles to compare the virus with the Terminator. Viruses were much like machines, they had a purpose, to replicate themselves, but it was strictly a mechanical process. There was no real intelligence behind their methods. They simply did what they do, and they would never stop.

Jim always had these thoughts in the back of his head when working in his lab. He knew how bad things could get. He had seen the results of bio-warfare experiments. At first his fascination had overridden any moral dilemma and he had pursued his experiments with great curiosity. By the time he was able to fully comprehend what he and a few others had created it was too late. He had left the program as quickly as he could. He now worked with vaccines, creating ways to stop viruses instead of creating newer, more powerful ones.

But in order to beat a virus one first had to identify it. Pick it apart, learn its mission, and then find a way to weaken it. Once weakened it could be introduced to the host and the host's natural defenses would do battle and learn to defeat it in the future.

He reached for a stack of Petri dishes and set about filling them with blood agar in order to culture whatever was in the vials. It would take some time. Fortunately he determined his own schedule.

$$*\qquad\qquad*\qquad\qquad*$$

"So what's next?" Jack asked his boss.

They sat in a quiet Georgetown bar for an after hours meeting. To Jack's surprise it had been Deacon's idea. Evidently his radar was giving him signals he didn't like, just as Jack's had been.

Deacon swallowed a healthy amount of Bombay before he gave Jack his reply.

"I'm not sure. You're being reassigned to the DC office as a liaison with Homeland Security. Evidently the brass feels you're in a good position after this last mission to help us all play nice together. I can't really say that I disagree with that. Homeland just seems to get bigger every day. No doubt this bombing will kill any efforts to rein in their budget. They'll get whatever they want for awhile."

"But?" Jack prompted.

"But it may be just a ploy by the senator to keep an eye on you for awhile. Remember, he sees just about everything. Most of us department heads don't like it. The damn Senate and Congress are the main source of the leaks that make it out. The CIA has the same grip. Every time they lose an agent or an operation gets exposed, its due to some politician playing "Guess what I know?" The Attorney General won't step up. He's in the senator's pocket. I get the feeling we're being used and I don't like it. Nobody uses us, not me, not you, and not the FBI. Not if I have anything to say about it."

"So what do you want me to do?"

Deacon swirled the ice and remaining gin in his glass before draining it. He set it down firmly before looking up at Jack.

"I went over the tape. The Senator never ordered us *not* to investigate the medication situation. So we're going to do what we do and investigate."

They shared a mischievous grin before Jack replied.

"I figured as much. I have the vials being analyzed. We hope to have the results soon. Wait, let me rephrase that. At least we'll know what it *isn't* fairly soon."

"Okay, let's keep this close to our chest for now. Is there anything you need?"

Jack thought this over for a moment while he finished his beer. "Do you know if any of our embassy liaisons are in DC right now? I mean ones from outside North America."

"I know Marty Ripaldi from the Peruvian office is in town for his daughter's wedding. Other than that I'd have to check. You know Marty?"

"Yeah, we've met once or twice. I may have to catch him before he leaves."

"I've got this trip to Israel with the director coming up. I won't be around to watch your back. Do I want to know what you're going to ask Marty about?"

Jack shook his head.

"Probably not."

PROFESSOR WARNS OF
GLOBAL FOOD RIOTS.
April 28, 2009—The Independent

—FOURTEEN—

KIMBALL LEANED BACK IN the chair as far as it would go and stretched out his legs. His lunch sat uneaten on the desk not far from his feet as he read the report on the test they had run.

It appeared to be a success. The dispersal devices, cleverly disguised as rocks, had distributed an aerosol spray of droplets 200 microns in size to a height of five feet for thirty seconds. All with a minimum amount of noise to prevent any birds in the area of being scared away before they'd had a chance to inhale the agent. It had been determined by earlier testing that the average bird needed a minimum of three to four particles in its lungs for the agent to take effect. Once it did, the infection would start, and the bird would suffer a few days of illness before it recovered and became a carrier—a natural world-wide distributor.

He flipped past a few pages of charts before he found what he needed next. The lab had also measured the agent's survivability in a variety of lab environments. It seemed to survive for only a few minutes in what was deemed average sunlight. The UV rays destroyed the genetic makeup of the agent's DNA, making it either dead or unable to reproduce. Either way it ceased to be infectious at that point. Introducing it in the dark increased its lifetime by only another forty percent. Other environmental factors such as cold, heat and humidity were also factored in, but were shown to be well within the parameters they had targeted.

John flipped the report shut and tossed it on the desk next to his lunch. He allowed himself a contented smile. They may have finally done it. After all the years of research and all the money spent, they may have found the keys to the solution. Not one key as they had striven for at first, but two. It was both an elegant and simple solution. There was still some testing to be done, but for the first time since he had entered the project, John felt they were very close.

His thoughts were interrupted by the ringing of the phone on the desk next to his feet and sandwich. He stared at it in irritation for another ring before moving to pick up the receiver.

"Kimball."

"We may have a problem. Are you alone?"

"Yes."

"I believe I was followed home yesterday. I can't be sure, but I thought it safer to tell you. Did you have anyone trailing me?"

"No. Did you get a look?"

"Not a good one. I only saw the tail twice. I may be wrong."

Kimball paused to consider the options. They had limited personnel, most of his people were expected to take care of themselves and basically operate alone.

"For now just keep an eye out and continue as normal. We'll break contact for awhile. Just report if you think it's truly necessary. I'll see if I can free someone up to follow you for awhile and spot any tails. Do you have anything new to report?"

"One item, more of a suspicion really, but I think the feds may have some of the agent. No more than a vial or two."

"What makes you say that?"

"Mr. Randall didn't seem too upset about losing it. He just seemed to dwell on the reason why it was destroyed. I think he may have pocketed a few vials before they were cleaned up. Or maybe the woman on his team, Sydney Lewis, she may have it."

"Both agents?"

"They were mixed together at the warehouse, strewn all over the red end like they were moving them when the blast happened. They had just been delivered that morning, right?"

"Yes, less than an hour before the detonation. Have you been questioned about them?"

"No, not yet. I'm waiting for the follow-up questions to my report to come in. So far I haven't been asked anything I didn't expect."

"Good, you know what to do if that happens?"

"Yes."

John hung up without another word. He stared at the receiver in his hand for a moment before checking the time. Was it a good time to make the call? Screw it, from what he heard the man was *always* busy. He dialed the number from memory.

"Yes?"

"One of my people is maybe being followed. I'm sending someone to confirm. Are you aware of whom this tail is?"

"No."

"They also suspect that Randall and Lewis may have samples of the agent."

There was a long pause as the man swallowed this information. Kimball waited patiently.

"I will have someone look into this. Anything else?"

"The test was conducted and everything looks good. I have forwarded a copy through to you. I believe we are ready to start the sea trials."

"I'd like to see the data before the trials start, but you may put things in motion."

"Yes, sir. You'll look into the tail situation?"

"Yes, but for now proceed as scheduled."

"Yes, sir."

Kimball stared at the dead receiver in his hand for a moment before cradling it. Were they just being paranoid? Were they paranoid enough? Taking action to determine some unknowns increased the chance of discovery if mistakes were made, and mistakes would be made. It was inevitable. The fact that this program had remained in operation without discovery was a miracle. Was it the fact that they were getting close to the end raising his paranoia? Maybe, but it was his job to be paranoid. Could they afford not to take action? He wasn't sure. He didn't have all the resources to know that. He could only hope the man on the other end of the phone did. He would have to just trust that the man did and make sure he was ready with his part of the project when the time came.

He picked up the phone yet again and dialed another number. The man on the other end answered in English with a hint of a Spanish accent. John had simple instructions;

"You may put phase one of the sea trials in motion. I'll need progress reports daily."

"Very good."

WARNING: OIL SUPPLIES ARE
RUNNING OUT FAST.

August 3, 2009—The Independent

—FIFTEEN—

JACK GUIDED THE CADILLAC through the streets of DC with practiced skill. He avoided the traffic circles and darting taxi cabs with ease. He knew his usual driving tended to cause his wife some tension, so tonight he was taking careful measures to avoid that. While the Cadillac was a luxurious car with available performance if he felt he needed it, it was not quite up to his Corvette. He felt strangely elevated in it as he was used to his butt being only inches from the road when he navigated the DC traffic.

But it was late evening in DC, and Jack had reserved a table for Debra and himself at the Cosmo Club. It was a place of impeccable food, an extensive wine list and extraordinary service. One of DC's finest. Debra had been hinting at a night out since his return.

Jack personally could do without the fancy club. While he knew the meal would be excellent, it was the people he knew they would run into that he could do without. The club was the primary place to see and be

seen by the Washington elite. Senators, congressman, White House staff-
ers, generals and admirals from every branch of service, and even the
occasional Supreme Court justice were all listed as members and fre-
quented the establishment regularly.

While that was bad enough, it got worse. Lobbyists from every cause
imaginable could be counted on every night. Most mingled in the bar or
were seen treating lawmakers to dinner as they shamelessly pushed their
agendas. Some would say that more lawmaking got done in the club bar
than in the capitol building, and they'd be right.

It was not Jack's first choice, but he had let Debra choose and that's
what she had decided on. He knew her real motivation. She desired to
regain their status lost during her husband's involvement in the sniper
shootings months ago. With Jack's new status as the nation's answer to
the embassy bombing, she felt it the right time to show their faces on the
power circuit again, and what better place than the Cosmo Club?

Debra squeezed his hand as he rested it on the shifter, a habit he
transferred from the Corvette. He returned her smile before lingering on
the dress. Something she pretended not to notice. She was decked out in
her finest tonight. She had come home from shopping with a new black
Vera Wang and had topped it off with the pearl choker he had given her
for Christmas last year. Every hair was in place and the makeup applied
with artistic quality. A multitude of shoes had been auditioned before
the current pair had been chosen. Jack had been offered several views
and questioned repeatedly. He had wisely approved every choice until
his wife had given up on him. Never one to dwell too deeply on fashion
choices, he had watched with amusement as his wife tore through his
closet, selecting and rejecting items until an ensemble of her approval
lay on the bed for him to wear. He knew when to fight and when to just
give in, and, on donning the suit, had to admit that his wife knew how to
make her husband look good. At least he had chosen his own cufflinks,
something he was currently proud of.

As he navigated another corner he also had to admit that her choice
of destinations was not entirely without some perks for him. There would

no doubt be some high level government types present tonight and they would not pass up a chance to congratulate him on his most resent mission. More importantly, be seen doing it. Others would note this as planned and follow their lead. Jack would be polite and humble, give the people what they wanted. His wife would bask in the glow of the attention given her husband and share knowing looks with the other wives. There would be friends as well as enemies in the room and the whole evening would resemble a high school popularity contest. Jack found it amazing that such successful and well-educated people placed so much value on this game of perpetual adolescence. He had no doubt in his mind he would be looking for the exit long before his wife.

As he approached the canopy entrance a valet ran up to the passenger side and assisted his wife as she emerged. Jack surrendered his keys to another and reclaimed her arm before they entered.

"Jack?"

"Yes, honey?"

"Could you at least smile?"

"Sorry." Jack put a grin on his face as the door was opened and the maître d' welcomed them in by name.

*   *   *

The valet quickly pulled the Cadillac around to the garage and parked it well out of sight of the guard at the entrance. As he left the driver's seat he scanned the area for his coworkers, but saw only one sprinting back to the restaurant entrance. He was alone.

He quickly examined the license plate and compared it to the numbers he had been provided. He had a match. He moved to the bag he had hidden behind a post in the garage earlier that night and extracted an object wrapped in a plain brown bag. Pulling the bag inside out over the object, he exposed it and wrapped his hand in the bag. Being careful not to get any dirt or grease on his uniform vest he dropped to the ground and secured the object to the frame of the car. Flicking the switch on the side, he was rewarded with a flashing red light for three seconds before it shut off. He extended the tiny antenna before scrambling to his feet.

Dusting himself off, he casually walked away from the car and back toward the entrance. Once past the guard he removed his cell phone and placed a call. It was answered on the first ring.

"Yes."

"It's done. They arrived about five minutes ago."

"Good, notify us immediately when they leave."

"Okay."

The line went dead and the valet pocketed the phone before sprinting back to his post. He wasn't sure what he had just done, but it was the easiest $1000 dollars he had ever made. Now all he had to do was keep an eye out for when the couple left.

*   *   *

The van was beginning to smell. The people had been packed in along with a variety of gear for several hours now and the tension combined with the close quarters had resulted in a rise in temperature. The 80s station preferred by the driver did not really help matters, but they bit their tongues. The driver was the one paying them.

The blare of the radio almost drowned out the ringing cell phone, but they were relieved when it was silenced in order for the phone to be answered. The conversation was short. The driver merely grunted a reply before hanging up.

"We're moving," he called back to them as he started the van.

The men in the back checked their gear and stretched out their cramping legs in preparation for the task they had been hired to do. While they were all experienced thieves, this was the first time they had been hired to *not* steal something. But the money offered was good and the job well within their abilities. Some examined the picture of what they were after. They had all been provided a shot about the size of a playing card to take with them. They also had digital cameras hanging around their necks as well as video cameras mounted to their heads over the masks they all wore. The cameras would feed out to the van to be monitored and recorded by the driver. Again, very strange to them, but it was not their job to question.

The van pulled through the neighborhood at just below the speed limit and approached the home without fanfare, pulling into the long driveway and right up to the garage door. Here the driver quickly exited, and holding his breath, punched in a code on the keypad located on the frame of the garage. He let out the breath as the door immediately opened. Not only had the code worked, but he was lucky enough to have chosen the door housing an empty space. He pulled the van in and quickly exited a second time to close the door behind it.

The van door stayed shut until the garage door was completely down. The driver stared at the blinking light on the alarm control panel next to the house entrance as the team spread out around him. One man elbowed his way to the front and examined the panel as well before noting the look of concern in the driver's eyes.

"Relax. We have two minutes before it goes off."

He pulled a small screwdriver from an inside pocket of his coverall and pried the cover off the panel. On the inside was a sticker with several numbers. He compared the numbers against a list held in his other hand until he found the code he needed. He snapped the panel back in place with his gloved hands before carefully punching in the code. The blinking red light turned to an inviting solid green. He then reached out and turned the knob on the door. It opened without resistance. The team quickly piled into the house.

"Maintenance code, direct from the manufacturer," the man explained to the driver before he followed the team inside. The driver just shook his head and returned to the truck. He pulled the small TV around in the passenger seat and turned it on. He was treated to a screen split into four views, each of them the bobbing head of a team member. Flashes went off as they took pictures of every room before they began their search. Everything must go back exactly as it was found without exception. No one could know they had been there. For thieves used to trashing the places they robbed it was taking some discipline to do this. It was helpful to know they would have plenty of advanced warning when the owner was returning. The driver settled in to wait and watched the action on the screen. Under his seat was a box of vials, exact duplicates of what they were searching for. Unknown to the driver, they were filled with this year's flu vaccine. He would swap them out if any vials were found.

He couldn't help but glance out the side window at the Corvette that shared the garage. A few more jobs like this and he could have one for himself.

*   *   *

Not far from where Jack and his wife were eating, a young man pushed a cart of cleaning equipment down a hallway at the Hoover Building. He considered himself lucky to have this job as they were hard to come by in the District. If he had not obtained this job when he did, the only other alternative was dealing crack. Something many of his friends had taken up.

While the job offered some security, it did not pay much, and he was always looking for an extra dollar. Tonight such an opportunity had come up. While he knew it was wrong, the money had been too good to pass up. He wasn't actually taking anything. They hadn't asked him to. Nor was he taking any pictures like the spy always did in the movies. They had just asked him to look and tell them what he saw. What could be the harm in that? They seemed to know he was escorted by security everywhere he went. He was never alone in any of the offices he cleaned, and there were cameras in the halls. So he would just look. It was up to him to tell them what he saw and he had already decided not to tell anything he felt was dangerous. Easy money.

"Hey, Tony."

Tony rose from his seat behind the desk and grabbed his hat.

"Ready when you are, Ricky."

The pair moved from office to office and Tony watched Ricky empty trash cans and dust shelves. Tonight wasn't a window cleaning night so the work went quickly. They talked of sports and little else as usual until they reached the office Ricky had been told of.

Here Ricky rounded the desk to fetch the trash can from under it. He was relieved to see it was half full. No red burn-bag for Tony to take care of. Ricky looked at Tony as he raised the can to dump it and purposefully missed the large bag hanging on his cart, dumping the contents on the floor.

"Missed an easy lay up there, kid." Tony smiled.

"Yeah, just take a second."

Ricky took his time cleaning up the papers, doing his best to scan each one as he reloaded the trashcan. He was able to make a few mental notes, but it was mostly nothing. He deposited the last piece before attempting another transfer into the large bag. He rounded the desk again and planted the now empty can under it. A glance at Tony showed him texting something on his phone, so Ricky took a chance and moved a couple of files on the desk to see the titles. Just numbers. He managed to memorize one before he heard Tony flip his phone shut. The only other paper on the desk were a couple of receipts, one from a gas station in New Jersey, and the other from a McDonalds in the same area. That was it.

Ricky pushed his cart out the door and followed Tony to the next office. As he waited for Tony to unlock the door he looked at the closed door of the one they had just left. The door said "Sydney Lewis." Ricky wondered what they wanted with her.

The Driver was getting anxious. They had been at the house for two hours and had not found anything yet. As rooms were cleared, he compared them to the shots taken as they had entered them. The crew was doing well for their first time. He had only had to make minor adjustments before he was satisfied. But they were running out of time and still had several rooms to go. So far they had eliminated places that people normally used—desk drawers, office cubbyholes, clever knick-knacks—and moved on to more serious hiding places. They had checked the refrigerator, removed access panels to appliances, and looked in every air duct. Still, nothing had been found. He understood that there was no way to be 100% sure the items weren't in the home, but he could at least make an effort.

He was considering moving a team member to the garage when the phone rang. He quickly thumbed it open and answered.

"Yeah?"

"They just sent me for the car."

"Got it."

The driver left the van and whispered into the mic. "Finish it up people. We are out in exactly eight minutes."

All four acknowledged as he made a quick sweep through the garage. He was careful not to move anything, just making a visual sweep. It was a typical garage, nothing out of the ordinary. He quickly gave up and returned to the van. Pressing a few buttons he now had a street map of DC on the screen. A red dot blinked at him from dead center. He glanced at his watch.

"Seven minutes," he voiced.

The dot on the map began to move.

$$* \qquad * \qquad *$$

Jack breathed a heavy sigh as they pulled away from the curb. It did not go unnoticed by his wife.

"What's the matter, honey?"

"I thought that damn congressman was going to go on forever. A freshman from California, Berkley no less, lecturing *me* on privacy rights. I should have decked him."

"That would have been a hell of a story for tomorrow's paper," she chided.

"And that general, acting like the Africa operation was all his idea. Really had to bite my tongue there."

"I thought you did very well, Jack, and everyone there knows who did what. That general is on his way out and was just puffing his chest. His wife dragged him out before he made a spectacle of himself."

"Sorry I missed that part."

"Let's just get home and I promise to do my best to make you forget all about it."

Jacks eyebrows peaked at that. He glanced at his wife and saw that look. Her hand crept across the center console and into his lap. Jack's foot tapped the accelerator to avoid the turning red light.

The tires only squealed slightly as he rounded the corner.

*   *   *

"Damn, he's moving," the driver voiced aloud.

"What?"

"The guys hauling ass home-get moving on that damn alarm!"

"I only get one chance at it."

"Well make it a fast one."

The team watched anxiously from the rear of the van. It felt strange to them. Usually they would be packed in among artwork and bags of items taken from the home. While they had all seen items they would have normally taken, they had left everything in place as they had been hired to do. Some were contemplating a return trip, but that was not an option per the agreement. Maybe in a year, they would save the code just in case.

"Let's go!"

"Almost there, open the door."

The man pushed buttons and the green light changed to a blinking red. He hustled around the van to enter the passenger side, his camera swinging wildly. While he was careful opening the door of the van he forgot about the camera. It struck the door of the Corvette with a loud thunk.

"Damn it!" the driver swore.

"Too late, let's roll."

The driver punched the door code and the garage slowly opened. He jumped behind the wheel and drummed his fingers as the he watched it creep up in his rearview mirror.

*   *   *

Jack swung the car into a wide left turn. With the hour being what it was, the streets were practically deserted and for once his wife was not complaining about his driving. One might say she was encouraging it at the moment.

She had slipped off her seatbelt and drawn her legs up onto the seat. The black Vera Wang had also ascended her legs and Jack was dividing his attention between them and the road ahead of him. His tie was long gone and what lipstick she had worn was now mostly on his neck and shirt collar.

His left foot twitched on the imaginary clutch as he pulled out of the turn and accelerated down the street, his wife ignoring his blatant disregard for the speed limit.

*　　　　　*　　　　　*

The driver noted the scratch in the door of the car as he backed out. It was spilled milk. Nothing he could do about it now. He gunned the engine till the van was out and exited to punch in the code again. The door responded and he was quickly behind the wheel again, backing out of the driveway. He had just put the van in gear and started forward when he saw the lights approaching.

*　　　　　*　　　　　*

Jack tapped the brakes when he saw the lights ahead. His wife let out a giggle as he swerved to the right to avoid the oncoming vehicle. Its lights were set on bright and made worse by the height. A large SUV or truck, he thought, as they passed within inches. He continued around the curve until the house came into view. He caught a glimpse of the vehicle in his rearview as it passed under a streetlight. A van?

"Are we home?" his wife asked.

"Yeah, we're home."

She gave him a final squeeze before she bolted out the car door and punched in the code to enter the house. She had it open before he could shut off the car and follow, and ran away from him down the hall, shedding clothes as she went.

Jack was no fool, he quickly did the same.

UN: DROUGHTS, MELTING ICE SIGNS OF
WORSENING CLIMATE CHANGE.
September 24, 2009—USA Today

-SIXTEEN-

SYDNEY WAS TIRED BUT doing her best not to show it. The last few days at work had consisted of multiple debriefings, conference calls, endless meetings and mountains of forensic evidence that all needed to be processed. While she realized the importance of it all, she hated being rushed. These things took time to do right, speeding through the process caused mistakes to happen. Something the political leaders didn't or wouldn't understand. They demanded everything immediately and God help you if you made a mistake. If you did, it was your fault, never theirs for rushing you.

"Screw 'em!" she spoke aloud.

Since there was nobody in the Mustang with her she didn't get a reply. She had the road to herself this morning as it was still a few hours before dawn. She needed to unwind, and since it was Friday she was giving herself a few hours to do so before work. She planned on a couple of boxes of 9mm at the range, followed by a few laps around the mall. She enjoyed watching the sun come up over the Potomac while the rat race was in progress all around her.

As she passed the White House she noticed lights already on in the West Wing. She tried to remember if she had ever seen them off, but couldn't recall. Good for them. If she was putting in the hours then so should they.

She stifled a yawn as she pulled up to the security point at the Hoover Building. It was going to be a long day.

*   *   *

Four hours later she finally made it to her office. Her official one anyway, after an hour at the range and another on the streets, she had used her dungeon office to change and get herself organized. She managed to keep two offices only because no one wanted her previous one in the basement. While she preferred it to her official one, she still had to put in time here so people could reach her. Otherwise the messages and memos piled up into a quantity too large to handle. So she transformed from running shorts and ponytail to up-do and business suit. As she carried a box of files down the hall she was pleased to see that she still got second looks from her male counterparts. Maybe someday she would have the time to look back, but not any time soon.

She managed to unlock her office while balancing the box on a raised knee. As she pushed it open and hit the lights her office presented itself as she had left it.

Almost.

She paused in the doorway and looked carefully at her desk. Something was wrong. Her Tell files were out of place. She examined the chair next to the door carefully before placing the box on it. Once her hands were free she checked the carpet. It had not been vacuumed since her last visit. She examined the windows and sniffed the air. The windows did not appear to have been cleaned recently and there was no lingering odor of a chemical cleaner in the air.

She carefully crossed the room until she was close to the two files lying on her desk. They had numbers she had pulled out of her head for file names and contained nothing but old information that had been public for years. She examined the surface for the hair. It was gone. The corners were no longer in line with the edges of her desk. Someone had moved the file. Someone had been in her office.

She walked around the desk, looking at the locks on her file cabinets and desk drawers. They appeared to be free of scratches. The Bureau used steel hardware with brass plating. Any attempt to force the locks would leave marks. She reached in her purse and found a Kleenex. Keeping her hand from disturbing any prints, she tugged on each drawer. Everything was secure. Finally she sat in her chair and thought about the last time she had been in the office. Did she forget to reset her Tell, or maybe bumped it on her way out? She had never forgotten before.

She rose and shut her door before returning to the desk and pushing the chair back. Hiking up her skirt, she got down on her hands and knees and combed through the carpet with her fingers. After a brief search she found the hair. She picked it up and set it on the blotter. Returning to her chair, she contemplated the hair.

Every employee of the FBI was encouraged to protect their office. Besides the usual locking of files and drawers they encouraged the use of the Tell, a personal way of determining if you've had a visitor. Each person's Tell was left up to them to construct and never shared with anyone. Sydney's was the two files. Every night when she left her office she arranged the files on her desk so the bottom corners of the bottom file touched the front and right sides of the desktop. Added to that, she placed one of her own hairs on top of the bottom file. It was all but invisible in the dark or low light such as moonlight coming in the window. If the file was disturbed or picked up the hair would fall. As the hair was on the floor and the files not left in their proper position, she knew someone had been in her office.

As she rocked in the chair she noticed the empty trash can. Maybe the cleaning crew had bumped it? That wouldn't account for the hair though, unless the files had been knocked to the floor. If something such as that happened the guard was supposed to log it in. The crews were escorted every night by security and instructed to never touch or move anything. Her first instinct was to go downstairs and get her print kit, but decided that was a little overkill. She would fill out an incident form and submit it. In a few days she was sure she would be told if it was the cleaning crew. Nothing else seemed to be disturbed, and she had too much work to do.

She pulled a handful of files from the box and spread them out on her desk. May as well get started.

*   *   *

Jack was doing much the same thing in his office. Unlike Sydney, he had three separate files to close. One for the embassy bombing, another for the ambush, and a third for the raid on the terrorist camp. As the evidence and supporting intelligence was processed and cataloged it was forwarded to Jack so he could assemble it into a final report. While the work of many would go into each file, his name would ultimately be the one signing at the bottom of each. He wouldn't get a second chance. It had to be right the first time.

Three hours later he was reading a heavily highlighted report on evidence found at the camp. The highlight would change to blackout if the file needed to be seen by someone without the necessary clearance. Jack was thinking that it would be an extremely fast read if that ever happened when he heard a knock on his door.

"Come."

Sydney opened the door with a tired smile on her face and a thick file in her hand.

"Hello, stranger," she greeted him.

"Hello to you, too. Seems we both got lost in the paperwork shuffle. Is that your final report on the embassy forensics?"

"I hope so. It's three inches thick already with possibly more to come later. But all the lab work is done and the only thing left is formalities."

"Such as?"

"Toxicology on the victims will take another few weeks, but I don't see how that will add anything to the investigation. If we find out that one of the embassy secretaries was smoking pot I really don't think it will be relevant."

"Okay, just set it on the desk if you can find a spot."

Sydney cleared a spot and deposited the thick file on the corner of Jack's desk. She then flopped into a chair before putting her feet up on the other.

Jack stopped reading and contemplated her raised feet. The strappy heels and her legs brought up a flash of memory of last night. He drove it away and sat back in his chair.

"Yes?"

"What? Just taking a break for a minute."

"You're hovering. What's on your mind?"

She looked around his office and took in the mess on his desk before answering.

"What's your office Tell?"

"It's mine. If I tell people, it's not really worth having is it?"

"Ever had it disturbed?"

Jack leaned forward and dropped the file on his desk.

"What happened?"

"When I came in today, my Tell was moved. Everything else was secure, nothing out of place, just my Tell. I figured the cleaning crew bumped it."

"You file a report?"

"Yeah, but who knows how long that will take to have an answer. Never happened to you?"

"Not me, but I've heard of others. Sometimes they like to test the new people. You know, make sure they follow procedure and file a report."

"I'm not new."

"No, you're not." Jack reached for the phone.

"Who are you calling?"

Jack just held up a finger while the phone rang.

"Security."

"Hello, this is Agent Randall. I need to know if a report was filed by your people regarding office..." Jack cupped the receiver and looked at Sydney.

She rolled her eyes before replying, "2789."

"...2789. Agent Sydney Lewis ...yes, I'll hold."

"Jack, it's probably nothing."

"I agree, let's just be sure."

They waited in silence for a full minute before the guard came back on the line. Jack had put the call on speaker.

"Sir?"

"Yes."

"I have no reports regarding Agent Lewis's office in the past week. It's due for vacuuming and windows in two days, other than that, just normal trash and dust. Is there an issue?"

"A Tell out of place, everything else seems secure."

"Any chance it was forgotten or just bumped, sir?"

Sydney shook her head.

"That's a negative."

"Did she file a report, sir?"

Sydney answered that one. "Yes, I submitted it around noon."

"Very well, ma'am, I can send a man up now if you'd like or I can consult with the night crew and get back to you in the morning?"

"Tomorrow will be fine. Thank you," Jack answered.

"Yes, sir."

Jack punched the button and broke the connection.

"More paperwork, thanks, Jack."

"A little procedure never hurt anyone." He smiled.

She took a good look at him before she rose to leave. Pausing at the door, she shot a question over her shoulder. "You seem to be in good spirits today. Have a nice night last night?"

Jack looked up at the surprise question and the look on his face was all she needed to see. He tried to maintain a neutral expression but ended up smiling anyway.

"Tell Debi I said hello," she called as she left the office.

"Go away," he called after her.

*   *   *

Kimball scanned through the stack of photos for the fourth time, but still failed to see anything worthy of a second attempt. The Randall home was very nice, tastefully decorated in simple colors and style. As he knew of Jack's wealth, he was surprised by this. He had expected a display of money as was often the case. But the Randall home had no such display. There were no priceless pieces of artwork adorning the walls or modern sculptures in the entryway. The wife's jewelry collection was extensive, but as a man he knew that could not be helped. The cars were quality and not flashy. The Corvette seemed to be the only indulgence, and for a sports car one could certainly spend a great deal more on such an item. If anything, it was the type of house Kimball could see himself in one day.

"Well?" a voice on the speakerphone asked.

"I see no reason for a second attempt. I doubt if the item would still be there if he did have it. He would most likely secure it at the Hoover Building or make some effort to find out what it is. What about the woman?"

"Same thing on her condo. She's a little messier than Randall, but we found nothing. She did have a bag packed like she had just returned from a short trip. The clothes were enough for maybe one or two day's tops. They'd been worn. She just hadn't unpacked them yet."

"Any idea where she went?"

"Not from the condo, but we have a possibility from her office. Our man could only take a quick look. He found a file with a number on it he managed to memorize, and he saw some receipts on her desk."

"From where?"

"Gas station in New Jersey just off the turnpike, and a McDonalds in the same area. Both of them dated the day after they got back from Africa."

"What town?"

"Parsippany."

"You're sure?"

"Positive. That mean anything to you?"

It meant a lot to Kimball but he wasn't going to voice his opinion to this man.

"I want you to get a locator on her car and call me if she starts heading that way again. Tail her, but don't get caught."

"Shouldn't be a problem. We can do it tonight. You think she'll move soon?"

"I don't know. Just be ready."

"Okay."

Kimball broke the connection and drummed his fingers on the desk. They were attempting to crack what was in the vial. They had no idea what they were dealing with. He had to find out who had it and where as soon as possible. They couldn't afford to have the agent released.

He pressed some keys on his computer and pulled up a map of New Jersey. Parsippany was right in the heart of the east coast biotech corridor. He had to find the lab that had the agent.

BIRDS FACE LONGER MIGRATIONS
DUE TO CLIMATE CHANGE.
April 14, 2009—Reuters

-SEVENTEEN-

PROFESSOR MILES SCRATCHED THE kitten's ears as he tried to read the latest edition of *Lancet* with his afternoon coffee. He sipped it slowly as he wanted it to last till he was done and also to prolong the time before he would have to disturb the kitten.

The kitten was a gift from the neighbor's kids. Unlike the professor, their father was a real farmer and the professor let him use his land to grow whatever he saw fit as he felt it wrong to waste it. As a result, the man's son would sneak over during the day while he was gone and mow the grass. A crate of vegetables was always waiting on the porch every Friday when he got home, often with a loaf of homemade bread. The cats were fed when he traveled and he never worried about the house while he was gone. It was a good arraignment.

A week ago he had been interrupted at breakfast by a knock on his door. He answered to find the farmer's young daughter standing at the bottom of the steps, her friends watching from the road on their bicycles.

"Yes?" he had asked.

The girl swallowed and looked to her friends for support before replying. She pulled her hands from behind her back and held up a small bundle of fur.

"He was born out in the barn. He's sick and …Daddy says I can't have any more. He calls you a doctor, can you fix him?"

Jim had frowned at first. Here he was, a man with two PhDs, yet he was being manipulated by a six-year-old girl. But who wouldn't be?

He sat down on the steps and contemplated the furball in her outstretched hand. Obviously the runt of the litter, it opened its eyes and let out a meow followed by a cough.

"Bring him here."

The girl deposited the kitten in his hands before retreating to the bottom step again. He looked the cat over. Its eyes were glued shut from a thick discharge and it coughed repeatedly as he turned it this way and that. He could feel ribs against his fingers. It was obviously not getting enough food.

"You feed him with all the others?" he asked.

"Yes, sir"

"The other cats are bigger?"

"Yes, some of them are sick, too, just not as bad. Can you fix him?"

"I can't, but I know a nice lady who can. Your Daddy knows you're here?"

She suddenly found her shoes. "No, sir."

"Well, we'll just keep this our little secret then, okay?"

"Okay."

"You better get on home before he starts looking."

The little girl offered a grin minus one tooth before turning and bolting down the driveway to her friends. He waved as they all pedaled away.

He raised the ball of fur up to eye level.

"What do I do with you now?"

He started with a bath. The cat proved to be even smaller once it was wet but it was too weak to put up much of a fuss. Luckily the professor had some flea shampoo left over from his other felines. Once the cat was dry he wrapped it in a warm towel and parked it in a chair while he made a phone call.

A ten minute ride in the car brought him to a nice suburban home. He tucked the kitten in his coat and made his way to the door. It opened before he had a chance to knock.

"Good morning, Professor."

"Morning, Lynda." Lynda was one of his people. A veterinarian and microbiologist, she worked on animal vaccines at the lab.

"Come in, where is the little guy?"

He reached in his coat and pulled out the kitten and handed it to her. "Neighbor's kid brought it over. He looks a little worse-for-wear."

"Yup, eye infection to start. Little guy have a name?"

"Tom?"

"Tom Cat, how original." She moved into the kitchen and set the fur-ball down on the counter. It proceeded to explore on wobbly feet while she donned a stethoscope.

"Lung infection, too," she announced.

"Fixable?"

"Oh yeah, pretty common for barn cats. They get it young and if it's summer they usually make it. This one's a runt and probably losing the fight for the food, so he's malnourished and susceptible. I've got some samples here I can give you that'll clear them both up pretty quick. Bring him in on Monday and I'll get him all his shots, too. He should be fine. How many is this for you?"

"This makes three. Do I qualify for the crazy cat man yet?"

"I saw a lady with over fifty once back when I was a tech in school working for the ASPCA. Now that's crazy."

"Well good. Least I know I have a ways to go. What do I owe ya?"

"Don't be silly," she countered as she pawed through her cupboards, pulling out the medications he needed. "I seem to recall free flu shots for me and my family every year. I'm sure I can play vet on the weekends for you. Besides, she's a cutie."

"She?"

"Afraid so, might want to rethink the name."

"Yeah."

So now a week had gone by and he had dubbed the kitten Tommi for lack of imagination. Unlike his other cats, Tommi was quite affectionate and preferred his lap as her primary napping location. Something he was slowly getting used to.

He jumped slightly as the phone rang. He stretched for it so as not to disturb the kitten in his lap and managed to grab it by the antenna.

"Hello?"

"Professor? It's Sydney."

"Well, hello, I'm still working on that puzzle you gave me. I've got to say I'm a bit perplexed by it."

"It's not a vaccine?"

"Oh no, it is. It came up in testing as the current flu vaccine, but it's got a lot of extras that I just can't figure out."

"Extras? I don't understand?"

"You remember your microbiology basics right? All DNA has sequences that are basically dormant. Our own human DNA has a vast quantity of what has proven to be remnants of viruses, basically defeated infections from throughout the lifespan of the human race. Well any strand of DNA, no matter what source it's from, has these leftovers. This flu vaccine is effective. I tried it on some mice and it performed as advertised. What I don't understand is vaccines are basically manipulated viruses. They don't traditionally have a lot of this extra stuff attached. This one has over one and a half times as much DNA material as it needs. It all appears to be dormant. I just don't know why it's there."

"Okay, so what do we do now?"

"I plan on running it through the machine until I have a full breakdown of what it is. I injected two monkeys with it yesterday afternoon. We'll just have to wait and see on that end. In the meantime I plan to start on the red vial. Maybe it will tell us something."

"I hope so. Did you have to bring anybody else into the loop?"

"No. Most of the stuff we do is proprietary. My people know not to ask too much."

"All right, Jack and I can't thank you enough. Is there anything you need?"

"Bring me some kitten toys next time you come up."

"You got another one?"

"Sort of a gift."

Sydney laughed, "Kitten toys, it's a deal."

*   *   *

The Deliveryman sat on the chair, sweating in the African heat. Something he had never gotten used to. The bottle of whiskey he was currently working on was his second in the last three days. Even with ice it tasted warm. He stared out over the city from his hotel balcony. He had been there for a week. Plenty of time to think.

He drained the last of the amber fluid from the glass and pulled himself up from the cheap chair to reenter the room. Lowering himself to the couch he took in the items on the table in front of him. A bag containing a large quantity of American C-notes. Several thousand worth, he had not bothered to count. An HK MP-5 sub-machinegun, well oiled against the humidity. A case of vials with red tops. A bottle of whiskey sitting next to a melting bucket of ice. His life had basically consisted of these items for the past several years. Yet here he was in a shithole hotel in the middle of Nairobi with nothing to show for it.

What the hell was he doing? So what if he was part of a grand plan? Was this the life he had imagined for himself? He had been a soldier once, something to be proud of. Or so he thought. After a few wars, the medals didn't shine so brightly anymore. Like most soldiers who make it far enough he realized no matter how hard he fought, it would really make very little difference in the end. No, in the end wars were inevitable. As long as men feared or coveted what other men had there would always be wars to fight.

"Plenty of work out there for all of us!" he yelled to the room.

When he got no answer he hurled the glass across the room where it shattered against the far wall. He didn't care. He had another one right there on the table.

No, war was always the same thing. Old men talking and young men dying. Well, he was done. And they owed him more than a few dollars and a piece of paper. A lot more.

He rearranged the money in the bag before adding the vials to it. He stuffed a couple of shirts and some items from the bathroom in as well. When it was full, he shouldered it and headed for the door, snagging the bottle in his fist on the way. It was his last day delivering little glass bottles around. He was retiring as of today. And he had his pension right here in this bag. Some cash, too.

If he started now he could make it to Mombasa by tomorrow.

—EIGHTEEN—

PROFESSOR MILES STEPPED OUT of the airlock and snagged a hose hanging from the ceiling. Once he was plugged back in and the roar of air once again filled his suit he made for the monkey room. During the usual breakfast routine he took a careful look at the two monkeys who had received the yellow vaccine. They appeared to have no change in their behavior as evidenced by the sheer volume of their screaming. He saw that their appetites were also intact as they scrambled for the biscuits he dropped into the feeding chutes. Trying to avoid direct eye contact (it tended to set them off) he examined them for any signs of respiratory distress or mucus discharge. Nothing. Well, in a few days he would give them the flu via another poke. Something they understandably hated, and to be honest, he hated it, too. Pinning them down with a special stick while injecting them was cruel, but it was the only way to test the vaccines. He took comfort in the fact that these monkeys, at the worst, would most likely only get some mild symptoms from the vaccine.

"Hello, ladies," he greeted Thelma and Louise, his two control monkeys. Although they had never received a shot from him, they had seen him do it to others and were extra wary today, as if the sight of a human in a space suit wasn't reason enough to be scared. The monkeys sensed the presence of danger and while they did not understand why, they knew it was around them everyday. While he was fond of his two control monkeys, he always regarded them as dangerous just for this reason.

Finished with his morning chores, he returned to the lab and picked up the tray he had brought with him holding the red top vial. After his disappointment in finding anything significant with the yellow top vial he was looking forward to the new puzzle of the red top. Today he would try to crack it.

First things first, he broke the vial down into several smaller samples as he had the first one. He fired up his bio-analyzer, placed a sample on a card and stuck it in the machine. This time he didn't wait to see what popped up before moving on to prep the rest of the samples. He still had some other trials going on that needed attention, too.

After a couple of hours he broke away from his other research and checked on the machine's progress. There were multiple readouts on the screen, but the primary was a surprise:

VIRUS CLASSIFICATION

GROUP:	Group V ((-)ssRNA
ORDER:	*Mononegavirales*
FAMILY:	*Paramyxoviridae*
GENUS:	*Avulavirus*
SPECIES:	*Newcastle disease virus (NDV)*

There were nothing but fragments listed after that. The usual suspects of flu, rhinovirus, TB. He scanned down the readout looking for any anomalies. On the second page he got a surprise. Smallpox. Although it showed up occasionally, it was rare. As long as it was a fragment it was nothing to worry about. He was surprised by the length of the list. It was up to three pages and the machine was still adding to it. He decided to run another sample after this one had played out just to be sure.

He reached up to scratch his nose but caught himself before he smudged his helmet. A glance at the clock told him he had been in the suit for over five hours. It was time for a break. He needed to know more about this Newcastle virus. He dealt primarily with the human infections and if he remembered right, Newcastle infected birds.

He pushed the print key and looked through the glass into the Level 3 lab to make sure the printer was working before heading out to the decontamination shower. He would have to consult an expert. Fortunately he had one.

An hour later he had Lynda sitting across from him in his office with the Terminator looking over her shoulder as she pet Tommi, who had found a warm perch in her lap.

"Newcastle huh? Is it a vaccine?"

"I don't know yet, I'm still getting more information, but the machine's chewed on it for a few hours now and that's the only primary it's spit out so far." He didn't feel it was the time to tell her about all the fragments that were attached. He'd dig into that himself.

"Do you know it?"

"The basics. Care to fill me in?"

"Well, it's a zoonotic bird disease that affects both domestic and wild species. If it got into the poultry industry it has the potential to wipe it out. There are vaccines already out there, but there's no cure. Depending on the strain, it has about a 90% or more mortality rate. Fortunately, we don't have it domestically. Last outbreak was back in '74, I think. Before my time."

"Tough bug?"

"Yes, mostly spread through direct contact. High concentrations are found in the droppings of the infected birds. They also have heavy secretions from the nose, mouth and eyes. They track it around, it gets in their feed. Stick an infected bird in a confined space with other birds, like say a commercial chicken farm, and they all have it pretty quick. We try to keep it from coming into the country, but the damn smugglers are gonna get it past us sooner or later."

"Chicken smugglers?"

"No, silly, Amazon parrots are the main threat. Illegal pet parrots from Latin America are high dollar and we require a lengthy quarantine and testing process. The smugglers do their best to get around it and increase their profit margin. Incubation runs from two to fifteen days. We cage 'em for thirty. Sooner or later some chicken farmer's gonna buy an illegal parrot for his kid and end the poultry business here in the US for a while."

"Don't we vaccinate?"

"Yeah, but it doesn't always take. Like I said, there are several strains. Some aren't even lethal, just cause a mild sickness that most people wouldn't even notice in their flock. Worst thing it can do to humans is cause conjunctivitis."

"So what's the best way to go about testing it? How do we know if it's a vaccine?"

"If you give me a sample, I can run an Enzyme Linked Immunosorbant Assay and a PCR. That'll narrow it down. I can give you some birds to test from my department. You have a space to keep them?"

"I have some room in my monkey cage in Bio-4. Will they be okay together?"

"Should be, so long as they aren't in contact. I'd just keep a distance between them. Newcastle doesn't have a thing for monkeys." She paused while Tommi stretched out and rolled over in her lap. "She's gaining weight already. She looks good. How you two getting along?"

"She likes to sleep on my head."

"Just keep shooing her away, she'll get the idea."

"I hope she gets it soon."

Lynda laughed and scooped up the kitten as she stood. She deposited it in his lap before she turned to leave.

"I've got a meeting. Call me if you need anything else. I'll send over the birds this afternoon."

"Okay, thanks for the help."

He thought about the incubation period as Tommi chewed on his knuckle. Two to fifteen days. He would inject the birds as soon as they arrived. He didn't want to wait too long to see what he had.

*   *   *

Jack relaxed as he worked the clutch and wheel with practiced hands. He was currently heading east on the Blue Star Highway and for once traffic was in his favor. The Corvette responded to his every wish as he threaded his way through trucks and slower traffic. He glanced across the divider at the rush hour traffic moving into DC and smiled.

His car was his sanctuary and he had indulged himself when ordering it. While he certainly could have afforded any of the exotic sports cars available these days, he had never been one to flaunt his wealth. The Corvette had every option offered, along with a few after-market improvements as well, all in a package that appeared to match any other model on the road. It was what car buffs called a "sleeper," a car that looked normal on the outside, but once past the skin was anything but.

So whenever Jack could, he drove. At the speed he wanted, with the radio tuned to the music he enjoyed. And while he had a Bluetooth headset handy, it rarely left the cup holder. It seemed to him that the faster he went, the more relaxed he became, and outside disturbances were not welcome.

So while he had cursed himself for his error last night, he found himself enjoying the results at the moment. He and Debra had spent the weekend at the beach house on the Delaware shore. He had, of course, brought some work along, despite the looks his wife gave him. Part of which was a computer disc he had mistakenly left behind when they'd departed the previous evening. It was both current to his embassy report as well as somewhat secret, so he had been forced to call Larry to provide some cover for him while he ran to the beach to retrieve it.

But it gave him time to think. As he slowed for a construction zone he thought about the phone call he had gotten from Sydney. The professor was confused as to what the vial contained. He said it was the flu vaccine plus something else. Jack had done his best to follow Sydney's explanation about DNA and virus strands, but had quickly gotten lost. She had the head for that he never would, so he just followed along until she ran out of steam. While she seemed to be excited about the mystery of the vial's contents, he'd had to prod her back to the original question.

Why would someone be willing to risk their life and be willing to kill others for the vials? Despite the professor's findings, they still didn't know. Maybe the red top vial would have some answers. He hoped so.

As he rounded a truck he reached up to adjust the visor as the sun was creeping higher. The man had said another week, so they would just have to wait. But right now he had plenty of pavement for him and his car to play. Jack slipped on his sunglasses and pressed down on the accelerator. The Corvette responded with a throaty roar.

*   *   *

Jack kept the car at barely above idle speed as he crept down the crushed shell street to the beach house. The shells were rough on the car's paint. He automatically took note of his neighbors' places as he passed. It was something they all did for each other as they were all part-time residents. Surprisingly, his neighbors had a van parked in the driveway. As he moved the Corvette closer he read "Bob's Heating and Air" on the side. There was nobody visible in the cab. The door to the house was closed as well as the garage door. Funny, the Johnsons usually weren't back for another week or two. Should he stop and check it out? No, he had to get the disc and get back, maybe on his way out.

Jack exited the car, leaving the door hanging open. He only planned on grabbing the disc and leaving.

He fumbled with the door code before throwing it open and striding for the bedroom. He found the disc on the dresser next to the DVD they had watched while it was raining. This time he checked the labels, it would be pretty bad to turn in an Adam Sandler movie rather than the FBI report he was putting together. He grabbed the right one and moved back into the hallway.

For some reason he glanced into the guestroom as he turned the corner. Something caught his eye. There was a boot print on the carpet. He tried to recall if they had entered the room over the weekend but he knew he hadn't. It was definitely a man's boot, much too big to be his wife's. The room had been cleaned and the carpet vacuumed on the previous weekend and the telltale lines of the vacuum were still in the carpet. It was as if someone had stepped in and then back out. One print.

Jack's instincts flared. He reached for his Browning before he realized it was in the center console of the Corvette. It became a pain in the ribs on long drives. His backup was at the office. But Jack was a Boy Scout once—he was prepared.

He stepped out into the hallway and silently opened a linen closet. Reaching around in back of a stack of sheets he pulled out a loaded Glock 17 along with an extra clip. Tucking the clip in his belt, he returned to the bedroom and cleared it. Picking up the bedside phone he dialed 911 and stuffed the receiver under the pillow before it made noise in the quiet house. He repeated the clearing process on the guest room before returning to the hallway and moving back toward the living area. Pausing at the end of the hallway, he used the reflections off the pictures on the walls and windows to examine the room. He saw nothing.

That left the kitchen, the office, a small sitting room and the garage. There was also a laundry room small enough to hide one person. He decided to go through the kitchen. As he advanced, the sound of the Corvette's engine running helped silence his approach, as did the black athletic shoes he now wore every day. The shoes had gotten a few looks from his coworkers, but after running through the snow-covered streets of DC on his last mission he had vowed to never wear office shoes again. Goodwill had some very good contributions that month.

He ducked low to see under the hanging pots and pans. The kitchen was clear. He now had to move down a small hallway past the laundry room to get to the garage. There was no other way.

*   *   *

Pure frickin' luck, the thief was thinking to himself. He had just happened to step into the guestroom when he saw the Corvette ease down the street. He had quickly left the room and made for the door, but it was already too late. He remembered the laundry room and quickly hid behind its bi-fold doors. He forced himself to stay calm and breathe easy. Jack wasn't here to do laundry. Since he was without a team this time, he had replaced everything as he went, so there shouldn't be anything out of place for him to notice. He heard the *tisk-tisk* of a warning in his earbud mic. Kinda late, but the man was in the back of the van and probably didn't see Jack approach until it was too late. He strained to hear anything as he looked through the gaps in the louvered door. He would just watch for Jack to leave and then complete the job. He just hoped that whatever it was Jack was after, it wasn't his favorite shirt.

That wish died as he saw Jack move around the corner with a gun in his hand.

*   *   *

The driver cursed when he saw the car pull past the van. He kept still so Jack would not see any movement from the back as he passed. He was clearly eyeballing the van though. He hissed a warning to the man inside and then slowly moved to the driver's seat and adjusted the power mirror so he could see the front door of the beach house. If his guy came out quick he would be ready. If Jack came out, well, he had a clipboard to hide behind when he passed. He reached out and started the van.

*   *   *

Jack's concentration was broken only for an instant when he glanced in the direction of the sound of the van starting, but that was all it took. The door to the laundry room he had been approaching flew out at him, followed by a masked man. Jack managed to avoid the elbow coming at his head, but caught the knee squarely in his gut, knocking the wind from him and planting him on the floor. He rolled toward the garage once and managed to catch a glimpse of the man rounding the corner

into the kitchen, heading for the front door. Jack aimed but held his fire
when he saw no weapon in the man's hand. Grunting against the pain
he rose and forced himself to follow. By the time he made the front door
he had his wind back and was pissed. He paused on the porch to see the
man running toward the van parked next door. He leveled the gun and
was rewarded with a round tearing into the frame of the deck in front of
him from the driver of the van. He dropped and rolled to the left before
rising and pumping two rounds back in return. They impacted the side
of the van as it fishtailed in the crushed shell street, its engine roaring as
the driver stomped the accelerator.

Jack vaulted the railing and raced for the Corvette's open door. He
remembered to buckle his belt before slamming the transmission in reverse and spinning the tires after the van. Thoughts of the paint job did
not enter his mind this time.

—NINETEEN—

DEPUTY BOBBY HAYNES HAD only been on duty for a few hours. So far his day had consisted of roll call, a quick drive through town and a lap around the high school followed by breakfast at his favorite diner that included a half hour of flirtation with Julie, his favorite waitress.

Their conversation had been interrupted by the call from dispatch. 911 call with no one on the phone. Most likely a kid or someone who had it programmed in their speed-dial and had accidentally pushed the button. It happened once in awhile in this little town. The house belonged to a VIP though, so he would check it out promptly.

He said his good-byes to Julie and made it to the car before dispatch called again. He was informed that the VIP was FBI. Not wanting to look bad with the feds, he put the car in gear and got moving. He considered the lights and siren, but with traffic so low he really didn't need them. It was only a mile or two anyway.

He crossed the small bridge and was soon at the entrance to the street.

As he turned he saw a large white van hurtling toward him. Instinctively he dropped his coffee and yanked the wheel to avoid a collision. The van driver did the same, but the rear end broke loose on the shells and the van impacted the side of the car with enough force to shove it off the road. Bobby grit his teeth against the coffee burning his lap and the coming rollover, but the unit chose to stop leaning and slid on its wheels into the intercoastal water. Fortunately the tide was low and the soft mud stopped the car from going any farther. He scrambled out of the unit in case it changed its mind and looked after the retreating van. A cloud of dust was his only reward. He was about to go back in the car for the radio when a Corvette came flying up the road after the van. The driver slammed on the brakes and showered Bobby with shells.

"You all right?"

Bobby could only nod his head.

"Call for back up!" the man ordered.

Bobby was once again pelted with seashells as the car raced after the van. He managed to find the microphone in the cloud of white dust and call dispatch.

"Dispatch, this is Bobby. I'm 10-7 in the ditch on the east side of the bridge. A white late model van ran me off the road. There's a man in a black Corvette in pursuit of the van. I believe he may be the homeowner. They're heading north at this time. Hauling ass. We better get Dan headed that way and call the sheriff and the state boys."

"Roger, Bobby, you okay?"

Bobby looked down at his coffee stained pants. So much for looking good to the feds.

"Yeah, I'm good."

*   *   *

Jack made it through the cloud of dust just in time to see the van take a right and disappear behind some trees, the driver barely keeping it on two wheels as they rounded the turn. Jack smiled as he knew he had the upper hand once they were on the blacktop. He snatched the Bluetooth headset up and managed to get it in his ear before he needed his hands free to make the turn. The Corvette took the high speed maneuver without complaint and Jack accelerated after the van in the distance. He fumbled with the phone and turned it on, the polite beep telling him it was ready. He held it up to his face before speaking.

"Call 911."

The voice activation software quickly complied and he heard the dial tone sound twice in his ear before it was picked up.

"911, what is your emergency?"

"This is Agent Jack Randall of the FBI. I'm currently in pursuit of a white van northbound on Savanna at Colonial. I discovered them in my home and they are fleeing. Shots have been fired. At least one of them is armed. Again, a white late model van with Maryland plates, northbound on Savanna. Can you send me any backup?"

"I understand, sir, can you give me your name again and what you are driving?"

"My name is Jack Randall of the FBI and I'm in a black Corvette."

"Okay, you said shots fired? From whom and what type of weapon?"

"From them, a handgun of unknown type."

"Any injuries?"

"Hold on."

Jack swung the car into another high speed turn, this time the tires squealed in protest but still kept their grip. Jack grunted against the pain in his gut as he straightened out of the turn and once again slammed his foot down on the accelerator. He caught a glimpse of a retired couple in the other lane as he passed, their mouths hanging open.

"Okay, what was your question?"

Uhh ...any injuries sir?"

"The van shoved one of the local deputies into the ditch, he's okay, they missed me."

"Okay, where are you now sir?"

Jack looked at the GPS screen on the dash. "Hollymount and Midway, westbound."

"We have a local sheriff department unit en route and the state police have been notified."

"Good, we're getting into the country. They can't outrun me, so they may try something stupid."

"I understand, sir. EMS has been notified, also."

"What's your name?"

"My name is Susan, sir."

"Okay, Susan, it's you and me for now. Don't go anywhere."

"I won't."

*　　　　　*　　　　　*

"Do something, he's gaining!"

"No shit he's gaining! He's in a damn Corvette and we're in a fucking van! What am I supposed to do?" the driver yelled back in return.

The thief weighed the situation. The driver was right, they couldn't beat the Corvette. If the chase went on too much longer there would be other cars, roadblocks and possibly a helicopter. They had to end it soon. Getting caught was not on his list of options. He had been caught once before and had vowed never to let that happen again.

"Find a stretch of road with trees on both sides."

"For what?"

"Just do it, and be ready to stop." Reaching into the driver's lap he took his pistol. Now with two, he made his way to the back door.

"Your trees are coming up!"

"Let him get closer, then stop the van across the road!"

The driver muttered a curse under his breath as he prepared to do so. He understood the situation as well as his partner, but still didn't like what he had in mind. But they really had no choice. As the van crested a small hill and entered a wooded area he chose his spot at the bottom of the next hill. As soon as the car behind him disappeared from view he stood on the brakes and cranked the wheel, putting the van into a sliding stop that blocked the road. He heard the back door open before the van stopped rocking.

*   *   *

Jack topped the hill and caught sight of the van blocking the road. He knew he was too late to stop and saw no way around the van. Training kicked in before he even thought about it.

He threw the Corvette into a high speed 180 degree turn just as he had been taught at the Farm during his training days. His instructor had demonstrated it with an armored stretch limousine and Jack had been impressed—impressed enough to return for some continued classes with friends from the Secret Service. The Corvette responded to everything he asked of it and he watched the kaleidoscope view of trees and sky slide by the windshield. As he spun the tires to put the body of the Corvette between him and the van he heard the sounds of bullets impacting the fiberglass and composite body of his car. He thumbed the belt release and snatched up the Glock from between his legs before tumbling out of the car. He moved to the front, placing the engine block between himself and the incoming bullets and looked for the van. Time was on his side, he could hear the sirens approaching, but they were a long ways off yet. Looking through the spider-webbed windshield he saw the van still sitting in the road. He forced himself to ignore the man at the rear of the van and took aim at the van's tires. Firing off three rounds in quick succession he was rewarded with the explosive deflation of the right rear wheel, the one that pushed. He ducked down as more rounds whizzed by him and his car, a couple more splintering the fiberglass.

He listened for the sirens through his ringing ears but it was impossible to know if they were any closer. He snuck another look toward the van and was surprised to see it trying to leave. The engine howled as the blown tire spun on the pavement.

*   *   *

"What the hell are you doing!" the thief yelled at his partner.

The driver ignored him as he floored the gas pedal and shut the door, obviously not waiting for his partner to re-board the van. He was leaving.

The thief threw a couple of rounds his way out of frustration before the slide locked back on the pistol. Enraged, he threw the empty handgun at the departing van. The driver smiled at him in his rearview mirror and worked to keep the van under control as he sped away.

*   *   *

Jack watched it all happen from a prone position in back of the Corvette. It sat so low he had trouble seeing everything, but he could see enough. He relaxed slightly when he saw the man throw the pistol away, only to tense again as he reloaded the second one. The man made for the trees while again firing in Jack's direction. A gunman fleeing through the woods would be hard to find and capture. He would most likely approach one of the local farmhouses and take what he needed there, maybe with the use of the gun. He made Jack's decision for him.

*   *   *

The driver thought he just might make it to the next farmhouse when the State Police cruiser came over the rise in front of him. It immediately swerved to block the road and the driver exited with a shotgun in hand. He reflexively turned the wheel to exit the road, but forgot about the lost rear tire. The van caught the edge of the road and flipped, its square cross shape contributed to the multiple rolls it took before impacting the cruiser. The trooper scrambled out of the way in time to watch his unit get crushed.

When it was over, he approached the van and looked inside. He turned his face from the scene in disgust before reaching for the radio on his belt.

"Dispatch, Unit 6, suspect van is Signal 4 at Kings and Beaver Dam Road. One person occupant."

"Roger Unit 6, do you need EMS Rich?"

"That's a negative."

*   *   *

"Randall, R-A-N-D-A-L-L, first name Jack."

Jack was talking with the state trooper as he surveyed the damage to his beloved car. The trooper was filling out paperwork. He paused to take in the damage, too.

"Looks like he sent quite a few your way. You just used the Glock?"

Jack had counted twelve holes in the bodywork so far. Amazingly the car still ran. He watched the exhaust and listened to the engine. One muffler had a hole in it, but that seemed to be it. It seemed to be running fine.

"Yeah, my regular weapon is in the center console. The Glock is from my beach house."

"Backup?"

"I use a 410 derringer. It's at the office."

"A derringer, a Browning BDM, and a Glock. Do I dare ask you to pop the trunk?"

Jack just smiled and shook his head. The trooper was showing some professional courtesy. He was still waiting for the "not equipped for pursuit lecture" but so far it hadn't come. The trooper had every right to give it as Jack had no business doing what he did in his personal car. It was a danger to the public and he knew it. But in the heat of the moment he had done it anyway, let the chips fall. Obviously the trooper felt the same. Jack eyeballed him as he worked the pen and clipboard. Big guy, his tag said Richard Titus, and there was a Marine Corps tattoo on his forearm. That helped explain the lack of a lecture, and the haircut.

"I'm gonna have to take both your weapons and impound the car I'm afraid. We'll get your statement and then I'll get you a ride home. Any idea what they were after?"

"What do you mean?"

"There was nothing in that van except the headless horseman. No valuables or stolen goods. No ID on either of them."

"Nothing?"

Jack thought about that as he watched the coroner's people circle the body at the edge of the woods. He left the trooper at the car and walked to the body. A younger trooper moved to block him, but was waved aside by Titus who had followed. Jack walked up to the body and knelt down for a closer look."

"Two in the ten-ring; that's good shooting from this range." Titus commented.

Jack just offered a nod for the compliment. He reached up and snagged a pair of gloves from the coroner's pocket and put them on. He rolled up the man's sleeves and pant legs until he saw it—a patch of scar tissue on his calf.

"Hey, Doc, what's this look like to you?

The M.E. took a good look before voicing his opinion. "Looks like a scar that got covered with a tattoo at one point, then removed. I'd say within the past year or so."

"That's what I thought, too"

CHINA HAS OVER 13 MILLION
ABORTIONS A YEAR.
August 2009—CNN

-TWENTY-

PROFESSOR MILES SHOOK HIS head behind the plastic faceplate as he examined the birds, as he had for the last few days. They appeared normal and healthy for the most part, but he had been told what to look for and he was now seeing it.

The ducks were showing slight swelling around the eyes and neck and one of the chickens had greenish stool when he had cleaned the cages that morning. One duck would sneeze every few minutes, but he noted no nasal discharge. It was Newcastle.

He reviewed the blood work he had run. It showed the virus strain as Lentogenic, the most mild of the four strains of Newcastle. This meant the birds would produce only mild signs of infection, and would survive as the strain was not lethal. They were now carriers. Parrots had been shown to carry the virus yet not show symptoms. This left them capable of shedding NDV for up to 400 days.

Miles documented his findings before walking past the monkey cages and leaving the room. He found a chair and flopped into it.

400 days. He marveled at the figure. A virus that lived that long in birds could be a truly scary thing. It was a tough virus, too, capable of surviving for several weeks with sufficient warmth and humidity. It could live on the bird's feathers, in its feces, in its mucosal discharge. It would live indefinitely if frozen.

He reached out to the keyboard in front of him and punched up the research data he had gathered. Newcastle Disease Virus (NDV)-avian paramyxoviruses was a single stranded linear RNA virus with an elliptical symmetry. The total genome was roughly 16,000 nucleotides.

This was the problem he had. The vial contained the same type of virus, yet the RNA strand was almost double the number of nucleotides. He had no explanation for the excess. As far as he could tell, it was made up of virus fragments and additional proteins for which, at this point, he could see no reason. Furthermore, it was appearing to be anything but a vaccine. If anything it *gave* the birds Newcastle, albeit the mildest form. It was still infectious.

There was only one reason on the books to introduce Newcastle and that was for a specific cancer treatment. In 2006 it was used to target certain types of brain and lung cancers. The virus preferred to target and replicate in the cancer cells, destroying them while leaving normal cells unaffected. But that was a completely different strain and certainly did nothing to explain why pallets of the medication were being stored in African warehouses. None of this was making any sense.

He put down the clipboard and, shaking his arm repeatedly, managed to pull it out of its sleeve and inside his suit. He first reached up and scratched a spot on his nose that had been bugging him all day. He then turned his back to the windows before reaching into his waistband and pulling out the candy bar he had tucked in there earlier. It was a violation of his own rules, but since he was alone in the lab he felt it was okay. He could be a do-as-I-say-not-as-I-do-guy for a few minutes.

He peeled the wrapper with his teeth and munched away as he read some more of the blood work report. At the bottom he discovered the report on his two monkeys. Both had been injected with this year's strain of flu that was now making its way through China. The monkeys were showing the correct antibodies, and it looked as though they would make a full recovery. Despite this, their white cell counts were higher than expected. As if they were gearing up for a long battle. Maybe the vaccine was experimental. He would keep a closer eye on them.

*   *   *

It was his first meeting of the day, or his last, depending on one's point of view. At 2:30 a.m. he had risen silently from the bed so as not to disturb his wife. He dressed quietly in casual attire before opening the bedroom door. His escort was patiently waiting with his nighttime security people. They exchanged no words as he was quickly led away. They passed numerous paintings as they strode through the building, paintings of important men, some great leaders, some not. He deliberately avoided their gaze and kept his eyes on the shoes of the man leading him. They descended to the ground floor and then on into the basement. The hallways were void of any people as the cleaning crews had been cleared for the evening. Security was also unusually sparse and soon just he and his escort were walking the hall. Other than time spent in his bedroom with his wife, it was the most he had been alone in several years. They descended again to a subbasement and were soon in front of a large heavy door. The escort placed his palm on the screen next to it and the door unlocked itself with three dull metallic thuds. A small indicator light turned green and the escort tugged the door open to reveal a long hallway lit at regular intervals. He followed the escort through the door and waited patiently while it was locked behind them before once again being led down the hallway. Muted sounds of traffic could be heard at one point, but otherwise the only sound was of their shoes on the tile floor. After what seemed like over two blocks they came to an identical door and the palm scan and heavy door were repeated. They walked down a carpeted corridor with several turns and twists until they arrived at a door blocked by a large, stern looking man. He said nothing as the escort turned and walked away, his job for the early morning hour over. The two men stood looking at one another until the escort was out of earshot down the long hallway.

"Assignation," the man spoke.

The guard nodded and opened the door behind him, allowing the man to enter the dimly lit room. He slowly surveyed the room, noting all that were present. As usual, he was the last to arrive. He took his place at the table without greeting or acknowledgement from the others. There were five of them total, a representative from each of the major continents and centers of population. They met only twice a year, as had their predecessors, in this room and never outside it. There were no papers in the room, no phones, not even a pen among them. These meetings never existed.

"Status?" he asked.

The African representative spoke. "We had a minor problem with the storage of the agent due to the embassy bombing in Tanzania. The agent was mixed as a result. We attempted to recover it while the remainder was being transported, but were forced to destroy it in place instead. It is believed to be totally contained. The remaining B agent is being moved from the area storage facilities. The A agent will remain as it currently is so as not to arouse suspicion."

"Very well," the man answered. "I have people monitoring those involved just in case. We will take action, if needed. Production is on schedule. We should be shipping to South America within four weeks. You are prepared to receive the agents?"

The South American representative cleared his throat before replying. "We have to be careful with Chavez in Venezuela. He's a paranoid fool and suspects everything. The other distribution points are ready. We hope to have the continent fully staged within a year."

The man nodded and the others stayed silent, awaiting his next thought.

"No more testing? We're sure we have the right agent this time?"

The Russian placed his hands on the table as the question fell to him.

"The test currently started in Mexico is revealing good results. They've dubbed it the 'Swine Flu.' We've identified the speed and coordination efforts of the public health entities involved. I would rate their response as good to excellent. Containment is still the deciding factor. While the zero-patient was located quickly and the virus source traced soon after, we've proved that containment is virtually impossible. The virus was in three countries in a matter of days, and worldwide in weeks. I believe we have solved the problems of transmission, virility, stability and effectiveness. We estimate a 1/3, or 2 billion reduction with the current agent."

There was a long pause as they all contemplated the number. It helped to deal in percentages instead.

"The cause will still appear natural?"

"Yes, as did all the previous tests. This agent offers a …quicker …solution as well."

"Good. There will be no more frog-boiling, we can all agree on this?"

There were nods all around the table. The agent that had been dubbed AIDS was an attempt to produce a stealth virus, one that would manifest itself slowly, thereby avoiding detection until it had already gained a foothold. The years it took to take effect, coupled with the suffering involved, had proven it to be a poor choice by their predecessors. The frog boiling statement, while crude, was accurate. If one dropped a frog in boiling water it would immediately take action to escape, but if one placed the frog in the water and then slowly brought it to a boil, it would sit quietly while it cooked to death.

"Production?" he asked next.

Again the Russian. "Our facilities are at full production capacity as are the units here in the United States. We estimate to have the required amount produced by early next year, with a backup supply stored at each site."

"Very good. How are we in the east?"

The Chinese representative addressed them with his usual soft-spoken voice and the others strained to hear. "Our distribution is complete.

We are adding more sites in Indonesia and removing the site from Yap as we discussed previously. The island is now considered a safety zone, along with the rest of Micronesia."

The leader again nodded his head and there was a long pause as they all contemplated the enormity of what they were discussing.

"Gentleman, I wish I had never inherited this task as I know you all do as well. Nevertheless, it has fallen to us to see it through. The plan must be in place within the designated timeline. Reports by my country's scientists paint a poor future for our world. We must be ready for the day the decision has to be made. Let us all hope it does not fall on one of us to make."

He got solemn nods of agreement from all around the table.

"I shall see you all again in six months." He rose to leave as the others kept their seats. They would leave at separate intervals so as not to be seen together. He opened the door to find a different escort waiting. He was led back through the maze of corridors and stairwells, through the tunnel and back into the building where he'd started.

"The office," he spoke to the escort, who quickly changed direction to accommodate. Another corridor followed by a stairwell and he was back in familiar territory. He hardly noticed as the escort disappeared and was replaced by one of his own security men. He walked past his secretary's desk and into his office only to find an elderly woman dusting the shelves. A security man kept watch. She quickly stopped and gathered her supplies before addressing him.

"Good morning, sir."

"Good morning, Betty."

*   *   *

"Still no ID on either of them, sir?"

"Nothing yet. We're still sifting through the trace from the van, but this isn't CSI, Jack. Test results actually take time to run in the real world and I don't really have a good reason to bump this to the front of the line. Someone will eventually ask why."

"You're the Deputy Director. How about 'Because I said so?'"

"It doesn't work that way and you know it. Now calm down and we'll go over it from the beginning."

Jack stopped pacing and found a seat in front of the man's desk. Jack had to admit that Deacon was right, and blowing his stack over the pace of the work was stupid.

"You're sure there were only two of them?"

"No. There could have been more in the house that I didn't see, but I doubt one would bail out while his partner was still in there."

"You said the van left the guy there on the road with you," Deacon pointed out.

"Yeah, but that could have been planned or just desperation forcing their hand."

"Tell me about the scar you saw."

"The one I shot had an old bullet wound on his calf, a through and through. It looked like he covered it with a tattoo but then later had it removed. The M.E. agreed. Ring any bells?"

"Your sterile guy from Africa."

"Yeah, obviously they want something, I just don't know what."

"Nothing missing from the house?"

"Nope, nothing even disturbed. It was like they had never been there. If it wasn't for that boot print in the carpet I never would have known they were there."

They both sat in silence for a few minutes while they looked for a motive. Jack broke the silence with a statement that surprised Deacon.

"Somebody was in Sydney's office."

"Say that again?"

"She told me her office Tell was moved the other day. I ran it by security but got nothing. No report of accidental movement and the cleaning man denies it. Guy's been here a few years. Guard says he's a good man." Jack let the statement hang for a moment before asking a question. "How're our two new friends behaving?"

"Murphy seems to be as advertised. No strange behavior. We let him see our tail once and he reported it. We said it was a training exercise and that seemed to satisfy them. Ms. Sachs, on the other hand, has a few strange quirks. She leaves the house to make phone calls every once in awhile. Evidently she has multiple cell phones, but we can't find the numbers in any database. She does her job well, but outside of work she has few friends. We're still keeping an eye on her."

Jack thought about their options. He'd been shot at twice now by whoever was behind this and he still had no real clue as to why. Basically they had two options at this point. Sit back and wait to see what came at them next, or take the fight to them.

"Let's go on offense."

"And how do you propose we do that?"

"Simple, we call Murphy over for a visit and grill him on what he knows."

"And if he knows nothing?"

"We recruit him."

*　　　　　　*　　　　　　*

Professor Miles opened the door to the monkey cage for the morning feeding. Thelma and Louise greeted him with their usual screams and quickly tackled the biscuits as they were dropped into the cages. The noise in the cage had changed slightly and he could hear the calls of the ducks at the end of the room over the roar of air in the suit. He would get to them as soon as he finished with the monkeys.

"Hello, boys, I've got…" He stopped when he saw the monkey's condition. Two were not screaming as the others were. They instead sat in their cages with a dull expression on their faces. A trail of mucus could be seen draining from their nostrils. Their normally bright eyes were dull and they didn't respond to his direct eye contact. His monkeys were sick.

They were the two he had injected with the yellow top vaccine.

—TWENTY-ONE—

"WHERE DID THE VIALS come from, Sydney? I have to know!"

"Slow down, Professor, what's the problem? What did you find?" Sydney worked to calm him so she could understand what he was saying. He spoke fast when he was agitated and for some reason he clearly was.

"The monkeys I injected with the yellow vial are sick. I pulled a blood sample from both and ran it through the analyzer. It came up as Influenza A."

"Okay. And?"

"So they shouldn't have anything! It was a vaccine. This year's to be exact. They have the wrong strain."

"They have the wrong strain, who, the CDC?"

"No, the monkeys!"

"Professor, slow down and start all over. I'm not following you."

The professor pulled the phone from his ear and forced a couple of deep breaths. It had taken all he had to not end the decontamination shower early and run to his office. He'd forced himself to decon properly and walk out of the lab. He gathered the printout off the printer before anyone could see it and called Sydney only after he had shut the office door. Something he rarely did. He mopped the sweat from his head as he sank into his chair.

"Okay, I'm back. Try to follow me here. The current flu vaccine is for three strains; A/Brisbane/59/2007 which is an H1N1-like virus, A/Brisbane/10/2007 which is an H3N2 virus and a B/Brisbane/60/2008-like virus."

"Okay."

"So the monkeys I injected with your yellow top vaccine have active flu when they shouldn't. Somehow they got sick."

"From another monkey maybe?"

"They've been housed in a Level-4 Bio-containment lab for the last two months and quarantined for months before that. They were clean. Anyway, I pulled a blood sample from each of them and ran it through the analyzer. I sent it to GenBank and it came back as Influenza A, H1N1."

"So they have the flu and it's not the flu the vaccine is for?"

"Yes, but it's much worse."

"I don't understand."

"The GenBank database identified the strain. There's no mistake, I ran it three times. It's H1N1 Influenza …from 1918."

"You mean…"

"It's the Spanish flu. The same flu that killed over 100 million people."

*   *   *

"Thanks for coming in. We just have a few questions for you," Deacon said as he gestured toward the remaining office seat. Jack shook the offered hand without getting up as Murphy made himself comfortable.

"Jack, how's the ankle?"

"All healed up, thanks."

"So what can I do for the FBI today?"

"We're investigating the ambush and the medication theft. We'd like to know what your thoughts are."

"Not too much I'm afraid. I thought it was chalked up to black marketers."

"That's the official version. We just have some open ends yet."

"Such as?"

"Why did they take the risk of shooting their own man and blowing up the cargo, why not just let it go?"

Murphy rubbed his chin as he thought about it. "Shooting their guy I can understand. He could talk and lead us back to them. Ruthless, but effective. As for blowing up the cargo, I really don't know. Maybe just to deny it to the competition."

"What do you know about the competition?" Deacon asked.

"AIDS drugs are expensive in Africa, and I don't mean just by their standards, I mean ours too. One unit in Africa goes for $62 while the same unit in Sweden goes for half that. As a result they get black-market drugs from Pakistan and India for a fraction of the cost. On top of all that you have to deal with a lot of government corruption. It's estimated that close to half of the drugs shipped don't even get to the people they were intended for."

"What about other vaccines?"

"Those are a lot cheaper and more plentiful. Flu and TB vaccines seem to get out without much of a problem. The drug companies work with the embassies to get them distributed. There's no money in it for the black marketers, so they tend to leave them alone. If they do grab some, it's usually by mistake."

"You ever have a hand in that? Drug distribution, I mean?"

Murphy shifted in his seat so he could look Jack in the eye. Jack read his face and was surprised to see a puzzled look.

"To what end are you asking these questions? Am I under investigation by the FBI?"

Jack looked at Deacon and got a nod.

"Yesterday I caught two men going through my house at the beach. A chase ensued and I shot and killed one of them. The other rolled the van he was driving and took his own head off. Maybe you heard about it?"

"That was you?"

"Since then we've determined that my home was also searched a few nights ago and one of my people's office here was also disturbed. By whom, we have no idea yet."

"Okay, so what does this have to do with me? You think I had something to do with it?"

"No, we're reasonably sure at this point that you didn't."

"Reasonably sure ...you've been following me."

"Yes, we have."

"Those training guys? That was bullshit?"

"Yes. We needed to see if you would report it."

Murphy sat back in his chair and glowered at the two men. Jack waited for him to say something so he could judge his reaction. He didn't have to wait long for Murphy to think it through and he saw the emotions travel across his face as he did.

"So, if I'm innocent, why am I here?"

Jack smiled as he got the response he was hoping for. "Simple, we need your help."

"You need *my* help?"

"You and Heather were the only two people on my crew I didn't know. We figure somebody tipped off the ambush party as to when we were leaving and what we were carrying. We've checked you out and decided that you're clean. Heather, on the other hand, has some strange habits. What can you tell us about her?"

"Wait a minute. You checked me out how?"

Jack held up a file. "We pulled your CIA file and did a background on you. There's actually not a whole lot we don't know about you at this point. You can tell your sister happy birthday for me by the way."

Murphy eyes traveled from the file in Jack's lap across the desk to Deacon's face and back to Jack before he closed his mouth. He'd been ambushed. By a couple of pros he had to admit. He pulled himself together.

"Heather Sachs? Not a whole lot. She's CDC. Works with the vaccination efforts. Her name comes up a couple of times in some reports. She seems to get the job done. Has some connections."

"What kind of connections?"

"She's shown the ability to cut through red tape on occasion. How I'm not really sure. She's been known to make a few calls and suddenly the blockage is cleared. Whether it's on our side or theirs, somehow she makes it happen. Family connection? Maybe her boss. Far as I know, the agency has never really looked into it."

"We are. Perhaps the agency could do so also?"

"Okay. How about some quid pro quo?"

"Shoot."

"What are these people after?"

"We think they believe that myself or one of my people have some of the medications."

"Do you?"

"Yes."

"What is it?"

"We're still trying to determine that."

Murphy thought that over for a moment before asking his next question.

"I've seen it in other embassies, I think. Have you looked for it?"

"I have a friend looking into that now. We've decided to keep this very tight," Deacon broke in. "We've asked to borrow you for a few more days so consider yourself on the team. Jack's been reassigned as our Homeland Security liaison and you'll be working with him. Get your normal duties done and don't let on that you're working on this to anyone. Don't use official communications. I don't want NSA picking up on this. We don't know who all the players are yet."

Murphy nodded in agreement as he looked from face to face.

"What's next?"

*   *   *

The Deliveryman stretched out on the cramped bunk and listened to the engines of the ship as they vibrated the walls of the small room he had been given. It had only taken him three tries before he found a ship leaving the country and heading south. A small amount of *baksheesh* had convinced the captain to take on a passenger with no questions asked. The captain had been surprised to see no cargo other than the Deliveryman's small bag. He had heard it rattle as the man adjusted it on his shoulder. Diamonds were his guess. Any thoughts he had of robbing the man were forgotten when he saw the pistol tucked into the waistband of the man's pants and the look on his face. He was more than happy to take the money and forget about his extra passenger. The man had paid well for passage to Cape Town, a simple day and a night's travel. It was not worth the risk to rob him.

The Deliveryman now lay as he had for the last several hours in the dark, damp cabin. He occupied the time by flicking the flashlight in his hand on and off, revealing the bag of medications lying on the chair across the room. He had implemented the first part of his plan—getting out of Africa without being detected. In Cape Town he would board a plane to Brazil. There he could get lost in the sea of humanity that made up Sao Paolo or go on to the United States. Either way, he had made the decision, there was no turning back. Now he just had to devise a way to get what he wanted in exchange for the medications. He was not sure of the whole plan, but he had his suspicions. If they were correct, then the bag was very valuable, very valuable indeed.

He made sure the safety was on before he settled back into the thin pillow. He had a whole day and night to think about his next move. He wasn't short of funding and he had a few passports he could use to get around the world if the need came up. He decided to stick to the current plan and see what opportunities came up.

With the flashlight in one hand and the pistol in the other, he allowed the ship to rock him into a light sleep.

−TWENTY-TWO−

THE MONKEYS LOOKED WORSE today. They sat hunched in the farthest corners of their cages, a dull expression on their faces. Their morning biscuits sat uneaten next to them. It was only the second day of the infection and already they were showing signs of respiratory failure. Both were coughing repeatedly and producing large amounts of mucus. Neither of them showed the usual monkey behavior of their neighbors. They had no energy. There was no cage rattling or the usual hooting and grunting. The large male was very weak and showed signs of cyanosis, his lips and fingers turning a bluish tint. Neither of them did more than offer a vague look toward the two people observing them through the cage door.

Lynda took in the sight with some regret. As a veterinarian, she was devoted to easing the suffering of animals and it pained her to see the monkeys in such condition, knowing it was introduced by them. But as a researcher she also knew this was the only way vaccines came to be. She put the thought aside and touched her helmet to the professor's to better conduct the sound of her voice.

"I think the male is the better choice!"

"I agree!" he yelled back. "Be careful!"

She turned to make sure the door to the room had closed all the way before stooping to pick up her equipment. She first pulled the protective plastic cover off the end of the syringe and loaded it into the end of the pole. This allowed her to inject the monkey with the drug without her getting within range of his claws or teeth. The monkeys were equipped with big teeth, capable of biting through a space suit with ease and exposing the worker to the Level-4 environment. These were not the cute and fuzzy monkeys one saw on TV, they were big and powerful animals with surprising speed and agility. Letting one loose in the lab would be a major problem that they didn't need right now.

When the syringe was ready she retrieved the pinning stick from between her legs and handed it to the professor. They carefully circled each other and untangled their hoses before taking up their positions in front of the cage.

"Ready?" the professor mouthed silently through his face shield.

Getting a nod from Lynda he pushed the business end of the pole through the opening and maneuvered it toward the monkey. The monkey eyed the pole but did little to avoid it. A few grunts of protest and a brief struggle ended with the monkey pinned to the corner of his cage. Lynda quickly inserted the pole into the cage, worked the mechanism to inject the monkey with a fatal dose of sedative. The professor held the monkey firm until he went limp. They waited for two minutes with the monkey not moving before touching helmets again.

"I think he's down!"

Lynda carefully opened the cage and reached out a hand to pinch the monkey's leg. When she got no response she pulled the animal toward her and flipped him on his stomach. Pinning his arms to his sides, she carefully lifted him clear of the cage. Monkeys had been known to come back to life if the dose had been too little and she took every precaution in case that was to happen.

The professor carefully examined the monkey for any signs of life. Finding none he opened the door for her and she carried the monkey out and placed him on the necropsy table they had set up in the lab. Before entering the monkey cage, they had carefully laid out every item listed on a printed checklist sealed in plastic. There were no unnecessary blades or other sharp instruments. A variety of hemostats sat in a tray ready to clamp off any bleeding. The only glass in the room consisted of slides and blood tubes. Everything else was plastic. Glass could break and produce shards capable of piercing a space suit, so they were kept to a minimum.

The professor placed a large bowl at the head of the table and poured EnviroChem into it. It resembled antifreeze with its pale green color. They would periodically dip their gloved hands into the liquid as it destroyed viruses. Once finished, he reached around to crimp his hose before leaning his helmet across the table. Lynda mirrored his movements until they could speak.

"I'll prep the samples, you do the cutting?" he asked.

"Okay."

Lynda smiled as they broke away. The professor was senior to her in every way, yet he was wise enough to know she was the better person for this and was giving her the lead. She dismissed the compliment until later and gloved up before reaching for the scalpel. The professor stepped back and held his hands in the classic safety stance—clasped together and on his chest. Both to show her where they were, and keep him from reaching in.

Lynda carefully performed a Y incision and opened the monkey's chest and abdomen. She performed each cut in steps, never cutting toward her opposite hand. Once the initial incisions were made, she traded the scalpel in favor of a pair of blunt tip scissors to expand the opening until the monkey's internal organs were fully exposed.

She forced herself to work slowly and methodically, stopping frequently to rinse her gloves in the bowl and the blood turned the mixture a dark brown color. She paused whenever the professor's hands entered the carcass to clamp off blood vessels or sponge away fluids. They soon developed a good working rhythm and Lynda began removing organs and cutting them open. They would carefully inspect each as it was removed.

The spleen was engorged and split easily with a touch of the scalpel. She sliced thin specimens from it and the professor carefully pressed them onto slides. The intestines were laid open and showed no signs of blood or other abnormalities. The stomach, while unusually empty, also showed no problems. The liver was cut into wedges and prepared for later viewing. Samples were also placed in plastic jars of alcohol and chemical preservative. The small ribcage was cut away with pruning shears and the lungs were removed. Here Lynda first noticed the problem.

As she held the lungs in her hand the problem was clearly evident, but she needed numbers. She looked at the professor and mouthed one word: scale. He retrieved it from a nearby bench and laying a steel pan on top zeroed the display.

She laid the lungs in the pan and watched the number climb. As she suspected, the lungs were grossly overweight. They were full of fluid. The monkey had been slowly drowning in his own secretions. As the professor recorded the number she opened the lungs with the scalpel. Clear fluid, with a tinge of blood, poured forth and covered the bottom of the tray. She exchanged a look of horror with the professor. What they were seeing was unlike any flu virus they had ever seen. Only two days into the infection and this monkey was already close to death. She felt the sudden urge to rinse her hands and did so.

"Get a hold of yourself, girl," she told herself inside the suit. She took a couple of deep breaths before looking up to see the professor watching her. He offered a reassuring smile before leaning his head forward. She did likewise and they butted heads over the table.

"You're doing fine. Take a minute if you need to. We have all the time in the world."

She smiled and nodded. "I can finish."

Nevertheless, they took a short break and checked each other's suits.

A fresh bowl of EnviroChem was poured as a confidence booster and they returned to the table.

Lynda steeled herself over the monkey and gave herself a pep talk. "You owe it to the monkey," she told herself. The monkey had given his life so that they might discover the mechanism of this disease. As a vet she felt obligated to finish the necropsy. But every drop of blood held a potential million viruses. The sight of the lungs had spooked her and she felt a slight tremor in her hands. She willed the shaking to stop and it did.

The professor pulled the monkey carcass up the table and clamped the head into a set of blocks. Once in place he hosed down the table, clearing it of any fluids. He then made a show of organizing the instruments on the tray. Lynda watched patiently until it dawned on her what he was doing. His little display of housekeeping was his way of giving her a few moments to collect herself without embarrassing her. For some reason it struck her as funny and by the time he was done, she was biting her lip to keep from grinning. She looked at her hands. The shaking was gone.

Taking up a position at the head of the table, she reached for the gnawer. Using it to open the skull, the professor helped until they were able to pop it with a pair of pliers. The brain showed no signs of disease and they quickly removed it as well as the eyes and spinal cord before dropping them all in preservatives.

At this point they were done and both were glad. They quickly triple-bagged what was left of the monkey and cleaned the table and instruments, both of which would be autoclaved before being used again. The decontamination shower seemed to take forever and the professor made a mental note to install a timer in the damn thing so at least one knew how long they had left to go.

He found Lynda sitting on a bench in the locker room, her hair matted and her scrubs sweaty. The air pumped into the suits was cool and very dry so as not to fog their space suits. It took some stress to produce sweat.

"How ya doing, kiddo?"

"I've never seen lungs like that before, not after a two-day infection. Just what the hell is this thing?"

"I'm not sure yet." He sank down onto the bench next to her, "But I aim to find out."

*   *   *

Murphy strode into the room with several thick files under his arm. He laid them on the table before sitting back in a chair and rubbing his eyes. Jack took in the rumpled suit and the shadow of beard on his face. Evidently he had pulled an all-nighter.

"So what do you have?" Jack asked.

Murphy shot a questioning look toward Sydney, Larry and Eric before he answered with a question of his own. "They in the loop now?"

"Yeah, she's got some information for you, too. You can speak freely here."

"Okay, well, as you may have guessed I was up most of the night digging into our friend Heather. She appears to be as advertised. I could only find one gap in her history. Six months before she came to the CDC she fell off the earth. She explains it away in a letter as an extended backpacking trip to Asia and parts of Europe. So I called a few friends at some embassies and I can't find one visa or any record of her traveling during that period of time. Her address at that time was listed as Raleigh, North Carolina, but that turned out to be an old roommate who was working at Duke and collecting her mail for her. This roommate said she would show up once a month or so and pick it up. So that blows the backpacking trip out of the water. Whatever she was doing it was in the North Carolina area. That's about it. Everything else checks out."

"You have three files there?" Sydney pointed out.

"Yup. One for Mom and one for Dad. It makes for some interesting reading." He shoved the files down the table. Jack opened one while Sydney flipped open the second while Murphy continued his briefing.

"Daddy was a professor of biology at Berkley. Published several papers and did a fair amount of research. Was pretty well respected for a while."

"For a while?" Jack asked.

"Seems he went off the deep end after a trip to the north slope of Alaska. Came back a soldier for the environment. Started making speeches and publishing articles. It got worse over a few years and eventually his classes started turning into nothing but environmental propaganda. He got booted out of Berkley and wound up joining Greenpeace. His wife was an oceanographer and she joined him. They gave the movement some much needed credibility. Anyway, Heather was brought up in this environment until they got even more radical and Greenpeace threw them out. Sometime after that they got involved in all kinds of other groups. There were raids on labs doing research on animals and sabotage to some fishing vessels in New England. Nothing they could tie them to, but their name was on it. Finally they got caught burning the ski resorts down out west to save the lynx and did some jail time. Heather went to live with an aunt, then changed her name and went to school. Evidently she no longer has contact with them, but we can't be sure."

Jack thumbed through the pages before addressing Sydney. "You grilled her on the plane, Syd, she mention anything like this to you?"

"No. I think she described them as hippies from the Midwest. Never let on about any of the environmental stuff. Can't say I blame her though. If my parents were in jail I don't think I'd be volunteering that information to everyone either."

"I wonder just how much the parents influence dug in?" Murphy asked.

"Now that I think about it, she didn't have any leather on. I remember her shoes were canvas. So were her bags and purse. She never wore makeup either. I just thought it was due to the climate."

"They test makeup on animals, and leather goes without saying. Anything else you remember?"

She shook her head and stayed silent as they all read the files. After several minutes, they had all skimmed through them and were contemplating the information. Murphy was doing his best to stay awake. His eyes snapped open when Eric broke the silence.

"I remember one thing she said. It sounded like nothing at the time but after reading all this, I'm not so sure."

"Go ahead," Jack prompted.

"Well, it was right when we pulled up to the hospital and we had fought our way through all those people. I had never seen anything like it before and I made a comment."

They waited while he gathered the memory together.

"I'm paraphrasing here, but I remember I said something like, 'I can't imagine or I never imagined.'"

"What did she say?"

"There're too many people."

They all sat in silence for a moment. Murphy saw the looks on their faces and didn't quite understand.

"So what does that mean?" he asked.

"Tell him about the vials, Syd."

Murphy listened intently until he too had the same look on his face.

"So what's our next move?"

"Let's get her in here," Jack said.

*   *   *

The Deliveryman sat in the airport bar, his bag in a pile at his feet with the strap wrapped around his ankle. He nursed his beer slowly and watched the eyes of the people behind him in the mirror behind the bar. Usually his size and appearance were enough to change the minds of most thieves, but the ones here in Sao Paolo were especially brazen. He couldn't afford to lose the bag right now.

He finished his scan and moved his eyes back to the letter in front of him. He read it over and decided it was enough. Twenty million dollars was a nice round number. More than he could possibly need in his life. He would need some to change his appearance and to find a corner of the world he could hide in. The rest would provide a comfortable but not lavish lifestyle. No reason to get greedy. No, twenty million was enough. A small figure to the people he was sending the letter to.

He sealed the letter and affixed the stamp. The address he had already penned on the front along with the proper mail code number, assuring it would get to the person intended without delay. He had read the pick-up times on the mail box and had watched as it was collected just a few minutes ago. He would drop the letter on the way to his gate. The letter would follow him to the States in two days, giving him plenty of time to put things in place for when it arrived. He had already spent the morning making phone calls and had been assured everything would be ready as he had requested.

They called his flight in Portuguese and then again in English. He drained his beer and retrieved his bag before striding to the mailbox and dropping the letter. He couldn't help but grin as he slung the bag of vials over his shoulder and walked down the gateway toward his plane. He was about to be a rich man.

EBOLA FOUND IN PHILIPPINE
PIGS FOR FIRST TIME.
July 10, 2009—The Associated Press

—TWENTY-THREE—

PROFESSOR MILES READ THE test results for the third time. Part of him wished he never had. After repeated tests and hours of contemplation, where he had thrown idea after idea onto the white board in his office, he had only come up with one theory. He now sat in his chair, staring at the board covered in questions and arrows. Dozens of items crossed out. Test results retried and confirmed. He had finally admitted that what he was looking at was true. He just didn't want to believe it.

He looked at the clock. It was after midnight and he was sure he was the only one still left in the lab except for the security people. Should he call now or wait till tomorrow? Could he afford to wait? He found himself looking up at the Terminator poster on the wall. The machine's red eyes stared back at him with a bare toothed grin. The Terminator was alive and living in his lab. He had to call now.

"What are you looking at?" he asked the poster as he reached for the phone.

It rang several times before it was picked up.

"...Hello?"

"Sydney, it's Professor Miles."

"Hello, Professor ...what ...what time is it?"

"It's late and I apologize, but I have something very important to tell you and it just couldn't wait."

"...Okay?"

"Are you awake? I need you to hear this."

He heard the sounds of rustling sheets and a creaking floor as she got out of bed.

"I'm awake now, go ahead."

"Today I did a necropsy on one of the infected monkeys with an assistant of mine. The monkey was only in the second day of the infection, but already it was showing signs of severe respiratory distress. The lungs on removal were saturated with bloody sputum. It appears to target not just the lining of the main branches of the respiratory tract, but also deep into the lungs, down to the alveoli. The lungs were bad. You could feel the weight in your hands, very heavy and dense. I've never seen anything like it. The monkey was very cyanotic prior to the necropsy, its lips, ears and fingers all blue, and it had a high fever. I estimate it would have been dead in a matter of hours. The female we injected has already died. When rigor set in the fluid poured from the mouth and nose. This flu shows no signs for six days and then kills in less than forty-eight hours."

"My God."

"It gets worse. We injected the female with the top three anti-virals on the market. Sydney, we got nothing. Nothing! It didn't even slow it down. We're running more tests now, but I don't expect anything different. But it's how they got it that's the worst part."

"What do you mean?"

"Remember when I said the yellow top vial was a vaccine? Well it is. I just couldn't figure out how the monkeys got this new strain of Spanish Flu. It just didn't add up. Then I got the new blood work back. They tested positive for the new flu *and* Newcastle."

"I thought you said the red top vial had the Newcastle virus?"

"It does, and it should only have affected the birds I gave it to. The birds were at the opposite end of the room. Newcastle shouldn't have had any effect on the monkeys anyway. They don't have the receptors for it."

"So how did it happen?"

"I'm not totally sure yet, but I can tell you my theory."

"Okay?"

"Both of the viruses had a number of additional fragments attached as well as several protein markers. I mean a lot of them. Fragments from all kinds of viruses. It's not unusual to find fragments, just not in this quantity. Both monkeys have a combination of the two virus structures showing in their blood. The viruses combined somehow to produce this new flu, and it killed the monkeys in less than two days. What you have here is some kind of binary virus. The first half is the yellow top vaccine. Anyone inoculated with it is fine. It will even protect them from the coming flu strains. But if they come into contact with a bird with the red top Newcastle strain, they'll develop the new flu, be carriers for a few days and then be dead forty-eight hours from the first sign of symptoms."

There was silence on the phone as Sydney thought through what she was being told.

"Sydney?"

"I'm here, I …I don't know what to say. Is this thing natural?"

"If I hadn't gotten it from the vials you had sent me, I would have to say maybe. It would appear natural if detected from the animals. But coming from a vial? That tells me it's an engineered virus or somebody has harnessed a naturally occurring one."

"I see. You have this all on paper?"

"Yes."

"And you're sure of what you're telling me."

"Yes."

"How fast can you get to DC?"

"I can be there by morning."

"Come to the Hoover Building. I'll have someone escort you up."

"All right. Sydney?"

"Yes?"

"Where did you get these vials?"

"We'll have to discuss that when you get here."

"…Okay."

*   *   *

"Let me get this straight, Professor. What you're telling me is that someone has a lethal flu virus disguised as a vaccine and they're housing it in American embassies?"

"It would appear so, yes."

Larry slumped back in his chair. They had been listening to the professor since early that morning as he explained his findings. It was now approaching three and they were still wrapping their heads around the idea.

"What happens if it gets out?"

"A worldwide pandemic like we've never had in history. If the birds are migratory the virus will spread across the earth even if we ground every plane and quarantine everyone who got the vaccine. There will be no way to control it. Right now it takes two parts. The initial inoculation followed by contact with an infected bird. But if the virus becomes airborne, you now have person-to-person transmission. It could sweep the globe. Some will survive as the virus mutates, some will have a natural immunity, but millions will die within days of being infected."

"How many total?"

"I estimate the number as high as two to three billion. That's one-third of the world's population."

They sat in silence, stunned by the number.

"What about a vaccine?" Eric asked.

The professor rubbed his chin before replying. He was clearly exhausted and the thoughts in his head seemed to make him even more tired.

"The pharmaceutical companies would have to convert their production to mass produce any vaccine. The technical difficulties would be astronomical. Flu vaccines are made by inoculating the seed virus in embryonated hen's eggs, you purify them and chemically treat them to remove the ineffective portion. Then the concentration is adjusted to known biological standards. Huge vaccine-ready flocks would have to be hatched six months ahead of time so that they're mature enough to lay eggs. It takes at least a half a year to prepare a flu vaccine. It then has to be tested and approved by the FDA. We use five million hens just to produce the annual flu vaccine, and that's just enough to give out to select target groups like the elderly and healthcare workers. To make enough vaccine for this? It would never be ready in time. The virus burns to quickly, it kills in days. The pandemic would be worldwide before the eggs were even hatched."

"So what *can* we do?" Larry asked.

"Find the source of this vaccine and eliminate it. Destroy the red top vials before they can be spread. I'll get my people started on a vaccine."

Jack had listened silently for most of the professor's lecture. The suspicions he'd had were true. It was the scale he was unprepared for. There was one thing he still didn't understand.

"Professor, you said there was no way to stop the spread. If this was man-made, what's its purpose?"

"That is for you and your people to find out, Mr. Randall. I prefer not to think about it."

They sat in silence once again until the professor's phone rang. He frowned at the disturbance, but on looking at the screen his face clouded.

"If you will excuse me for a moment?"

"Of course."

The professor rose and walked out to the hallway, closing the door behind him. They followed his progress until they were alone.

Larry spoke first. "Syd, you believe this guy?"

"I trust him Larry. He's one of the world's leading experts on virology. He has no reason to lie to us."

"What are you thinking, Jack?" Murphy asked.

"At first I thought it had to be a weapon. But he says there's no way to control it. How do you steer something like this? It will go after everyone. Unless you've already vaccinated all of your own soldiers and civilians first, it will turn on whoever releases it. Then what about your allies and third party countries? It's too …indiscriminant …to be a weapon. I just don't understand the purpose."

They all stared at the two vials in the middle of the table. The professor had sterilized them and brought them back with him on the chance that the FBI needed them to help determine the source. As they had listened to him for the last few hours the vials had kept drawing their gaze. They now looked at them with a new respect. Sydney couldn't believe what she and Jack had been casually carrying around in their pockets all that time.

"So how do we figure that part out?"

"I'm hoping our friend Heather can shed some light on that. She's due here in about an hour. I have some pointed questions for her."

He was interrupted by the professor reentering the room. His face was pale and he slowly sat down as if he had lost the strength to stand.

Sydney rose and went to him. "Dr. Miles, what is it?"

He spoke to the glass of water in front of him.

"Thelma and Louise."

"Who?"

"My control monkeys. That was Lynda on the phone, my assistant. She says they've crashed."

"What do you mean?"

"The virus …it's airborne."

＊　　　　＊　　　　＊

"I don't recall asking you to bring anyone with you, Ms. Sachs. Who might this gentleman be that you insist on being here with you?"

Heather glanced at her companion, but said nothing. They had arrived at the Hoover Building that afternoon together and been stopped at the desk. Security people called Jack after being informed that she re-fused to see him without her unknown companion. He had reluctantly allowed it. They took seats at the table and met the looks of the people across from them.

"He's not my lawyer, he's my boss."

Jack merely waited. The man finally spoke.

"Mr. Randall, if you would ask these people to leave for a few mo-ments, I think I can provide some answers to your questions."

Jack played with his pen for a moment as he contemplated the offer. Heather obviously deferred to the man. Jack had no charges against her and no reason to hold her. He couldn't force her to talk. But obviously they were close to something, something this man had information on. He decided to hear him out.

He nodded to his people and then watched as they filed out of the room. To his surprise, Heather rose and followed. Soon they were alone in the room.

"Mr. Randall, my name is John Kimball. I've been sent to arrange a meeting for you."

*   *   *

Jack and Sydney sat on the cold steps and stared at the star filled sky. They had been there for over an hour and their butts were beginning to get cold. She pulled her coat a little tighter and drew her knees up to her chin.

"Why am I here, Jack?"

"I need you with me. I need a witness and you're the only one I have that they can't touch."

"I don't follow."

"If we're meeting who I think we are then most people will be intimi-dated by his power. I need a witness who will do what's right, regardless of who it is telling them how things are or how they should be."

She smiled. "And that's me?"

He looked at her and returned her smile. "That's you."

"So who are we going to meet?"

"You'll see."

"Are we going to arrest him?"

"I don't know."

"Why are we going if we aren't going to arrest him?"

"I believe we'll get an explanation."

"That's it?"

"That's it."

Jack offered nothing more so she let her questions die as she waited. A glance behind her was met by the stern look of Abe Lincoln sitting in his chair. He offered no assistance. She felt Jack tense as a car approached.

Kimball pulled up to the curb and saw Jack sitting on the steps. The two of them stood and approached the car. He thumbed the button and the tinted glass slide down.

"We agreed it would just be you. Why is she here?"

"You showed up uninvited. She goes, too, or there's no deal."

Kimball examined his face in the light of the streetlamps. He saw no room for negotiation.

"All right, get in."

They entered the back seat and the car swiftly pulled away from the curb and turned left to drive down the mall toward the Capitol Building. They traveled in silence through the rain-wet streets, virtually devoid of any traffic at this early morning hour. The Washington Monument glowed in its spotlights and the bronze soldiers of the World War Two memorial could be seen as they forever patrolled the mall. As they neared the Capitol Building, Jack couldn't help but recall that night a few months ago chasing his friend through the DC subway after he had shot the senator. He drove the thought from his mind. He had other things to think about.

He felt Sydney's hand creep into his and give a squeeze. He turned to see a look of concern on her face as she watched him. He gave a squeeze back. The car committed a series of turns before they found themselves going back down the mall past the White House. They turned right and stopped in front of the Old Executive Office Building.

"That man on the curb will lead us. Don't say anything to him or anybody we may run into."

They all exited the car and gathered on the curb. The man approached slowly and nodded to Kimball. He then turned and silently led them into the building.

It appeared to be a service entrance and they immediately entered a stairwell, descending several flights before stopping at the bottom and entering a room. Here the man reached into a closet and pulled out a wand. With a gesture they all assumed the position and were thoroughly checked with both the wand and a careful pat down. Kimball included. When satisfied they were clean the man simply opened the door and led them away. After a series of twists and turns, where they saw no other people, they came to a door with a large man standing in front. He and the escort exchanged a look before the escort spun on his heel and silently left.

The large man simply stood until Kimball spoke.

"Assignation."

The door was opened and they were allowed to enter. The room was strangely silent. As if all sound were sucked into it and swallowed. They made no noise as they traveled down the short entryway and turned the corner.

The man sat alone at a large table. He was dressed casually in a pair of jeans and a sweater. A glass of water sat on the table in front of him and nothing else. He rose slowly to greet them.

"Good evening, gentleman, and to you young lady."

Sydney gaped at the man until a nudge from Jack shook her out of it.

"Good evening, Mr. President."

WHO ALERTS COUNTRIES TO WATCH
SUSPICIOUS FLU CASES.
April 25, 2009—USA Today

—TWENTY-FOUR—

"MR. RANDALL, I'M AFRAID I don't know this young lady with you."

"Forgive me, sir, this is Sydney Lewis of the FBI. She's one of my people."

"Moral support, Mr. Randall?"

"Something like that, Mr. President."

"We may all need it after tonight, please sit."

They all took seats at the table. The President sat heavily in his chair and rubbed his face and hair before gazing across the table at the three of them.

"You've had an interesting past few weeks, Mr. Randall. An embassy bombing, a raid on a terrorist camp, a shoot-out in the Delaware countryside…"

"Yes, sir."

"But that's not what you're here about today at this ungodly hour, is it?"

"No."

"You have some questions?"

"Yes, sir."

"Then please ask."

"Sir, in the course of our investigating the embassy bombing, we've discovered a quantity of medications that have proven to be what we believe is a biological weapon of some kind. This is in violation of numerous treaties as well as being highly controversial. Several people have died, and there have been numerous breaches of security at my agency as well as my home. We have reason to believe this is being carried out with the backing of a government agency of some type. To make a long story short, we came here tonight to discuss this with you before we go to the press and the proper authorities."

The President nodded before replying, "Do you intend to go to the press?"

"We haven't yet made that decision."

"I really have no problem with you going to the authorities as you say, that has been handled already." He gave a nod in Kimball's direction. Jack looked at him for his reaction but the man was stone faced. "But the press could be a nuisance."

The President rose from his chair while motioning them all to remain seated. "If you don't mind, I was a teacher once and I just find it more comfortable to stand while giving a lecture.

"You stumbled onto something quite big, Mr. Randall, and you might be surprised to know that I've learned a great deal more about your actions these last few weeks than you would think. You and Miss Lewis here have really done yourselves a job. I wish I could commend you. But if you'll allow me a few minutes, I think you'll understand why I cannot.

"This all started well before my time, before yours to be sure. In the late '60s the United States was still fighting the Cold War. The nuclear arms race was still in full swing. Vietnam was happening. The space race was progressing. But there was another cold war being fought, one the public had little knowledge of and never really understood. It was a biological war, and it was fought in secret by both parties. It went on for several years. The US had several labs throughout the country working on all manner of bacterial and viral concoctions. As did the Soviets. They were actually ahead of us for some time."

"No one knew of this?" Jack asked.

"It's a lot easier to hide a lab with a few bioreactors than it is to hide an intercontinental ballistic missile. We kept everything very close to our chest. Just not close enough. The spy game was going full tilt. Leaks on both sides were rampant and the other country's advances were well known. Fear was tantamount. People could wrap their minds around the idea of nuclear war, no matter how horrific. But compared to a deadly virus eating its way through the population, it was beyond the minds of all involved. Both sides had arsenals large enough to end the human race several times over. Vats of smallpox as large as this room, plague, Ebola, Marburg and anthrax, to name just a few. We also had the means to deliver it. Everything from aerosolizers that would fit in your pocket, to ICBM's capable of air bursting the virus over an entire city. Submarine-launched missiles, bombers. The list went on and on."

"But didn't President Nixon sign a treaty?"

"Correct, in 1969 Nixon ordered the total dismantlement of the US biological warfare program. Up until then, seven hundred million dollars had been spent developing agents. About this time several of the scientists involved began to question what they were doing. One of which was your friend Doctor Miles. They called it a perversion of science, and I tend to agree with them. Unfortunately, the threat still remained and the advances being made in vaccine technology were the direct result of the offensive side of the research. The program had to continue, treaty or not. Our intelligence at the time revealed a massive program being run by the Soviets. Over fifty labs and 65,000 researchers all working in closed cities on nothing but germ warfare."

"But Nixon went public with the treaty. Why?"

"The historians never asked did they? They simply assumed it was from a desire to formulate a relationship with the USSR, perhaps from the belief that bio-weapons were both unreliable as offensive weapons and difficult to stockpile safely. There was also the fear that Third World countries would be encouraged to start their own weapons programs, setting off an arms race among them. Why would the United States, the most powerful country on the face of the earth, with its massive arsenal of technically superior nuclear weapons, make the possession of weapons of mass destruction cheap and easy for other nations? No, we wanted the arms race to be on our terms. We made it official in 1972 with the Convention on the Prohibition of the Development, Production and Stockpiling of Bacteriological and Toxin Weapons, more conveniently known as the Biological Weapons Convention. Everyone thought Nixon was a fool, that the Soviets would never adhere to the treaty."

"They didn't," Jack stated.

"Not to the treaty, no, but they did adhere to another."

"I don't understand."

"Nixon was no fool. He knew that such a program was too easy to hide. Luckily there were cooler heads behind the public blustering of the leaders at the time. Both countries agreed to continue research in secret. He made a deal like no other. Delivery devices were scrapped. Large quantities of agent were eliminated, but the research went on, with both sides sharing the results."

"What? Why would they agree to that?" Sydney blurted out.

"The Cold War forced men in my position to look far down the road into the future. A new threat was beginning to show, and it was one that could not be defeated or deterred by nuclear weapons. But I'll get to that in a moment."

"This was now the late '70s and early '80s. The Soviet Union was still the Soviet Union and being what it was, it suffered a long list of defectors. These defectors leaked stories of the country's bio-weapons program thinking them great bargaining chips to smooth the way for them into the United States. They were simple researchers and had no idea of Nixon's plan, which now had been inherited twice by succeeding presidents. The defectors were quieted as best they could be, or discredited if the need presented. An accidental release of anthrax from one of their research cities killed a number of people and also made things difficult for awhile. But mostly the agreement held and the process continued, as it does to this day."

"You mentioned another threat, sir?"

"Yes, one that has gotten closer and closer over the years until today it's known to everyone on the planet. A threat of our own making."

"In the '60s India, Pakistan, and several other countries around the world experienced great food shortages. This, combined with the post World War II jump in population, gave us our first hint at what the future held. Fortunately Norman Borlaug came along with his invention of dwarf wheat and these countries could increase their wheat production and feed the exploding population. But we had already seen the edge, and we knew there wouldn't always be a Norman Borlaug to save us."

"Mankind is capable of many things. Unfortunately many of these things are also to our own detriment. The world population stands today at just under seven billion people. Economic growth is the highest it's ever been, exceeding predictions made decades ago. Resources are being used at an alarming rate. The very basics such as food and fresh water are once again becoming scarce. Food production is nearing its peak output. The world's fish stocks are dwindling each year. They tell me 90% of the edible fish stocks will be gone by 2048. China has been the only country thus far to make any attempt to control population growth. Their one-child-per-family law was seen by the world as barbaric and criminal. Yet the population of China increases every year by millions. The developing world screams for energy and we pump oil at a record pace. Climatologists tell me we can't burn much more of the oil available without increasing the global temperature greatly. Some say peak oil is already here. The ice caps are melting. If the Greenland icepack slides into the north Atlantic we'll see a stop of the Gulf Stream current. This will bring an ice age to Europe, making its climate on par with that of Siberia. The ocean will rise and flood most coastal areas. Low-lying countries such as Bangladesh will cease to exist. Deforestation continues despite efforts to confront it. It all comes back to population."

"The headlines have been screaming this for years, but the world keeps on going as if nothing is happening. My predecessors saw all this coming, and they have taken steps to slow it and if need be …to fix it."

"Slow it, sir? How exactly?"

The President returned to his seat and took a sip of the water in front of him before lifting his head to meet their eyes.

"How would you slow the population growth, Mr. Randall? Or you, Ms. Lewis? Short of starting a nuclear war or all-out genocide they had only one choice."

"Disease," Sydney whispered.

"Exactly. Efforts were made to find a virus that would cause infertility, but it has proven to be beyond our grasp. The alternative, while distasteful as it may be, is the introduction of disease."

"This has been done?"

"Yes, several times in the past four decades."

"My God."

"God *has* tried. But our scientists keep defeating him. It seems to be up to us now. In nature there is a natural check and balance process. When a population grows too large for its environment the inhabitants become crowded together. This becomes a natural breeding environment for viruses and they soon mutate into a deadly form and thin the population to a more sustainable level. It has happened throughout documented history. Modern medicine defeats this process. Our population has gone unchecked by disease for some time. There are still some diseases out there. The flu takes an average of 30,000 people a year here in the United States alone. Malaria outbreaks do the same in Africa and South America. Every corner of the globe has its viruses that do their damnedest to thin the population. But medicine has proven stronger. We vaccinate every year for the flu. We wiped smallpox from the face of the earth. Defeated polio. Yellow fever was conquered to build the Panama Canal. Yet we never once thought that we *needed* these diseases for the balance they provide. Not once. There hasn't been a deadly world pandemic since the

1918 Spanish Flu, and, as a result, the population has exploded. So the decision was made to force the issue. In the late '70s HIV was introduced into the world. It was thought that it would start what's called a slow burn over the globe and hopefully stem growth for a few decades before being defeated. While its success was not what was predicted, it served to teach us many things. Since then others have been tried. SARS, bird flu, West Nile, to name a few. The current swine flu is a test of the world's response to a pandemic. It has shown a predictable outcome. It won't be enough to stop the spread, but the virus lacks the strength to cause much change.

"Since its conception, the program has grown. It's overseen by a committee of five people, all of whom represent the major population centers of this earth. I inherited my position from my predecessor. Mr. Kimball here heads our research and production facility here in North America as well as taking care of ...operational issues."

"God's little soldier."

The President's head snapped up at the remark. Jack met his glare with his own.

"I do *not* consider myself God, Mr. Randall! I did not choose this task for myself. Every day I look for an alternative, but four decades of looking by myself and many others has failed to come up with one, so before you go showing me your superior moral character, let's hear your solution!"

The President sat back and relaxed his hands that had become fists during his statement. His glare however did not falter.

"I have done everything I can to avoid further introductions. You have no idea."

Jack sat in silence, not quite believing what he'd just been told. The enormity of it was beyond his thought process. What the professor had told them was not only true, it had been planned for decades.

"AIDS is horrible. How could you do such a thing?" Sydney asked.

The President's glare softened as he looked at her face. He took on a more fatherly tone with his reply.

"It was not my decision, and knowing what we know now, I don't feel it was the right one. The virus works too slowly and causes too much suffering. I would have voted against its introduction. I'm told a vaccine is almost ready for trial, the era of AIDS will soon be over."

"You said you were avoiding future introductions. Just what does that mean, sir?" Jack asked.

"Technology. While we have no choice but to pursue the program, we also are constantly looking for ways to avoid it. The new surge in environmentalism will help, but most experts agree it will be too little too late. The main things are energy, water and food. Our best bet for energy is coming out of the space program. The development of the space elevator will change everything. Advances in new carbon nanotube cable technology will enable us to create such a device. The rest of the required engineering already exists. With such an item in use we can finally place heavy payloads into space for a small fraction of the cost of current rocket or shuttle technology. It will enable us to place vast solar power stations in space with the ability to beam an endless supply of clean energy to earth. This would virtually end the need to burn fossil fuels. A permanent station on the moon would be the next step. It would also make it possible to manufacture and ship enormous quantities of fluorocarbons to Mars. Our scientist tell us it may be possible to warm the red planet enough to melt its icecaps, releasing the stored oxygen there and producing an atmosphere much like that of earth. Perhaps even by the end of this century. Humanity would have a whole other world to expand to.

"Water is another problem that may be solved with a few more advances. High volume desalination plants may produce enough fresh water to turn many of the world's desert climates to suitable farmland. Right now the American plains are the breadbasket of the United States as well as several other nations. We produce enough food for ourselves many times over. With global warming, much of northern Canada will become a major agricultural producing area. But with the projected growth in population it will not be enough. The desert areas of Mexico, the United States, Africa, and Australia will need to be harnessed for more production. This can only be done with high volume desalination and unlimited clean energy to pump it wherever it is needed. If enough is supplied there may be no more need for the damming of our rivers and streams other than flood control. The natural flow will return the environment to a more suitable balance.

"If these few advances can be made, there may be no need to activate the program. But the program must be in place if the time comes that it's needed."

"And when is that determined?"

"We constantly monitor global temperature, atmospheric carbon levels and icecap degeneration. Grain production and fish catch levels. If … certain parameters are exceeded …the program will be implemented."

"Who made this decision?"

"The committee."

"And who do they answer to, sir?"

The President just shook his head.

"No one, the committee decides all! That's it, isn't it?"

The President locked Jack in his powerful stare. He was a man used to the mantle of power and he was not about to accept Jack's accusation.

"*I* have no intention of apologizing to you, Mr. Randall. *I* did not make these decisions, *I* did not make these problems the world is facing, *I* did not ask for this task. I did, however, inherit it when I took office and I have done what I feel *has to be done* to safeguard this planet! This is not some theoretical exercise! This is science, and the numbers *do not lie!* The alternatives are global famine and all out war over the earth's resources. Something I am not willing to accept!"

The room fell silent after the outburst and Jack sank into his chair. It lasted for a full minute before Sydney summoned the courage to speak.

"How does the virus work?"

The President had spoken enough. He rose and gestured to Kimball before picking up his glass of water and turning his back on the room to pace. Kimball cleared his throat loudly before speaking.

"It's a binary virus, a two-part cocktail. Efforts to find one virus always failed to produce a viable strain. So our people developed a new way of delivery. Part one is introduced through a vaccine program. We were able to dig up some corpses in the permafrost of an Alaskan village that was wiped out by the Spanish Flu virus. From this we were able to culture the strain and genetically modify it, making it more virulent and deadly. We then found a way to split the virus and encase it in proteins that would test as benign. Part one would sit dormant in anyone vaccinated, waiting for part two."

"The virus has to appear as naturally occurring. We were able to attach the second half to the Newcastle virus, a virus that would affect birds only. The birds would not even appear sick to the untrained person. By using migratory birds the virus would spread naturally over the earth with no way to stop it. As it is transmitted though the air, it would infect anyone who came in contact with a host bird. The ducks and geese people feed in the pond at the park. Seagulls at the beach. Pigeons. Any of these are viable carriers. Once introduced, the virus would combine and become infective. There would be no way to trace the source. Once infected, the person would be able to transmit the virus, as easily as the flu, to other people. It is engineered to allow mutation while also proving to be quickly lethal. A person would be sick for a minimum amount of time before expiring, and the virus would eventually mutate and burn out. It would all be over in six to ten months."

"And you have this all in place?" she asked.

"The vials as you found them are in place in various places around the world. A dispersal device has just been tested to deliver the virus to the birds. We have started phase one trials in the natural setting with an inert test virus. The program could be started with one or two birds now, or with the new devices, a whole flock at a time at several places around the...."

"Stop!" Jack spoke.

The President spun to face Jack.

"Why are you telling us that? The rest I can understand, but we don't need to know that, unless we aren't going to make it out of this building."

The President shared a look with Kimball before answering. "I have no intention of harming you or Ms. Lewis here. This meeting, I'm afraid, has several purposes."

Kimball reached inside his coat and Jack tensed. When he withdrew his hand it held nothing but an envelope. He slid the paper across the table to Jack. The President nursed his drink and watched silently.

"I received this letter yesterday, about the time of your summons of Ms. Sachs. It's postmarked Sao Paolo, Brazil and dated two days ago. The man who wrote it was one of our delivery people. The same one who initiated the ambush for the agent in Africa, if that helps. He is quite capable, but I'm afraid he has ...lost his way."

Jack opened the letter and read it slowly twice. He then folded it and handed it to Sydney who did likewise. The horror was evident on her face.

"He doesn't know what he really has. We keep the program as compartmented as possible. But like I said, he's capable. He may have figured it out."

"So pay him," Jack said.

"It may come to that, but unfortunately that may not be enough."

"He has to be eliminated?"

Kimball offered no answer.

"Yes," the President spoke.

"So that's why we're still alive? You need me to find this guy?"

"You think this is easy, Mr. Randall? You're assuming Mr. Kimball and I are safe from the virus, aren't you. You couldn't be more wrong. *Nobody* is safe. We don't get a pass. No one does. There's no vaccine, although this man thinks he was given one. We're all subject to the program, every last one of us. But while there is still hope that the program will not be needed, we must do everything in our power to safeguard the agent. If this man should release it, we will all be at its mercy. He must be found, and found quickly."

.

—TWENTY-FIVE—

THE DELIVERYMAN PULLED THE pickup slowly down the dirt
road, taking the time to carefully navigate around large potholes full of
standing green water. The trees closed tighter around the pickup as he
pushed ahead, the sun increasingly blocked out by the massive trees and
hanging moss. An opening in the trees revealed a canal off to his right
and he caught sight of the broad back of a Florida gator moving in the
opposite direction.

He rounded a blind corner and was soon met by a large dog sunning
himself in the middle of the road. The dog twitched and jumped to its
feet, sounding the alarm for all within earshot. He was soon joined by
two others and the trio now paced the truck as he maneuvered around
another bend.

The house suddenly appeared out of the surrounding vegetation
and he slowed to a stop in front of it. Knowing his friend like he did, he
sounded the horn twice before stepping out of the cab. The dogs circled

him warily, but to his relief made no hostile moves. He watched them as best he could while scanning the area around the house.

It looked like it was right out of a movie. A small dilapidated shack stuck out in the middle of the Everglades swamp. It had the usual packed dirt driveway and open-sided barn accompanying it. He spotted an air-boat parked in the barn along with an old pickup truck. Several machines in various stages of disassembly shared the small space. The ocean breeze somehow made it through the trees to tug at the loose metal roof, producing a rhythmic beat.

He was considering honking the horn again when a voice spoke from close behind him. He flinched.

"My sister ain't here."

He raised his hands and turned slowly to face the voice and was met by a large man dressed in canvas shorts and a large vest full of pockets. A well worn hat sat on his head shielding his eyes from the Florida sun. He was wet from the waist down, but the shotgun aimed at his head was bone dry. He hadn't made a sound, seeming to step right out of the swamp.

"That's too bad. That means I'll have to settle for you."

The man tried hard to maintain his mean stare but it soon failed, replaced by a wide grin, minus one tooth.

"Maybe, but you'll be real tired when we're done! How the hell are ya?"

"I'm good, you swamp rat. Could ya aim that thing somewhere else?"

"My safety still works!" He moved the barrel until it aimed at the sky and held up his trigger finger. He flexed it twice as proof before rounding the truck and grabbing his friend in a bear hug.

"About damn time you stopped by. I was beginning to think somebody put a hole out your back or some woman had tamed ya. Where the hell ya been?"

"You know me. Everywhere."

"Well come on in and let's have a beer."

The Deliveryman watched as Toby turned and hobbled toward the house. While the pace would equal that of an average man, the movement of the leg was out of rhythm and painful to watch, the massive scar and the large amount of missing muscle evident on the exposed leg. He remembered the day it had happened, on a bloody road in the desert not far from Eden. If not for him, his friend would have died that day, but there was no debt owed by either of them. They had long ago lost count of who was ahead on that scoreboard. He followed until they were in the small home. He found a chair while his friend fetched four cold ones, just like they had always done. The first two always went quickly.

"So what brings you out to my seaside resort?" He flopped on the couch and was promptly joined by one of the dogs. He scratched its head while he drained half of the first beer.

"Just passing through, I'm afraid. I got some things I have to take care of, and then I'll be on my way out of the country again …maybe for good."

"For good? What, you gonna retire now, is that it?"

He hesitated before he replied and Toby took a long pull on his beer as he watched his friend's face.

"I think I'm done. I've had enough and I got an opportunity to leave with a nice pile."

"*They* say that? Or you got something else going?"

"Something else."

Toby thought that over as he finished the first beer and picked up the second. He asked the obvious question first. "Sure you want to cross Uncle Sam like that?"

"After seeing how well they took care of you? It wasn't a hard decision."

"You know better than that. It was our decision to go, nobody forced us."

"Come on, Toby, you gave them a leg for fuck's sake, and what do they give you in return; a shiny piece of tin and a thanks-a-lot-there's-the-door! Good thing your dad left you this place or you'd be out on the street!"

"I get a check every month and the VA takes care of the leg. I'm doing fine."

"Yea well, it's not like I have a lot of civilian world job skills. I'm aiming a little higher."

"Do I want to know what you got planned? You need some help?"

The Deliveryman calmed down. He looked at his friend and smiled. He had to admire Toby. Here he was, with his blown-up leg, deaf in one ear, bad concussion, seizure medication and chronic pain, yet he was always in good spirits. Never complained about the hand he had been dealt, and ready to help his friend even though he had no idea what was involved. He wished he could be more like him.

But he wasn't. He had already set the game in motion and he would have to see it through till the end. But he couldn't get his friend involved. He had already done enough.

"No, this is a one-man show. Could use some of those things I stashed here with you, though."

"They haven't moved." Toby performed the pull and twist motion he used to get himself to his feet. He stopped in the kitchen for two more bottles before leading his friend out to the barn. Chickens scattered as he strode past the pickup and set his beer on the hood. A large freezer sat in the corner with engine parts and other bits of scrap piled on the hood. All of it coated with a thick layer of dust. They worked together and the chest was soon open. Toby removed package after package of "steaks," as he called them, from the freezer, piling them on the truck's hood. The Deliveryman saw that most of them were shaped like a gator's tail, but he said nothing. The freezer soon appeared to be empty until Toby reached down and tugged on a string lying in one corner. The false bottom popped free after a couple of good tugs and a pair of duffle bags could be seen sitting on the bottom. Toby drew back and let his friend remove the bags. He lugged them to the bed of the truck while Toby replaced the steaks.

Unzipping the bags, he examined the contents. While he had worried when he first saw the layer of dust on top of the freezer, his doubts were soon gone as Toby had obviously taken good care of the items. There was no rust showing on anything and the tape on the boxes was still secure. He could trust Toby not to open anything he had sealed and he obviously hadn't.

He fell into a practiced routine as he stripped, checked and reassembled the items one by one. He made mental notes of things he would need and separated the items he could leave behind. Toby watched him patiently, nursing his beer while his friend's went ignored and warmed in the sun. After twenty minutes the task was complete.

"You need anything else?"

The Deliveryman smiled. "No, I think this will be enough. I can get the rest of what I need on the road. I have something I want you to hold on to for me."

"Could've mentioned that before I put all them steaks back in the freezer."

"No, this stuff can't be frozen. It needs to stay someplace where nobody will bother it, somewhere out of the sun."

"How big?"

The Deliveryman reached into the cab of the truck and pulled out his backpack. From inside he took out a small bag and a cigar box. The bag clinked when he moved it, the box did not. He handed them to his friend.

"The bag is the stuff. It's kind of dangerous. Don't let any visitors see it or handle it. It has to stay out of the sun, too."

Toby held up the bag and gave it a look. "Can I see it?"

"Go ahead."

Toby looked into the bag before reaching in and removing a vial. He held it up to examine closer.

"What is it? Drugs? You know I don't do anything with that shit."

"No. Nothing like that. You really don't want to know. Just hold on to it. If I don't come back it could be worth a lot of money someday."

"All right." Toby shrugged. "What about the box?"

"It's for you, buddy."

Toby gave his friend a look before he peeled the tape off the lid and opened the box. Inside he found four bundles of crisp $100 bills. He started shaking his head right away.

"Don't even think of saying no. The people I got it from won't be missing it and I don't have anybody else to give it to. Just be a friend and take it, buy a new boat or something, or just give it away. It's up to you."

"I don't need it!"

"Toby, come on. That truck ain't gonna last forever. What if the next hurricane knocks the house down? Just save it till you need it."

Toby grumbled under his breath, but he could see his friend was serious. If he refused it he'd probably just find it in the mailbox tomorrow or under the seat of his truck. He closed the lid and taking off his hat, smacked his friend with it.

"Damn you."

"Hey, at least you could buy some more beer with it. I'll even help you drink it."

"There's an idea. Let's put this shit away and grab a few bottles and take out the boat. The gators'll be stirring and I've got some room in the freezer now."

"Deal." He followed Toby back to the house, a beer in one hand and his new gifts in the other.

SWINE FLU EPIDEMIC: ONE IN THREE FATAL VICTIMS
HAD NO SERIOUS UNDERLYING HEALTH PROBLEMS.
July 23, 2009—Daily Mail

-TWENTY-SIX-

JACK SCANNED THE CROWD. There were more government agencies represented in the room than he had thought possible. There were people from the US Marshall's office, the Department of Homeland Security, the DEA, the FBI, the CIA, Defense Intelligence and a slew of others. Today they all had one common goal: the largest domestic manhunt in history.

That morning he had made another trip up Pennsylvania Avenue, this time to the West Wing of the White House. Unlike his meeting just a few hours prior, there was no hiding from the press this time, and he made sure he was seen both entering and leaving the building. In the hours that followed, the phones had rung in every intelligence and law enforcement agency of the United States. Presidential orders went out and agency heads scrambled to comply. In a short time Jack had information flowing to his desk. A search of available people had been conducted and individuals screened and now a team had been assembled. None of which had any history or past working relationship with the target. It was going to take a bit of interservice cooperation to get the job done. Something the services represented here were not really known for. Jack would have to play diplomat to get the job done. For that he would have a little help from the man waiting in the room next door.

He walked to the front of the room but the conversations failed to stop. Jack was not known to all of them. He looked to the door on the right of the room where Sydney waited. He gave her a nod and she opened it. A man emerged and walked to the front of the room to stand next to Jack. The conversations all quickly died.

Glen Hendrix was only five foot six in height, yet he carried a presence few men could aspire to. An impeccable dresser, today was no different, and he stood next to the podium in a tailored English suit that equaled what most people in the room made in a month. But none of them would fault him for it. The man had made his own money. Born poor in the Bronx of New York, he made it to Harvard, become a captain of industry, head of the labor department, and now White House Chief of Staff. His presence here today spoke volumes. Glen Hendrix did not come see you, you went to see him. When he spoke there was no doubt that he had the total backing of the President and carried the full weight and power of the White House.

He looked down at the file he carried with him, purposely forcing the room to wait in silence. When he did finally look up it was with a look of contempt, as if he had much better things to do then be here addressing them. The room braced for what was coming.

"First of all, thank you all for coming on such short notice. You may have noticed that there are quite a few different agencies represented here and the reasons for that will become clear in few minutes. All I can say is that we have a credible threat like we have never had. This is not a drill. The President has authorized this mission as the result of a direct threat to the United States as well as the rest of the world.

"However, the threat will, at this time, remain classified. This is to prevent widespread panic. This decision was made by the President just a few hours ago in consultation with expert council, including the Secretary of Defense and the National Security Advisor. You people have all been carefully selected to meet this threat. I've been told that any leaks will result in immediate termination and/or bad conduct discharge. Charges will be filed. This is no joke, people, there will be no resignations. The President's own words.

"There will also be no interservice rivalry. If anyone is caught withholding information or not sharing any and all intelligence, the same rules apply." He turned and pointed directly at Jack who was standing off to his left. "This is the man in charge. Period. What he says goes, as of now he outranks *all* of you. If that's a problem, leave now." When nobody stirred, he moved on. "If it sounds like I'm being tough, it's because we have no time for the usual party games on this one. One way or the other, this will all be over in a few days. We need the best you have, of yourselves and of your agencies. You have my full support and faith as well as that of the President. While this has the potential to be a dark day, I believe it could also be our finest. So ...that's all I have. Do a job."

He retrieved his file from the podium and silently left the room. All eyes followed him until the door shut behind him. They then focused on Jack.

Jack got a reassuring nod from Sydney as he took the Chief of Staffs place at the podium. He cleared his throat and looked out over the room. The faces he met were all experienced people, most of them older and much more accomplished than he. Yet he was the one in charge. He regretted that his first words to them would be a lie, but they really had no choice at this point.

"Good afternoon. For those of you that don't know me, my name is Jack Randall and I am with the FBI. I recently headed the investigation into the embassy bombing in Tanzania and the follow-up raid and capture of Mohammed Al-Nasser. In the intelligence gathered on that raid we uncovered a threat to the United States. The threat is from a biological weapon. This weapon was developed, we believe, in the former Soviet Union, and either sold to or stolen by the terrorist group. It is a strain of the influenza virus. If the intelligence is correct, the virus has the potential to infect up to 300 million people and kill at least a third of those infected."

A rumble went through the crowd and Jack silenced it with a wave of his hand. The lights dimmed and a picture of a man was projected on the wall in back of him. The picture changed from the head-on face shot to a few other candid photos and returned. Jack continued while the images rotated on the screen.

"This man is our target. His name is Steven Cascabel, but he has several aliases. He's an American, formally with US Army Special Operations. Discharged after the first Gulf war, he is believed to have become a hired gun working mostly in Africa and the Middle East. We believe he has loose ties to some terrorism networks, but mostly works as a supplier of weapons and intelligence. We have no reason to believe he's a member of any organization at this time. It seems to be purely a money making venture for him, which brings us to our problem."

"Two days ago my office received a letter from Mr. Cascabel. He sent pictures of a vial we believe to be the agent I described. We've been able to confirm that this vial is missing from secured stockpiles and contains the agent. The letter was postmarked Sao Paolo, Brazil. We've gone over video and records of every flight from Brazil to the States over the last few days and we can confirm that he arrived in Miami two days ago. His location is unknown at this time."

"I don't understand, sir? If he's already in the country aren't we too late?" a woman from the DEA spoke up.

"Fortunately, his goal is not to release the virus. He only wants one thing. Money."

"So let's just pay him off and then hunt him down. Isn't that the safest choice?"

"We have reasons to believe that the subject doesn't really know the virus's capabilities. If for some reason he became exposed or allowed the virus to be exposed to the environment there would be no stopping it. He would become a carrier and anyone exposed to him would become ill and pass the virus on, resulting in a worldwide pandemic. We also must locate him as soon as possible to prevent him from dividing the virus into several locations. He's believed to have a total of forty vials, enough to carry on his person easily. We have to account for every vial and do it fast.

"You will all be receiving a file on this man containing everything that's been gathered so far. I want to meet with the heads of all departments after this meeting. I need everyone to mine their databases for any information on him. Contact information is included. Let's get the information flowing. I don't like saying this, people, but Mr. Hendrix was not lying. When this is over it will be gone over with a magnifying glass. Just keep that in mind and do a job we can all be proud of. That's it."

*　　　*　　　*

The Deliveryman smiled when he saw the boat. After stopping to pick up some supplies he had followed the directions Toby had supplied him and found the home with ease. A large Mediterranean-style three-story vacation home owned by a successful businessman from Connecticut, it sat in a secluded area separated by thick Florida vegetation from the prying eyes of the neighbors. Toby worked as a boat maintenance tech and had serviced the man's boat many times. When he had described what kind of boat he needed, Toby had immediately thought of the house. He pulled the pickup into the driveway and exited the cab. He looked left and right as he walked casually to the house and punched in the security code. The garage door opened and he pulled the truck in and out of sight. As it was spring, the man and his family were back home up north and would not reappear until October. A quick walk through the home confirmed this and he focused his gaze out the large windows. Looking out through the lanai and over the pool he saw the boat moored off to one side, only partially blocking off the view of the bay. It was perfect. He moved to the kitchen were he found the keys hanging on the wall just where Toby had said they would be. The owner obviously put a lot of faith in his security system. He checked his watch and looked at the angle of the sun. It was late enough in the day for him to get started, he thought.

He didn't want to come early and chance running into the pool man or a yard maintenance crew. He dropped his duffle bags and backpack by the door and moved slowly down the walk to the boat, checking for nosy neighbors as he went. He was pleased to see the man had landscaped to prevent this.

After spending a few minutes removing canvas covers from the windows, he stored everything below and did a quick evaluation. The owner was obviously a no-nonsense captain, an ex-navy man Toby had said, and the boat was decked out with the finest gear that money could buy.

His seaman's eye took in the boat and he cataloged the information he would need once he was underway. The boat was forty-one feet of white fiberglass with twin diesel engines, the owner preferring two strong engines as opposed to smaller straining ones. The flying bridge was fully equipped to handle rough weather and the safety equipment was new and plentiful. Despite its length, the boat only drew four and a half feet of water, which would enable him to enter most marinas. He stored his duffels below before returning to the house and scouring it for needed items. He assembled a box of food and filed a large cooler with ice. The man of the house was not his size in the pants department, but he found a few comfortable fishing shirts and some warmer clothes he would need later. A few CDs from the collection by the fireplace were added, as well as a bottle of Johnny Walker Blue that was just too good to pass up.

The sun was going down as he stored the final items aboard. He slipped the extra lines the owner had placed in the event of a hurricane, freeing the boat of all but two. Once the sun had disappeared he flipped on the bilge blowers, letting them blow for two minutes before he started the starboard-side engine. It rumbled to life and he checked the gauges before starting the port engine. Since the sound traveled well across the water he quickly slipped the remaining mooring lines and returned to the bridge to advance the throttles forward. He checked the tide and weather as he eased out into the bay, using the engines to steer as opposed to the wheel. After picking up a steady five knots he relaxed and fired up the GPS. As it synced with the satellite network, he pulled out the chart he had worked up that morning. He punched in the grease-penciled numbers he had written on the chart and smiled as the GPS digested the information and laid out the plot on the screen. He checked his position against a nearby marker and nodded approval as it confirmed that the GPS was correct. The radar came on next and was also thoroughly checked and determined to be functioning well. These two items would determine how much sleep he got over the next couple of days and he was relieved to see they were both functioning.

He was soon cruising past the channel markers and out of the manatee protection zone. He advanced the throttles more and the boat accelerated nicely, the trim tabs keeping her on a level plane. A cruise ship was departing the city and he soon caught up to its wake. The boat pitched up and down and he expertly maneuvered the boat to avoid the worst of it.

Once past the cruise ship he found the ocean to be agreeably flat and was able to keep the boat at an even sixteen knots. Altering his course north, he worked his way out into the Gulf Stream. He could have stuck to the intercoastal waterway, but it was much too slow and he was more likely to be spotted. Preferring to stay out in the blue water, avoid the shipping channels and the Coast Guard, and cutting across the curve of the east coast was the better plan. He should be in DC soon, as long as the weather held. He went below and stocked up on snacks and caffeine as the plan called for going straight through the night.

With the auto-helm engaged he settled in and let his mind wander a little. He tried not to think about it but the thought kept entering his head. What kind of boat would he buy with his twenty million dollars? Maybe he would just keep this one and go find a nice island somewhere. Find something young and soft to keep him company and forget about the life he'd had up till now. He had plenty to forget, that was for sure. Maybe getting lost in the Caribbean was just what he needed. But first he had to get the money. He forced himself to quit counting his chickens and concentrated instead on how to get what he wanted without getting caught.

ARCTIC ICE MELT OPENS
NORTHWEST PASSAGE.
September 16, 2009—USA Today

-TWENTY-SEVEN-

THE VOLUME OF INFORMATION one could produce with a few phone calls never ceased to amaze Jack. If the call came from the President, the volume increased tenfold. Jack and his team where forced out of their usual working area, affectionately known as the Pit, and into a larger one at Homeland Security. The heads of every department attached to him spread out around the room. Phone lines had been added and the local takeout food vendors were doing a brisk business. Jack had an office behind glass, but found himself spending most of his time in a large conference room receiving briefing after briefing.

So far they had compiled the target's history all the way back to grade school and once the information was confirmed, they started talking to every person he'd had contact with. Everyone from high school football teammates to old girlfriends to army buddies. They were all receiving quiet visits from the FBI or the Marshall's office. Some were reluctant to talk and some just played dumb. Those were being tailed and observed, their phones were tapped and their histories being investigated. Some names hadn't been found yet and a large part of the team was involved in the search for them. The IRS had even been tapped as a source and there were over ten people from that office alone digging into tax records. Jack viewed this as good solid police work, and, given enough time, it would bring results. The problem being that they didn't have a lot of time. He had purposely kept his people out of the search for just that reason, although he did have Eric sorting through each report and pulling out the key information. He would consolidate it and was publishing a kind of investigative newsletter to everyone so no one involved got left out or got behind. The last thing they wanted was to have people working on the same stuff and not know about it. The department heads quickly caught on and now every report had a one-page summary on top. Jack wanted his own people focused on the future, trying to figure out what the target's next move would be.

Jack stared at the report in his hand, but his mind was elsewhere. Where was the man going? How did he intend to do the exchange? What was his escape plan? He had all these questions and a million more.

"Did you get any sleep last night?"

Jack looked up to see Sydney standing in the door with two cups of coffee in her hands. She had the concerned girlfriend look on her face.

"I got two hours on the couch in my office."

"You think that's enough?" She came forward and set the coffee down in front of him. He quickly swapped the cold coffee in front of him for the fresh Starbucks.

"You went out for coffee?"

"I needed a break from the Mountain Dew. It's just across the street."

Jack sniffed his. "White chocolate mocha?"

"You think I forgot?" she grinned.

Jack just smiled and closed the lid before taking a careful sip.

"How about you, you sleep any?"

"I got about four hours down in my dungeon office. Did a sprint on the treadmill and took a shower. I feel like a new woman. You should try it."

"I'll sleep when this is over."

"What if it kills you?"

"Then I'll sleep then."

Jack glanced toward the door before lowering his voice. "Anybody getting close?"

"To the truth? No. Not yet. When our guy disappeared, he really did a good job. I've talked to Kimball every few hours and they aren't getting any hits on their radar. When they erased him they did a good job. I'll stay on it, but we need to end this quick. Sooner or later, somebody's going to get two pieces of information that go together. Only way to avoid that is to end it first."

"Yeah, I know."

Sydney fell silent for a moment and Jack turned to face her.

"What is it?"

She twirled a lock of hair around her finger and sipped her coffee. Jack knew from experience he wasn't going to like this.

"I don't like lying to Larry and the others."

Jack sat back in the chair and let it recline him. He should have seen this coming.

"I don't either, Syd, but we made a deal and I think it was the right one."

"I still don't like it. Have you thought about what to do when this is all over?"

"Yes. I have some ideas."

"Like what?"

"I'll have to tell you later." Jack was looking over her shoulder at someone approaching. Sydney twirled in her chair to see two men in uniform enter the room. Both were wearing body armor and packing sidearms in the open. The first stopped at a desk and questioned the occupant who then turned and pointed to Jack. The two men quickly closed the distance and entered the room. Sydney could now see a locked security bag handcuffed to the first man's wrist. He approached while the other man stood in the doorway.

"Mr. Randall?"

"I'm Jack Randall."

"Some ID please, sir?"

Jack removed his Homeland Security badge as well as his FBI credentials and laid them on the table. They were scrutinized by both men before the man asked the next question.

"This woman is cleared for this, sir?"

"Yes, she's with me."

Sydney watched the exchange in confusion as did some others through the glass. Jack signed a form twice before the man uncuffed himself and set the bag, cuffs, and keys on the table. Jack opened the bag and briefly looked inside before nodding and shaking the guard's hand.

"Very good. Thank you."

"Yes, sir." The two men left as quickly as they had come.

Jack sat down and examined the papers in front of him. The crowd outside the glass, realizing that that was it, also went back to work. Sydney waited patiently for three whole seconds.

"Well?"

"Well what?"

"What's in the bag?"

Jack shrugged. "Take a look."

Sydney grabbed the bag and pulled it close to her, keeping the opening hidden from the prying eyes with her body. She looked inside to see a stack of what looked like diplomas to her. She had to read the top one to be sure of what she was looking at.

"Bearer Bonds?"

"Yup."

"How many?"

"Twenty million dollars worth."

"Holy shit!"

Jack sighed and echoed her response. "Holy shit."

*   *   *

The Deliveryman examined himself in the mirror. The hair was growing out from his usual short cut. He had been careful to avoid a military style cut for years, but it had actually become quite popular in the American civilian population so he wasn't too worried about it right now. The beard was coming in, too, but needed another day or two before it would really change his features. He was close enough to shore that he was able to pick up some TV broadcast and was surprised to see that he wasn't a part of the news cycle yet. While he couldn't get cable on the boat, he was close enough to get internet on his laptop. He had visited all the news sites as well as a few government ones and not seen anything on him yet. There were some brief stories about roadblocks and checkpoints around the DC area, but it was being explained away as training exercises for the Department of Homeland Security. He would have to be careful.

He pulled away from the mirror and went back up on deck. He first examined the angle of the boat in relation to the sun. The wind had changed direction by a few degrees but so far there was no need for any adjustments. He checked on the two anchors he had set earlier that morning and was pleased to see that neither of them had dragged. The two fishing poles he had out with lines in the water were for show and had not moved. He gazed out over Chesapeake Bay and watched the boat traffic move back and forth. After the marathon run up from Miami, he was exhausted. Despite the auto-helm and the radar, he had not slept much. Catnaps in the bridge chair were the best he could manage due to the amount of traffic on the east coast. He had dodged cargo ships and oil tankers, as well as a small armada of warships leaving Norfolk harbor, all without attracting too much attention. Once he'd arrived in the Chesapeake he had quickly found a secluded anchorage and fell asleep to the rain pelting the deck. Now rested and fed, he was relaxing on deck while he figured out his next move and surfed the internet.

The internet was a wonderful thing. In a matter of minutes he had the man's address, date of birth, hometown and a complete credit check. He was careful not to dig too deep as he didn't want to set off any warnings. He just copied down the information he needed, along with a few maps, and he was ready for the next step.

He glanced at the GPS one more time to confirm the distance to the marina. He wanted to arrive just as the weekenders would be showing up to go out. The marina would be busy and he could hopefully get lost in the shuffle. By that time his hair would be a different color and the beard would be more grown out. It meant another day, but he had learned to be patient a long time ago.

He pawed in his backpack and extracted the passport he planned to use. He would have to get the hair as close to the picture as possible. Fortunately, he had been schooled in just how to do this and he already had the necessary box on board in his cut-and-run kit. All he needed the ID for anyway was for the rental car. He could always steal one, but that was always taking a chance. Right now he needed to keep the chances to a minimum. He rooted around in the bag for the other needed items. A quick trip to the post office would have to happen soon, also, and he didn't want to forget anything.

Tomorrow would be a big day. He would become another spring tourist in the DC area, only his pictures wouldn't interest anyone else. He settled back in the padded deck chair for a nap. Soon he would be running on little sleep again, and like most soldiers, he knew when to bank it up.

OVER-FISHING IMPERILS
FISH IN DEEP WATERS.
February 19, 2007—The Associated Press

—TWENTY-EIGHT—

THE SUN WAS NO longer streaming in through the windows, but Jack didn't notice as he continued to peck at the keyboard. Although his office had a secure computer with more speed and power, he was currently using his laptop, something the government discouraged, yet it happened every day. People just preferred to work on the machines they were used to, transferring work back and forth as needed. It had made for some embarrassing leaks when laptops were stolen or left on the table at Starbucks. But there was no real way to enforce the policy.

Jacks reasons for using his laptop at this late hour were not for convenience. As he pecked, he kept an eye on the door. He had closed the shades of his glass cubicle but people had a knack of just tapping on the door as they entered without warning. He understood why, but still hated it. At least they were all professional enough to do it only when it was important.

He proofread what he had written before burning four copies to disc.

These he slid into sleeves which then found the inside pocket of his coat. Only then did he delete the document on the screen. The computer asked him, was he sure he wished to delete it? Yes, very. He glanced at the clock before standing and slipping the coat on.

He stepped out of the office to see Sydney behind the glass of the conference room. The entire table was covered in paper and she was pacing around the room. He knew she worked better when she had space so he had let her take over the room. He caught her eye and patted the pocket of his coat. She nodded. Message received.

"I'm going home to kiss my wife and get some clean clothes. I'll be back in an hour," Jack told the room as he walked out.

Sydney's eyes followed him until he was out of sight.

*   *   *

Jack pulled the Cadillac up to the garage door but didn't bother waiting to pull it in. He wouldn't be home that long. The garage door was slow opening and he had to duck his head to enter. He was greeted by some soft rock music and the lingering smell of something Italian as he entered the kitchen. He found the remains of some chicken Florentine on the counter and sampled a piece with his fingers. He munched as he followed the music down the hall to a small sitting area looking out over the backyard. His wife was curled up on the couch with her feet tucked under her, reading a book.

"Well, hello, stranger," she greeted him.

"Don't get up." He stepped across the room and gave her a kiss.

She smiled as the kiss broke. "You found the chicken."

Jack smiled. "Yes, wish I had time to eat it, but I'm afraid I'm just here long enough to get some clothes."

Debra pouted at the statement but said nothing. He had already warned her of the job he had and that he would be gone for awhile. She didn't like it, but she was slowly coming to terms with it.

"It's delicious by the way," Jack called as he moved down the hall toward the bedroom.

"I could heat some up and you could take it with you?"

"That would be great!" She could barely hear him now.

She moved to the kitchen and got out some Tupperware. After spooning a generous helping into one bowl she stopped and got a bigger one that would hold it all. Jack wouldn't be alone and it would just go to waste if it stayed here. She added a few forks so he could share it with his crew. She put it all in a bag and added some bread before sealing it. She put it on the counter next to the keys to the Cadillac so he wouldn't miss it before moving down the hall toward the bedroom.

The carpet masked the sound of her bare feet and she arrived without Jack hearing her. She found him on his knees in front of the closet where they kept a small floor safe. He had it open and was looking at some computer discs he held in his hands. The look on his face was one she hadn't seen before. Conflict. The expression lasted for only a moment before he placed the discs in the safe and closed it. He replaced the carpet and shoes over the safe and began pulling clothes from the hangers and tossing them on the bed.

"How are you doing?" she asked.

Jack swiveled to see her leaning in the door. "Slow, but we're making progress."

"Anything you can tell me?"

"Not really, honey. I'm sorry, it's just..."

"Its okay. I get it, secret agent man." She smiled, disarming the situation. She changed the subject. "You're not going to wear that shirt with those pants, are you?"

Jack froze over the bed, looking at his selections and trying to figure out which ones she was talking about. He quickly gave up.

"Help me?"

Debra set down her wine and quickly sorted through the clothes on the bed. Rejecting some, re-pairing others until Jack had a suitable wardrobe set before him. He quickly grabbed a garment bag and packaged the selections while his wife added ties and belts. Shoes were not a problem since Jack had adopted his athletic-shoes-only policy. Fortunately, she had found several pair that were workable.

She sat back on the bed and watched as her husband disrobed and took a quick shower. Seeing he was preoccupied, she stayed silent until she saw the look on his face again as he stared at his reflection before he shaved. Something was bothering him. She had never seen such unease in him before. Jack was never one to shy away from difficult decisions. She noticed that he would never have doubts before making an important decision, only after. It made him strong in her eyes. Yet he was worried about something tonight, and she didn't know if the decision was made or yet to come. What was on those discs? Should she ask?

Jack finished shaving, brushed his teeth and quickly got dressed. She followed him to the door where she pointed out the bag of food. He turned for a good-bye kiss and a long hug. She straightened an imaginary flaw in his collar so she could get a good look at him.

"Jack?"

"Yeah, babe?"

"Is the water over your head?"

He looked into her concerned face, realizing he couldn't hide things from her as easily as he used to.

"No, the water's right at my head."

*   *   *

The Deliveryman let the shutter cycle twice more and captured them in their embrace. He had thought the shots of Jack's wife on the couch were all he was going to get and had been pleasantly surprised to see Jack show up at such a late hour. It was obviously going to be a short stay as Jack had some clothes and a bag of food with him. He hadn't even bothered pulling the car into the garage.

He had over fifty shots to show for his day of crisscrossing the DC area. After dyeing his hair and trimming his beard just so, he had docked the boat at one of the many marinas on the bay and rented a car. He had chosen his tourist outfit carefully as Washington was one of the few cities in the nation with video surveillance coupled with facial recognition software. A baseball hat, sunglasses, and trimming the beard to change the shape of his mouth would work to defeat this. He also dressed as a tourist complete with a map sticking out of his pocket and a camera around his neck. It had only taken him one lap around the mall to note the heightened security and heavier than usual police presence. He had avoided the White House and Capitol Building and had found a bar where he could sit and nurse a beer while studying his map and the entrance to the Hoover Building. His patience had been rewarded by Sydney Lewis visiting the Starbucks across the street. He had managed to get several shots of her as she waited in line and more as she crossed the street. He had then made a trip to Georgetown and taken a few more of her condo before venturing into the suburbs to find the Randall home. Here he had found a good place to observe the home from the seclusion of a vacationing neighbor's backyard. He had watched Jack's wife cook a dinner for herself while watching the evening news only to eat alone in front of the TV before doing the few dishes and finding a book. He had been about to leave when Jack showed up.

He snapped a couple more as Jack walked outside to his car. He saw him pull out his cell phone as he backed out.

"Soon, Jack. You and me. Real soon."

*   *   *

"This is my dream job?" Danny asked himself as he stared at the computer screen. The cursor blinked at him patiently as if encouraging him to write. Danny had to fight the urge to turn it off. He looked at the notes he had taken and wondered why he didn't just print himself up a form. They were the same notes he had taken two days ago and again four days before that. Only the names and the locations had changed. Just another gun battle in southeast DC. The ongoing turf war was good for a murder or two a week lately and Danny was growing quickly tired of it. He could only write the same story so many times. Occasionally an innocent bystander was brought down, too, and there would be a brief public outcry, but that was all. When the mayor of the town smoked crack and still got reelected, what more was there to say? The people got exactly what they asked for.

At least he was no longer in Orlando, although he admitted he missed the weather. He would trade cold and damp DC for hot and damp Orlando any day. But sometimes he questioned his desire to work for the *Washington Post*. After his story about the sniper shootings a few months ago he had finally received a call from the paper and offered a starting position in the Metro section. He had taken it without a second thought and was now putting in the hours necessary to work his way up again. So far he had kept his editor pleased and not stepped on his dick. Tonight though was not the opportunity to shine he had been waiting for. But a man had to pay his dues.

He was tapping out the story, wondering if he could just cut and paste it from a previous one, when his phone rang. Although he had assigned ringtones to certain people, he hadn't heard this one in awhile and answered it without checking the caller ID.

"Metro, you got Danny."

"They still got you in Metro, Danny?"

It took Danny a moment to recognize the voice. He pulled the phone from his ear long enough to check the screen before answering.

"Uh …yeah, gotta start somewhere."

"I've been reading your stuff, Danny. You're doing well."

"Thanks."

"Busy tonight?"

"Not especially."

"How about a walk through Rock Creek Park?"

"Okay."

"Same place we met before, say about fifteen minutes?

"Uh …hold on …yeah, I remember. I'll see you there."

"All right. Just you, though, Danny."

"No problem."

The connection broke and Danny sat looking at the phone in his hand for a long minute. He hadn't spoken to Jack since before the interview with the sniper's brother-in-law. He hadn't even been sure if Jack knew he worked for the *Post* until now. He shook it off and tapped the keys to save his story before grabbing his coat and racing out the door.

FLOW OF INVESTMENT DOLLARS
TO FARMS SEEN GROWING.
June 23, 2009—Reuters

—TWENTY-NINE—

DANNY PULLED INTO THE small parking lot and parked two spots over from the Cadillac. He looked the park over and was not surprised to see it deserted this late on a weeknight. He finally saw the shape of a man sitting on top of a picnic table over by the tree line. It was Jack. He waved him over.

"Hey, Danny, good to see you." They shook hands.

"You too."

"Wondering why I got you out here this late on a school night?"

"Well …yeah. You're not gonna get all deep throat on me are you? I'm too young to go to jail."

"No, nothing like that. I'm afraid I don't have any hot tips for you tonight. Nothing like that at all really."

"If this was social we could find a bar with cute waitresses," Danny pointed out.

"No. I'm afraid that wouldn't work either. I need you to safeguard something for me. And I can't tell you what it is or why. Can you do that for me?"

Danny was confused and let it show. "I'm not quite sure I understand. What is it you want me to hold on to for you?"

"These." Jack reached in his pocket and pulled out the two discs. One was labeled with Danny's name and work address, the other for Senator Teague at his office. They had FBI security seals on them, the kind that had to be destroyed in order to release the disc. The seals had Jack's signature on them and the date. Danny examined them without saying anything.

"There are only four of these in existence. One is with me and the other is with Sydney Lewis. You remember her?"

"Yes."

"Something big is going to happen in the next few days, maybe here in the District, maybe not. It's a lot worse than it's going to appear. I can't really say more than that right now, but the whole story is on those discs and it goes right to the top. I'd like you to hold on to them in case something happens to myself or Sydney. If we should end up dead, I need you to deliver the disc to Senator Teague. What you do with your copy is up to you, but the senator will know what's best and …I would hope you would listen to him. No one can know you have it, Danny. I'm afraid I'm putting you in some danger here, but I don't have anybody else. You showed some real stones before and I thought you could handle it."

"Is it because I'm a reporter?"

"Some. Mostly it's because you're a good guy."

"And if you live? You want them back?"

"Yes."

"Will I get an explanation then?"

"If I can give one, you're my guy."

Danny tapped the discs against his leg and thought it out. Just hold on to the discs for a little while. It's not like it was a kilo of cocaine Jack was asking him to hide. Jack had always played straight with him in the past. He had no reason to believe he wasn't now.

"Okay, you got a deal. On one condition."

"What's that?"

"Next time we meet in a bar. My ass is freezing on this damn table."

Jack laughed. "Deal."

*   *   *

The low light setting on the digital camera was just enough for him to get a few shots of the meeting with the help of the streetlight. He had punched in the route from Jack's home back to the office on the GPS and had decided to do a loose tail on him as far as the city. He was surprised to see he had pulled over into Rock Creek Park. After passing, he had carefully circled around and found a place to park where he could approach on foot. Getting into camera range without being seen was not too hard, thanks to the springtime vegetation, and he settled in just as Danny had arrived. Not knowing who he was he got several shots, including them exchanging the disc. He wasn't sure what Jack was doing, but the meeting was short and both of them were soon on their way. He waited until he was sure they were gone, and looking for tails of his own, he returned to the rental.

After thinking about it for awhile, he made the decision that DC was not going to work as the exchange site. He needed more familiar ground, something more crowded that he could take advantage of. It would require further thought, but he had an idea.

He crossed the bridge again and left the District, heading for Georgetown University. Somewhere in the area he would find a Kinko's that was open all night. He quickly had the photos printed off and returning to his car, he selected the best shots. He added them to the items in the box and sealed it before reentering the store and mailing it overnight across the river. The clerk didn't even question him. He just processed the shipment and added it to the outgoing bin. He returned to studying his textbook before the man had left the store.

Step two was done. Now he just had to get back to the boat without being seen.

*   *   *

"You hungry?" Jack asked as he set the bag down in front of her.

Sydney frowned at the bag but changed her mind when the smell hit her nose.

"Italian? Where did you get Italian this late at night?"

"Debra made chicken Florentine. It's good. There's enough for two. Serve it up while I ditch my clothes."

Jack unpacked his bag and hung up the spare clothes so they wouldn't wrinkle. Sydney dug into the bag and had it all spread out by the time he returned and was already eating.

"Good?"

"Umm," Sydney replied through a mouth full of pasta.

Jack smiled as he picked up his fork. Amazingly, the food was still warm. He dug in also. It dawned on him that he should feel at least a little guilty for eating a meal prepared by his wife with his ex-girlfriend. But he was really too tired and hungry to dwell on it.

"No wine?" Sydney asked.

"Quit yur bitchin," Jack replied.

She just smiled and dug her fork in for another bite. Sydney couldn't cook like this and she was a little jealous of the fact that Debra could. Not enough to stop eating though.

"I took care of the other thing. Your copy is in my coat."

Sydney swiped her mouth with a napkin and unconsciously looked through the glass at the people in the outer office before replying.

"Will he play along?"

"Yes."

"How do you know, Jack? I mean, he *is* a reporter."

"I know. I just do, I guess. You trust me on this?"

"You know I do."

Jack sighed. "Just stick close on this one, Syd. I got the feeling it may come down to just you and me at some point. If we fail, we have to trust that Danny will tell them why."

OVER-FISHING IMPERILS
FISH IN DEEP WATERS.
February 19, 2007——The Associated Press

—THIRTY—

THE FULL MOON AIDED in his navigation and he felt confident
enough to push the throttles up a notch. Boat traffic was heavy in the
bay and too many captains were distracted by the ever present skyline
of Manhattan to watch for other boats. He altered course two degrees to
starboard to avoid a large ferry coming from Staten Island. He had been
forced to stick closer to shore all the way up from the Chesapeake Bay in
order to stay within cell phone range. After working the phones for hours
and dropping the right names and dollar amounts he was finally able to
secure a berth at the marina he needed. It was for two nights only, but
that was all he thought he would need. The plan had been growing in his
mind the whole day and he kept refining it as the time went by.

A helicopter buzzed overhead, heading for the terminal just east of
Battery Park. He eyeballed it long enough to determine that it was pri-
vately owned and not a federal bird. His paranoia would be at its maximum when he entered the city and he would take every precaution he

could think of to blend in. New York City held the largest FBI field office in the US and the city crawled with security people. But it had also been home at one time and he knew it well.

He nudged the wheel farther to starboard and pushed the throttles up some more to combat the Hudson current. He stared up at the gap in the skyline where the World Trade Center had been. He had never been a great fan of the twin towers, always thinking they lacked style. They never really had the grace of the Empire State Building or the beauty of the Chrysler Building. But the day they had fallen still burned in his gut. But that was a lifetime ago. He had new battles to fight.

The moon was giving way to the early dawn and he slowed the boat till he had just enough forward momentum to meet the current and steer, keeping the bow aimed upstream long enough for a ferry to depart the marina. Once it was past, he let the starboard engine feather and allowed the current to push the bow to the right until he was aimed at the entrance. A push of the throttles had him through the breakwater and out of the current. The slips were clearly marked and he angled for the one he had reserved. A young man with a radio walked swiftly down the dock to assist him and the Deliveryman left the bridge long enough to throw the line over his head. It landed in his outstretched hands and he quickly had the bow in control as the boat coasted into the slip.

The Deliveryman scanned the dock and surrounding buildings before he shut down the engines. The dock worker quickly had positioned the fenders, tied the stern off, and waited on the deck for him to depart. If the feds were going to make a move, they would make it now. He watched and waited for a full minute before leaving the bridge.

"Anything I can do for you, sir?" the boy asked.

He peeled off a couple of hundreds and gave them to the boy.

"I'm just delivering her, son, you don't have to call me sir. I'll need the tanks topped off and the fresh water filled. Empty the waste tank also if you would. Hose her down and make her presentable. The owner will be here to take her home in two days."

"Yes, sir."

"If you add a case of beer to the galley fridge, that would be good, too. Make sure you get a few for yourself, the old man can afford it," he added with a wink.

"Will do, sir."

The Deliveryman snagged his backpack and stepped off the deck. He moved quickly out of the marina and into the busy streets of New York. Despite the shadows cast by the surrounding buildings, he kept his sunglasses on and scanned the faces of those around him, looking for that one face that looked too long or too intently. He worked his way into the city, changing direction at every corner, backtracking occasionally and changing speed. He crossed the street through traffic and used the reflection in the building glass to watch for tails. After ten blocks of this he darted down a subway entrance. He bought several passes, and at the last second, jumped on a train heading uptown. He changed cars after a few stops and found a chair in the corner where he could watch everyone. Nobody made eye contact on the car, most pretending to read their papers or magazines, some typing out emails on their cell phones. No one seemed to be interested in him. But he kept an eye out anyway.

Eventually, near the Village, he left the subway car just before the doors closed. He repeated his random walk for several blocks before finally deciding he wasn't being tailed. He then checked the address he had scribbled on a piece of paper before setting off to find it.

Twenty minutes later found him looking through the glass of a bike shop. Bikes costing several thousand dollars were on display to attract the customer's attention. Although he could presently afford it, he was not in the market for such a high tech machine. He scanned the crowd behind him in the reflection before entering the store. A man in his fifties looked up from a bike he was working on at a bench in the back of the store. He had the long lean look of a biker or marathon runner. His hands were callused and his hair still had the imprint of the bike helmet he had worn on his ride to work.

"Can I help you?"

"I hope so. I need a new bike. Somebody stole my last one."

"Sorry to hear that. What kind of riding do you do?"

"Just here in the city. Some of my friends were bike messengers. I try to keep up."

"Dangerous job. I was dumb enough to do it for a few years, though. Got a price range we can work with?"

"Under a grand?" the Deliveryman asked.

"I can get you on a cheap new one for that much, and I have some decent old ones. How soon you need it?" The man returned to the bench briefly to grab a cloth tape measure. He hung it around his neck so he now looked like a tailor.

"I'd like to ride it home, if I could."

"Okay. Well let's measure those legs of yours and see what I got."

An hour later, and $900 lighter, the Deliveryman pedaled down a path in Central Park, getting his skills back and becoming acquainted with his new purchase. After an hour he ventured out onto the street and worked his way toward downtown. He avoided darting cabs and took an assist from the occasional delivery truck. He soon had a rhythm going and passed the World Trade Center on his right. He turned left and made his way into the financial district, stopping to look around and watch the traffic on Wall Street. He snapped a few photos with the digital before returning it to his backpack. Numerous bike messengers could be seen playing their dangerous game of weaving in and out of traffic. After counting the cars and gauging the flow of traffic, he checked the time and pushed off again. Making his way farther south, he pedaled his way to Battery Park. He stopped and took several more shots, once again checking the time and counting the traffic. He sat on a bench and watched until rush hour started once more and traffic slowed to a crawl. Once this happened, he started his stopwatch function and pedaled into the traffic. He passed car after car and was even able to skip through intersections clogged by traffic. He made it to the financial district again in much faster time. He pedaled into a small alley, stopping briefly before pedaling on, heading for the dock and the boat. He arrived just as the traffic was beginning to thin and checked his watch again.

Pleased with his progress for the day, he found a bench to rest on while he waited for the day crew to leave the marina. Tomorrow was Friday and he hoped the traffic would be even heavier.

*   *   *

Jack stared at the pile of items on the desk and tried to think clearly. Everyone was giving him some space after the meeting they had all had. When the package had arrived that morning it had been carefully screened as all packages were. When the electronic device was detected, it was opened by someone from EOD as a further precaution and discovered to be just what the X-ray showed it to be—a cell phone. The items was quickly processed by Sydney's people before being forwarded to Jack. On seeing the photos, Jack had called a meeting and raised hell. The man they had been looking for had made it all the way from Florida to DC without being detected and had even followed Jack around and gotten photos! Some of them right across the street from the Hoover Building! The speech was short, but everyone got the message. Now Jack sat alone and seethed as the others were afraid to approach him just yet.

Except for one. Larry walked into the conference room and sat down with a stack of files and a can of Coke. The chair creaked under his considerable bulk. He leafed through a few pages before looking up to see Jack watching him. He returned his eyes to the page before he spoke.

"Ever tell you how I got my first commendation?" Before Jack could reply he went on. "I was working in the St. Louis office and we had busted a small drug running operation. Three redneck brothers moving some coke and meth back and forth to Kansas City. Anyway, we raid their place out in BFE and take them all down. We only had one van so we cuffed them all together and stuffed them in the back. My partner drove the van and I followed him all the way back to town. We stopped at this gas station to fill up, one of those chain stations in front of an old motel. My partner fills the tank and I wait in the car with the van in front of me.

"I'm playing with the radio or something and I hear this yell. I look up to see the three rednecks pile out of the back of the van and take off running. My partner forgot to lock the damn door. Anyway, I hop out of the car and take off after them. Please keep in mind that I was younger then and in slightly better shape than I am now. So they disappear around the corner of the motel and I go charging after them. They're all younger, but they're cuffed together, so I think I got a chance to catch them. This motel was the kind with the doors on the outside and an awning going all the way around, right? So I round the corner and what do I see? One redneck is dragging the other two with both hands and trying to get across the lot. The other two are out cold. I draw down on the one and he gives up. The other two are limp as rags.

"Seems these idiots were so intent on getting away that they forgot they were cuffed together. The two small ones chose opposite sides of an awning pole to run around and when they got jerked to a stop they butted heads and knocked each other cold. The big one gets up off the ground and just starts dragging 'em till I showed up.

"So I'm standing there with my gun on them and my mouth hanging open and here comes a crowd of people. Well, the big one starts screaming police brutality and tells everyone that I beat the other two unconscious. My partner shows up then and takes in the scene and before I can tell him otherwise, he believes the big idiot. Well redneck number three wakes up so we have the two of them carry the one in the middle back to the van. We call an ambulance and they come and check 'em out. Eventually we get back to St. Louis and get them processed in. Well, the next day I go on vacation, right? When I get back I get called on the carpet and they give me a piece of tin. Seems my partner put me in for it so the mistake of the door lock would get overlooked. I didn't want to get him in trouble, so I just bit my tongue. But if you ask anybody from the St. Louis office they'll tell you the story of how I took on three redneck drug dealers and knocked two of them out cold."

Jack fought hard not to smile. He managed to keep his composure and ask a question. "Is there a moral in this story for me somewhere?"

"Mistakes are going to be made, Jack. We just have to roll with them."

Jack played with his pen for a moment. Larry was right and he knew it. The tension was gone.

"I know, and I don't believe carelessness has to exist in order for a mistake to be made. I just gave that speech to assure that there wouldn't be any."

Larry smiled. "Well, if it helps any, I'd say you got the message across."

Jack smiled back and toyed with the pen some more.

"Those boys must have been running pretty fast?"

Larry nodded. "Matching shiners. Made for some great mug shots!"

They were both still laughing when Sydney stepped into the doorway.

*   *   *

"Okay, we've cataloged everything and dusted it all. I picked up a few prints but no hits on any of them. Most likely they're from the producers. The cell phone is pre-paid and was purchased in Miami the day our boy arrived in-country along with another. We've obtained extra batteries for it so you can keep it on you until he calls. The backpack is clean and one of thousands made and marketed everywhere. There's no way to trace it, but we did confirm it was sold in the same store. The letter is from an HP printer. We should be able to match it if we ever find it. The pictures …the pictures were all printed last night at the Kinko's in Georgetown. He was here in the last twenty-four hours. That's all I can really tell you."

They all absorbed Sydney's news in silence. Somehow the man had gotten out of Florida and into DC without being seen by any of the measures they had taken. It was as if he had leapfrogged over them and simply landed in their backyard.

"Why did he do this?" Eric asked, holding up a photo of Jack. "I don't understand what he hopes to accomplish by taking the pictures?"

"It's a message to me, Eric," Jack answered. "In the letter he's picked me to do the exchange. The pictures say don't try to double cross me, I can get to you."

"So what do we do now?" asked Murphy.

"Simple." Jack reached out for the phone lying on the table and held it up. "We wait."

AMAZON DEFORESTATION
SPEEDS UP.
August 4, 2009—AFP

-THIRTY-ONE-

THE EARLY MORNING MEETING had degenerated somewhat but instead of stopping it, Jack let it happen. Jack loved a good team and the discussion among these professionals was both informative and passionate. It told him what they felt most strongly about as well as what they thought they were all doing wrong. The volume was steadily increasing and Jack was about to step in, when they all fell silent.

The phone sitting on the table was ringing.

Jack jumped from his chair and snatched it up. He gestured frantically to the man outside the glass and he donned his headphones and tapped keys on the computer in front of him before giving Jack the go-ahead nod. Jack looked around the room to see everyone frozen in place and silent. He answered the phone on the fourth ring.

"Randall."

"Good morning, Jack, and everyone else listening. I'll be brief. There's a bench in Central Park across from the Essex Motel. You need to be sitting on it with the phone and the backpack today at noon. Wait for my call. Got it?"

"Yes."

"Good."

The connection ended.

Jack looked out the glass at the technician. The man just frowned and shook his head. The call was just too short. Jack dismissed it. It didn't matter anyway. He knew where the man was now anyway.

The room stayed silent as everyone waited for Jack to speak. When he did, it was a mouthful.

"I want HRT, the NBC team, and the homeland security response team all in New York City, ASAP. Call Andrews and warm up the jet. Notify the New York office and get me all the assets they can free up. Give the NYPD and the fire department a head's up and tell every borough that they're having a bio-warfare drill in real time today. I want every guy on duty to be suited up and all decon and containment procedures tested. I want the rapid response units to fill all their tanks with bleach and to be ready by 1100. Get me helicopters, every one you can find and fill them with tracking equipment. I want at least two tracking devices embedded in this backpack with some serious battery life. Tell TSA to upgrade to level four security at all the area airports and get air traffic control to clear all low flying traffic from the area until otherwise notified. We leave in one hour, people, make it happen."

Everyone scrambled to comply and soon every phone line in the room had someone on it. Jack mentally reviewed the checklist, trying to see if he had missed anything. Sydney tugged on his sleeve.

"What about the hospitals? What do we tell them?"

Jack nodded at her question. "What do you think?"

"We have to warn them. We can tell them it's a drill or something for now."

"Find out who handles that with Homeland Security and pull the real time drill scenario on all of them. Tell them they're being tested and graded on their response. That should be good for now. At least they'll be leaning forward in their foxholes if we have to change it to an actual response."

"Okay, where do you want me for all of this?"

"You ride with Greg and his guys. Bring your toys and get some armor. Be careful."

"You're sure?"

"I know Greg won't like it, but I want you close."

"All right."

*　　　*　　　*

The Deliveryman closed the phone and took a deep breath. Today was the day. He would either come away clean or end up in a federal prison. He went over his plan again in his mind, seeing the streets as he had the day before. He had spent a restless night on the boat, going over the maps and notes he had taken. He'd made contingency plans for everything he could think of, and even had a plan to abort the operation if he thought the odds of escape were too long. He could always wait and try this again in another city.

But that would be harder. He didn't know any other city like he knew New York. Other cities might provide the crowds and traffic he needed, but he wouldn't be able to work from memory like he could here, and that could mean all the difference.

He turned the phone off and removed the battery before pocketing it and placing it with the others in his backpack. Once they were stored, he donned his sunglasses and got up off the park bench. The same bench he had described to Jack a few moments ago. He threw a leg over the bike and set out west on 59th Street. He would go over the route one more time before parking the bike. His new bike messenger outfit fit snugly on his body and he blended in with the traffic. He latched on to the back of a truck and coasted along under its power for half a block, watching for car doors that might suddenly open in front of him. It was his biggest fear while riding, the door. But he hoped to never have that problem again after today.

*   *   *

Walter Putnam was also starting his day. After the long climb up to his seat he paused for a rest and took in the view as the sun came up over the city. It was one of the perks of his job and he enjoyed it every day. Some of the richer inhabitants of Manhattan may have had a higher or more comfortable view, but he doubted it was better than his.

Walter was an ironworker, a member of the Local 361 and one of the best crane operators they had ever had. He'd started at the age of nineteen, like his father and his father before him. He remembered stories of the buildings they had built and had visited every one of them throughout the city. His father had been especially proud to help build the World Trade Center and Walter had often looked skyward to see those twin towers. He had also been told the towers would outlast him, but that had not been the case. Sitting in his crane, Walter had watched the towers fall just two months after his father's death from cancer. It was just as well, they all thought, as the sight would have killed him. Walter and the other ironworkers had labored for months alongside the firemen to clear the debris and recover what bodies they could. And now he returned every day to erect the new World Trade Center. He liked to think his father and grandfather were watching, and he hoped they were proud.

Today would be a busy day of laying more concrete. The foundations for the new buildings were going in and some of the locations were not reachable by boom or truck, so they would load hoppers of concrete which Walter would transport to the men waiting in the rebar jungle. They would have to work quickly. The cement was a special formula and was mixed offsite before being trucked in. It had to be poured within a certain time or it was no longer usable. A lot of money was being spent today and Walter and his crane were a big part of the process. He fired up his machine and took it through a test run, his hands moving the two joysticks with practiced skill. His sharp eyes didn't miss a thing and he did a radio check with his safety officers before lowering the hook to accept the hopper and its dumping apparatus. Once it had performed as required and the men on the ground confirmed it, they were ready. He looked down the street to see the first wave of cement trucks approaching. He sipped his coffee before securing it in the cup holder. Time to go to work.

*   *   *

The G-5 screamed in protest as the speed brakes engaged and the plane slowed to a halt on Teterborro's main runway. The pilot quickly taxied clear and headed for the hangar surrounded by security people. He parked just outside its open door and watched as a ground crewman moved forward with the tug to pull the plane the rest of the way into the hangar. The doors would be shut before anyone exited the aircraft and he saw several men in dark suits waiting against the wall. The airport was used to VIPs coming and going, but few government flights landed there. Measures had been taken to accommodate the plane on very short notice.

Jack hardly noticed the landing. He had been going over emergency preparedness plans with the Homeland Security people who had placed a conference call to the New York office while en route from DC.

"I'll have my people and their birds and crews here in about two hours, Jack. What's first on the list?" Greg asked.

"The UN is in assembly. They have some visiting speakers. I'd like you to check in with their security people and give them a head's up. They may not take you seriously. They tend to be the suspicious type. But offer them any help you think they might need. You'll have to be a diplomat on this one, Greg, can you do that?"

"You mean can I kiss ass and grovel? Not really, but for you I'll try."

"Thanks. Meet me at the New York office when you're done, okay?"

"I'm on it."

Jack turned to meet the approaching men in the suits. One he recognized immediately as Nick Matson, head of the New York office. A man many years his senior and some said the next director of the FBI. Jack would also have to be diplomatic if he expected the man's cooperation.

But he knew him from a case they had worked when Jack was still a new agent and they had developed a mutual respect. Jack stuck out a hand before Matson had a chance to.

"Good morning, sir."

"Jack, it's good to see you again. You really started a mess here."

"I know, sir. If I hadn't gotten this started in Africa, we'd all be home right now. With the Director in Israel it kind of fell to me."

"Don't worry about that, Jack. I got a call from the Attorney General yesterday and he says it was the President's choice to put you in charge. That's all I need to know, don't worry about stepping on my head. Let's just find this guy and get this done."

Jack smiled at his old boss, a silent thank you for making an uncomfortable situation easy.

Matson dismissed it and got down to business. "Let me tell you what we've got so far. We have the word out and the hospitals are running their drills and they'll last until 9 p.m. tonight. NYPD is calling in all the extra people they can and we're blanketing the city with blue. We're running checks on every hotel in the city, but that will take some time. We've beefed up the security at all the major attractions, but it's New York City. There's no way to cover it all. The pictures you sent were printed up and every cop has a copy in his hand. The fire department has rigged six of their trucks with the bleach/water disinfectant and they'll be ready to do any decontamination we may need. We've spread them out around the city and they have people from the army's NBC teams riding with them. We're not 100% ready yet, but we should be close in a few hours."

They paused as they all entered cars waiting outside the hangar. Inside they were able to speak clearly once the sound of jet engines was blocked out. The cars immediately left the airport and headed for the George Washington Bridge.

"That sounds great, sir. I appreciate the effort."

"So, Jack, just what is it this guy has? Is what I'm hearing true?"

"Yes, maybe even worse."

"Well okay then, let's get to work."

BEACH POLLUTION STILL
WORLDWIDE PROBLEM.
July 9, 2009—USA Today

—THIRTY-TWO—

IT WAS HIS THIRD elevator ride of the day, but he had to keep up appearances. He had been circling around the financial district for a few hours, getting familiar with the traffic and any obstacles he might face. So far he had scouted out three routes that offered the best options of speed and cover. One had a construction site that he could duck into if need be. It also offered a place to change clothes.

The other occupants of the elevator ignored him. He was just another bike messenger with his backpack and front wheel. He kept the helmet and sunglasses on, but there was little need for it here. Most just fiddled with their cell phones or stared at the floor indicator. A bike messenger was clearly beneath them on the social scale. One of dozens they saw every day. Something he was counting on.

He noted the two officers standing on the corner as he left the building. They seemed to be just scanning the crowd as it flowed past. Looking for him? Maybe. One of them had a picture in his hand he kept referring to. Luckily his bike was locked to a pole in the other direction. He kept an eye on the cops in the reflection of the glass as he mounted the front wheel back onto the bike and unlocked it. They didn't move, just stood in place and scanned the passing crowd, sipping on their coffee. They looked like they were prepared to be there for a long time.

The Deliveryman mounted the bike and pedaled away from the cops. He quickly entered the traffic and headed south toward Battery Park. He noted other pairs of cops on the street corners, also scanning the crowds with pictures in their hands. He couldn't avoid riding right by two of them, but was ignored as he had been on the elevator. He blended in. He'd become part of the landscape. He smiled at his success, but also knew not to push it. He headed for the spot he had found earlier. Jack should be in place soon and it was time to get things rolling.

He hitched up the backpack and heard the reassuring sound of the vials clinking together. He jumped a curb and cut the corner in time to beat traffic. Soon he would be out of the city for good, but he had one last ride. He locked up the bike again outside a building not far from Battery Park. He then walked a block before hailing a cab.

"Where to, buddy?"

"Central Park. East side."

*   *   *

Jack casually walked through the park at an even pace. The car had dropped him off a few hundred yards away and he was slowly making his way to the bench as instructed. They'd had a pair of agents sitting on it already for the last hour, casually reading the paper and talking while sipping cups of coffee. Looking like any other New York couple killing an afternoon in the park. There were no less than four cameras on them and others scanning the area. But the foot traffic and congestion on the street were heavy. There were a million places to hide and not be seen. The man had picked a good spot and they all knew it.

Jack paused at the corner of Center Drive and 59th street and scanned the crowd before turning right and moving toward the bench. The crowd moved with him and he matched their pace.

"I'm in sight of the bench," he spoke into the microphone hidden in his collar. The earpiece, custom made for him by an FBI electronics wizard the night before, fit perfectly in his ear and out of sight unless one was standing right next to him.

"We got you, Jack," he heard Greg reply loud and clear in his ear.

On cue, the couple folded their papers and rose from the bench just as Jack walked up and took their place. He set the backpack on the bench next to him to prevent company, but kept a loop of strap around his arm. It would be a really bad time for some thief to try and snatch it. Jack squirmed a little in his seat to keep the derringer in his pants from poking him somewhere he was fond of. The letter had specified that Jack wear shorts and a T-shirt to the meet. The shirt was tucked in and tight as instructed. This was to prevent him from being armed, with no place to hide a weapon. But they had managed to sew a pouch to hold Jack's derringer in the crotch of his shorts at his insistence and it was all but invisible. It only gave him two shots of .410 number six shot, but Jack felt it was worth the risk. He also had a short metal spike in the sole of one running shoe, courtesy of Greg.

"Where did you get this?" Jack had asked.

"From a catalog," was his reply. Jack had chosen not to inquire further.

Jack sat on the bench and sweated, scanning the crowd. He had another twenty minutes to wait until noon. He could feel the eyes on him as he waited. He felt like bait and didn't like it.

Sydney's voice in his ear made him jump a little. It was as if they were all in his head. But he could hear her over the sounds of the traffic and chatter of the people passing by, and that was more important.

"Jack, we have the decon crews in their trucks and the plan is to have them follow you from a distance, sort of keeping you in a bubble. If something should happen, they should be no more than a few blocks away."

Jack just nodded his head and continued to scan the crowd. He wasn't sure what he hoped to see but he couldn't help but do it. He hated the waiting. All he could think about was what if they missed him? What if a vial was broken in the exchange? Had they planned for every contingency? Everyone had wargamed the scenario to death, but there was always the unknown, something they just hadn't thought of. Jack racked his brain to think of what that might be. He watched a man on the next bench feed pigeons.

His thoughts were interrupted by the phone on his belt ringing. Ten minutes early.

"We hear it, Jack," Sydney voiced.

Jack picked up the phone and pushed the answer button.

"Yes?"

"Afternoon, Jack. I like the outfit. First things first. How about you stand up and play the ballerina for me?"

"Okay." Jack stood and holding the bag over his head, made a show of stretching his arms up and slowly turning around.

"Good, have a seat."

Jack sat back down as instructed before speaking.

"We need to talk…"

"No, Jack. No talking on your part, just listen, and don't fuck this up. Reach under your seat and grab what's taped there."

Jack felt under the bench and pulled out a plastic zip tie. It was an accountability seal, bright orange with a number on it. The kind one could break with their hands but was only good for one use.

"Good. Now I want you to apply the seal to the backpack and make sure it's at the top where I can see it."

Jack did as he was told. He would now have to break the seal in order to get back into the backpack.

"Done? Good. Now put on the backpack and don't take it off till I tell you. Grab a cab and head toward Morningside and West 123rd. I'll be calling." The connection broke.

Jack stood up and walked to the curb, raising his arm. He only had to wait a few seconds before a cab pulled up. As he got in he heard Sydney's voice in his ear.

"We're moving with you, Jack."

*   *   *

The Deliveryman watched through the binoculars as Jack entered the cab and it pulled away toward Central Park West. He would not be following. He stowed the binoculars and left the building by the service entrance. A quick walk down an alley brought him to the street. Instead of heading uptown, he headed the opposite way. After a block, he hailed a cab.

"Washington Square Park," he told the driver. He checked his watch as they pulled away and consulted his notes. He should beat Jack by a few minutes. So far, so good.

He smiled as a fire truck flew past them in the opposite direction with their sirens blaring. The city was going to hear a lot of that today.

*   *   *

"Why the seal? I don't get it," Eric asked.

"It prevents Jack from pulling a gun or some other surprise out of the bag for one, and it also serves to confirm that it's the same bag he wore to the park. He knows we'd have a hell of a time finding a duplicate and getting it to Jack. This guy is smart. He's thought this through," was Greg's reply.

"So now what? We just follow along?"

"What choice do we have? We try to beat Jack to each location and be prepared. We keep moving the pumper trucks and keep them around Jack as best we can. The trackers are working. We know right where he is."

They all watched the screen as the red dot moved slowly up Central Park West. The fire chief was on the radio, moving his trucks to keep Jack surrounded. The blue dots depicting them were moving faster and were already in a loose circle around him. One looked like it would be at the park in a few minutes.

Sydney let out a long sigh and realized she had been holding her breath.

"Talk to him, Sydney," Greg told her.

She nodded and moved the mic closer before speaking. "Jack?"

"I hear you, Syd."

"We're right with you. We should have a fire crew there in just a minute. We'll be a block away. Can you tell us anything?"

"The seal is just a regular seal you can buy anywhere. The number is 2707 if that helps. Even if you could get me a copy, I don't think we should attempt it. Let's just roll with what we've got right now. Greg?"

"I agree, Jack. I think we're just getting started."

"Me, too. Let's just stick to the plan and be quick on our feet."

"Got it. I need to make some calls."

"Okay."

Jack stared out the window at the park as it moved by. The cab driver wasn't the aggressive type and Jack had some time to think. He studied the folded map of the city in his hands and tried to predict where he might be headed next.

ONE BILLION WORLDWIDE
FACE STARVATION.
November 15, 2009—CNN

—THIRTY-THREE—

JACK DID HIS BEST to ignore the eyes on him. His outfit and backpack screamed tourist to the casual observer and he got a few strange looks as he stood on the corner. He had arrived a few moments ago and had carefully scanned the buildings and surrounding people but nothing jumped out to his trained eye. He didn't really expect anything. He had no doubt that this was one of several stops he would make today. Sooner or later he would be told to leave the backpack somewhere or hand it off to someone. He could only comply with the man's demands at this point and hope the vials he was carrying did not become damaged during the exchange. He had made it very clear to everyone on the team that the recovery of the vials was priority one. The capture of the Deliveryman and the money were a distant second and third. There had been some muttering in the ranks, but he had been adamant. One way or the other, it would most likely be over by the end of today. Jack looked up just as an HRT helicopter flew overhead. As the sound faded he heard the phone ringing in his hand.

"This is Jack."

"I would hope so, Jack. Very good job on your first assignment. Now if you would just dance for me once again."

Jack raised his arms and moved in a slow circle, which only drew more strange looks from the people around him.

"Satisfied?"

"Yes, Jack. Time for another cab ride. This time let's go to Washington Square Park. Check out the coeds, maybe play a little chess."

"You're enjoying this?"

"Not really, Jack, just trying to keep things light. Get out on MacDougal and walk through the park to University. I'll call you back."

*   *   *

The Deliveryman ended the call and then settled in to watch the chess match. Friday was a popular day for people in the park and several students as well as a number of tourists always gathered to watch the chess players. A young man, maybe twelve, was currently holding his own against one of the park's regulars and the Deliveryman took advantage of the crowd to blend in. He would wait to see Jack walk past and confirm that he was unarmed and that the seal was in place before he sent him on his next trip. He checked his watch against the notes he had taken and figured he had a long wait. On the next leg he would start giving Jack time limits. That's when it would get interesting.

*   *   *

Sydney watched as the red dot representing her boss moved south toward New York University. She heard the babble of radio chatter behind her as the fire chief moved the trucks again and Greg positioned his people, but mostly she just watched the dot. She was worried about Jack, but refused to let it show or to voice her concerns to anyone. It would disappoint him if he knew, so she pushed her worry aside and tried to think. What would Jack want her to be doing? Thinking ahead. She tried to see the situation as he would. She knew everyone else was thinking about the exchange and the vials, but had anyone thought of how this guy may have planned his escape? Suppose he did manage to get the money and slip away. How would he exit the city? They had the bridges and tunnels all being watched. The airports were all manned with as many agents and officers as they had been able to scramble. They had people on every subway train and in every station. Every ferry in and out of the city was being watched. The helipads had agents at the desks. Where was he going to go?

The van tilted to the side as they took another corner at high speed. The mobile command center was heavy on the suspension, but light on comfort. She gripped her chair as they leveled off.

She concentrated on the screen again. Think ahead, Sydney. Where was he going?

*   *   *

Jack thought the same thing as he exited the cab and stepped out into the park. Foot traffic here was heavy as the spring weather drew the students out in mass numbers. He worked his way through the crowded park, looking for a face that held his for just a little too long. The park was perfect for what the man needed. Not only was there a sea of people, there was a sea of backpacks. People on bikes and rollerblades flew past and loud music from people dancing on the sidewalks mixed with even louder music from passing cars. Jack was quickly swallowed up in the mass of people.

*   *   *

The Deliveryman caught sight of Jack as he worked his way past the crowd at the chess tables. He kept his head aimed at the contest in front of him, but his eyes behind the sunglasses followed Jack as he passed. He examined him carefully from head to toe as he walked by not ten feet away. He saw no bulges that might hide a weapon or any telltale ear buds or wires that could be communication devices. The backpack looked to be the one he had mailed him and the seal was affixed to the closed zippers and in full display, just as he had instructed. He saw Jack scanning the crowd as he walked past, but he didn't linger on him and moved on without breaking stride. He'd let him get to the other side of the park before leaving the area to call him. Maybe it was time for Jack to walk a few blocks. Things would be speeding up soon. He casually left the chess game and skipped through traffic to stand on the steps of Judson Memorial Church. He pulled out the phone and pretended to send a text message as he scanned the crowd for Jack's retreating figure. He saw him in the distance, Jack's height giving him an advantage over the students and other people in the park. He flipped the phone shut and headed in the opposite direction.

*   *   *

Jack walked all the way to the curb before stopping and scanning the crowd waiting on the other side. He palmed the phone in his hand, waiting for it to ring.

"I'm at University, just north of Fourth," he spoke into the mic, "no call yet."

"We have you, Jack. The trucks are in position and we're two blocks north of you," Greg replied in his ear.

"Okay. Any sign of our guy?"

"No, nothing concrete. We're interrogating your two cab drivers but looks like they don't know anything. So far it appears this guy is still acting alone."

Jack tilted his head and took in the surrounding buildings. There were a million places he could be watching from right this second and there was no way to check them all. He was at the mercy of the next phone call. He just had to wait.

The wait wasn't long before the phone rang. He looked at the screen. So far the calls had been from a different number each time. The first one they had already traced to a pre-paid cell. Jack had no hope in the other numbers being any different, but they would trace them all anyway. He punched the answer button.

"Yes?"

"Good job, Jack. You're doing well. I'm glad to see you wore some comfortable shoes today. Nike Shocks? I have a pair, too. Let's put some wear on them okay? Take a left on Fourth and go east to Broadway. Head south on foot until I call you back. Got it?"

"Yes."

The connection broke. The man knew better than to get into a long conversation or say too much. Technology had improved to the point he was sure they could track the call in seconds.

"Did you guys get all that?" Jack asked.

"Fourth to Broadway and south till he calls," Greg echoed the instructions. Jack heard him address the others in the truck. "Leapfrog the decon trucks south, no sirens, and start deploying the backup officers around the lower Manhattan area. This guy seems to prefer staying on the island."

"I agree," Jack spoke. "I'm moving."

He waited for the light and then moved across with the crowd.

NEW FLU "UNSTOPPABLE," WHO
SAYS, CALLS FOR VACCINE.
July 13, 2009—Reuters

-THIRTY-FOUR-

FOUR HOURS LATER, JACK and the team were getting frustrated. The man on the phone had Jack on a marathon. He had seen the Chrysler Building and Tomkins Square Park, taken a walk through Chinatown and Wall Street and was now sitting on a bench in Battery Park. He had been in three more cabs and walked countless blocks of pavement. But the exchange had not been mentioned yet. The only thing accomplished so far was to make Jack tired.

The frustration for Jack was on a whole other level. Not only was he tired from all the walking, his patience was at its limit. Twice more the man had commented on Jack's appearance or movements and that made them all angry as it was obvious the man had Jack in sight when he said it. Yet they could not locate him. The phone numbers changed with every call and while they could quickly track them to a certain tower in the city, the towers covered a range of several blocks in all directions. With the city having one of the highest populations per square mile in America,

it was a lost cause as the man kept him constantly moving. Jack had no choice but to play the mouse to his cat, and the team just had to follow along as best they could. He had managed to buy a bottle of water from a street vendor and now sat on the bench waiting for the next call. He noticed that traffic was quickly increasing as the afternoon rush hour was just starting. Since it was Friday, it looked to be even heavier than usual. He watched a bike messenger weave in and out of traffic with a skill and dexterity that kept him always seconds away from being killed.

Jack sipped the water and waited. "Anything?" he asked.

Sydney's voice was in his ear this time. "Nothing, Jack, we're looking."

"Okay."

They had been nervous twice. Once when it looked like they were heading toward the United Nations building, and again in Chinatown, as it was close to the bridge. Both times they had turned away. After a quick conversation, they had decided that if Jack was told to approach what they considered a high profile target, he would refuse. If the guy wanted his money he would just have to change the destination. So far they had not had to do so.

His thoughts were interrupted by the phone ringing in his hand.

"We're on," Jack spoke.

"We're with you," was Sydney's quick reply.

Jack punched the answer button. "Yes?"

"You look a little tired, Jack. Don't worry, this won't last all day. Grab a cab and tell the driver to take you up William Street to the financial district again. Leave the windows down this time, Jack. I like to see you."

"Are we going to do this or not?"

"Patience, Jack, patience."

Jack stared at the dead phone in his hand, rose and hailed a cab. A car edged out two vans to beat them to the curb. Jack climbed in the back and looked up to see the driver looking over his shoulder.

"Where to today?"

"Wall Street. I need you to take Williams."

The driver made a face. "You sure? Traffic will be bad. Hope you're not in a hurry."

Jack shook his head. "Look in my hand for me."

The driver made another face, thinking he was getting robbed again. Didn't these guys know that all cabs had cameras in them now? This guy didn't really look the type though so he looked down and saw a badge instead of a gun. He looked back at Jack with a questioning look.

"What gives?"

"I'm FBI. I don't really have time to explain, but I need you to do what I asked exactly how I asked it, okay? When I get out someone will talk to you and explain."

The driver turned around and put the car in motion. "No problem. Just tell me what you need." They entered the traffic and soon slowed to a pace matched by those on the sidewalk.

Jack read the nametag on the back of the seat and relayed the information and the cab number into his mic. Once Sydney answered, he took a minute and examined the driver over the seat. He had a large scar on his unshaven face and long hair. But his eyes were clear and sharp and he handled the cab with a practiced skill. As he rotated the wheel his sleeve ran up his biceps and Jack caught sight of the bottom half of a red-white-and-blue tattoo.

"82nd Airborne?" he asked.

The driver caught his eyes in the rearview mirror. "Yup, Gulf One. Name's Jerry."

"I'm Jack. How long you been driving the cab?"

"Off and on since I got back. Figured if I could drive a Hummer halfway to Bagdad I could handle the streets here. Sometimes it's not much different, ya know?"

"Yeah, I can imagine."

"Anything I should know?"

Jack shook his head. "Not really. I've been waiting to meet a man all day. If he should show, just roll with it okay?"

"Got it."

*   *   *

The Deliveryman passed a fellow bike messenger going *against* the one-way traffic and they performed the obligatory wave as they flashed by. He changed lanes so he was out of the middle and gaining on the cab in front of him. He rose up in the pedals and looked over the cab, judging the traffic in front. They were a block or two short of Wall Street and it being just after the market closed on a Friday, it was crowded with messengers. Now was the time.

He cranked the pedals and pulled up next to the cab, grabbing onto the B-post between Jack's window and the driver's as they all moved down the street. He looked down to see Jack's startled face.

"Hello, Jack. Don't speak, just take off the pack and show me what's inside."

Jack closed his mouth and complied. He tore the seal open and unzipped the backpack, holding it wide open for the man's scrutiny. Once the man looked and smiled, he shut it and simply waited.

"Fair enough." The Deliveryman unbuckled the pack from his back and slid it around in front of him, the vials making noise as they tumbled on one another. Jack cringed at the sound. He opened it to show Jack a bag full of vials.

"We do this at the same time," he said. Jack grit his teeth but nodded in agreement.

They both placed the identical bags on the frame of the window and with a nod exchanged them. The Deliveryman added a small bag hanging on his handlebar before zipping the bag closed and slinging it over his back.

"Good-bye, Jack. Nice doing business." He let go of the window and pedaled into traffic, leaving the cab behind.

"Greg, it's the bike messenger! He just did the exchange and he's moving up Williams! Red and black shirt! Black bike! Wearing a white helmet! He exchanged the backpack for a duplicate."

"He just turned west on Pine!" Jerry added.

Jack rooted through the bag quickly and got a count. There were only half of them here! There was also a note. He quickly unfolded it and read it out loud.

"Location of the rest when I'm clear," Jack read aloud. "Shit. Are you tracking him, Greg, he only gave us half the stuff!"

"We lost the signal! Can you follow him?"

Jerry looked over his shoulder. "That thing he dropped in the bag before he closed it?"

"Yeah …Damn it!"

"What do you want to do?"

Jack shook his head and gazed out the window before returning Jerry's gaze.

"Can you catch him, Jerry?"

Jerry's face cracked into an evil grin. "I thought you'd never ask." He quickly swiveled around and gripped the wheel. "Hold on."

Jack scrambled for a handhold as the cab jumped the curb and darted around the gridlock and into the intersection. With one hand on the horn, Jerry spun the tires as they took off after the man on the bike.

*   *   *

Greg was in a frenzy of activity. After the constant movement from place to place all afternoon he had been caught by surprise by the rapid exchange.

"Bravo two, do you have signal?"

"Negative, no signal on the package."

"Alpha two?"

"Negative also."

"Anyone have a visual?"

All he got was silence. "Damn it, people! How did we lose him so fast? I want a six-block perimeter around his last location. Guy on a bike with a black backpack. Red and black shirt and a white helmet. Find him!"

"Charlie three, I've got two that match that at Wall and Pearl."

"Charlie seven, I've got one at Gold and John."

Greg looked around the unit in confusion, "What the hell?"

"A uniform maybe? Do those guys wear uniforms?" Sydney offered.

"I don't know," Greg answered.

"What do we do?" Sydney asked.

Greg thought about it for a few seconds while he stared at the screen. More locations were being called in and the dots were popping up on the screen.

"Fuck it. Start arresting people! Stop every one of them and hold them!"

Everyone stopped what they were doing and turned.

"You heard me! Do it!"

Everyone scrambled to comply.

Greg turned back to the screen and tried to figure out his next move. Somehow the man had defeated the tracking device and had also found a way to not only disguise himself, but to move through heavy traffic quickly. It was so simple it was stupid and he kicked himself for not seeing it sooner. He still had one chance though.

"Where's Jack?"

NEW FLU RESEMBLES
FEARED 1918 VIRUS.
July 22, 2009—Reuters

—THIRTY-FIVE—

THE DELIVERYMAN PEDALED HARD. When he heard screeching tires behind him, he had looked back in time to see Jack's cab jump the curb and just miss getting hit as it crossed the intersection after him. Just his luck, Jack had found a cab driver crazy as he was. He had thought of this when he planned the exchange and now increased speed in order to ditch the cab.

At the last second he made his turn onto Pine and angled up on the sidewalk. Jerking the front wheel up, he climbed the two short flights of stairs and angled between the large flower pots at the top. He had to stand on the brakes to avoid a crowd of people, but he quickly recovered and angled right around the fountain and headed for the gap between the buildings. He was essentially cutting diagonally across an entire city block, and there was no way Jack could follow.

        *   *   *

Jerry pounded on the horn again as he cut across the front of traffic and made a left on Pine. Jack had crawled into the front seat, doing his best to keep the Deliveryman in sight as he pedaled through traffic. He shut his eyes involuntarily as they just missed a delivery truck parked in the street. Jerry pulled up onto the curb on the right and stopped just in time for Jack to see the Deliveryman pedal away at the top of the stairs. The stairs were shallow and the car could certainly make it up them, but the heavy concrete flower pots at the top could not be breached.

"Damn it!" Jack moved to get out but was stopped by Jerry grabbing his arm.

"Don't leave yet, Chief, Jerry's not out of tricks yet. Hold on, we'll catch up to him on Liberty."

He grinned again as he once more leaned on the horn and gunned the engine. People in suits and street vendors all scrambled to get out of the way and he and Jack were roundly cursed, as only New Yorkers could deliver, as they jumped the curb back into the street and headed west on Pine. Jerry gunned the engine and hit the horn as they raced up the block, barely keeping between the parked cars lining both sides. Jack waited for a door to open in front of them, but they made the intersection without hitting anything or anybody. Jerry used every inch of the open intersection and put the car into a controlled drift around the corner before slamming on the brakes.

There was construction going on to the building on the right and a large dumpster blocked half the street, making the narrow opening even worse. Two workers were carrying a load of wood across the street while another stopped traffic. The two men froze at the sight of the car, unsure which way to exit. The man blocking traffic just held up a hand with a sneer. Cabs could all wait in his view.

That view changed when Jack leaned out the window with his badge in his fist.

"Move your ass! Now!"

The men quickly changed their minds and found new strength, moving the materials aside before staring after the cab as it raced by. Jack returned his view out the windshield just in time to see the Deliveryman ride down the stairs at the end of the block. He quickly crossed the intersection and headed west on Liberty.

"That street's one-way. We'll get jammed if we follow him!" Jerry shouted. Before Jack could answer he stood on the brakes and slid to a stop. Slamming the transmission in reverse he spun the tires as they backed up a few yards.

Sydney's voice suddenly sounded in his ear.

"Jack, where are you?"

"Where the hell are we, Jerry?"

"West on Cedar at Nassau! He's west on Liberty heading for Broadway!" Jerry replied as he spun the wheel.

"Did you get that?" Jack asked.

"Got it. We're north of you. Southbound on Broadway at …Fulton."

"Where are the damn birds? We can't get some eyes on this guy?"

"These streets are like canyons, Jack and they're over thirty stories deep. A lot of shadows. They're trying. Can you see him?"

"Not right now." Jack grunted as Jerry swerved around a double-parked car. His eyes widened as Jerry showed no signs of stopping as they approached Broadway. Jerry leaned forward and judged the traffic. Evidently making a decision he tapped the brakes enough to loosen the rear end before sliding sideways into the intersection. Jack closed his eyes and waited for the impact.

*   *   *

The Deliveryman was sweating now. Moving up Liberty against traffic was bad enough and he had been shocked to see the cab just half a block away when he had rounded the corner of Manhattan Plaza. From the elevated position he could see the cab clearly and had been lucky that the one-way street was right in front of him. He wasn't sure if Jack would try taking a shot at him in these crowded streets, but he didn't really wish to find out. He spotted an NYPD cruiser parked on the corner but there was no sign of the officers. A Starbucks on the corner was their most likely location. Foot traffic on the sidewalk was not as heavy as the vehicular traffic, so he jumped the curb between two cars and continued west. As he approached Broadway he cut across the corner past the big orange cube with the hole in it and looked north to find a gap in the traffic which he could use to cross Broadway. On the other side was Zuccotti Park, really just a landscaped concrete gap in the surrounding high-rise buildings with a few trees, but it allowed him some cover. He could now hear sirens echoing off the buildings coming from the north. It was impossible to determine just how far away they were.

He saw a suitable gap in the traffic and made for it.

*   *   *

Jack opened his eyes to find the cab in the middle of the intersection and aimed north, facing oncoming traffic. Several cars screeched to a halt and there was one minor impact. Jerry had placed the cab in park and was now sitting in the window on his side looking north over the traffic. Jack quickly matched him on his side.

"I don't see him!" Jerry shouted over the multiple horns and yells of the drivers. One man exited his car with the obvious intent of killing Jerry, but Jack waved him off with his badge. Jack scrambled out the window and stood on the cab's hood. He scanned the street before him and the park off to their left, but saw nothing.

"You think he turned?" Jerry asked.

"I don't know. Any idea where he might have gone?"

Jerry had the entire city firmly implanted in his head, but after a few second's thought just shook his head. "There was nothing but buildings on his route. No place to go unless he turned around."

"Or stopped?"

"Maybe." Jerry shrugged.

Jack was just about to jump down from the hood when he saw a flash of color dart out into the traffic. The cars were now going around the cab to his right and traffic was moving again. He followed the biker and got another look as he jumped up on the curb and entered the park.

"That's him!" Jack pointed. "Let's go."

Jerry dropped back into his seat as Jack dove into the passenger side. Jerry spun the wheel and they were once again racing down Cedar Street.

*   *   *

Sydney pounded the dash in frustration as the driver fought his way through the traffic. They had become their own enemy as all responding units were stopping the flow of traffic all across lower Manhattan. The four fire trucks had superior sirens and weight to back them up, not to mention the universal respect of the city's inhabitants. People tended to yield to them more readily than an unmarked panel truck with the same lights flashing. She looked at the map and was about to yell to Jack on the radio when he beat her to it.

"He's crossing Zuccotti Park heading west!" Jack yelled in her ear.

"Got it!" she yelled back.

She looked at her map and then up at the coming street sign just in time.

"Turn right!"

The HRT driver didn't hesitate. He just threw the truck into a sweeping right turn and they were now on John Street.

"Sydney, what the hell?" Greg emerged from the back.

She held up her map and pointed. "If he turns north on Church we can head him off. He'll be stuck up against the World Trade Center site."

Greg looked it over before replying, "And if he doesn't?"

She looked into his face and frowned. "I don't know."

*   *   *

Walter paused to watch the fire trucks speed down the West Side Highway. There had been quite a few of them out today and he had lost count of how many times they had passed. He took a sip of his now cold coffee and watched the crews covering the concrete with sheets of plastic. The forecast had only predicted a small chance of rain, but they would cover the newly laid foundations just in case. Too much money and too many labor hours had been invested to let a little rain screw it all up. The trucks had come at a steady pace all day and he had been rushed for most of the afternoon. He now took a short break while the guys downstairs cleaned some stray mix from the dumping mechanism. It wouldn't do to have it lock up on them right now.

"You still awake up there?" his safety crew asked over the radio.

His hand gripped one of the joysticks and found the button for the mic. He keyed it up with a smile.

"Just barely. You guys about done screwing around? I'm getting bored up here."

"Couple more minutes it looks like, Walt. Hang tight."

He could barely hear him over the sounds of the sirens.

"No problem. Hey, what's going on in the city today? I haven't seen that many fire trucks and PD out in a long time."

"We're not sure, but they've been running back and forth all day. Joe checked the news but didn't hear anything. You see anything from up there?"

"No, they seem to be going in all directions."

"Maybe a drill or something. You ready?"

"Yup." He put down the coffee and grabbed both joysticks.

"Give her a test run or two for us."

The bucket responded and he quickly moved it over to the waiting trucks for another load. The sirens faded from his mind as he concentrated on his work.

WARNING: OIL SUPPLIES
ARE RUNNING OUT FAST.
August 3, 2009——The Independent

–THIRTY-SIX–

"SHIT!" JERRY YELLED AS the truck pulled out in front of them. Past the truck they could see that traffic was at a stop on Church Street. Lower Manhattan was in gridlock due to all the emergency vehicles trying to get through. Everyone was confused and just trying to get to their destinations. Jack watched helplessly through the park's trees as the Deliveryman pulled away.

"Damn it, Jerry, do something!"

Jerry looked from the street in front of them to the park on their right.

"Jack, you better back me up when this is over."

Before Jack could ask, Jerry spun the wheel, jumped the curb and entered the park. He laid on the horn as they slalomed through the trees and down the broad steps. Pedestrians scrambled out of the way of the mad cab driver and Jack just held on for his life as they bounced over the steps. He could barely make out the figure on the bike as the scene through the window bucked up and down, left and right. For some reason his gaze was drawn to the meter as it billed him for their impromptu trip through the park. The bottom of the cab made a metallic tearing noise and the cab suddenly got louder as they ducked around even more trees. The park had a gentle slope, too, and they met short flights of steps every twenty yards or so. Somehow Jerry stayed in control as they plummeted over one flight after another. They avoided the last set of four and bounded out onto Liberty going the wrong way.

Here Jerry's skill and luck became moot as the cab could take no more punishment. The right front tire blew as they impacted the curb and Jerry managed to steer them into a parked car rather than the stunned people on the sidewalk. Traffic in the intersection, while moving slowly, still managed to swerve into each other in a vain attempt to avoid an accident. The streets in all directions became an instant parking lot.

"You okay?" Jack asked.

"Yeah, I'm sorry, Jack. Damn tire blew."

"Don't be," Jack replied as he scrambled to climb out the window. He hung his badge around his neck as he climbed up onto the roof and gazed west.

*   *   *

The Deliveryman was busy weaving in and out of the gridlock when he heard the crash behind him. Taking advantage of a small straightaway he gazed over his shoulder to see the vehicular carnage in the intersection. If it had not been for the slightly downhill grade of Liberty Street next to the park, he may not have beaten Jack to the intersection. The sight of the cab coming at him through the park had almost caused him to crash into a parked car. Jack was obviously determined to catch him. Maybe he should have just given him all the vials to begin with instead of keeping ten with him? He fully intended to leave them at the marina in a dock locker and phone Jack the location as soon as he was in the blue water.

He smiled as he saw Jack climb up on the roof of the cab. He was obviously on foot now and had no way of catching up to him. He would be back at the boat in a couple of blocks and then out of the city soon after. His plan was working.

Or, so he thought. Just as he turned his attention back to the road a car door opened directly in his path. Its owner's wrist was crushed by the bike's front wheel as it impacted the handle and the Deliveryman was thrown clear over the framed window and onto the concrete. The bike with its now mangled front wheel and twisted handle bars came to rest in the car driver's lap as he screamed in pain.

The helmet saved his head, but the impact of his body with the door frame had broken a rib or two on the right side and the Deliveryman now lay in the street, gasping for breath as he stared up at the sky. The view was quickly blocked by pedestrians gazing down at him. He could see their mouths moving, but could not make out their words. Willing his legs to move, he was relieved to have no pain as they responded. He unbuckled the helmet chin strap in an effort to breathe easier.

"elp me nup."

"What did you say, son?" a man asked.

"Help me up."

"Are you sure?" The man reached out a hand and pulled even while he asked.

"I'm okay," he managed to croak. Once upright he looked back to where he saw Jack. He was no longer standing on the cab, but was now running through the crowd toward him.

The Deliveryman pushed the man aside and ran down the street away from Jack. Within a few yards the pain in his ribs told him he would not be able to get away on foot. He needed a place to hide, somewhere he could shake Jack. The stores on his left were nothing but single storefronts, if he entered one he would be trapped. On the other side was the World Trade Center construction site. He really had no choice.

He grit his teeth against the pain and vaulted up onto the fence where there was a gatepost. Using the gatepost, he picked his way over the barbed wire at the top and dropped down into the site, yelping in pain as he rolled to his feet. He moved quickly behind the trailers and other parked equipment and was soon lost from sight.

*   *   *

"Syd, he's jumped the fence into the World Trade Center site! I lost sight of him! Have the cops surround the site. Nobody leaves! Stop all the construction traffic too!" Jack yelled into the mic as he ran down the street. People all stared after him. While strange people were not unusual to New Yorkers, an FBI man running down the street screaming at someone that evidently only he could see was new. Jack slowed when he came upon the wreckage of the bike. The driver of the car was cradling his broken wrist and cursing while the others were gazing through the fence into the construction site.

"I got it, Jack," she replied.

"Where did he go?" Jack asked the people still there.

They all tried to answer at once until Jack waved them all quiet and pointed to the man who had helped the biker.

"He just jumped the fence and ran behind that blue trailer. I haven't seen him since."

"Okay. Okay. Was he hurt?"

"I thought so, but he sure went over that fence with no problem," the man replied.

Two NYPD officers approached from the west. They had abandoned their cars and followed the chase on foot until they found Jack. An HRT helicopter buzzed over the site and began to circle the area.

Jack addressed the two cops. "I need you two to secure the entrances. Get all the help you can on the radio and surround this place. Tell them I'm going in after him." Jack paused and pulled out the collar of his shirt and spoke into it. "You get that, Syd?"

"We got it, Jack," Greg answered. "I have the chopper overhead and the team from the truck is securing the entrance on the north and east sides. Wait for her, Jack, she's almost there."

"What?"

"Look behind you."

Jack turned to see Sydney running toward him, complete with body armor and an HRT jumpsuit. She ran up and stopped with a smile. She wasn't even out of breath."

He checked her face. She looked determined. Okay.

"He crossed here, you ready?"

"Yeah." She moved to climb the fence.

"Wait." One of the cops stopped them.

Jack turned to see the man stripping off his own vest. "You're about my size, right?"

"Thanks." Jack donned the armor and accepted Sydney's backup pistol from her ankle holster. It felt small in Jack's hand, but it was better than the derringer for what they were doing now. He thumbed the slide back and saw gleaming brass in the chamber.

"Ready?" He got a nod and a bit lip in return before she turned to climb the fence. Jack quickly followed and was surprised to get a helping hand or two from the crowd. He looked back through the fence to see Jerry grinning back.

"Go get him, Jack. Just don't forget."

Jack just smiled back. "Forget what?"

"You still owe me for the ride."

"I'll come find you when I'm done here."

"Okay."

With a shake of his head, Jack turned and followed Sydney to the cover of the first trailer. They quickly slipped around it and were lost from sight.

*   *   *

The Deliveryman was quietly cursing his luck as he surveyed the workers standing around the truck. The maze of construction equipment and building materials on the other side of the road was what he needed. If he could just get there he could maybe make it to the other side of the site and exit close to the marina. His only other choice was to exit the site somewhere else and hope to hide in the city until he could get to the boat. Although the days weren't getting longer, it would be dark in just a few hours and that would be to his advantage. He slipped the backpack from his back and rooted around inside. The bag he had dropped in contained two items. One, a device that gave off a signal that defeated most tracking devices. He couldn't be sure if it was working or not, but he had no doubt the backpack contained at least one. He didn't have time to search for it right now. The other item was a small handgun. He pulled it from the bag and palmed it in his gloved hand. With a last look at the stack of bonds he zipped the bag shut and slung it back on his back.

He had to move. The longer he stayed in one place the more cops they would surround him with. Mobility was his best friend. He eyeballed the men around the truck again. He could approach them and with the gun take control of the truck. Maybe even drive it right out the door? But the men all had radios on their belts. They would have the word out before he got fifty yards.

The decision was made for him as the men all climbed into the cab or up onto the flatbed and the truck soon moved off down the road. As soon as it was around the corner he bolted for the stacks of materials. His ribs screamed in protest, but he had learned to ignore such pain long ago.

FLOW OF INVESTMENT DOLLARS
TO FARMS SEEN GROWING.
June 23, 2009—Reuters

—THIRTY-SEVEN—

WALTER CAUGHT THE MOVEMENT of the running man out of the corner of his eye and turned his head in time to see him disappear into the stacks of materials in the supply yard. He immediately felt something was wrong. First, the man was not dressed as his fellow ironworkers, and second, he was running. Nobody ran on the site. It was against the regs. The dangers on the site were high and potentially lethal. They could come from any and all directions. A running man had no way of watching for all these dangers and that was why it was never done.

He stopped the crane with the bucket safely in the air and keyed the radio for his ground crew.

"Hey, Bobby."

"Yeah, Walt?"

"I just saw some guy run across the road and into the stacks in G-8. He's not one of our guys. Maybe you better call security and go find him?"

"Say that again?"

Walter rolled his eyes before keying the mic again. "Listen. I just saw a guy run across the road and into the supply stacks. He's not one of our guys. Wearing a black and red shirt and a backpack. I can't see him now, but he's gotta still be in there."

"Okay, buddy, I'll call security and they can hunt him down."

Walter took a last look toward the stacks were the man had disappeared but saw nothing. He was about to grab the joysticks and resume moving cement when his sharp eyes caught some more movement. This time he watched two people climb the fence on Liberty Street and run across the gap toward the trailers. They both had black vests on and what looked like guns in their hands. He saw what were obviously two NYPD uniformed cops on the sidewalk. They made no move to stop them or follow.

"Hey, Bobby, I got two more now. They just jumped the fence on Liberty, too. I think they may be cops after the first guy. What the hell's going on down there?"

"I called it in, Walt. They said they're on the way. If you see them again sing out."

"Okay."

He looked down to see the crews waiting for the bucket, shielding their eyes from the setting sun shining through a gap in the skyline. He moved the joysticks and the bucket descended for another load. While they were filling it, Walter scanned the site for the first man. He also noted cops at the main entrance and along the fence on Liberty. Maybe this was what all the sirens had been about all day? Walter shrugged and kept looking.

*　　　　　*　　　　　*

"Jack, look." Sydney pointed to two men walking up the road. They both had radios in their hands and holstered weapons on their hips. One turned around long enough for them to see the emblem of a security firm printed on the back of his jacket.

"Make sure your badge is showing," Jack told her as he left the cover of the trailer's shadow and approached them. He got within a few yards until they noticed him as they were busy scanning the stacks of materials on the right side of the road.

"Who are you?" one demanded.

"Agents Jack Randall and Sydney Lewis, we're from the FBI. We just followed a guy over the fence and into your site. We need you to move everybody out and help us secure a perimeter."

"Damn, what'd this guy do?" the younger guard asked.

Jack took a deep breath. Just how much should he tell them?

"He may be carrying something very dangerous in a backpack. It's essential that we stop him."

"Really? What is it?" the guard asked.

Sydney broke in. "We don't have time to explain. Are you here looking for him?"

The older guard waved the younger one silent. "Yeah. Our crane operator saw him running into these stacks. It's all building materials and other construction stuff. But it's a maze. Our own guys get lost in it sometimes."

Jack looked skyward and saw the crane operator high in his glassed-in seat.

"Is there anyway you can let me talk to him?"

*   *   *

Greg scanned the screen in front of him and watched as more and more assets converged on the trade center. The dots moved like ants as FBI units, fire crews and New York's finest all moved to surround the site. He now had two helicopters orbiting around the site and sniper teams were moving into the surrounding buildings and taking up positions where they could scan the area. The problem was the area was both open and not open at the same time. At this point, the trade center site was really nothing more than a big hole in the ground full of construction equipment, trailers, ramps, tunnels, barricades and ironworkers. The fact that it was below ground meant that a good portion of it was unseen from any angle. The cranes and surrounding buildings kept the helicopters too high to provide good surveillance and his agents were leaning out the doors with binoculars while the pilots fought the updrafts and crosswinds created by the flow of the wind around the high-rises. He had the Port Authority people closing off the subway tunnels and he was told they were already in place. In another twenty minutes he would have the place so locked down a rat couldn't get out without being seen. But a lot could happen in twenty minutes.

"Come on, Jack, get this guy," he muttered to himself.

*   *   *

Walter had just picked up another hopper full of high quality cement and hoisted it high over the site when his radio squawked.

"Walter? My name is Jack Randall and I'm with the FBI. The man you saw go into the stacks is very dangerous and we need to locate him as soon as possible. Can you see him from your position?"

Walters eyebrows rose to new heights when he heard this. It was about the last thing he expected to hear on his radio.

"Hold on one second, Mr. Randall, and I'll take a look."

First thing Walter did was find a safe spot to park the hopper over. If he should hit the wrong button or the crane should fail he didn't want a few tons of cement landing on any of his coworkers. Once he found the spot he wanted, he locked the controls and scanned the area where he last saw the man.

"I don't see anything right now, but he could be anywhere in there. Those stacks cover more than a football field."

"The site's being shut down and all the men pulled out. You're safe up there and we could use your eyes. Can you hang tight for us and help us out?"

"No problem. I sit here all day. But that cement in that hopper can't stay there for too long or it'll start to set up. Sooner or later, I'll have to dump it."

Jack looked at the construction foreman who had joined them. The man nodded in agreement.

"He's right. If he doesn't dump it soon it'll become a solid block in the hopper and ruin the whole thing. Expensive."

Jack nodded. He could really care less about the cost of a new hopper right now, but he didn't want to piss off the man for no reason.

"Well, let's just hope we find the guy quickly." He pulled his collar out and spoke into it.

"Greg, how do we look?"

"Perimeter's coming together nicely. The fire trucks are one and two blocks away, but they're in gridlock. We're trying to free them up. Main entrance is under control and no more traffic is moving in or out. I have two sniper teams in position, but their views are limited by the fact that you're in a damn hole in the ground. I'm afraid I can't give you much intel from them. I'm told it'll be another twenty minutes until we can say it's locked up tight. What are you thinking, Jack?"

"I'm thinking he could squeeze through somewhere and be long gone in twenty minutes. What about the subways?"

"Port authority has them locked down with some ESU guys. They practice it, you can tell."

Jack spun in a circle and tried to scan the whole site, looking for any holes, but he couldn't see it all or even picture it. It was just too complex. What he did see were a lot of birds. Pigeons and gulls seemed to favor the site. He made a decision.

"Greg, I'm gonna push it. Sydney and I will go in and try to flush him out. I'm gonna give you the frequency of the on-site construction team. The crane operator saw the guy run into the stacks and he's up there watching for us right now. See if Eric can put us all on one net."

Greg closed his eyes and didn't reply right away. He would normally protest such a move and ask Jack to wait for his team so they could clear the stacks more carefully and in greater numbers. But he also knew that what the man had in the backpack was very dangerous. Jack was the man on the ground. He had to trust his judgment.

"Okay, Jack. I'll keep working on the perimeter and get some more sniper teams deployed. Take it slow. Check your six and be careful."

"Yes, Mother."

"What now, Jack?" Sydney asked.

"You and I are going to flush him out." He turned to address the two security guards. "Can you stay here and make sure nobody else goes in there and that he doesn't come out?"

"You got it."

"Okay, Syd. Let's roll."

—THIRTY-EIGHT—

THE DELIVERYMAN GAZED UP at the circling choppers. Why were they so high? He saw them bobbing around as they slowly circled. Maybe the winds were bad that high up? Either way, he had to watch them. He was hidden from everyone's view except for them. He watched one as it circled past the top of the crane. He couldn't tell if there was anyone in the crane or not. It wasn't moving and the angle of the sun shone off the glass in such a way that it defeated his eyes from seeing inside. He pushed the thoughts aside and concentrated on his situation.

One of the backpack straps had failed on his way over the fence so he now paused to tie the strap down. As an afterthought, he took the trailing ends and tied them together across his chest, doubling and then tripling the knot to take up the slack. He couldn't afford to have it happen again at a critical time.

The area he was in reminded him of an urban combat training area. It was like a building with the roof torn off, and he moved from corner to corner, automatically clearing the way before him and moving on. The stacks were taller than he could see over and the only outside objects were the circling helicopters and the crane. He made an effort to stay out of the line of sight of all three, but it was unavoidable if he wanted to move. And there was no doubt he wanted to move.

*   *   *

Jack looked left to see Sydney peering into the stacks of materials. They were two stacks apart and the plan was to stay that way. Jack was a little worried. While he had been through extensive training for this kind of scenario, he knew that hers was limited. The last time they had done something like this she had mistaken him for the person they were after and taken a shot at him. Luckily for Jack she'd missed. But she seemed to hold her new weapon with confidence and her hands automatically followed her eyes and the barrel was pointed where it needed to be. Maybe she had been practicing. He'd have to ask her later.

He palmed the smaller handgun and made sure there was a round in the chamber before returning his gaze to Sydney. She was watching him and waiting for his signal. With a hand gesture she probably didn't understand he waved her into the maze. He matched her and soon they were lost from sight.

"Greg, we're in the stacks and moving west. Anything from the crane operator?"

"That's a negative, Jack. He's watching. We told him not to move the crane. I don't want your guy knowing he's up there."

"Okay, just keep him looking. How about the snipers?"

"All the angles suck. I have the spotters looking for better views, but I wouldn't count on anything better than the crane guy."

"You're just full of good news," Jack whispered.

"Sorry, buddy, I'm working on it."

"All right, well do it quietly, I need my ears."

"Roger." Greg fell silent and ordered the noise in the van cut also. Jack didn't need any background chatter in his ear right now.

Jack caught sight of Sydney as they cleared the first row of materials. They both shook their heads and Jack waved her on to the next row.

*   *   *

The Deliveryman looked both ways up and down the row but still saw nothing. The gap was wider here for some reason and he would be in full view of the helicopters and the crane when he crossed it. He needed a better crossing point but no options were presenting themselves. Why can't it be dark? Or better yet, a nice drenching rain, a torrential downpour with lots of thunder to cover him from view as well as mask any noise he made?

"Wish in one hand, jackass," he told himself.

With a last look down the stacks he launched himself across the gap. He counted to three before he was behind cover again. He quickly moved deeper into the shadows edged farther to the right.

*   *   *

Walter saw the movement and quickly keyed the mic.

"I saw him, I saw him! He's about halfway through. He just crossed the center aisle and he's right in the middle. Still heading toward the Hudson!"

"We hear you, Walter. Can you give us a better location?" Greg asked. He keyed both mics so Jack could hear what Walter was saying.

"There's an aisle about halfway through the stacks and he just crossed it. He's still right in the middle looking north-south."

"Walter, this is Jack. I'm in the stacks with my partner? Can you see us?" Jack stepped out into a gap and waved in the crane's direction.

"Uhhh ….Yeah! I see you. You're about …eight stacks away from the aisle. You need to come toward me about two stacks also. Just move and I can tell you where to stop."

"Okay, you see us both now?"

"Yup, you need to go two toward me and eight to the west."

"All right, we're moving. Do you see him?"

"No, but he'll pop up. The stacks are lining up with my point of view. I'll see him when he crosses the gaps."

"Okay, Walter. You're the only eyes we've got right now. Just don't lose him okay?"

"I'll do the best I can."

Jack turned to see Sydney's questioning gaze. She could only hear Jack's side of the conversation.

"What are we doing?"

"Our eye in the sky saw our guy. We can pick up some speed." He pointed. "Two down and eight across. We stop at six and split up again. There's a large gap we need to cross. We cross apart and one at a time, okay?"

"Got it."

Jack led off with her jogging behind him.

*   *   *

The sounds of the sirens were constant and there were more and more of them. He could hear them as he wound his way through the stacks and they almost caused him to run. They told him that time was working against him and if he didn't escape soon his chances would be slim of making the harbor and the boat. He shortened his looks and sped up his dashes. This worked the ribs more and he was forced to grunt against the pain. Something he admonished himself for. He had been taught to do this sort of thing silently as noise would give away his position. The background noise here was so loud he knew he really didn't need to worry about it, but the self-scolding came automatically.

Another five rows without encountering anyone was making him wonder why. Were they just going to surround the area and then come after him? He had heard some noise behind him and just assumed they were coming his way. Maybe they were hoping to flush him out? If so, what should he do? Only a fool knowingly entered an ambush. Just how many were behind him?

He decided to find out.

*   *   *

Walter saw more movement, but it wasn't what he expected. He keyed the mic again.

"Hey guys, I saw some more movement. How many guys you got down there in the stacks?"

"Just two, Walter, the man and the woman you saw earlier. Why?" Greg answered.

"Because I just saw some movement heading toward them. I think it's the guy we're chasing. I mean, if you say you have nobody else in there?"

"Hold on, Walter, I gotta tell Jack!" Greg switched mics.

"Jack!"

Jack quickly waved Sydney to a halt and stuck a finger in his ear. "Not so loud, Greg. What is it?"

"Sorry. Walter says the guy's moving toward you."

"What?"

"The guy's coming back at you. Just hold your ground and he's gonna try to get us a location."

"Okay."

Sydney had moved to Jack's position while he was talking. He turned to give her the information.

"He may be coming back our way. Let's spread out but stay in sight. Find a corner in the shadow behind something solid if you can. Look behind you."

She nodded and moved to comply.

"Hey, Jack? It's Walter." Greg was keying both mics again.

"I'm here, Walter."

"I was thinking. Just what does this guy have gun-wise?"

"We assume a handgun of some type, why?"

"No rifle or anything?"

"No."

"So his chances of hitting me up in this cage are slim-to-none?"

"What are thinking, Walt?" Greg cut in.

"Well, how about I put the hopper right over him? That way everyone will know right where he's at."

"He'll shoot at you for sure, Walter, I can't ask you to do that," Jack answered.

"I know. That's why I'm offering."

"It's not your fight, Walter."

"The hell it's not! This is *my* city he's fucking with! You telling me it wouldn't help you if I did it?"

Jack didn't know what to say. His silence was all Walter needed.

"It's not like you can climb up here and stop me. Just tell 'em I did it on my own. Stand by. I'll show you what I can do with this thing."

THE PLANET'S FUTURE: CLIMATE CHANGE
'WILL CAUSE CIVILIZATION TO COLLAPSE.'
July 12, 2009—The Independent

—THIRTY-NINE—

THE LOUD SQUEAL OF moving metal drew his eyes skyward and he looked up to see the crane rotating, the large hopper of cement was once again swinging through the air. So there was an operator still up there. He would definitely have to keep himself hidden from his view now. He watched the hopper swing in his direction and then lower until it hung over the stack he had run behind in the last row. He realized with horror that the crane operator was giving away his position. He moved to the other side of the stack and looked back in the direction he had first come.

*   *   *

Jack hadn't realized how fast the crane was. He had moved to Sydney's position to inform her of the situation when the hopper swung down and hovered not two rows away from where they were.

"Stay here. I'm going to circle around," he whispered.

Jack ducked low and sprinted across a gap. If the man was that close he would try to get around him and maybe he and Sydney could get him stuck between the two of them. After another scan around a corner of stacked rebar he sprinted across another gap.

*   *   *

The Deliveryman saw the movement, but had no time to react. He moved deeper into the shadow of the stack he was up against and looked toward the next gap. The angle only gave him a two-foot window to see through so he leveled the pistol and waited. If more than one person was after him, as he suspected, he couldn't afford to be surrounded. If he could wound one he would take them both out of the action as the remaining one would take care of his wounded partner. He could eliminate two pursuers with one shot. He adopted a shooting position while still in a crouch and waited. If the first shot hit, he had plans for a second.

*   *   *

Jack scanned again without seeing anything and once again looked at the hopper hovering in the air. Should he move over a row? No, he would cut the corner west and get behind him. If Sydney stayed in place, he would be the hammer to her anvil. He adjusted the derringer that was still holstered in his crotch to a more comfortable position before taking one more deep breath.

He once again sprinted to the next stack. He was almost there when the sledgehammer hit his chest and spun him to the ground.

*   *   *

Sydney bit her lip to keep from screaming Jack's name. She didn't know if it was Jack who had shot or the man they were chasing. Another shot quickly followed. She forced herself to control her breathing and moved slowly around the stack in the direction of the shot. She had moved two rows when she saw the prone body of Jack lying in the shadow of some plastic wrapped boxes. She heard running footsteps moving away to the west so she sprinted to his side.

She found him lying in the dirt gasping for breath and tugging at the collar of his vest. She quickly ran her hands down the front and felt the deformity on the right side. She peeled the Velcro straps off and pulled the vest and shirt away from the skin.

A bruise. Just a large ugly bruise. No blood. No holes. Jack would be fine. He was already getting his breathing back.

"Damn you!" she cursed him before sitting him up and hugging him.

"Okay, okay," he gasped out. "I'm all right. Help me up."

She pulled him to his feet. Jack took several shallow breaths but held his own when she let go. He reattached the Velcro straps and nodded to Sydney's questioning look. He was fine.

He pointed with her HK at the hopper in the sky. It was slowly moving west.

"Let's go." He took off running after it. Sydney stood open-mouthed, watching him, before shaking it off and sprinting after him.

*   *   *

The Deliveryman was running flat out. He had shot one man and then sent a round at the crane operator. He had hoped to deter the man from using the hopper any further but obviously it hadn't worked as it was following him now like an alien spacecraft. He weaved around the stacks but the hopper stayed right with him. He cussed the crane operator and weaved some more. He had to lose him before he came out the other side.

A round whizzing past him quickly followed by the sound of the shot behind him made him duck around another stack. They were coming.

*   *   *

"Shoot at me again, you little bastard!" Walter railed away to himself up in the seat of the crane. When the muzzle flash lit up the stack where the man was hiding, he had just assumed the shots were aimed at Jack. When the bullet had caromed off the housing he was in, he had realized that wasn't the case.

Like most people, Walter had never been shot at before. His mind processed it like most people. First with disbelief: Is he shooting at me? Then, once he realized he wasn't shot, with anger. He's shooting at *me!* So now Walter was a pissed off crane operator. He fought back with the only weapon he had.

He kept the hopper glued to the air over the shooter's head as he zigzagged through the stacks, even lowering it a bit as if he aimed to squash the man like a bug. As much as he would have liked to, he didn't think the FBI men would approve. But then again, he hadn't asked. He could hear voices on the radio, so he just kept quiet and worked the crane, muttering more curses under his breath. He could see the two feds chasing after the man, the woman's hair waving behind her as she sprinted.

✳   ✳   ✳

Sydney sprinted hard to keep up with Jack. She remembered what a runner he had been but hadn't realized he had kept up on it. She ran everyday! She should be kicking his ass! He had longer legs though—she would blame it on that. She heard him yelling into the radio as he rounded the stacks, following the moving hopper full of cement.

"Greg, he took a couple of shots at us. We're chasing him at a run now west through the stacks. We're following the hopper. Can you get some shooters on the other side?"

"I've got one with a decent view and I'm moving others in place. I still don't have a solid perimeter yet, Jack. You need to stop him or slow him down!"

"I'm trying!"

"I know. I'll have some help there in two minutes."

"This may be over in one."

✳   ✳   ✳

The Deliveryman paused when he reached the end of the stacks. He was now close to one of the large ramps that descended into the pit from

street level. There were more supplies stacked tightly under the structure and a large open area off to the side that looked like it held a newly
poured foundation. Large expanses of cement could be seen. Some had
already been floated and covered in plastic, while others still showed pro-
truding rebar. He had obviously interrupted a large project. But at least
it explained the hopper. He glanced around the stack to see it hovering
about twenty yards to his left. Obviously he had lost the crane operator
in the last few rows, but he was still close enough to mark his position.
A group of seagulls wandered around the yard, but no workers could be
seen. The flashing lights of police cars seemed to be everywhere up on
the street level. It pissed him off.

All he had asked for was a lousy twenty million. It was pocket change
to the damn feds. Why all the trouble for some lousy secret medications?
They were just going to screw him right up till the end, weren't they? Well
if that's the way they wanted it, he sure as hell wasn't going to go down
without a fight. The boat was only a block way. If he had to shoot his way
there, he would.

*   *   *

"Jack, it stopped!" Sydney yelled.

Jack turned around and looked at her, only to see her pointing skyward. He followed her gaze.

The hopper hung motionless in the air. Either the man had stopped
or Walter had lost sight of him. He felt for the radio.

"Walter?"

"I'm here."

"Did he stop?"

"I think so. He was zigzagging a lot and I may be a row off, but I
haven't seen him come back your way and I've been watching real close.
I think he stopped at the edge."

"Can you see us?"

"Yeah, her hair helps."

Jack looked at Syd with confusion, but quickly dismissed the comment.

"We're only two stacks over from the hopper. I need to know exactly where he is."

"I can't see him, Jack. But I'd put money on him being no farther than one row away from the hopper. Closer to the south, I think. That's my best guess at this point. Sorry."

"That's okay, you did great."

Jack pictured the area in his mind and looked for any possibilities. He could ask for more men to enter the site, but that would pull them off the perimeter and Greg needed every guy he had. If they put more people in now there was a good chance of a friendly-fire accident. The fewer people in the pit meant the less chance of someone being exposed if something happened. No, the best plan was still the original one. Set up a perimeter and deny any escape. Then they could go in after him, if they had to. Maybe if they could just get him out in the open? Perhaps he would give it up. The Deliveryman had been a soldier once. He had to know his odds were bad. Most would give up at this point, or some, like a cornered animal, would turn and fight.

"Here's what we're going to do. I want you to go down at least five rows to the north. I'm going to put some pressure on him here. If he moves out into the open, take him out. Don't expose yourself, stay behind cover. I may throw a round his way to get him to move. You got it?"

"I don't know, Jack. You really think we should separate?" she asked.

"I know. You tend to want to stick together in this situation, but this is the best idea I have for us right now. Those vials *can't* get away."

She nodded. "Okay, just remember, the vials are in the backpack."

"Yeah?"

"Let's try not to shoot them?"

"Right."

EDIBLE FISH WON'T DISAPPEAR
IF OVER-FISHING STOPS.
July 30, 2009—USA Today

—FORTY—

"WHAT DO YOU SEE, Walter?" Greg asked.

"It looks like the girl is moving toward me. She's about five, no six, stacks from where they both stopped. Now she's moving out to the edge. She stopped. She waved to me! Tell her I see her." He waved back.

"Okay. How about Jack?"

"He moved the opposite way, just not as far. I see him …no, he just disappeared into the stacks again. What's up? What's he going to do?"

"Ever been hunting, Walter? I think Jack's gonna flush the game for Sydney."

"Oh."

"Just hang tight, Walter, you're doing great."

"I was thinking. You want me to hit him with the hopper?"

Greg looked at the mic in disbelief. Hit him with the hopper? The thing weighed tons. How was he going to pull that off? He had to ask. "How would you do it?"

"Well, not to brag, but I've been doing this a long time and I'm pretty good at it. This crane is real sensitive and I've actually been moving pretty slowly with it up to now. If he decides to move out into the open I can probably knock his little dick in the dirt with it."

"I don't know, Walter. The stuff he has in that backpack is real fragile. If Jack asks for it, give it to him, but until then let's try to get him in one piece. What's in the hopper anyway?"

"Few tons of cement."

"Still liquid?"

Walter checked his watch. "Yeah, not for much longer though."

"Okay. It's Jack's call. Right now just do the shadowing thing, it's working well."

"You got it."

*   *   *

Jack lay on his belly in the dirt and looked around the stack at ground level. He scanned for no more than a second before pulling his head back. He had repeated the maneuver three times now and the bruised tissue over his right lung protested more every time. His breathing was a little more rapid and shallow. May have a bruised lung, he thought to himself. He'd have to get it checked out later. Right now he pushed it from his mind.

He gazed up at the hopper. It was nearly overhead. The man had to be close by. Enough time had passed for Sydney to be in position. He rose to his feet and placed both hands on the gun.

"Greg, I'm gonna fire one shot to flush him out."

"Got it." Jack heard him relay the information to the other team members. He took a deep breath and fired a round into the stacks across the row from him and then spun to go around it in the opposite direction.

*   *   *

The round had its desired effect as it ricocheted off the stacked steel and whizzed past the Deliveryman before embedding itself in the lumber he was currently hiding behind. He was measuring the distance to the cover of the ramp when the shot happened and he automatically moved toward it at a sprint, sending a few rounds in the direction of the shot. He was halfway there when he was bathed in shadow from above. He looked over his shoulder to see the hopper swinging down at him only a foot off the ground. He dove to the ground and it missed him by inches. He scrambled to his feet to see it now between himself and the cover of the ramp. He sprinted away toward the new foundations, only to see a woman emerge from the stacks and aim a gun at him. He fired off a round in her direction, but all she did was sink into a crouched shooting position and return fire.

The round impacted his chest and spun him around. He ran on for a few steps until another struck him in the lower back, he collapsed into the dirt just short of the new foundation concrete.

*   *   *

Jack had made it around the stack just in time to see the Deliveryman running through the flock of seagulls he had scared into the air with the gunshot. He took off after him only to see the hopper nearly swing into the man. As he rose from the dirt and changed directions, Jack was horrified to see him run directly toward Sydney while firing in her direction. Before he could get a shot off he saw a bullet impact the man's chest and spin him around. Yet somehow the man stayed upright and once again raised his arm to shoot. Jack fought his training to shoot center-mass and put a round through his lower back. The man crumbled to the ground.

*   *   *

No! Sydney screamed in her head even as she pulled the trigger. The round entered the man's chest and she watched helplessly as he spun around only to be hit again by Jack. As the man's lifeless body skidded to a halt in the dirt she was already running toward him.

"Jack, help me!"

She ran to the body and flipped him over just as Jack got there. They both looked in horror at the growing spot of fluid leaking from the backpack. Sydney's round had passed straight through his chest and also through the backpack.

"Blood?" Jack asked hopefully.

"You want to chance it?" she shot back.

Jack grabbed his collar. "Greg, we need the decon team here now!"

"Two minutes!" was Greg's reply.

"Two minutes," he told Sydney.

She looked around. The seagulls were already landing back around them and the breeze was blowing in swirls around the pit.

"That's too long!" She pulled a garbage bag from her pocket and shook it out. "Help me get the backpack off!"

They flipped the body back over and attacked the knots. They were rock hard, too tight to move.

"Gimme a knife!" she demanded.

"I don't have one!"

Sydney scanned the area around them but nothing offered a solution …unless.

"The cement! We throw him in the cement!" she announced.

"Will that work?"

"Better than leaving it exposed to these birds!"

Jack didn't argue, he just grabbed a strap on his side while she did the same on hers. Together they dragged the man five yards and threw him into the new concrete. The body impacted with a dull splat but failed to sink into the hardening mix.

"Now what?" Sydney cried.

"Hold on!" Jack pulled on his collar.

"Walter!"

"Yeah, Jack?"

"Bury this guy! Hurry!"

"Okay …get back!"

Jack grabbed Sydney's hand and pulled her down as Walter swung the hopper in not four feet off the ground. He quickly centered it over the man and despite it still swinging opened the chute.

Three tons of concrete quickly covered the man and then just kept on coming. Walter figured if it was important enough for Jack to want it done, he was going to get the whole thing. Besides, in twenty minutes the hopper would have been ruined.

Sydney and Jack sat in the dirt and watched the growing pile of concrete erase any sign of the man beneath it. Once the hopper was empty and hanging much higher in the air, they collapsed onto their backs.

"What happened to not shooting the vials?" Jack asked after a few silent moments.

Sydney turned her head to see his grinning face lying next to hers.

"Hey, at least I didn't shoot at you this time."

"And I should thank you for that?"

"Yes you should."

They were still laughing when they heard Walter's voice on the radio.

"Is it okay if I come down now?" This launched even more laughter.

Jack finally sat up. He noticed a team of six men walking down the ramp toward them. They were all wearing blue space suits. A pumper truck was following them at a slow pace, the remote nozzle on the front already turning around. The men started shaking out what looked like body bags, but were actually containment suits. One for each of them, this was not going to be pleasant.

"Well, Walter, it's over, but if I were you I'd just stay up there for a little while longer."

HOPES RAISED FOR
UNIVERSAL FLU DRUG.
February 23, 2009—The Independent

—EPILOGUE—

THEY ALL WATCHED THE video of the decontamination process. After Jack and Sydney had been bagged in their plastic cocoons and loaded into nearby ambulances, the fire department sprayed the entire area down with bleach and water. Even Walters's hopper had received a good soaking and, to his relief, all the leftover concrete was washed away. He was worried they'd somehow blame him for the hopper being ruined if the concrete had managed to set up. But it hadn't, and Walter was treated to a rigorous debriefing by the feds where he was given a cover story that was even believable. The city had a new hero to stand next to the firemen and police officers involved that day and Walter and his wife Florence were being treated to the best restaurants in town as well as visits from the mayor and the governor.

Jack smiled at the TV as he thumbed the remote to turn it off. He hoped Walter enjoyed his fame more than he did. Unfortunately several news cameras had his mug on film and the whole thing had blown up again. The only good thing about it was he and Sydney had been in quarantine for several days and had an excellent excuse to deny interviews.

He spun in the chair and faced the man sitting across from him. He and Sydney had requested the meeting and the man had readily complied. It was unofficial. As far as the press knew, the man was on vacation. He had arrived at Jack's beach house in secret and would leave that way.

"So the story is still a wacko who made some homemade anthrax? Is the story going to hold?"

"I believe so. All the elements are in place and nobody has any other theories outside of the usual conspiracy theory crackpot websites. I think this will blow over without too much of a problem, and to top it off, the FBI and Homeland Security get a win in front of the home crowd. It's nice when the public can see their tax dollars at work."

"There was no trace of the virus found?" Sydney asked.

"No. We'll test for a couple weeks after the body is exhumed, but I'm told we dodged a bullet. Once we chip the guy out of the cement, we'll see how many vials he had just to make sure we got it all. But that will take some time. We don't want to rush this, but the sooner we get that big tent out of the World Trade Center, the sooner they'll quit showing it on the news, and I can quit doing the damn Sunday morning news shows."

"What about the bonds?" Jack asked.

"Soaked with agent and blood? Did you want them?"

Jack shook his head with a smile. "No, sir."

"Didn't think so." The man stirred his drink. "On a more serious note, I've talked to a few people and the consensus is that the program will stay in place. I know that's not what you wanted to hear, but that's what some very smart people have convinced me of. I didn't make the decision lightly, I want you to know that. I'm a numbers man, Jack. If you want to convince me of something you have to show me numbers. Well, I've seen a lot of numbers in the last month and I've verified almost all of them. I'm having the data forwarded to you. Numbers don't lie. So for now, the program stays.

"However, I'm also looking at some other numbers. Funding for

NASA, seawater desalination, and crop research will enjoy a large boost in the near future, as will population control measures. The global warming initiative is also getting a boost. Next month, the new fishing treaties go into effect and the penalties have been raised significantly for all violators. It's a start, but hopefully it will grow from there and we can get ahead of the problem. That's about all we can hope for right now."

Jack sipped his drink while he thought about what the man had said. Sydney caught his eye and after a moment gave an almost imperceptible nod. He agreed.

"I like what I'm hearing, sir, but I think I'll need to hold on to the discs I spoke of, for awhile, just the same. But you have my word that they won't go any further."

"That's a reasonable agreement, Mr. Randall."

"Then you can tell him we have a deal."

"Yes. He won't like it, but hey, most of them only get one term anyway. He'll run a decent campaign, but his people will fumble it at the end. It won't be a landslide. It'll look like it was a tight race all along."

The man rose to leave but stopped to take one last look out at the ocean.

"Nice place you have here, Jack. I always did love the ocean. Maybe I'll have to get a place like this in a few years."

"You're welcome here anytime, Senator."

"Miss Lewis." He shook Sydney's hand before straightening his hat and walking down the deck toward his car. There he did something he rarely did and sat down behind the wheel. The seashell driveway crackled under the wheels as Senator Teague pulled away. It was a long drive back to the District.

*　　　　*　　　　*

Toby scratched his head as he gazed into the bag. He counted twenty of the small vials and was at a loss as to what they were. All he knew was that he had to hold on to them. The bag they were in was opaque and had a waterproof seal so he could put it just about anywhere. Whatever it was, he was sure he didn't want it in the house. If someone ever came looking for it, he wanted to have deniability.

He sealed the bag tight and walked out of the house. Following a narrow path he walked through the vegetation to his small chicken coop. The birds scattered as he stepped through the door. He'd built the roost up to the ceiling and the hens had made the most of every space. He selected a spot up in one corner of the roof where they couldn't get to it and stuffed the package in and out of sight. The roof was new with a steel covering over thick tar paper. He had screwed it down with twice the number needed and it had survived two hurricanes without budging. He wondered how long it would be till he saw his friend again. Maybe a year, maybe five? You never really knew with him. But he would hold on to the stuff for him for as long as it took. He was sure that sooner or later he would forget all about it.

The package should be safe there with the birds.

— AUTHOR'S NOTE —

WHILE I UTILIZE THE use of vaccines for an evil purpose in this body of work, I wish to convey that I, in no means, am against vaccines in any way. The twisted use I penned was in no way factual, I simply pulled it from my somewhat odd imagination. While I took careful steps to remain as accurate as possible in all other areas of biological research, I bent the rules on occasion for the sake of the story. I, myself, have traveled this world extensively, both with the military and as a civilian, and as a result have been inoculated too many times to count.

I will continue to do so.

Randall Wood is the author of the novels *Closure, Pestilence* and *Scarcity*. After a life spent in occupations such as paratrooper, teacher and flight paramedic, he eventually listened to the little voices in his head and now writes full time. He currently resides on the Gulf coast of Florida with his wife, their three children, two cats and one Great Dane puppy.

He welcomes readers, and fellow writers, to his website at: www.randallwoodauthor.com

I welcome any comments, feedback, or questions at

mail@randallwoodauthor.com

I also welcome any input as to mistakes I may have missed, not necessarily typos or grammar, as they are self-explanatory, but mistakes pertaining to procedures or content. Mistakes of this nature tend to pull the reader out of the story and make it less enjoyable. If you should find such an error please fire off an email in my direction. The beauty of e-books and print-on-demand physical books is that they can always be updated to fix such things. I'll post the mistake on my website with full credit to the person who found it. If you wish to remain anonymous, that's fine too, the help is always appreciated.

I also welcome any and all reviews, with one small request. With the controversy over fake reviews garnering so much attention, it gives your review greater credibility if you do so in your real name and with the verified purchase icon. Doing so helps all readers call honest attention to their favored writers, and helps keep the integrity of the online review process intact.

Who knows?

Your review may end up on the back of the next book.

Please visit my blog at www.randallwoodauthor.com to learn about current and future projects.

www.TensionBookworks.com